TAINTED SOUL

Sam C. Leonhard

Dreamspinner Press

Published by
Dreamspinner Press
382 NE 191st Street #88329
Miami, FL 33179-3899, USA
http://www.dreamspinnerpress.com/

Tainted Soul

Cover Art by Anne Cain   annecain.art@gmail.com
Cover Design by Mara McKennen

ISBN: 978-1-61372-238-1

Printed in the United States of America
First Edition
December 2011

eBook edition available
eBook ISBN: 978-1-61372-239-8

To Nicole
The dragon is *so* your fault!

ACKNOWLEDGMENTS

I would like to thank the following people for betaing, support, and virtual hugs during my writing time:

- Theresa for reading and correcting the first draft. I know it's not easy to correct my many mistakes, and you know I would be lost without your fabulous skills.

- Mary M. Ardagna for doing the final edit before submission. I'm looking forward to meeting you sometime soon, dear!

- Zahra Owens for friendship and last-second support.

- Lots of hugs to my friend Gabi, for reading and commenting so thoroughly on anything I ask you to read.

- Maria for precisely the same reason.

- Elizabeth North, Lynn West, and my editors at Dreamspinner Press, for being out there and being absolutely fine about the strange fantasies people like me entertain. Special thanks to Anne Cain for the lovely cover!

PROLOGUE

THE grass was soft and dewy so close to sunrise. The old gray wolf trotted slowly through the woods, tail hanging low and eyes half-closed. It was a female, and as she hadn't managed to catch the hare—again—her spirits were dampened and her stomach empty.

The wolf was hungry and tired, but then she always was nowadays. Too old to catch her prey; too slow to survive much longer.

This world was too cold for her. Snow covered large parts of it, and at night, an icy wind ruffled her fur, making it brilliantly clear she would freeze to death sooner rather than later. Coming here had seemed like a good idea; now she wasn't so sure.

Dying wouldn't be the worst thing that could happen to her. Death lost its terror when one grew old and rusty. She had lived a long life. She had survived her only child, she had done too many stupid things, and she yearned for a nice, long, dreamless sleep.

Years had passed since she'd thought of her cub. With sudden clarity, she had his smell in her nose: sweet and slightly fruity, like freshly plucked oranges. Until a moment ago, she hadn't even known she still could remember the smell of oranges.

The sun would be up soon. Hopefully, it would warm her.

With aching bones, the wolf curled up on a mossy patch underneath a tree. She had slept here before. No one had discovered her hiding place so far, and she closed her eyes, trying to ignore her growling, empty stomach.

A lone bird began to chirp right above her head. As a human, she'd always loved this time of day and the sound of birds singing before her window.

But when she'd been human, she hadn't been able to withstand the calling. It had driven her crazy, being called by a soundless, silent voice, and so she had turned into a wolf underneath the full moon one night and had refused to change back ever since. The voice had dimmed to a mere whisper. And to make sure it would stay that way, she had fled her world and her home, had run from world to world, from portal to portal whenever she'd found one that was open. Slipping through behind others, risking being seen but without another choice. She would have run to the end of the universe to escape the calling.

It hadn't worked. Not for good. The voice was there again, calling her, tormenting her already tormented soul.

Had she heard it before she'd come to this world? Was the voice the real reason why she had come to this ferociously cold place?

Whatever. She could hear the voice, but she was able to ignore it. Wolves were mostly immune to the wishes of others; the calling was annoying, but nothing she needed to obey.

She was sure of it.

She liked being a wolf. A wolf's life was easy—at least it had been when she was young. On the other hand, as a wolf she couldn't look after her grandson anymore.

Not yet asleep but not fully awake either, the wolf thought she heard a sound above the wind, which was rustling the few leaves still fighting winter. A soft sound, harmless and unobtrusive. Nothing she needed to worry about.

Her ears twitched. Sound was more prominent to a wolf, and she'd learned long ago to separate good sounds from bad. A fleeing hare was good, and the crunch the bones made when she cracked them. Blood dropping to the ground was a good sound, and her paws trotting over grass and earth.

Hooves were bad, as hooves often meant centaurs. Wings were sometimes bad, especially when belonging to eagles or harpies. Not that she'd met many harpies, and not that they tended to chase old wolves. But nevertheless, wings that size made her run or even hide underground if necessary.

This world seemed to be safe aside from the cold weather. No creature making sounds that soft would be a threat to her.

Opening one eye, the wolf found she'd slept for a while, but not long enough for the sun to come up. How she longed for the warmth to dry her fur; maybe, once she was warm, she could even forget her body's aching bones for a while.

Darkness was all around her, and the wind turned from merely cold to icy. The wolf shivered, her empty stomach growling for food.

So that sound she'd heard: had it really been harmless? Or had she dreamed it?

The one who called her was dangerous. She'd met the creature only once, and for years she'd believed it had caused her only child's death. Nowadays, she wasn't sure anymore. Staying in a wolf's body for nearly two decades wasn't good for thinking straight.

She got up on stiff legs, shook the leaves out of her fur, and sniffed the wind for game. Being a wolf had its advantages. Fresh meat was one of them. If she managed to catch the prey.

No. Too early. And she was too tired. A bit more sleep before she went hunting again.

With a growl, she turned herself around once and slumped back onto the patch of moss. It was still warm from her body's heat.

As a human, she had been too mad to stay in the human world. As a wolf, she had had to leave her grandson behind despite his young age and despite the love she felt for him. Had she stayed, she might have killed him, in either shape. Had she stayed, the creature might have found him and done him harm.

She didn't have a choice. Madness, in combination with walking on four legs, strange as it was, offered safety. The one who called her didn't know how to deal with madness, couldn't sense her in her wolf form, and thus had lost track of her many years ago.

Or so she believed.

Her grandson would be an adult man by now, if he'd survived his childhood.

Sadness claimed the wolf, a lonely, longing feeling, ripping her heart to pieces. Her boy; her sunshine. Unlike his father, he'd never suffered from depression. He had been a charming, bright child, and keeping him out of his drug addict mother's reach had been one of her main goals.

He'd been a beautiful child, wild and free and clinging to her once it became clear his mother was incapable of keeping her hands off the drugs. He'd loved his grandmother, and she'd loved him.

She'd loved him enough to leave him behind once it became necessary. She'd loved him enough to have a rune tattooed on his neck, one that would hide his existence, one that would make him as invisible as possible. The creature would have loved to get her claws into her grandson, tearing him apart, devouring him. The rune would make it a lot harder for the banshee to do so. She was certain of it. Or at least she had been, once.

The wolf's paws twitched in her dreams. She'd fallen back asleep, an easy thing for a wolf no matter how cold it was. Her human part, the small part still not entirely drowned by her wolf-self, regretted what she'd done to her boy. The tattoo on his neck would keep him safe and hidden, but it would also make it very hard, if not impossible, for him to make friends or find a partner. He very likely would have to go through life alone, and she grieved for him.

But if she hadn't done it, he would be dead already, slaughtered by the creature that called her.

In her dreams, the wolf saw the boy's face, freckled and lovely. Red hair and strange, beautiful eyes, long, slender legs, a quick, cheeky smile, and a handsome face. And he had been a good child, neither cruel nor stupid. Her grandson had reflected the best parts of his heritage. He had surely grown into a beautiful, intelligent man.

Last time she had seen him, Gabriel had been about eight years old.

The wolf's legs restlessly chased dream bunnies or, maybe, ran from nameless fears. A low whine emerged from her throat; in the tree above, it disturbed a squirrel, which had been trying to find one of last year's buried nuts.

She was safe in this world. It was too cold for anyone but wolves and the occasional prey.

She was safe here.

THROUGH the woods, a creature slithered, its scaly tail leaving snakelike tracks on the snowy ground. Where its eyes should have been, only holes could be seen, had anyone been there to look. Where its mouth should have been, there was only a gap, toothless and round, slashing the air it sucked in greedily.

It was too warm down here. Had it not been necessary, she would never have left her mountains. It was safe up there, secluded and cold. Cold was important. Cold was the elixir of life, and without it, she couldn't think properly.

But it had been necessary to come down onto the plains. The wolf was here, now, this very moment.

The banshee had waited so very long for this, had called her for years, only to get nothing but disobedience in response. Staying in the mountains now the wolf had arrived was not an option. The moment she had crawled through the portal, the banshee had been aware of her presence. Finally, the wolf had followed her call. It had taken long enough to lure her here; now was the time to face her, even if it meant missing the coldness she craved.

If only the wretched thing hadn't resisted her call for so long. The banshee was old herself now, and the warmth down here made her feel even older.

And she had to protect her cave.

On the other hand, her cave was hard to reach, and it was protected by barriers. This wouldn't take long, and the banshee was not yet too old to end a wolf's life.

There she was, hidden under a tree.

The banshee's cold claw touched the wolf's fur, dug deep into her flesh. The wolf had been fast asleep, exhausted, half-starved. Otherwise, she might have sensed the danger in time. Now it was too late.

The wolf yelped, struggled, still half-asleep. But the banshee didn't let go of her. Shaking the wolf, the creature just waited, silently, for her to wake up fully, and ignored the wolf's increasing howls.

The wolf changed. The paws became hands; the limbs stretched into arms and legs. The graying snout was replaced by the nose, mouth, and sunken cheeks of an old woman.

No more fur. Just long, tangled hair, matted and dirty.

No more howls. The screams of a human echoed through the quiet woods, scaring the last remaining animals away into the darkness.

The banshee dropped her prey, knowing the old woman couldn't run away from her. Even in wolf form, she wouldn't have stood a chance, but to be certain, she'd waited for her to change back into human. It was one of the banshee's few magical skills—in her presence, no one could stay in another form for long.

If only the wolf-woman weren't a shapeshifter. If only she'd listened to her call sooner.

Well, she wasn't a wolf now. She could answer questions.

When the banshee let go of her, the woman dropped to the ground like a puppet whose strings had been cut. Where the banshee had touched her, her white, fragile skin was red and marred, like freshly burned flesh. She whimpered, her hands clutched to her face.

You came to me.

There was no voice, just an echo in the woman's mind. She jerked as if struck; she didn't look up.

I called and you came. But it is too late. I found him. He is mine now.

The frail old woman gasped in shock. "You're lying," she whispered hoarsely. "He's safe from your eyes. I hid him. You won't ever be able to put your filthy claws on him."

The banshee would have laughed were she actually able to laugh. As it was, the sound she made resembled an animal's death cry more than anything else. *He went through a portal. I saw him. I watch him. He cannot hide anymore.*

Now the woman looked up. Her eyes were bloodshot, her lips blue with cold. She wouldn't live much longer even if the banshee should decide not to kill her. "A portal? My Gabriel? No! Never taught him runes."

Awkwardly, the banshee bent and put her claws around the old woman's throat. *He found a mate,* she hissed. *The rune you put on him was useless. A fae fell in love with him. The fae showed him how to use runes. He learned. He knows. Portals are friendly to him. Sooner or later, he will hear my call and follow it into this world. Where I will await him. Where his destiny awaits him.*

Gentle pressure to the woman's main veins caused her to struggle and scratch at the banshee's gray, stone-like skin.

You lost your way, did you not? the banshee asked and allowed the woman to take another breath. *You are old and weak. You could not resist my call any longer, not even in your wolf disguise. But it is too late. I do not need you anymore.*

Limp as freshly killed prey, the old woman hung in the banshee's claws. Tears ran down her cheeks and froze before they could drop to the ground. "Gabriel," she murmured. "I tried to protect you. I'm so sorry."

Her near death didn't seem to be of any concern to her.

With the last bit of dignity she could muster, the old woman got to her feet, stood as straight as the banshee's claws around her throat would allow. "My Gabriel hasn't been born for any destiny," she said proudly. "You might have fiddled with my genes, and he might be part of you somehow, but he doesn't belong to you. He'll fight you, and he'll win." Wiping a strand of gray hair out of her eyes, she refused to look away.

The dead gray sockets showed neither concern nor mercy. *So many tries; so many failures.* The banshee sighed, faint like the wind. *You are one of them. Your son was one of them. You were all weak or useless, or both. But you were necessary to create my child. This boy who once was yours, he is different. He's strong. He will do what is expected of him.*

And as an afterthought, she added, *His love won't last.*

Gradually, the banshee increased the pressure around the old woman's neck.

The old woman struggled. Once, she had raised her grandson because her son was dead and her daughter-in-law a drug addict. Once, she had realized how different the boy was and in what danger, and had taken the baby to a wise man who'd tattooed the rune onto his neck, shielding him from curious eyes. Gabriel had cried bitterly, complaining about the pain and the strong grip she'd used to hold him still.

Once, she'd been human. Her name had been Bellatrice, and she'd lived in the human world, raising a mostly human child.

Then, when the calls and the madness had become unbearable, she'd turned into a wolf, hoping the calling would end.

Now she realized she hadn't been able to ignore it at all. The creature had called her to this world, and although it had taken some time, she had finally followed. And now she was lost.

Knowing Gabriel was lost as well broke her heart.

"I hate you," she said with as much self-assurance as she could muster.

Your hate is of no concern to me, the banshee whispered, strengthening her grip, and she watched as the old woman suffocated. Bellatrice's legs kicked out, and she gurgled, her lungs screaming for breath.

In vain. There was no escape once a banshee got that close.

When the old woman was dead, the banshee dropped the body into the snow and sniffed the corpse. It was not good to eat. Too old; too desperate.

Still, she didn't turn to leave. Not yet. The mountains could wait, and her egg could wait.

This was more important.

Gabriel, the old woman had said.

The banshee hadn't known the boy's name. She'd found him, and she'd watched him, and she had tried to call him. Useless. He would not hear her. He was like her, but only partly. His ears were deaf to her calls due to what else he was.

But now she knew his name. Names were powerful, and now she had all the power over him she needed.

She briefly considered the consequences of the calling. She could call animals; she could call her kin. She could even call a wolf that was sometimes a human, like the now-dead woman lying in a crumpled heap at her feet.

But Gabriel was different. He was so much more than just banshee. Calling him might upset the balance of the worlds, might harm the portals, might bring discord into the gentle harmonies of power.

She shrugged her shoulders. She had no mind anymore for the dead woman. Snow fell; the body would be covered by noon and rot to bones in a few months.

The banshee hurried to get back to her cave. The discord, the failing balance—she didn't care if the worlds sank into chaos or the portals erupted and killed anyone near them. She wanted revenge more than anything else.

Only her wishes counted. Her wishes, her needs, and maybe her egg, awaiting her return.

There shall be discord, she thought. *There shall be chaos and death, if only the boy follows my call.*

Gabriel.

Cold ice greeted the banshee when she entered her cave. It coated the walls and floor; it made the banshee shiver with relief. She was home. A hole in the ground was where the banshee slept, if she slept, which happened rarely. It also held her egg, small and fragile. Briefly, she checked on it. Yes. All was well.

Now she was hungry. A snow fox would be good, or a young polar bear.

They'd follow her call. They all did.

Gabriel would as well. Now that she knew his name, he would be here before the year was over.

CHAPTER ONE

I'M GOING to die.

The thought emerged from the deep recesses of his three-quarters sleeping brain. Crystal clear, it felt much more real than, for example, the dream that was already fleeing his mind or the bed he was lying in.

I'm going to die. Soon.

It was late on a nice, sunny October afternoon. Exhausted after a long night, Gabriel hadn't managed to keep his eyes open after lunch, so Aleksei had sent him to bed for a nap.

But he hadn't slept well. He'd been dreaming of nameless fears and a voice calling him. Again.

Motionless, Gabriel lay on his back, partly covered by the blanket he'd pulled over himself some hours before. Sunlight painted patterns on the bed and floor, rearranged constantly by the gently moving branches outside the window.

Staring at the ceiling, Gabriel tried to remember the words from his dream but failed.

He took a shaky breath and sat up. "Damn naps. I always feel worse afterwards instead of refreshed."

It was hard to keep his eyes open. He was still sleepy; the bed was calling, the dream, too, in a weird, scary kind of way, and what would be the harm of going back to sleep for another half an hour? He was home, wasn't he? He could take a nap if he wanted to, even a long one lasting until dinner. Today, he didn't have much else to do. And maybe Aleksei would join him. Maybe a bit of sex would chase those strange dreams from his mind for good.

But….

Lately, there was always a *but*. A *but* standing in the way of sex, in fact. *But* it was too late. *But* he was too tired. *But* he had to work. *So sorry, love, I won't make it home before morning. Another time, surely.*

Another month, more likely.

Anger welled up. He should feel great, not worse than ever. He should be fully awake, and he shouldn't be trying to find yet another reason not to have sex with Aleksei!

A quick glance at the clock confirmed he'd slept for about two hours. Aleksei was somewhere in the house, waiting for him to get up. They'd make plans for the evening. One of them would think of something for dinner. Nothing special. Normal life happening.

So why did he feel so out of sorts?

"Easy answer to that one. I'm feeling out of sorts because something is wrong. If only I knew what."

With a sigh, he got up and pulled on his jeans. Lately, he felt uncomfortable walking around the house naked, as if someone was watching him.

"Should take a shower," he murmured, already pulling on a shirt. "But I won't."

Aleksei had often joined him in the shower. Until recently, Gabriel had craved it. The fae was a skillful lover, always aware of Gabriel's moods and wishes.

But not anymore, and not because Aleksei didn't try. It was because Gabriel didn't want him to.

Why don't I want him near me?

With shaking legs, Gabriel sat back down on the bed. To keep his hands occupied, he fished for the leather string in the front pocket of his jeans, braided his long hair, and bound it with the string. "I love him," he said.

He didn't sound as if he believed it.

"It's Aleksei! I love him, for fuck's sake!"

Nope, still didn't sound right. Just desperate.

His heart pounded. He felt pale, weak, and for a moment, he believed his thoughts and fears were the result of an empty stomach and maybe the sort of strange, half-forgotten nightmares an afternoon nap sometimes brought. He had been having more nightmares recently, hadn't he? Occasionally, he would wake up bathed in sweat, his eyes wide open, his mouth dry with fear. He never remembered any of the dreams, but surely they could trigger some false emotions?

He almost had himself convinced. But then his gaze fell onto his hands and he blushed.

He loved Aleksei and had never betrayed him. Well, not really. Not completely.

Gritting his teeth, Gabriel faced the memories flaring up in his mind. It had been a week ago. He'd visited Gray Oak's world, and he'd run into one of the tree nymphs guarding Sweet Rain's sleeping soul. Nothing special, really. He'd seen tree nymphs before, had talked to them, and once had found one of their lost children. Never had he felt even remotely attracted to one of them. They were wiry people, dark-skinned and with long, tangled hair. Their clothes were made of grass, and often, butterflies or small birds followed their every movement.

This guy, though….

In the safety of his bedroom, Gabriel hugged himself in despair. He loved Aleksei! From the moment he'd set eyes on the fae, there had been a mutual attraction neither of them had been able to deny. They'd been drawn to each other and eventually landed in bed together.

"Three years," Gabriel muttered. "I am risking his love and a three-year relationship for a quick fuck with a damn tree nymph."

Okay, he hadn't fucked the guy. Not really. But he had kissed him. And he had allowed him to undress him. They'd landed in the grass together, and the reason Gabriel was staring at his hand with a mixture of hate and confusion was because he so clearly remembered the contrast of his white hand on the man's dark ass.

A cold shiver ran through him upon thinking about the tree nymph. He'd been so hot! Young and direct and greedy and so very different from any human he knew, and equally different from Aleksei. His kiss had been demanding, his tongue eager, his cock impressive.

Gabriel tried to convince himself he hadn't stood a chance against the man, but he failed. He had wanted the kiss. He had wanted more.

When the tree nymph had opened his shirt, Gabriel had kissed his throat. When he'd dropped his loincloth, Gabriel had swallowed dryly, leaned in for another kiss, and cupped his balls.

The tree nymph's skin had smelled of earth and leaves. His hands, long and strong, had wrapped around Gabriel's cock, stroking him slowly into hardness. All the time, the tree nymph had smiled, and when Gabriel had slipped two fingers into his tight hole, he'd pushed against him repeatedly until he'd spilled before leaning over, taking Gabriel's length between his sharp little teeth, and sucking him off.

Gabriel absently wiped the back of his hand across his mouth. He'd felt ashamed the moment he came and had dressed without a word. He'd never even asked the tree nymph's name.

"But I love him," he said helplessly to his hands, which were resting like dead little animals on his knees. "I love Aleksei. I am nothing without him, I don't want to lose him, and why the hell have I been so stupid?"

Two days ago, he'd kissed Conchita.

The thought alone made him shudder. Conchita was generous with the charms of her large-breasted, big-hipped body, and before he'd met Aleksei, they'd shared a bed every now and then. He liked her, always had and always would.

He'd never kissed her, though; he would have sworn an oath he never would.

And yet, two days ago he *had* kissed her. And it had been disgusting, not because of her or anything she'd done or said, but because he didn't want to be with her. He knew it would be awful the moment she'd smiled at him, but he had still kissed her.

Throat tight with fear, Gabriel wondered if he was going mad. Maybe he'd gone through the portals a few times too often—after all, he'd never really been trained to do so, and Aleksei still didn't understand how he did it. Going through the portals, crossing the bridge into another world, was fatal for anyone who didn't know how to do it properly. But Gabriel had done it instinctively from the first moment on. So it was unlikely the portals had caused his condition.

"I just need some rest," Gabriel muttered. "Yeah. Been a long week. And I'm hungry. Everything will be okay once I've eaten."

Determined, he got up, straightened the bedcovers, and went to find Aleksei.

Of course he knew he was fooling himself. He didn't need rest. The past weeks and months had been relatively quiet, with few crossings to other worlds. There'd been enough sleep, enough to eat, and definitely enough leisure time to recharge his energy tanks. He had no reason to betray his lover. He had no reason to feel so lost and restless, as if somewhere else a better life awaited him.

"My life is here."

Strangely enough, saying it aloud seemed to help. The feeling of being pulled away ceased, and the first smile of the afternoon appeared on his face.

"Aleksei?" Gabriel called. "Where are you? I'm starving here!"

There was no answer. The house was silent, which was unusual. When Aleksei was home, there was usually some sort of music in the background, small noises from the kitchen when he felt like cooking, or at least the soft steps of bare feet on the light wooden planks. Gabriel's ears could pick up even the smallest sound—one of the positive side effects of having shapeshifter blood running through his veins.

"Aleksei?"

The living room was empty. Only the small scarred cat that had moved in with them a while back lay curled up on the sofa. He opened one alert eye when Gabriel walked in; when he saw there was no danger, he went back to sleep.

Aleksei wasn't in the kitchen. A lone cup of tea sat on the table, already cool.

Which meant his lover could only be in his workroom.

A deeper smile spread over Gabriel's face, chasing away his fears and guilt as well as the strange thoughts concerning his imminent death.

Not worrying felt good. Thinking about Aleksei... well. It might feel a bit awkward, but it definitely felt good too.

He was too fed up with riddles to ponder his problems right now. Later, maybe. Or never.

"Aleksei? What are you up to this time?" Pushing open the door to the workroom, Gabriel experienced a sudden rush of heat at the sight of his lover. Aleksei sat bent over his microscope, black hair curled wetly on his neck. He must have had a shower not too long ago.

Alone. Without waking him, and without waiting for him.

Gabriel sighed. Only some minutes ago he'd worried Aleksei would join him in the shower. Now that he'd found out his partner had showered without him, he wasn't happy, either.

This was not good.

Think about it later.

Gabriel closed his eyes for a moment and breathed in the faint scent of Aleksei's freshly scrubbed skin. To a human—one without werewolf ancestors, anyway—the scent would have been imperceptible. To Gabriel, it was but another facet of Aleksei's complex and complicated nature.

His uneasiness lessened with every step he took, until he completely forgot about it.

"Hey, love." Gabriel was already next to the fae when Aleksei finally looked up.

"Hmm?"

"I've been calling for five minutes now. Thought you'd gone out or something."

Aleksei raised an eyebrow, a small gesture that still made Gabriel's heart flip. It was such an insignificant habit; for Gabriel, it summoned up the fae's nature perfectly. Slightly arrogant and dominant without needing words; curious, judging, and exceptionally sexy.

His encounter with the tree nymph was pushed into a dark corner of his mind. The kiss he'd shared with Conchita vanished completely.

"Love you," Gabriel said, meaning it with all his heart and mind.

Aleksei smiled. "Good to know. Did you enjoy your nap?" He picked up a pen, peeked through the ocular of the microscope, and quickly scribbled something onto a scrap of paper in that cryptic handwriting Gabriel had never managed to decipher properly.

"Must've been tired. Can't imagine why." Gabriel moved closer to Aleksei and placed a light kiss on his exposed neck. "What are you doing there, Doc? Not trying to unravel the mystery of my ancestors again, are you?"

Aleksei absently reached out and patted Gabriel's hip, simply because it came into range of his hand first. "I decided that since I cannot figure out where the strange stripe in your genes comes from, I could at least try and rule out which races played no part in your creation. Easy, really. There are only about sixty known races. Once I am through with my list, I will have figured out what exactly you are not. What is left must be the correct answer." He looked up, frowning. "Did you just wonder why you were tired? I thought that to be obvious. You went running this morning. For hours, if I remember correctly. And last night, you went to bed late. Both reasons explain your fatigue, as well as the fact you had a nap." He smiled. "I even thought about joining you in bed. If you hadn't been asleep already, I might have done it."

Gabriel had to force a grin onto his face. Apparently, his uneasiness had been lurking behind the next corner, waiting to jump at him at the first possible moment. "Hoping for a cuddle?"

Aleksei's smile vanished. "Hoping against hope, yes. Lately, we have both been too busy for cuddles, it seems. Although you are, as you know, an exceptionally arousing sight, especially when your legs are spread and you're gasping for breath." He sounded casual; he turned back to his microscope, his mind clearly on the blood sample he was examining.

Something in his voice made it obvious he knew something was wrong between them.

Gabriel shuddered. There it was again, that sudden, overwhelming chill. As if someone was walking over his grave. As if he were dead already.

To keep Aleksei from talking about cuddling or spread legs, Gabriel leaned over and had a look at the list on the counter. "I know the first few races," he said. "Yours can be ruled out because it doesn't produce redheads, true?"

"True. Fae tend to be dark-haired with the occasional blond in between. I have never seen anyone with ginger hair, even, never mind the dark red of your strands." Curling one of said strands—escaped from the string—around his fingers, Aleksei unexpectedly pulled Gabriel down for a kiss.

Gabriel's initial reaction was to pull away, but the thought vanished as quickly as it had flared up. *This is Aleksei!* Warmth and love flooded him, along with the overwhelming relief the kiss brought. He wanted this! He needed this, and how had he survived so long without physical contact with his lover?

Their tongues touched. Gabriel's plait slipped over his shoulder, brushing his lover's cheek. Aleksei caught it; he deepened the kiss, then broke it right before Gabriel began to seriously consider using the workbench for a quick afternoon fuck.

He couldn't believe he'd ever thought about another man, never mind kissing one.

He couldn't believe a moment ago he'd felt disgust at the thought of kissing Aleksei.

And he couldn't believe there was still that feeling of being watched, or hearing that faint, insistent call.

Called to go where? Called by whom? He didn't know. All he knew was that a part of his soul wasn't into this.

Part of his soul, part of *him*, was being held hostage elsewhere.

I'm going to die.

The very thought that had ripped him out of his sleep made him flinch when it popped up in his mind like a New Year's rocket. This time it was even clearer, less a thought and more like a prediction.

If I die, at least I cannot betray him.

Equally clear, only this was an answer, a challenge to the one who was calling, if it was a someone at all and not simply a product of his crazy mind.

Torn between his fears, his longings, and his doubts, Gabriel took another look at the list. "So I'm not a fae and not a vampire. And not a—what's that word?"

Aleksei snatched the paper out of his hand, took a pen, and crossed out another name. "Not a riverghost, not a merman, and not a tree nymph. Also, I checked your blood against mine. I now have proof you are definitely not fae. Oh, and you're not troll, either."

Gabriel, who'd been about to take a sip of water from Aleksei's glass, spilled it on his shirt. "A—what? Troll? There are *trolls* out there?"

Once more, Aleksei raised an eyebrow. "I thought you made yourself familiar with the races living in the worlds you visit? It appears I was wrong." With precise movements, he changed the thin piece of glass under the microscope. "Yes, there are trolls. Large creatures who tend to keep to themselves. They prefer cold weather; you would find them in Pandora's world, high up north. I assume you remember Pandora?" He tilted his head mockingly.

Gabriel took in Aleksei's naturally pale skin and the dark, strange patterns decorating it. When he'd first seen them, he'd thought them to be tattoos. Later, he'd learned them to be part of the fae physiognomy, skin patterns that changed with age, health, and emotional state. A woman would have different patterns than a man, a sane fae different than a mad one. Not that there were many mad fae. The only one Gabriel had met had been Aleksei's brother Petresh, who had had hardly any skin patterns at all.

Just underneath his lover's shirt, Gabriel could see the necklace he wore. A rune pendant hid the patterns as well as his true looks. To the casual observer, Aleksei appeared as a shortish, slightly overweight man with mousy brown hair and equally mousy eyes. No one would spare him a second glance. No one would bother to challenge him, attack him, or ask him out for a drink. Although politics concerning the hidden worlds had changed in recent years, members of other races were still not widely welcomed. Aleksei knew this and had taken measures. He always wore the necklace. In addition, he was still trying to figure out why Gabriel was immune to its powers.

With a pang, Gabriel realized Aleksei was waiting for an answer. "Pandora... um... just a second. Tall, dark-haired, gorgeous?"

"Small, four-legged, vicious. She's a gorgon, and we met her last year. Say, beloved, is there something wrong with you?" Putting the pen down, Aleksei suddenly focused his attention fully on Gabriel. His ice-blue eyes showed nothing but concern and maybe slight curiosity.

To Gabriel, it seemed as if Aleksei was able to look right into his soul, see all his sins, even see the stolen kisses as well as the guilty orgasm he'd had with the tree nymph. He paled and looked away.

"Just a bit tired still," he bit out. "The gorgon. Pandora. Yep, now I remember her. Strange creature. And there are trolls living in her world?"

"Trolls and dwarfs, as you would call them, although if you did so to their faces, they'd chop your head off. Or your knees, rather. They are a small and light-boned race, living in symbiosis with the trolls. However, neither race has played a part in your heritage."

Once more, Gabriel took the list, scanning through the names. "It will take you weeks to rule each race out," he said. "Always assuming you can get blood samples from all of them and compare them with mine. You sure you want to bother?"

"Absolutely. You might not like to talk about it, but something *is* wrong, Gabriel. While sleeping, you often suffer from nightmares, yet in the morning, you don't seem to remember any of them. During the day, you are absentminded. I would say you are hiding something, only I tend to believe otherwise. Something is bothering you. It might have to do with one of your ancestors."

"That's a fairly long shot."

Gabriel hadn't intended that to come out so harshly. To take the edge off his words, he desperately tried to find something else to talk about—and found it on the list.

He grinned. "You've forgotten some races," he said. "Tsk, tsk, Doc, I've never known you to lack thoroughness in your research."

Aleksei frowned. "I have forgotten no one. The list contains every race I am aware of."

"Apart from dragons." Deep down, he felt like he was on an emotional roller coaster, needing to flee Aleksei one moment and wanting to kiss him the next. On the outside, he managed to behave. More or less. "When you were fighting with your lovely brother, you called him a stupid idiot and said if you were to go back far enough, you might even find dragon blood in your genes. So. Where are the dragons on your list?"

It was a rare thing to see Aleksei off balance. The fae knew everything, had seen everything, and was always well informed about any given event. He read more in a day than Gabriel did in a month, had visited every known world, and when he didn't know something, he vanished into his workroom or library until he'd learned what there was to learn about the question. Nothing surprised him.

Now, a look of deep sadness showed in his eyes, as if Gabriel's question had opened an old wound.

"Dragons? There is no use adding dragons to the list, beloved. They once existed, but since they've last been seen, centuries have passed. And although we still keep a seat for them at the fae council, not many dare to say they believe in their return for fear of getting called foolish. Nowadays, most of us believe that they are creatures of legends, Gabriel. And even if dragon blood happened to get mingled with yours, there is no way I could prove it, given I have no dragon blood sample to crosscheck your blood with."

Dropping the list onto the table, Gabriel crossed his arms over his chest. There had been something in Aleksei's voice that told him the fae grieved the absence of dragons, and he wondered why that would be. "You'd wish huge flying reptiles to soar across the sky?" he asked. "Sorry, Doc, but that sounds like a bit much, even for me. They'd eat people, burn the harvest, terrorize mankind, wouldn't they?"

Aleksei snorted, then gently touched Gabriel's face. "Truly, I tend to forget the silly stories humans came up with to explain everything they were too frightened to accept. No, dragons wouldn't terrorize anyone. They were intelligent creatures, even wise, as the tales say. The fae council always listened to their advice. Actually, we are bound to obey their orders should they decide to show up ever again."

"Well. I could have read a bit more, I guess." Grumbling, Gabriel leaned into Aleksei's touch. "Any other creatures you ought to tell me about? Do unicorns exist?"

"Of course."

"Aha. And they truly like virgins?"

"If they can get them. Basically, they eat anything they can hunt down."

At Gabriel's stunned expression, Aleksei had to laugh. "I have the strong feeling you need some lessons, Gabriel. You clearly do not spend enough time in the library, or you would know unicorns are even more vicious than gorgons, worse than centaurs, and much more deadly than harpies."

Gabriel pinched his nose in mock exasperation. "You're making my head hurt with all this info, Doc. Give me a break, okay? How about something to eat instead? And maybe we can go out tonight? I have to deliver a file to one of my clients."

With a sigh, Aleksei put the cover over his microscope, but not before he'd stored away all blood samples. "I won't get any work done as long as you are peeking over my shoulder anyway. Dinner, then. And a visit to your client afterwards. As you wish, beloved." But his lips twitched as he said it. Gabriel knew he liked to accompany him when delivering files, always taking the opportunity to meet new people.

And Aleksei was in for a surprise tonight. Gabriel had had something in mind for months now, but he'd never dared to do it. Tonight would be perfect, and hopefully, his strange aversion to getting too close to his lover would vanish for good.

As they ate, the strange feeling of being watched lessened until it was totally gone. Gabriel began to wonder if he'd only imagined it, and when they did the washing up together, he was certain of it. Nothing was wrong. Nothing had ever been wrong.

And the tree nymph…. Well. With a bit of an effort, he could surely forget about him too.

IT WAS a quiet autumn night, a bit too warm for October but neither as wet nor as foggy as would be normal for this time of year. Aleksei wore a long gray coat—the man just didn't know how to feel comfortable in common clothes—and Gabriel had the file on his client's mother in his knapsack. The same old knapsack he'd had when he first met the fae. Thoroughly washed and cleaned, of course, but as it once had been the only personal thing belonging to him, he'd kept it when he moved in with Aleksei.

Gabriel casually looked over his shoulder, checking the street behind them. It had become a habit, not only because he needed to prevent any bystanders from seeing him opening a portal—whenever he opened a portal—but also because the hidden worlds weren't safe places. There were hardly any cities, aside from one built by the elves. And even that one was in the middle of the woods and high up in the trees. Danger lurked everywhere, so a careful survey of his surroundings had become a habit that had saved his life more than once.

"No one is following us," Aleksei said, and Gabriel cringed. He was good at his job; he was good at hiding. And it bothered him that Aleksei had seen him checking the streets behind them, although he couldn't have said why.

"I know," he replied. "It's just... I don't know. Better safe than sorry. The last job wasn't easy. I was threatened by more people than I care to remember, and I always fear one will be angry enough to follow me back home and finish me off on my own doorstep."

Not a lie. But not exactly the truth, either. He had been threatened. He felt a slight fear of someone following him home. But he was checking the streets because he felt as if he was under surveillance again.

Probably the security camera at the corner. Nothing to worry about. Security cameras were everywhere nowadays.

To his surprise, Aleksei put a hand on his arm. "You didn't tell me you've been scared." There was concern in his voice. "There are runes that can hide your tracks. You should be able to use them without any problems. Had I known about your worries, I would already have shown them to you. I thought I had. I must have been mistaken."

The hand on his arm felt warm, even through the leather of his jacket. As a fae, Aleksei had a higher body temperature than a human, and it was always a pleasure to get into bed with him, especially on a cold night.

Or used to be. Tonight, like so many nights before, the thought of sharing a bed was highly unwelcome. Tonight, the heat the fae radiated burned him. Gabriel had a sudden urge to turn and find a portal, run away from his home world, his job and his duties, and most of all, away from his lover.

Aleksei watched him silently. He seemed to sense his inner turmoil; taking his hand off Gabriel's arm, he waited until Gabriel swallowed hard and got his trembling muscles under control.

"You need to tell me what's wrong with you," Aleksei said calmly. "Whether this is about us or if something else is bothering you."

His cool words hurt. *He knows,* Gabriel thought, anger welling up. *He's not supposed to bloody know anything about me!*

Then his heart clenched, and the anger was drowned by panic. If Aleksei knew about his strange fears, and more importantly, about his problems with their relationship, he would surely leave him.

The simple thought of losing Aleksei was too dreadful to bear.

He felt his muscles trembling. *Keep calm,* he told himself, and he forced a smile upon his lips. *Just keep calm and all will be well.*

He didn't believe it. This was getting out of hand; if he didn't do something about it, the evening would end a lot earlier than planned, and a lot worse than he could possibly have imagined.

Gabriel had chosen his usual outfit: jeans and leather jacket. Although he earned enough money with his business, *Lost and Found,* he rarely bothered to spend it, and his lack of interest showed in his casual clothing. Sometimes he got a present for Aleksei, though even then, he tended to bring him rarities from the hidden worlds he visited rather than buying something fancy and useless. For himself, it was always stuff he needed anyway. A new pair of running shoes. Food. A book every now and then. Clothes were unimportant. His jeans he bought secondhand; his shirts were often stolen from Aleksei's wardrobe. And most of all, he just didn't feel comfortable dressing up. He'd probably lived on the streets for too long to have much use for money, and he knew that, in some ways, he hadn't changed all that much since he'd moved in with Aleksei.

Gabriel took a deep breath and halted his steps. They were running late for meeting his client, but what the hell. This was more important. Aleksei was more important!

"Nothing's wrong," he said, and he took Aleksei's face between his hands.

Though he was an impulsive man, Gabriel rarely showed his affection in public. For one thing, the need to act unseen and unobserved was built into his genetic code. No shapeshifter, not even one whose genes had been tangled up with human blood for generations, liked to be watched. The second reason lay in his past: although the rune on his neck hid him from curious eyes, he had grown up as a runaway and a thief, always avoiding the police. Showing affection in public meant drawing attention, and that took some courage for him.

Now was a good time to bite the bullet as well as fight the irrational feelings about Aleksei that tormented him.

Gabriel kissed him, and he could sense Aleksei's surprise as well as his joy. Since they'd been together, he'd developed a deep insight into the fae's thoughts, hopes, and wishes, and he knew with certainty Aleksei was as worried about his behavior as he was himself. This kiss was meant to prove all was well.

Although it wasn't. And although they both knew the "nothing is wrong" part was a huge lie.

His hands on his lover's hips, Gabriel moved as close as possible without taking their clothes off, and he let his hands wander downward. "It's been a while since I've taken you real hard," he whispered into Aleksei's ear. "When did we last use the handcuffs?"

Aleksei's breath quickened. "Months ago," he murmured. "As you know."

And once more the feeling of being watched vanished. The world around him seemed to shift back into normal mode: nothing was wrong, really nothing; no one was on his trail, and there were no nightmares and no uneasy feelings. Maybe this was it. Maybe all he needed to do was to make love to Aleksei to come back to his senses.

Gabriel's cock was straining against his jeans. Through the fabric of Aleksei's trousers, he traced the outline of his lover's length.

"Let's deliver the file," Gabriel murmured, stroking along Aleksei's thigh and wishing they were at home, naked in their bed. Sex with Aleksei was still the best sex he'd ever had, not only because the fae had grown into an exceptional lover once he'd shed his self-chosen virginity, but mainly because there was so much emotion with every stroke, each push, each kiss. With him, Gabriel could shed his fears and his doubts.

"It's the house on the corner," Gabriel said. "My client likes to sleep in, so he asked me to drop by his club after sunset. Another few steps, half an hour of business chat at the most, and then we'll be able to play. All night, if you like."

Aleksei relaxed in his embrace. "In other words, you suggest dropping the subject of whatever is wrong with you until my lust is sated?"

Gabriel grinned. So typical for Aleksei never to let go. "Yep. Let's talk in the morning. Although I doubt you will be awake enough by then."

Side by side, they walked to the tall red house Gabriel had pointed out. There was no bell, only a rusty old knocker. It creaked when Gabriel used it. A moment later, a narrow slot opened and a pair of dark eyes looked them up and down.

"What d'you want? Members only," a voice snarled.

Gabriel, having foreseen something like this, handed the person behind the door his business card. "I'm Gabriel Jordan. Your boss is awaiting my report."

The silence behind the door and the absence of the eyes indicated that the card was being closely examined.

Two years ago, that wouldn't have worked, at least not this smoothly. For one, back then he didn't have a business card. Second, he probably would have lacked the courage to get face to face with the security guard. He would have sneaked in, avoiding being seen even if he'd had an appointment, and it would have worked. He was good at sneaking, and he was really good at not being seen.

Back then, he would have expected the security guard to take a look at him and call the cops.

Back then, not many people had heard of *Lost and Found*, the firm Gabriel had taken over from Luis Mallfrick shortly after Aleksei's mad brother had killed the vampire. He'd changed the firm's reputation and had set out to find people connected to the hidden worlds: daughters chased away by their parents because they'd become pregnant by riverghosts. Children left for dead and saved by the hidden races. Brothers and uncles, nieces and mothers and fathers—Gabriel had told the world he'd find them, not expecting much response.

At first, few had sought him out. At first, he survived only because he lived with Aleksei, who made sure he ate and slept on a regular basis.

But then, Senator Dubaku had ordered him to find his one and only daughter. And Gabriel, without even knowing where to start searching, had found her. And her husband. And her children.

The senator had been beside himself with delight and relief. He'd thought his daughter dead for the better part of twenty years, since she'd fled his house and his hard hand at the tender age of sixteen. Getting her back—and finding himself to be a grandfather—had meant enough to him that he had carefully but persistently worked on changing the laws. Nowadays, the hidden races could live in the human world unchallenged. Children of mixed race weren't called abominations any longer, at least not openly.

No one had the right to call the cops just because a neighbor looked slightly ghoulish.

Not all was settled yet, but Dubaku was working on it. Once he was president, things would become even easier.

In addition, he'd made public who'd found his daughter. Overnight, *Lost and Found* became famous. Policemen had rushed into

Gabriel's office, demanding that he reveal his sources, which he'd refused to do. Journalists had tried to interview him, greedy for details about his past, which he'd refused to give as well. No one needed to know his mother was a drug addict. No one needed to know his grandmother was a wolf.

Eventually, the police accepted—with pressure from the senator—that Gabriel was off-limits. The occasional journalist still turned up, and every now and then, a blurry picture of him appeared in the newspapers. But his relationship with Aleksei was still a secret, and his shapeshifter blood was unknown to the press, so he didn't mind too much.

The security guard opened the door, admitting entrance. "Second floor, second door on the right," he said.

The staircase was dark, lit only by candles, the walls covered in black velvet. Not a sound could be heard. "You said this is a club?" Aleksei asked. "What sort of club doesn't have any members visible?"

"Oh, there are members," Gabriel replied. Suddenly, he couldn't wait to hand over the file and enter one of the rooms this very special club was famous for. "At least, so I've heard. My client is a rich guy. He bought this house five years ago, and ever since, his business has flourished. He offers… well, you'll see what this club is all about once I've delivered the news about his mom."

A broad-shouldered, tall woman with short, spiky blond hair awaited them at the top of the staircase, a sheet of paper in her hand. Looking from the paper to Gabriel and back, she finally nodded. "Did a bit of Internet research when you took the job for Mr. Taylor," she said. Her voice was deep and mellow, like liquid caramel. "Pleased to meet you, Mr. Jordan." Then she looked Aleksei up and down. "And you would be?" She held her hand out encouragingly so Aleksei would give her his name.

"Bill Bonnetemps," he said curtly as he took her hand and shook it heartily.

Gabriel suppressed a grin. Aleksei had given a false identity, as usual. Some things never changed. He beamed one of his more charming smiles at the woman. "He's with me."

"Yes, I can see that," the woman replied dryly. "Still, I need to know who he is before I can let him anywhere near the boss's office. Mr. Taylor'd slay me alive if he turns out to be a mass murderer. See my problem, Mr. Jordan?"

"You go ahead," Aleksei said smoothly. "I'll keep Miss—what's your name?—company until you are done. If that would be okay with you?" His raised eyebrow seemed to do the trick. The woman relaxed—not much, but enough to make it clear Aleksei would be allowed to keep her company.

A surprisingly soft smile appeared on her full lips. "Name's Tanith. Afraid you've got to stand. No seats out here, see. No one usually wants to stay on this side of the doors for long. All eager to get in ASAP." She indicated the corridor with a nod. It was about fifty feet long. On each side, there were five doors. Thick, solid doors, and soundproofed, by the looks of them.

"There are members of the club currently present?" Aleksei asked.

Gabriel could tell he was really curious. He always was. That's why it was practically impossible to keep a secret from him. For long, anyway.

He sighed. Later. Right now he had to deliver a file.

Tanith was, not surprisingly, already answering each and every one of Aleksei's questions when Gabriel turned his back to them. He was pretty sure she'd also give him her phone number before long. Although with the necklace on Aleksei looked anything but appealing, it was just what people did when the fae set his mind to being charming. Aleksei could turn his charm on like a switch, and he did so shamelessly if it served his purpose. Whatever his purpose might be at the moment.

"You coming in sometime tonight?"

The voice ripped him out of his thoughts. He hadn't even realized he'd opened the door to his client's office.

One last glance at Aleksei. The fae was clearly flirting with Tanith, and witnessing it was harder than Gabriel had expected.

Gabriel left Aleksei in the caring hands of Tanith, hoping what she told him about this club wouldn't make his lover leave before he was done. Aleksei could be strangely old-fashioned at times. Gabriel wasn't entirely sure he would be open to the surprise he had in store.

"Close the door behind you, Mr. Jordan. I do not want my employees to know what you have to tell me. You do have something to tell me, don't you?"

The man behind the large desk tapped his fingers impatiently against the smooth surface. He was in his thirties, relatively young to own one of the most expensive private clubs in town. Not massively tall, he was good-looking in an uncommon way, with a shock of black hair and warm brown eyes. Or at least they could appear warm, if he so chose. When he'd asked Gabriel to find out about his mother, they had been warm until he'd made it clear he wouldn't accept a negative response. At that point, they had developed a hard, nearly cruel glitter that told Gabriel the man would stop at nothing to get what he wanted.

Closing the door and stepping up to the desk, Gabriel shook his hand. "Mr. Taylor. Thank you for seeing me this late. I do hope it is not a problem I brought my partner?"

Taylor nodded to a small screen on his desk. "I saw you arrive. Had it been a problem, he wouldn't have been allowed in. What do you have for me?"

Patience was definitely not one of the man's virtues. Fine.

Gabriel took the file out of his knapsack and placed it on the desk. "Would you like me to summarize what I found?" he asked. Usually, people didn't much like having to read through twenty or more pages in search of a long-awaited answer, and Taylor was no exception.

The man behind the desk nodded. His attention was fully on Gabriel, a somewhat unnerving experience, as Gabriel usually avoided being noticed in any given situation.

Guess I haven't been in the business long enough or I would have got used to it by now, Gabriel thought and cleared his throat.

"Well, I have found your mother," he began.

The only reaction he got was a curt nod.

"She lives in Nebraska. You will find her name and address in the file. Should you consider contacting her, please know she is willing to meet you only under the condition her family doesn't learn of your existence."

"Family?" Taylor leaned forward ever so slightly in his chair.

"She is married and has two kids, ages twelve and seventeen."

"I see. Continue."

Admittedly, Gabriel had expected an outburst. Or at least some well-placed swear words. Brian Taylor was known as an impulsive man who never shied away from a fight, be it with fists or money. He usually won. Even now, while sitting motionless in his chair, he radiated energy and a raw sexuality that were breathtaking. His reacting so calmly to the news his mother had built a new family after she'd left him and his father was nothing less than a huge relief.

"After she left you, your mother traveled the world, spending substantial time in Italy and Southern Germany. She speaks both languages fluently. In Spain she met her husband, Carlos Fuegares. They married, they moved to the States, and now she seems to have settled down. I spent an afternoon with her once I tracked her down. She doesn't regret having left your father. She regrets having left you, hence her offer for a meeting."

Brian Taylor placed his palms flat on the desk. It was, apart from the file he hadn't even touched yet, completely empty. "Tell me in which of the hidden worlds she's been. Tell me about her parents; tell me what race's blood runs in my veins."

Gabriel frowned, then slowly opened the folder and took out a single sheet of paper. "I had her blood tested, Mr. Taylor. Your mother is 100 percent human. She's never visited the hidden worlds and is only vaguely aware of the other races. In any case, she's never been interested in meeting one of them. She met Carlos, fell in love, and that was it. If you want to know why she left your father, she said you'd have to ask her yourself if you want to find out. But in her family runs no other blood than human."

Seeing Brian Taylor's mouth sag open nearly made Gabriel smile.

"I'm…. Are you saying there are no traces of non-human blood in me?" Taylor sounded dumbstruck. And disappointed. He certainly wasn't as relieved as he should be. All of Gabriel's former clients had been scared of the answers he would bring back. All of them had feared the same thing: that they weren't human, not fully, that they therefore were disqualified from being called good Christians, that they were suddenly sub-human, dirt on the shoes of everyone else with a clean genetic code.

Tainted blood.

Most of those he'd told about their non-human heritage had cried. Or cursed.

"I thought she'd run away because there was something else in her blood, something driving her away from us," Taylor said thoughtfully. "I truly believed she'd gone to one of the hidden worlds, living with her true family and finding herself a husband more fitting for her needs. But a Spaniard? That's ridiculous. It doesn't explain—"

He broke off in midsentence. His fists were clenched, his jaw set, and after a moment of controlled fury, he banged his hands hard on the desk. "Fuck," he hissed. "I thought... I'd hoped...."

Gabriel looked at the man behind the desk. He was a smart guy. He'd made it far in a very short amount of time by outwitting his opponents, by ruthlessly getting them out of the way, and by putting everything he had into each bargain he made. There was no holding back once he'd set his mind on something. Taylor was a killer when it came to business. Gabriel was certain this man was one of the few people who knew himself inside and out. There were no hidden secrets buried inside him. Taylor could look into a mirror unblinking for hours as only a man who is not afraid of the darkness in his soul can do.

Disappointed. That could only mean there was a part he knew existed but couldn't name.

A non-human part.

"Would it help if I told you that you are part vampire?" Gabriel had to suppress a grin when he asked; grinning would definitely not have been good for the business.

Taylor jerked his head up. "What?"

In a calming gesture, Gabriel raised his hands. "I wasn't finished with my report. Usually, I have to break the news a bit more carefully to my clients. You seem to want to have non-human blood running through your veins. Well, here it is. Your grandfather was a full-blooded vampire. Your father's father, to be precise. Which makes you—"

"Which makes me one-quarter vampire."

Gabriel wasn't surprised to see the man close his eyes with relief. "You were suspicious?"

Taylor's nostrils flared, the only visible sign of his obvious inner turmoil. "Damn fucking sure I was. The way I live—at night—and the way I act, even how and what I eat were strong indicators. I love to hunt, and although I rarely shed blood in business, I still kill my opponents with a few well-placed words. Vampire, yes? Does that mean I have an unnatural craving for virgin blood?"

Gabriel shrugged his shoulders. "I don't know. Do you?"

Taylor was completely at ease now, and for the first time, he picked up the file and leafed through its contents. "I like my steaks bloody," he mused. "But my women have to be of age as well as experienced. My current girlfriend is a year older than I am and certainly hasn't been a virgin for over a decade. Is there anything else I need to know?"

Gabriel recognized when he was being thrown out, even when it was being done politely. He got up and picked up his knapsack. "Should you decide to have children, make sure the mother-to-be knows about your heritage beforehand," he said. "I have seen many families destroyed because either father or mother was shocked by the newborn's appearance. Vampire babies are nearly translucent at birth, with black eyes and very sharp nails. Do yourself a favor and tell the lady in question what you are should you ever desire to become a father. Given you are only one-quarter vampire, the telltale signs in your children will vanish about an hour after birth, but they will be there."

Taylor nodded, then frowned. "My mother gave birth at home. My father wasn't there, he was held up in a plane over New York."

Gabriel saw him take a deep breath.

"She was alone. She cut the umbilical cord with nail clippers, then wrapped me in a blanket, put me on the bed, and left." He looked at Gabriel. "My mother knew something was wrong with me."

Again, Gabriel shrugged his shoulders. "Nothing wrong. Just different. And according to the file, she was nineteen when she gave birth to you. I cannot even imagine the shock when she set eyes on her newborn. If your unexpected—and unusual—appearance was really the reason for her leaving, do not judge her too harshly."

The silence stretched for a few heartbeats, during which Gabriel pondered the possibility of Taylor finally losing his controlled manners and beginning to shout at him for the unwanted advice.

Taylor opened a drawer, took out a check, and signed it. Holding it out to Gabriel, he said, "The outstanding fee. I will recommend your firm."

Gabriel took the check and stored it in the inner pocket of his leather jacket. Monique would cash it on Monday. Time to get out of here.

"One more thing," Taylor said. "Last time, you asked one of my employees if there's a chance of using one of the club rooms."

Gabriel sighed. Damn. It seemed his plans for the night had just been cancelled. "They're for members only. I know," he said. "I thought asking wouldn't hurt."

Taylor's attention was on the file. "The information about my mother and my grandfather is valuable. You may use room number eight tonight. For free."

Gabriel blushed ever so slightly. "Look," he said, "I didn't have any intention of prying favors from you. Of course I will pay for—"

"Have fun, Mr. Jordan. And goodnight."

CHAPTER TWO

THE young elf was about to open a portal for the very first time, and he was excited about it. He had spent last night awake and alert, sharpening his senses as well as calming his soul.

Opening a portal was nothing one should do lightly.

His older brother had opened his first portal at the age of fifteen. When he came back, not only their parents but also the whole village had been there, greeting him and cheering when he stepped through the golden light.

The portals were sacred, created at the dawn of time. Only one who knew the right runes and managed to feed them with power could open them.

He would earn his name today by opening a portal and stepping into another world, one of his choice and liking. He had chosen the unicorns' world, and he would kill the first one he could find. A large, strong unicorn would die at his hands; he would bring back the bloodied horn, and his people would reward him with the name he would carry until he died.

He was a bit nervous, but he knew that was to be expected. His older brother had been nervous too. He had told him so.

The sun rose above the mists; the young elf put down his weapons. He knew it would take a hard fight to kill his unicorn, but he still wore nothing but a string of leather around his hips. Clothes would only slow him down during the hunt, and he couldn't carry a weapon either, as no metal must soil the unicorn's hair.

The first line of the rune was easy. At the second one, his hand trembled, but he swiftly steadied himself. He knew the rune necessary to open the portal. Knew it by heart. In the past few months, he had done nothing else but learn how to paint this one rune and how to feed it with power. He knew what he was doing.

A name was most important among his people. A man without a name couldn't marry and couldn't have children and wasn't allowed to stay with his family. A man without a name was nothing but a shadow, and the young elf didn't want to become a shadow.

He had also learned how to protect himself from the portal's powers. It wouldn't be able to harm him. Safely, he would step through it, and safely, he would return.

The last line. The rune flared up and the portal opened, bright and frightening.

No use waiting any longer. The longer he waited, the longer his family had to wait for their son to return.

He lifted his eyes to the portal and took the first step, shielding his mind against its powers. It was easy. Much easier than he had thought.

The young elf began to laugh. Unable to stop, he dropped to his knees at the portal's doorstep with tears running down his face. It was so easy! Why had no one ever told him how easy it was to step through a portal?

The discord hummed in his blood, but he was not aware of it. He'd never opened a portal before; he did not know how it should look and taste and sound. His mind was torn apart without him even noticing it. His body, bereft of the mind's protection, shriveled to dust.

Long past midnight, his family arrived and waited for him to return. When the moon went down, they hung their heads in shame, believing he'd been too much of a coward to step through the portal. They believed him to have chosen the life of a shadow without a name.

They never mentioned him again, not knowing how he had died or that he had died at all.

CHAPTER THREE

TANITH and Aleksei were laughing and talking when Gabriel closed the door to Taylor's office behind him. Her hand was on his lover's arm; her eyes were sparkling, and when she said something, he rewarded her with a crooked, knowing smile.

A sudden, harsh rush of unexpected jealousy threatened to strangle Gabriel; when he cleared his throat, trying to keep his face calm, Aleksei turned to him.

The smile deepened. And now there was that special extra something in it that made it a real smile, one for Gabriel alone to see.

The jealousy vanished as quickly as it had developed.

Gabriel loved this special smile. It made him feel safe, and until recently, it had made him want to rip the clothes off his lover and fuck him senseless.

Yep. Exactly. *Forget about the odd feelings and emotions plaguing you today. Think about the room awaiting Aleksei and you.*

Until now, he hadn't even noticed how hard he was.

"Well, have fun, then, Bill," Tanith said. "And don't forget what I've told you: trust no one, especially not the nice ones." She winked at Gabriel and then fished for a key in her tight leather trousers. "Here's room number eight," she said, unlocking the door. "You have until sunrise, because at sunrise, we close."

"I will be sure to make good use of the remaining time," Aleksei replied smoothly. "Many thanks for your advice, Miss Tanith. It is very much appreciated."

Her smile vanished, and she leaned closer, whispering into his ear. "Seen too much, Bill, not to warn a nice guy like you. You seem to trust your partner. All I say is he looks dangerous to me. Do be careful, won't you? Don't want to call an ambulance and the cops because he's beaten you bloody." Without another word, she went downstairs, leaving Aleksei and Gabriel alone in the corridor.

The door to room number eight was ajar; no way to see anything yet but darkness.

"What the hell was she talking about?"

Aleksei crossed the distance between them with a few long strides, wrapped his arms around Gabriel's waist, and pressed his groin against his leg. "She considers you dangerous," he replied lightly. "I can only agree. You didn't tell me this is a sex club, Gabe."

"I'm not dangerous!"

"And not just *any* sex club. This is the *Poison Prince*, the most exclusive club in town, if not in the state. Members only, and a membership is practically impossible to get if you aren't recommended by at least five trustworthy people. Who must be members as well. Open to everyone, regardless of sex or race."

Gabriel shook his head. "Is there anything you don't know?" he sighed. "Do you want to go home now you know what this place is?"

Aleksei pressed his whole body against Gabriel's. "You must be joking, beloved. Go now, before I unravel the secrets of this place in person? You brought me here for a reason. And behind me is an open door. I clearly recall your promise of taking me really hard."

There was a predatory smile on the fae's face that made clear once more that ultimately, Aleksei was in charge, even when he offered himself so blatantly.

Gabriel tightened his embrace. "You're not offended? I wasn't sure. We've never done it outside the house. You certainly don't strike me as the sort of person who'd enter such a club willingly. I know in some rooms there's equipment for torture, and in others you will find a direct line to the 'net with hundreds of people watching what you're doing. Live porn, whipping, gang bangs—name it and you will find it here. I am more surprised you don't want to leave than I would have been at your immediate rebuke of the sheer idea of staying a little while."

Without a word, Aleksei pushed the door further open.

Well, Gabriel had planned this, wanted this for months now, ever since he'd taken on the job. Now the room was his, and so was Aleksei. To hell with his strange thoughts about being called and cursed. To hell with his messing around. He must have been sick, drugged, maybe, or he wouldn't have even looked at the tree nymph.

His heart thumped loudly in his chest, as if to remind him he was alive.

To hell with his thoughts about death. A moment ago he'd been jealous of Tanith, but Aleksei was his, and was waiting for his attention.

He swallowed, then followed Aleksei into the darkness.

The door closed with a soft sound, barely audible.

He took in his surroundings.

It wasn't an overly large room, and it had clearly been designed to serve many desires. The walls were a dark, gleaming velvet, the floor polished redwood. Tiny bulbs were scattered across the ceiling, making it resemble the night sky and shedding just enough light that he could see where he was treading. A big, low bed dominated the room; at a second look, Gabriel saw it could be folded up should someone prefer the floor. The bed sheets were black satin. Handcuffs dangled from the headboard.

His jeans became tighter. Aleksei was very responsive to handcuffs.

The room didn't have a window, but there were several shelves along the walls. Gabriel watched as Aleksei picked up a whip, a rope, chains, and, last, an enormous dildo. It was unnerving, seeing his lover examine the thing: the sight made Gabriel feel small and unimportant, unworthy of the fae's love or, to be precise, anyone's love. If Aleksei wanted to play with the dildo, it could only mean he considered him, Gabriel, as not properly endowed, and that he was unsatisfied with their lovemaking.

Well. There hadn't been any lovemaking recently, and that was entirely his fault.

Aleksei turned, dildo in hand. He raised an eyebrow. "What on earth is one supposed to do with this thing?" he asked, sounding genuinely curious.

Gabriel swallowed. "Some men—and some women—have the need for a really large… item inside them. If you…. Do you…?"

Aleksei laughed. He flipped the dildo in his hand before putting it back on the shelf. "Ridiculous."

Then he picked up some candles, put them in holders placed along the shelves, and lit them with a single well-practiced rune. "A bit more light," he said. Then he turned to Gabriel and let his coat slip off his shoulders. "I want to see your face, beloved. And your body."

Gabriel gulped. Aleksei's admiration of his physique never ceased to amaze him—had someone asked him to describe himself, he would have called himself as common as muck. In his own eyes, there was no reason to look at him admiringly. Yet his lover did, even though Gabriel had neglected Aleksei's needs recently.

Gabriel lifted his hands to his shirt to unbutton it, but Aleksei stopped him.

"Don't," he said. "Let me get undressed first."

Gabriel couldn't do anything but nod.

Aleksei's long, slender fingers moved to his throat, where he took off the necklace disguising his true looks. Not that it made any difference to Gabriel if he wore it or not, as he was always able to see the fae as he was. Aleksei, though, preferred not to wear it during sex. He said it was like wearing a mask and that he disliked that feeling when he was with Gabriel.

Carefully, he placed the necklace onto one of the shelves. Slowly, he opened the first button of his shirt. Underneath, there was smooth skin, and when he opened the next button, Gabriel could also see the first tendrils of ivy painted on his lover's chest. The patterns glowed.

They only glowed when Aleksei was excited or very angry. Or aroused.

The shirt fluttered to the floor. Gabriel's eyes were glued to Aleksei's throat, where he could see the pulse beating fast and steady. Even across the distance, he could smell his lover's unique fragrance. As always, it reminded him of the first night they'd spent together. Back then, it had been a forced pairing. Now, in this strange room, Gabriel suddenly understood Aleksei had never offered himself so freely and completely.

He took a step and then halted. Aleksei had shaken his head ever so slightly, but with a smile on his face that made it clear it wasn't meant as rebuke.

Aleksei's hands moved to his belt. It tinkled gently when he opened it, the metal clanking against the top button of his trousers. Trousers that exquisitely clad his long, slender legs and his firm ass. They landed in a pool at Aleksei's feet, along with his briefs. Like a dancer, Aleksei stepped out of them, leaving them behind and taking a step toward Gabriel in one movement.

The candlelight reflected on his pale skin, adding an unusual golden cast. Gabriel had believed he was used to the sight because there were dozens of candles in their bedroom at home. He'd been wrong. Aleksei had never looked as gorgeous as he did tonight. In this strange room with its purple walls, the candlelight had a different effect on the fae. Maybe it was the tiny lights on the ceiling mingling with the candlelight. Maybe it was because Aleksei was so very aroused and— maybe—even a little scared of what Gabriel might have in mind for him. In any case, there was a richness to the tone of his skin that Gabriel hadn't seen before. More patterns appeared on his body, from tiny blossoms around his ankles and larger leaves on his biceps and shoulders to the ivy growing from his throat down to his abdomen. His thighs were decorated with lines and circles, and on his temples and cheeks were patterns Gabriel couldn't wait to touch.

The only thing Aleksei still wore was the silver bracelet Gabriel had given him, the first present he'd ever made to his lover. It accentuated his nudity in a way that was breathtaking.

Gabriel's eyes lingered on the bracelet for a long moment. Aleksei had promised he'd never take it off, and so far, he'd kept his promise. It meant more to Gabriel than he could express.

He took a step. His gaze wandered over his lover's body only to be drawn to his cock, rising hard and erect from a completely hairless groin.

Gabriel's own cock jerked in his trousers. Aleksei must have shaved himself today, something he had never done before. It looked glorious.

Patterns circled the base of Aleksei's cock, too delicate to be seen clearly from a distance. They wound up to the tip; it looked as if his manhood was bound, and the markings shone in a strong, icy blue just like the color of Aleksei's eyes.

Like a sleepwalker, Gabriel reached out and cupped his lover's balls. Squeezing them gently, he heard Aleksei gasp with pleasure as if from a distance. This could not be real. He must still be asleep, in his bed at home, no odd thoughts and fears and memories having ever bubbled up inside him.

Only—there was a need he couldn't name yet, a need to continue squeezing Aleksei's balls until they burst, until Aleksei howled with pain, leaving him bleeding and screaming on the bare floor.

Hurt him badly.

Ever so slightly, Gabriel shook his head, forcing the voice out of his mind. He did squeeze a bit harder, but not hard enough to cause even the slightest bit of pain. In addition, Gabriel's throat became dry with fear. But he couldn't leave now. Leaving would mean an end to the relationship.

He was in control. No stupid alien thoughts would ever make him hurt Aleksei!

Aleksei loved having his balls massaged. Usually, he would lie on the bed and spread his legs wide, urging Gabriel on to the next step. He wasn't a patient lover, whether he was top or bottom.

Right now, he just stood and waited, his cock swelling a bit more as Gabriel continued to squeeze.

Gently. He would never, ever hurt Aleksei, no matter what his brain demanded. Clearly, his mind could not be trusted. Clearly, it was better to act on instinct, for his instinct told him to simply fuck his lover senseless.

A dream. Yes. Maybe that was the right way to look at it. Or a nightmare, rather. The whole day had been a nightmare. It still was. But a nightmare, though frightening, was harmless. A nightmare, no matter how realistic, could not do harm.

Stick to that, Gabriel thought. *This is not real.*

Aleksei's balls were smooth and tight, the skin slightly oily. He must have taken great care in his grooming. Small sounds of delight escaped his lips each time Gabriel clenched his fingers.

I'm in command, Gabriel thought, and he had trouble believing it. *I can do this. I love him. He wants me and I want him, and damn this day and my urge to run away from him!*

Determined, he blocked out the uneasy feeling of eyes drilling into the back of his head. Determined, he blocked out the voice telling him to shed blood. No one apart from himself and his lover was in this room. He wasn't being watched, no one was calling him, and damn it, he needed to concentrate on the task at hand!

He ran his hand lightly up to the top of Aleksei's cock. "You're gorgeous," he whispered hoarsely. "Did you shave while I was asleep?"

"I thought you might like it." Aleksei's voice was soft with need.

"Love it. Love you!"

Aleksei met his eyes. "I understand this is a room to play," he said. "I am open to whatever you have in mind for me."

Gabriel continued to stroke his lover's cock. It lay large and hard in his hand, the head moist and swollen.

Bite it off. Hurt him. Kill him.

Gabriel closed his eyes, trying to keep the upcoming panic at bay. He kissed Aleksei's neck, right above one small blue blossom. "There's the bed," he murmured. "And there are handcuffs, if you like."

"There is more to this room than the bed," Aleksei objected, still not moving and not even bothering to look at the bed. Instead, he looked upward to the ceiling.

Gabriel followed his gaze. He hadn't noticed something was hanging up there—the room had been too dark at first, and then Aleksei had undressed, and now he was torn between thoughts of love and murder.

Hurt him. Kill him.

Echoes in his head. The small hairs at the back of his neck stood up.

On the other hand, if Aleksei wanted to play, he would do whatever he could to make this one night at the *Poison Prince* a memorable one.

He reluctantly let go of Aleksei's cock and stepped back so he could take a proper look at the ceiling. "Strings? Ropes? Is this—leather or fabric or what?"

"It is called a swing," Aleksei said. "If I understood Tanith correctly, the construction is supposed to carry a man's weight as well as bind him. Anyone sitting in the swing would be completely at the mercy of his or her partner. Unable to get free on one's own accord. Unable to touch oneself, should the dominant partner not allow it. There are shackles for ankles and wrists. I would consider it an ultimate proof of trust should anyone allow himself to be bound like that voluntarily."

An icy shiver ran over Gabriel. Trust—now that had always been an issue between them. Aleksei had lied to him practically from the first moment on. About his name, his race, his profession…. And it had also taken ages before Gabriel had been able to open up to Aleksei, to tell him about his mother, his grandmother, his lonely childhood, his miserable life.

He hadn't thought trust was still an issue between them. He hadn't known Aleksei doubted his trust in him.

Then another thought struck him. What if Aleksei not only doubted him but also knew about his near betrayal and was now challenging him to reveal this last shameful secret and end their relationship?

Just when he was about to blurt out the truth, every single bit of it, from his encounter with the tree nymph and his urge to run away from home to the kiss he'd shared with Conchita, a strange expression flashed over the fae's face.

"Look—" Gabriel began, but Aleksei interrupted him.

"You misunderstood me," Aleksei said quietly. "You seem to have drifted away from me recently. I dislike that. I am willing to prove my trust in you and this relationship. It's why we are here."

Gracefully, he dropped to his knees. Gracefully, he crossed his wrists behind his back.

Gabriel stared at him, dumbstruck. This couldn't be true! The Aleksei he knew was always in charge under any circumstances, even when helplessly writhing underneath him. The Aleksei he knew wouldn't kneel in front of him and wouldn't offer to be put in a swing and—

Hit him. Hurt him. Kill him.

Instinctively, Gabriel bared his teeth to the unknown enemy in his mind. It grew stronger every time it phrased one of those cruel, impossible commands. It was about to overpower his will, his intention to make love to his partner, to enjoy this night and repair what had gone awry between them.

The part of him that was wolf woke up suddenly, unexpectedly. It took over from one heartbeat to the next. The wolf pushed Gabriel's human mind aside, his fears and his doubts and his disbelief at the possibility of an enemy really trying to command him.

Gabriel's wolf part was strong, much stronger than he'd ever thought.

His vision blurred. Aleksei's black hair mingled with the darkness of the room. His pale skin looked like watercolor on a paper left out in the rain.

This wasn't real. So he could do what he wanted, no matter the consequences.

Everything.

He didn't know where that thought had come from, but it seemed a good one. Without even knowing he was doing it, Gabriel shed the part of himself that made him human and allowed the wolf to take over. The wolf didn't hear voices, and if he did, he didn't care about them. The wolf only cared about his need.

Here and now, he didn't have a name, no fears and no worries and no wish to hurt his mate. Here and now, he was someone else, someone who wasn't watched or called, someone who didn't need to be afraid of secrets, and definitely not someone who killed others.

Only the mating counted. The man on the floor had begged to be taken, had offered himself, was waiting for his attention.

A thin chain dangled from the ceiling. He pulled it, and the swing rattled down, all clinking leather and metal. It was tangled, but it gleamed with promise in the candlelight, so the wolf ran his hands along the catches and loops, the smaller and larger shackles, smelled the leather and the oil that kept the metal free of rust.

His cock ached for action. The wolf might rule his mind, but his body was still human. He had hands and arms; he knew how to do this.

The man on the floor didn't resist when the wolf lifted him up and put him into the swing. He didn't struggle when the web of leather was rearranged around him so the swing held the weight of his body. Large straps safely supported his back and neck. When the wolf took his wrists and let the cuffs snap closed, he never even flinched, nor when his naked feet were hooked up into stirrups. He complied fully; he never complained.

The metal was cold. The leather must feel alien to the man's body, especially because no words interrupted the silence, no touch was offered beyond what was necessary, and because the wolf never kissed his mate or even looked him in the eye.

Wolves didn't kiss.

The wolf had lost his sense of time, so he didn't know if it had taken mere minutes or hours to put the man into the swing. Closing all the snaps and holds, securing his wrists, and adjusting each leather strap was definitely tedious work.

But well worth it. When it was done, when his—mate? victim?—hung before him, his naked ass exactly at groin height, the wolf growled at the sight of the tight puckered hole and the shiny, shaven balls. Each of the man's limbs was bound in leather and metal. Long legs were spread, pale arms cuffed out of the way so the man had no chance to touch himself.

Ice-blue eyes were watching him. It was a disturbing thing, as if they were asking questions he couldn't answer, as if they could see a part of his soul he didn't want to be seen and wasn't even sure had been there before tonight. So the wolf found a long piece of fabric and blindfolded the man, in part to get him even more under his control, leaving him in the dark about what would happen to him, but mostly so he wouldn't have to look into those eyes.

He ran his hand along one long leg. The man shivered under his touch, and his cock jumped.

Not good enough. Not enough control.

Thoughtfully, the wolf watched the man in the swing, traced the lines on his skin and followed them to the crotch, where they circled balls and cock.

An idea sparked in what was left of his human mind. Yes, that would certainly give him the ultimate control.

The shelves along the wall were filled with toys. Clamps, whips, all sorts of lube, dildos....

Use it. Ram it into him, rip him apart, make him scream for mercy!

Stupid voice. Still audible, even now and although he'd hoped it had gone quiet.

Picking up one of the dildos, the wolf pondered its use, then looked at the man in the swing. He had been uneasy at the thought of it. True, he had laughed and called the thing ridiculous, but deep down, the wolf knew he had been scared of the idea of having it inside his body. It was large, too large, and it would hurt like hell.

Smooth rubber, plain black. It would make the man scream.

Do it! Use it! End it!

The voice was hysterical. It wanted him to obey, but wolves were free. They didn't obey orders. They were not dogs, and the voice knew it was losing its power over him.

The wolf growled and put the dildo back on the shelf. No. He wanted to fuck his mate, not use a tool on him. He wanted him to scream with pleasure, not pain.

He wanted him to remain his mate, not die in a pool of blood.

So the wolf went back to the swing in the middle of the room empty-handed. Candles flickered when he went past. A few went out.

Probably a stray draft of air.

When he stood between the legs of his mate, the wolf could not only see his heartbeat, he could also hear it. That was a first. His hearing was much better than average, but it wasn't that good. To prove himself right, he pressed his ear to the man's chest. Yes. Wild and fast. Maybe the man's complete and utter submission was doing this to him—improving and highlighting his senses.

Undoing the leather string binding back his hair, the wolf let it touch the man's glowing skin.

Another shiver, longer this time. The man's cock stood up straight like a soldier, with the foreskin revealing the velvet head and the wet, dripping slit on top.

Mine, the wolf thought.

He cupped the man's balls swiftly and wound the string around the base of his cock, tightening it and forcing a deep groan from the man. The string looked black against the man's skin. When he wound it another few times around the man's length, a thin smile curved the wolf's lips. Hadn't he thought the patterns resembled a binding? Now he was using a real one, and he bound cock and balls tight, restraining the blood flow in order to delay, if not forbid, orgasm.

The man's head fell back, only loosely supported by the ropes. His neck muscles stood out as he tried to find a more comfortable position, and as he did so, the swing swayed and with it his whole body. His legs, spread wide already, were pulled apart further by the movement; his hole, slack with anticipation, twitched.

The wolf cupped the man's balls again, roughly this time. Because of the tight binding, they appeared harder, the freshly shaved and slightly oily skin gleaming in the candlelight like dark marble.

A bead of precome was gliding down the man's shaft.

Damn, but he couldn't wait any longer. He needed to fuck, fuck that hole and come deep inside the man's ass before he exploded, and so the wolf stepped out of his jeans, throwing them into a corner and grabbing his own cock in the same movement. A bit of spit should do for easing the way—the wolf had completely forgotten about the lube on the shelves. In the wolf's mind, preparation was overrated, teasing and foreplay as well. Only the fuck itself counted, and the harsh yells he would rip out of the bound man.

A voice whispered in the back of his head, but he couldn't make out any words. Wordless orders, having no meaning to him. This was the wolf's hour. No other had the power to intervene.

Just one more moment, for the wolf liked the somewhat painful anticipation before he entered a hole, so he lingered at the man's entrance, letting his cockhead kiss the man's ass.

This time, the groan was really harsh.

No more lingering. No more empty promises. The wolf put one hand on the man's waist to still the swing's movement, kept hold of his cock, and pushed hard and deep, breaching the man's entrance without wasting any thought on whether he might be ready or not. A little pain was okay because very soon, it would be washed away by lust.

Oh, yeah, that was good. Tight and hot, and now he put his second hand on the man's hips, his grip as hard as his thrusts. He'd leave bruises.

So what.

Hard. Fast. Deep. No thoughts penetrated the wolf's mind, no emotions. Only his cock ruled, and his cock alone. This was better than drugs, better than alcohol, better than food and sleep and water on a parched tongue.

It was better than love. Love only made demands and restrictions. Love wanted rules and obedience.

He growled again—or maybe he howled—and when he came, he didn't even notice. There was no release with his orgasm, no satisfaction, not even the usual fatigue and wish to curl up and sleep. His cock stayed hard, and so did the man's.

He kept fucking and thrusting, his hands moving to his victim's ass so he could spread his cheeks wider for better access.

Maybe the man groaned. Maybe he begged for his release, for the wolf to undo the binding on his cock so he could come.

It was of no concern to him. This was for his pleasure only, and if he went a bit wild and a bit mad, it didn't matter.

Seconds, minutes, or hours—he didn't know. The thrusting was all, his need to find release, although he'd already come, his seed making his victim's tight hole slicker and easier to fuck. He was hard, which meant he continued fucking.

He howled again, like the wolf that was pacing restlessly inside him would have howled had he been able to surface completely. He fucked like a wolf, not caring about his mate and eager to bite his throat to mark him as his possession.

Before he knew it, the wolf had pulled the man up until he was sitting on him, supporting his weight and driving even deeper into him now that gravity helped him along. Before he knew it, he'd wrapped his arms around him, pulled him tight and even tighter until he could feel his mate's racing heartbeat against his sweaty chest.

Another little bit and he would break bones.

And before he knew he was doing it, the wolf had bitten him, drawing blood, coming again and this time feeling every moment of it, enjoying it, riding out his orgasm while licking over his mate's exposed throat. Blood trickled down his pale skin.

Nothing had ever tasted better.

Sated, the wolf let go of the man, who fell back into the swing's supporting chains with a groan. When the wolf pulled out his finally flaccid cock, seed trickled down his legs. He had come; the wolf could go to sleep now.

The man in the swing muttered words he didn't understand in a pleading, begging voice. At the sight of his dark-red cock, swollen and still bound by the leather string, he thought he could grasp their meaning. Obviously, the man wanted to be released from his bindings to take a hand to himself and end the pain in his member.

As quickly as he'd surfaced, the wolf retreated, and as expected, the voice was back, suggesting he let the man hang there, unable to get free and unable to touch himself, his cock stiff and erect and dripping with precome but unable to spill.

He could still hurt him. He could still end this damn useless relationship with a few well-placed lashes of the whip.

He could still use the dildo on him.

Surely lust had turned into pain by now. Surely if he left now, he would be free of this creature and his icy blue eyes and his emotions and his need.

"Gabe, please!"

His name and the way Aleksei said it, urgent, hoarsely, dropped into the blackness of his mind and blocked out the voice's cruelty. Quickly, Gabriel stepped back between Aleksei's legs and put one soothing hand on his heart while he wrapped the other around his lover's cock. It was hot to the touch; the leather string, partly obscuring the iridescent skin patterns, was tightly wrapped around it from base to tip, the knot tight just underneath the head.

For a split second, Gabriel wondered who'd done this to Aleksei; for a split second, he adored the gorgeous sight of his lover's swollen, painfully hard cock.

Then he tried to undo the knot. At first, he thought he wouldn't be able to do it. The leather was slick with sweat and precome, and Aleksei squirmed and wriggled underneath him. "Please," he rasped, his voice rough and hoarse and deep. "Please, Gabe."

Gabriel shivered with the fear he'd kept the leather string on for too long, doing serious harm to the fragile veins and muscles.

His fingers were too clumsy to do the job. He couldn't open the damn knot!

Finally, he used his teeth, trying to bite the string apart. When he nicked the tender skin, Aleksei's groans turned into a low scream.

Pleasure or pain?

Yes! Bite him harder, bite the vein open and let him bleed to death!

He ignored the voice. His tongue was dry; he struggled to bite the string apart without nicking Aleksei again.

Then the knot gave way, and with an awkward thrust, Aleksei came in his mouth. Gabriel just had time to wrap his lips around his lover's cock before Aleksei spilled his seed, screaming harshly in his orgasm, his muscles cramping after too long a time in the swing with his legs spread too wide and his hole getting fucked too hard.

Gabriel swallowed every drop his lover had for him, massaging his balls and keeping one arm underneath him for extra support. Only when Aleksei was empty and sated did he lower the swing to the ground, cold dread building up in him. With shaking hands, he undid the shackles and stretched the fae's legs carefully, easing the cramps out of his muscles. Finally, after he'd mustered all the courage he could find, he took off the blindfold.

With closed eyes, Aleksei lay on the floor, the swing sprawled disassembled around him. His breathing was fast, and so was his heartbeat; Gabriel could feel it under his palm.

Hadn't he been able to hear it not too long ago? Hadn't it added to his lust to sense the fae's fear at his own helplessness, at being blind and bound and at his mercy?

What have I done?

Hesitantly, he touched his lover's face. "Aleksei," he whispered. "Are you okay?"

What if he wasn't? He'd lost control, he was sure of it. What if whatever he'd done to Aleksei had been too much?

The thought shocked Gabriel into action. Jumping up, he tripped over one of the swing's chains, caught himself, and reached for the shelf where Aleksei had placed his necklace. With trembling hands, he picked it up and went back to his lover, where he barely managed to close the catch. If Aleksei needed medical help, at least the doctor wouldn't see his skin patterns.

"Gabe."

"Aleksei! Let me call—"

"Gabe!" Aleksei lifted his hand and touched Gabriel's face. "Stay with me for a little while, will you?"

Weak with relief his lover was at least able to talk, Gabriel settled next to him. Not knowing if his touch was welcome, he decided to give it a try anyway. With his fingertips, he touched Aleksei's lips and nearly cried when a lazy, sated smile curved the fae's mouth.

"Are you... I mean, do you need anything?" Gabriel asked anxiously.

"Just you," Aleksei whispered. "This was... very intense."

Gabriel gulped. He couldn't really remember what he'd done. He only knew his cock hurt and his legs trembled as if he'd run a few miles too many. "You aren't hurt? I can press the alarm button, and they will send a doctor up if it's what you want. Just—please, love, I'm sorry! I didn't mean to lose control like that!"

Now Aleksei opened his eyes. "Hurt?" His raised eyebrow spoke louder of his confusion than words could have done.

Gabriel didn't know what to say. He *had* hurt him, he was sure of it. Around Aleksei's wrists were bruises caused by the cuffs, his legs and his back would ache for days, and....

He frowned, trying to remember. They had fucked. Hard. And he'd come, which was a fact, as the dried traces on his legs and between Aleksei's buttocks proved.

Only—he couldn't remember. Why did he think he'd *wanted* to hurt the man he loved?

He stretched out next to Aleksei, resting his head on his lover's shoulder. He had to clench his teeth or a sound of utter despair would have emerged.

Aleksei pulled him closer, brushing his lips across his. "You did not hurt me," he said quietly. "On the contrary. What you did to me was amazing and unbelievably beautiful."

I can't even remember what I did, Gabriel thought, and had to fight hard not to cry.

CHAPTER FOUR

ARANI had grown up among thieves. Picking pockets came as naturally to her as breathing, and she'd been able to steal the rings from her mother's fingers before she was able to talk.

Not that she liked talking much. Talking led to problems, problems led to arguments and more talking, and all in all, she preferred silence. Especially the long silences while she waited for a portal to open, for the really good places for stealing were on the other side of them. So far, she'd sneaked into three of the hidden worlds, one of them being where the elves lived. They had a city high up in the trees. They had jewels and enough food to keep her family fed for an entire month.

The only problem was, of course, that she couldn't open a portal herself.

Her father had warned her about crossing into other worlds. "It's too dangerous," he would say. "One never knows how long one will be stuck there. Do you want to get stuck in the centaurs' world? Or in a world where harpies rip your heart out?"

Stupid prejudices. Harpies ate a mostly vegetarian diet, as Arani had found out. She was twenty-four, she had been the sole provider for her family ever since her father had lost his eyesight, and still, he treated her like a child.

She had been waiting since sunrise for the riverghost to open the portal. She was bound to arrive any moment now, carrying her basket with goods for her daughter, who lived in the elves' world. The riverghost crossed through the portals at least once a month, and always, Arani was waiting for her. Old and nearly as blind as Arani's father, the riverghost was no threat to her, and wouldn't see her were she to jump up right in front of her. She never noticed she wasn't on her own when painting the runes into the dust. She definitely didn't know Arani was going through with her, a silent, secret passenger, like a tick on a dog's neck.

Arani grinned. Excitement bubbled up in her when she thought of the town. It was so big and shiny and noisy, and occasionally, she dreamed of staying there and never coming back. After all, what did her world have to offer?

Precisely nothing. Eventually, someone would catch her thieving, and then her hands would get chopped off.

So she resolutely pushed the thought away. Thinking about the law's ax wasn't something she liked to do, especially not shortly before sneaking through a portal.

In theory, she knew how they worked, of course. More than once, she had tried to paint the lines onto the ground herself. Actually, she was sure she'd drawn them correctly, but nothing ever happened. No golden light erupted and no portal opened, no matter how much she prayed.

Surely she was doing something wrong. But as long as the old riverghost kept visiting her wayward daughter, Arani could visit the elves' world and, while there, steal what she liked. The protection the riverghost weaved around herself was strong enough to protect her as well. And so far, she'd always found someone to take her back, equally unaware she was at their tail.

"Finally." Stretching her aching back, Arani watched the old riverghost trotting along the path to the tree where she usually opened the portal. She'd never found out why the woman did it here and not somewhere else, but then, talking to the one giving her a free ride wasn't really an option.

Maybe it was because of the small pool underneath the trees. Maybe the riverghost just felt safer opening the portal next to water that wasn't too close to her home.

When the portal opened, the golden light seemed a bit less bright, but it was probably only because it was a hot day and the sun blazed even through the roof of leaves above.

Did the old woman seem a bit flustered, confused, even?

Arani didn't pay much attention to her. "Go through," she murmured. "I don't want to spend all day here in the woods when the city is awaiting me!"

She did notice the riverghost hesitate before the portal. Just for a fraction of a second and not long enough to make her worry, but she did notice.

She found out why when she stepped through the portal right after her, but by then it was too late.

Wrong! Arani's mind screamed while the portal's powers drained her life and her will. *Help!* she wanted to shout, but couldn't, as she didn't have a throat anymore, or a mouth.

She died before the old riverghost woman, but only by a matter of seconds. Parts of her body were found in both worlds, and her father grieved for her and cursed her with the same breath, weeping and mumbling "I told her" over and over again.

The old riverghost went missing, just like the young elf seeking his name. Just like the others who weren't strong enough to withstand the portal's powers now that a trip through the portals turned into something fatal every now and then because of the discord caused by the banshee's constant call.

CHAPTER FIVE

THE floor wasn't as cold as he'd thought, and as he was warmed by Aleksei's always slightly higher body heat, Gabriel eventually managed to suppress the shivers trying to claim him.

He didn't manage to keep his mind in check, though.

I lost control. I hurt Aleksei. He'll dump me the moment he comes back to his senses!

Carefully, so as not to disturb his lover, Gabriel licked his lips, swallowed, and wished desperately for water to wash away the taste of blood in his mouth.

I bit him.

No use denying it. Not only was Aleksei's blood still on his lips, he could also see the wound his teeth had caused. An irregular, deep bite between ear and shoulder, nasty-looking and surely painful.

He couldn't help himself. He kissed the wound gently, adding a silent apology and praying to all existent and imaginary gods that Aleksei would eventually be able to forgive him.

A smile ghosted over Aleksei's face; he reached out and placed a tired hand on Gabriel's waist.

It didn't make sense. How could he smile? How could he touch the man who… did whatever Gabriel had done to him?

Then a thought hit him. Gabriel moved back an inch or two, trying to get a better look at Aleksei's neck. There was the bite mark, clearly visible even in the candlelight. "This should be healed by now," he said, surprised his voice sounded so normal.

"You took off the bracelet." Aleksei sighed; it sounded content. To prove his words, he lifted his left hand. Slender wrist, bruised skin, and no bracelet whatsoever in sight.

Alarmed, Gabriel sat up. He couldn't remember any of it. "I didn't... I wouldn't.... Did I?"

"Hmmm. When you closed the cuffs. Very considerate of you given how tight they were. The bracelet must be somewhere on the floor."

"But I never did anything like this before!"

The shock and confusion in his voice caused Aleksei to open his eyes. "Nothing you did tonight have you ever done before," he pointed out. "You've never taken me to any kind of club. You've never blindfolded me. You've never taken me with such force, and no, you've never taken the bracelet off me. You did tonight. Where is the problem?"

"Everywhere," Gabriel wanted to answer, and, "It wasn't me who did it." But he remained silent. Instead, he patted his hands over the floor, found his jeans and his shirt and, finally, the silver bracelet. Runes were engraved in the metal. When the catch closed around Aleksei's wrist, the sound was so familiar Gabriel remembered having done it for the first time in every detail. Back then, he hadn't doubted his love, and back then, he hadn't felt as if a wild animal was lurking inside him, waiting for another opportunity to escape.

Back then, there hadn't been voices telling him to hurt his lover.

The wound on Aleksei's neck began to heal even as he watched. The runes were powerful, designed to take care of moderate and even larger injuries as well as simple muscle aches and bruises. It was his design; together with Marita, he'd made it, and he'd never been so relieved to see it work perfectly.

Gabriel gingerly traced his hand over his lover's belly, down toward his legs. They had trembled when he'd taken the fae out of the swing. They trembled now when he touched him.

Aleksei moved ever so slightly, sighing contently when Gabriel brushed his fingertips along his inner thigh and higher, toward the sensitive bridge between scrotum and anus.

"Don't you mind me touching you?"

Stupid question. Obviously Aleksei didn't mind or he wouldn't have spread his legs.

"But I hurt you!"

"You took me hard. As promised."

Aleksei's fingers caressed him. It felt as heavenly as it felt wrong.

"You didn't hurt me. You know I consider you binding me to be highly arousing. Any kind of binding. Beloved, why do you insist on regretting something you haven't done?"

Helplessly, Gabriel sank into his lover's arms, not knowing how to answer. He didn't have any answers anymore. He wasn't even sure if he knew the questions.

They stayed a little longer in the purple-colored room, until their heartbeats had calmed down and the sweat on their bodies had dried. When the floor became unpleasantly cool, they moved into the shower, standing silently under the warm spray until they were clean and getting too tired to remain standing upright for much longer. When they dressed, they didn't talk; when they stepped out into the corridor, it was empty.

No one was waiting for them.

His clothes felt odd on his skin. The silence rang in his ears, and Gabriel couldn't help but listening for the sound of sirens. Surely someone had heard Aleksei scream; surely someone had called the cops.

He had raped Aleksei. He knew it no matter his partner's denial, and it made him sick. Despite the shower, he felt filthy; despite the water's heat, there was a deep coldness claiming his body, and he doubted he would be able to get rid of it anytime soon.

He had to force himself toward the stairs, wishing he could jump out of a window. Only there weren't any; only Aleksei expected him to go home now.

Aleksei was already out of sight.

"Did you enjoy your time at the *Poison Prince*?"

Tanith's question came totally unexpectedly. Gabriel jumped two stairs back up, causing Aleksei to turn and look at him with a frown. *He knows something is wrong*, Gabriel thought; and then he bared his teeth in a bitter smile. Of course he knew, because everything was wrong. And Aleksei knew Gabriel inside out, much better than he knew himself.

Panic gripped him, but Gabriel managed to get it in check just in time, or a scream would have escaped him. *I'm getting real good at that*, he thought, on the edge of hysteria. *I just need to behave normally. No mad laughter. No casual kills. Normal. Can't be that hard.*

Cold sweat beading along his spine, Gabriel got a grip and went downstairs, then went into the small observation room where Tanith sat surrounded by computers and screens.

"It was perfect," Aleksei said. "Give Mr. Taylor our sincere regards and best thanks. The night in your club certainly exceeded our expectations."

Gabriel clenched his fist, expecting to feel claws. The room was too small for his liking; he was backing off when Aleksei put a hand on his arm.

"Would you show me the video from our room, please?" Aleksei said to Tanith; Gabriel saw him paint a small rune into the air.

Tanith's eyes became slightly glassy. She frowned, about to shake her head, then thought otherwise and nodded. Hesitantly, as if she had to think hard about how to perform the task, she pressed a few buttons, then leaned back in her chair, clearing the view to the largest monitor in the middle of the room.

"Video?" Gabriel whispered. He hadn't known there was camera surveillance in the rooms.

It made sense, of course. The staff needed to be able to intervene should someone go too far.

Then why Tanith hadn't intervened when he'd raped Aleksei, for fuck's sake?

Sound filled the room, and pictures, surprisingly clear given there hadn't been that much light. Instantly, Gabriel recognized the purple walls and the large bed in the background.

"Fast forward, if you please," Aleksei said, his hand still on Gabriel's arm. Without it, he would probably have jumped forward and strangled the woman. How dare she spy on them? How dare she put cameras in the room and tape them?

Had she watched? Maybe, then, she'd been too horrified at his actions to call the cops.

Transfixed, Gabriel stared at the screen, saw how Aleksei's features changed when he took off the necklace and his skin patterns became bright and prominent.

There was his lover, naked and bound, and he saw himself winding the leather string around his cock. Relieved, he noticed that he'd been gentle, and that at least in the beginning, there hadn't been pain.

On screen, Aleksei groaned. But when Gabriel looked at the man standing next to him, he saw a small, satisfied smile play on his lips.

No horror; no regret.

Gabriel couldn't watch any longer. Eyes focused on his feet, he waited for Aleksei to say something, do something. Curse him, maybe, or accuse him, or storm out, leaving him behind for good.

"Wild," Tanith said softly. "Haven't seen sex that hot in a long time. Seems you two are into the really kinky stuff. Do you even have a safe word? I bet you don't. But then, that's up to you. It's obvious you two trust each other entirely."

Gabriel's throat was too dry to swallow. Trust? After what he'd done?

The few bits he'd seen on screen and what he knew had happened didn't match. On screen, Aleksei and Tanith seemed to see sex. Compliant sex, hot and wild.

In his mind, his memory screamed "rape."

Gabriel would have fled the room if Aleksei hadn't held him back. "Burn the film onto a CD, please, Tanith," he ordered, not harshly, but without giving the woman even the smallest chance to disobey him. Another rune followed his words. It gleamed before it vanished, and Tanith did as she'd been told.

"Now delete the file and any copies you might have on your server."

It was fascinating to see her struggle. Aleksei's order clearly went against her work ethic, which told her not to go against her boss's wishes. "Gotta keep a file," she mumbled. "For security. If someone wants to sue us or... something." Her hands rested on the keyboard, her fingers twitching as they hovered over the delete button.

Aleksei sighed and wove another rune. Gabriel remembered it; the pattern was the one the fae had used when they'd first met. A Forgetting rune. It would erase any memory of the past minutes from Tanith's mind.

Her hands dropped loosely to her sides. Her head nodded toward her chest; her eyes slid closed. Obviously, Aleksei had added a Sleeping rune as well.

The fae pushed her chair aside swiftly. On the screen was a frozen picture of his face, wild with ecstasy and frighteningly beautiful. The patterns on his skin seemed to burn right into the watcher's retinas.

Of course Aleksei was eager to delete the file. He had taken his necklace off. Everyone who watched the video would see his true features, and everyone would know him not to be human. In the wrong hands, it could turn into a powerful weapon, no matter the protection the hidden races received nowadays.

Aleksei's fingers silently scurried across the keyboard. He searched the main drive for copies and found two. Delete. He searched external hard drives and found one. Delete. Finally, he checked a rack with CDs and took the one containing the nightly recordings of room number eight.

"Let's go home," he said when he was done. "She won't remember anything once she wakes up. I do hope she won't get fired for losing the files."

"I doubt Taylor will ask her, given I've told him some interesting news about his family," Gabriel said, impressed that he could actually form a sensible sentence. "He'll be too busy getting in contact with his mother."

"Let's hope you are right." Aleksei stored the CDs in the inner pocket of his coat. He was on his way out when finally Gabriel realized what was wrong with this whole scenario.

"There was a camera in the room."

Aleksei's lips twitched. "Yes, love. That's how they managed to put us on film."

"You knew about it?"

"Of course. She told me when I was waiting for you. I am surprised you didn't know."

Gabriel rubbed his neck uneasily. "Guess I didn't think of it. Point is, we were watched. When we went into the room, I could practically feel it, and it made me a bit edgy. Maybe."

Nice lie. You were edgy before, and you felt as if you were being watched before.

Gabriel gulped the words down before they could leave his mouth.

Then a thought struck him, dreadful and wonderful at the same time. What if—

"We need to get home," he urged. "Now. Quickly. Got to check something. You done here?"

"We can leave whenever you like," Aleksei replied, but Gabriel was already rushing out the front door.

ON THE verge of killing Aleksei should he stop at another red traffic light, Gabriel could not concentrate on anything but the thought he'd had in the *Poison Prince's* surveillance room.

There'd been a camera in room number eight. And in room number eight, the feeling of being watched had been strong. Strong enough to make him go wild; strong enough for his mind to snap, to make him feel like a wolf in a human body.

So what if there were other cameras around? What if there were cameras at home?

There *were* cameras at home, must be, because otherwise, he was going mad. The cameras would explain his feeling of being watched.

They wouldn't explain the voice in his head. But then, solve one problem at a time. Cameras first. The voice could wait.

"Look, can't you speed up a bit?" he urged. "It is really, really important I get home as quickly as possible."

"This *is* as quickly as possible," Aleksei replied. "Any faster and the police will stop us. I am not in the mood for using any more runes tonight, Gabe. Ten minutes at the most and you can search for whatever you are looking for."

The wheels of the old Jag, which had replaced the old Mercedes Aleksei had driven when they'd met, screeched when they took a corner. When they finally reached home, Gabriel was out of the car and halfway up the stairs before Aleksei had even turned off the motor. He didn't bother to switch on lights. His night vision was much better than average, and just recently, he had discovered his eyes had become more sensitive to artificial light. Leaving it to Aleksei to lock the car and the garage, Gabriel couldn't think about anything else but finding out whether there were unwanted intruders in their house.

Panting, Gabriel stood in the middle of the living room. He'd discarded his leather jacket on the cream-colored couch. His hair obscured his face; he'd bent his head because like that, it was easier to listen to the distant sound at the back of his mind, telling him to search for cameras, for intruders, for betrayal.

He placed his knife on the dinner table. It seemed to be too heavy all of a sudden, and anyway, he was home now. He wouldn't need it tonight.

"Would you like to tell me what this is all about?" Aleksei asked. "I know it was a long day, but I didn't expect you to insist upon going home so soon." There was an edge to his voice, indicating confusion and a slight blossoming anger at Gabe's refusal to explain himself.

"Shhh." Gabriel didn't even look up. "I'm trying to figure out how to find what I am looking for."

Aleksei dropped onto the couch, stretching out his long legs with a comfortable sigh. "Either you have a vague idea where you have lost the item in question and search the usual way, or there is a Tracking rune on whatever it is you are looking for and you use a Finding rune for retrieving your possession. I am not aware of any other ways."

Gabriel shook his head in frustration. Aleksei was distracting him, and distraction wasn't what he needed. "Just be quiet. Don't know yet how to do it, but...." His voice trailed off. He didn't know how to explain what he was doing because he had no idea himself.

Before his inner eye, a vague, smokelike idea popped up. "I could create a rune for it, couldn't I?" he murmured. "Yeah. Altered Finding rune, just without the counterpart of the Tracking rune."

Aleksei cast him an amused smile. "I thought I told you it is not possible to invent new runes. I'm sure I did."

Gabriel's fingers began to twitch. "Your brother said he created a rune allowing him to change his gender."

"He was lying," Aleksei replied briskly. He didn't like to talk about Petresh. "And he's always been a show-off. The rune he was using exists, but it is illegal to use it. My brother always liked to brag about his skills. You cannot invent new runes, Gabe. No one can."

A glow formed around Gabriel's fingertips. It wasn't golden, as it should be, as it always was when he used one of the more powerful runes. This light was as colorful as a rainbow.

Had he looked up, he would have seen Aleksei's mouth drop open.

Sometimes, learning a new rune hurt. They were tricky little beasts, and more often than not, Gabriel was sure they had a will of their own. So what he was doing now—inventing a new rune, although that was impossible—would have scared the life out of him had he been fully aware of what he was doing.

He wasn't.

His fingers moved. Fine. His brain told them what to do. Fine as well. But the color was all wrong, and what he was really worried about was Aleksei going bananas because of his messing around. Runes were dangerous; they both knew that.

Right now, Gabriel just didn't care.

The glow deepened and a pattern showed in the air, not overly complicated, but one he hadn't seen before. "Just a small, harmless rune," Gabriel murmured. "Just a way to find the damn cameras."

"Impossible," Aleksei breathed. Gabriel didn't even hear him.

Unlike normal runes, this one didn't vanish. Instead, the light spread out. Red, violet, and emerald sparks flew through the living room like little fireflies, vanishing behind books and pictures, curtains and furniture, only to reemerge seconds later and move on to the next place.

Aleksei watched in silence. Gabriel just stood and waited, not knowing what would happen once the rune was done doing its job.

The sparks didn't move fast, but they were thorough. Once they were through with the living room, they moved on to the kitchen, to the bathroom and hall, to the bedroom and downstairs into the garage.

One spark stayed behind, glowing a fierce red, but right now, Gabriel paid it no attention. His fingers were still moving, not creating a new rune but somehow maintaining the one that was already at work.

When Aleksei got up and moved toward the one red spark, Gabriel said, "Don't. They're not done yet."

"What exactly are you doing, Gabe?" Aleksei stood motionless in the middle of the room. "I have never seen anyone doing anything even remotely similar. I have never seen runes act like that. In fact, I am not sure whether to call those things runes at all."

Gabriel smiled, at ease with himself for the first time in days. "Oh, they are runes. Part of a rune, anyway. A Finding rune. Kind of. There! They are done."

The sparks rushed back into the room, formed a cloud of colors around Gabriel, and fell into place in the original lines he'd painted some minutes ago.

But the rune didn't vanish. A few sparks were missing.

Gabriel frowned. His hands built a protective shield over the rune, and he gently touched one of the tiny sparks. "Ah," he said. "I have to find the missing sparks. Hang on, I'll be back soon."

"One is in the corner above the bookshelf," Aleksei pointed out. "I wanted to examine it, but you held me back."

Excitement bubbled up in Gabriel. "Guess it worked," he said, then stepped to his lover and smacked a kiss onto his lips. "They found the bugs! Must have, and if I'm right, I finally know why I feel like I'm being watched all the time!"

Rushing to the bookshelf, he reached up but couldn't even get near the tiny red spark. "Damn," he muttered. "Did you have to build these shelves so high?" Without waiting for an answer, he dragged a chair over and jumped on it, but he still couldn't reach the place the firefly-thing was guarding. "Look," he bit out, "I'm really losing my patience here. Show me what you found!"

His fingers moved. The spark changed in color and form, became orange and clawlike, and a moment later, something small hit the floor.

The spark went back to the rune still glowing in the middle of the room, rejoining the others.

Gabriel jumped down and picked up the small item the spark had dropped. "Knew it," he said, by now nearly unimpressed that he'd been right. "A video bug. The same kind I use in the office. Damn it, Aleksei! Someone broke into our home and planted them. I bet I can find out who it was. Just means changing another rune. Just let me find the other bugs first."

"Gabe, wait a—" Aleksei began but Gabriel was too busy looking for the bugs to take any notice.

Fist clenched around the tiny camera, Gabriel went through the rooms in search of the other sparks. He found one in the hall and one outside, overlooking the street. The fourth one proved to be tricky until he thought about going into the garage, and there it was, sitting innocently above a stack of old tires.

Each time he found a video bug, the spark that had found it vanished, probably rejoining the rune in the living room. Gabriel nearly crushed the last bug getting it down, for once cherishing the rage soaring through him. Someone had been spying on him, driving him half crazy by doing so. Someone had intruded on his home, his privacy, and as soon as he managed to find out the person's name....

"Gabriel?"

Aleksei was calling him. His voice nearly drowned the other wordless voice deep inside him, the one he'd been hearing for so long now it had become somehow familiar.

"Yes," he called back. "Be right with you."

He needed to get the rage under control before he went upstairs or he would start to destroy furniture. Or better yet, he needed to go outside and hunt someone down, anyone, hunt and kill and devour.

Suddenly exhausted, Gabriel leaned his head against the garage's cool concrete wall. It was three in the morning, and he felt awful. "I just created a new rune although I shouldn't have been able to," he sighed. "Honestly, I don't think this could get any worse."

"Gabe, if you stay in the garage for much longer, I will come and get you."

Okay, making Aleksei angry was worse. "Coming," Gabriel said, but not nearly loud enough to be heard.

The staircase seemed steeper than before, the bugs in his fist pulling him down with each step he took.

Aleksei awaited him in the living room. At least the rune was gone, a relief for Gabriel, as he'd begun to feel guilty about doing something that was widely believed to be impossible. He didn't need another scolding, and when it came to runes and their proper use, Aleksei wasn't a patient man. He'd studied them all his life, he knew more about them than anyone else Gabriel had ever met—including Aleksei's sister, and that meant a lot—and he already looked quite unhappy.

"Sorry, Doc," Gabriel said. "I found the last one down there. Got them all now. Four bugs. Four cameras. I'll crush them, and then—"

"Gabe," Aleksei said, and from his tone, Gabriel knew he was in trouble.

"I said I'm sorry, okay?" he snapped, feeling uncomfortably caged by the room and his lover's presence. "I didn't mean to do anything wrong. You know I have a knack for runes, and I rarely play by the book. So I created a new one. Shoot me! I'm sure it's not forbidden. Kill me later, okay? Let's talk about those damn cameras first!"

"I planted them."

"Don't you get it? Someone's spying on us, someone means us harm, some—" He stopped midsentence. "What did you just say?"

"I planted the cameras. All of them. Or rather, I asked Monique to arrange getting the gear. She told Billy to use the stuff your office uses whenever necessary. He came here one day while you were at work, did what was necessary, and ever since, the bugs, as you call them, have been part of our home. You agreed to that, Gabe. You suggested to use office gear, and you suggested Billy for the job. So the question is, why can't you remember the cameras being here?"

The small hairs on the back of Gabriel's neck stood up. "What?" he asked again.

"You heard what I said. These are, ultimately, your bugs. Your secretary allowed me to use them; your friend installed them. They are here for our safety."

"No."

"The cameras have been here for nearly two years now. They cannot have had anything to do with your feeling of being watched. Which you didn't tell me about. Could it be you are hiding other things from me?"

Now Aleksei was angry. And suspicious.

Damn.

Repeatedly clenching his fists, Gabriel took a step backward.

Kill him. Break his neck. He spied on you. It's what you promised yourself you'd do. It's what you want to do!

The voice was very insistent about the killing part.

Another step backward. Gabriel tried to ask why Aleksei had broken his trust, but couldn't do it because his lips had revealed his teeth and he was growling like a wild animal.

A look of deep concern showed on Aleksei's face, washing away the anger. "I want you to sit down, Gabriel," he said. "You look awful. Let's talk about this, beloved."

The growl became louder. His nails dug little cuts into his palms; by morning, they'd be gone, but right now, it hurt.

Betrayal. Enemy. Danger. Come to me!

The same voice that had ordered him to hurt Aleksei, back in the club.

And still, he couldn't form words into sensible questions.

He very nearly jumped on Aleksei, toppling him over and biting his neck, showing his dominance as well as his hate. Only at the last moment did he turn and flee, because that was what he always did when in trouble: he ran away, leaving the problem and the person causing it behind and starting a new life without either. He didn't need trouble. He didn't need people.

He just needed to run.

The door was in the way, but Gabriel shouldered it open as if it were made of cardboard, and jumped into the street, breathing in the night air in deep gulps.

Come to me!

The voice was strong, and anyway, Aleksei had betrayed him. Planting bugs in the house and not telling him about it and lying on top of it, claiming he had told him. It had to be betrayal.

The wind tore at his hair, the cold bit his cheeks, and his fingers moved. They did that every now and then when he'd had a bit too much to drink or a nasty dream or, apparently, when he was creating new runes. Right now, they suggested he should open a portal and get into a world with less concrete and a lot more trees.

Running. Breathing. The streets were empty, the world bereft of noise. Just the blowing wind and the sound of his feet hitting the asphalt.

It felt good. And it would feel even better if he were barefoot, if his feet could get into direct contact with the ground, so he stopped and pulled off shoes and socks, threw them into the night, and went on running at an even faster speed.

A glass shard cut his foot and he swore. This world was bad and it stank. It was too bright and too loud and too warm. Sweat broke on his brow. He didn't like it here.

Before him, golden light glowed. Had he opened the portal already? Must have. No one else was around. Kyril's world, then. The centaurs' world. There was enough wood to satisfy the wolf in him, there were no cars, and he was too fast to be caught by the centaurs. Besides, they knew he belonged to....

No. He didn't belong to anyone.

With a long leap, Gabriel jumped through the portal. Maybe it felt a bit strange; maybe it hurt. But it didn't matter. He had left everything bad behind, and now he could run until he was too tired to set one foot before the other and fell asleep on the spot. No nightmares. No strange thoughts upon awaking. No one asking odd questions or looking at him as if he'd done something really, really stupid.

Grass under his feet and autumn leaves. The golden glow was gone, but with it also the pavement and the noise and the streetlamps hurting his eyes.

He stretched, feeling his muscles adjust to running faster than he usually did. The leaves under his feet crunched and crumpled to dust.

The forest smelled great, all trees and moss and earth. Above him were the stars, but he didn't have eyes for them—the darkness was colorful in itself, dozens of shades of gray, and then there were the various fragrances of rabbits and deer and the occasional fox. No other wolves were around.

Had he always been able to run this fast? And his clothes—jeans and shirts weren't good for running, restricting his movement and clinging to his skin once they were soaked with sweat. Clothes were a nuisance, so he shed them, and then he stretched again and growled, his body aching for movement, his mind at peace for once.

He was no longer sweating. He wasn't naked, either, although he wasn't wearing clothes. Somewhere behind him, along with his jeans and shirt, he'd also discarded his human body. Now, he wore fur instead of skin and had paws instead of hands and feet.

He hadn't known he could turn into a wolf. He hadn't even imagined it would feel so good. He was warm, and he could feel the wind in his fur and snow under his paws.

Not human anymore. Not fully wolf, either, because he was still able to think. Both? It didn't matter, for he was still running, on all fours now, with his snout telling him which way to go and his eyes searching for prey.

A young deer crossed his way and stood, transfixed, when he jumped at it, burying it under his weight. Bones cracked. Could a deer scream?

Blood on his snout and between his fangs. Blood running down his throat and the taste of fresh, hot flesh. He was hungry, ravenous, as if he'd never eaten in his life. Nothing was more important than the kill, nothing.

Devouring his kill, the wolf didn't pay much attention to his surroundings. Nothing could distract him from the deer lying slashed and bleeding in the snow. Gobbling down flesh and bones occupied his mind.

He didn't yet notice the faint rotten smell wafting through the winter night. He didn't notice the dark, dangerous shadow lurking in the darkness.

Before the wolf would have been lost for good, his survival instincts kicked in. He raised his snout from the deer; the hairs on his back rose, and he growled, protecting his catch and making it clear he was not prey. Another wolf would have thought twice before attacking him. He was larger than average, he radiated aggression, and his eyes spoke of hidden intelligence.

Now he flinched at the creature's rotten smell wafting toward him.

The wolf jumped backward, abandoning what was left of the dead deer in favor of surviving another minute or two. The creature approaching him was dangerous. It stank, and it wanted him dead.

The wolf shivered.

Whatever this was, it was too large for a wolf to deal with. A wolf couldn't fight that thing, so he howled, calling for help, calling for his mate, only to realize he was alone in this world and the one chasing him was closer than ever before. He couldn't see it yet. He could smell it and feel it, though, which was bad enough.

He turned and ran. Again. *Home!* he thought, and he continued running, although the creature's voice, deathly real in this winter world, turned into a scream of rage and thundering command. His human brain would have stopped to listen; his wolf body decided that the more distance between him and his pursuer, the better.

A thought, clear and sharp, pierced his mind. The first one in many hours.

Aleksei.

Aleksei would help him. Always had, no matter what. He was his mate.

Home. Home was a really good idea.

Only how to get home? And where was he, anyway?

Annoyance pushed away fear. He couldn't think while he was running, and once he stopped, being on all fours came as a shock.

Paws. Fur. A snout.

The body of a wolf.

The lack of hands was troublesome. How to create a rune without hands? He did have hands, usually. He didn't have fur and fangs.

The sheer need to become human again triggered the change. Changing back into human form was more painful than the other way around, but maybe Gabriel was only more aware of the differences between the two bodies. Expecting that strange, horrible-smelling creature would jump out at him and kill him, just like he himself had killed the deer, didn't help, either.

Better not to think of it.

Gasping and shaking violently, Gabriel found himself lying in a mesh of leaves and molten snow, covered in deer blood and aching all over. Above him, stars sparkled, and all around him were trees.

Next to him were his shirt and his jeans. For some reason, he must have retraced his steps, but he still didn't have a clue where he was or how he'd gotten there.

All he was sure about was that this wasn't Kyril's world.

When he heard a sound in the darkness, he jumped up on shaking legs. The creature was somewhere behind him; the rotten smell he could make out was proof of it. He didn't know what it wanted, but he knew he'd better try to get the hell out of here before it came any closer.

"Aleksei," Gabriel said helplessly. "I messed this up big-time. As always."

With half-frozen fingers, he painted the rune to his world—and failed. No golden glow. No portal.

"Shit, shit, shit." He was too nervous, too cold, too scared.

Again. More carefully this time.

There was a scream behind him, so damn close his heart skipped a few beats out of sheer panic. Frantically, he wasted several seconds to rummage through his wet clothes in search for his knife before he remembered he'd left it at home.

No chance to fight the creature. Not with his shaking hands as his only defense.

"Concentrate!"

His clothes pressed to his naked chest, he took a shaky breath and drew the rune that would take him home. This time, he stayed focused, trying not to listen to the sounds around him, trying not to smell the creature closing in on him, trying to concentrate. The thought of his knife, a present from Aleksei, helped him to do so. That, and his overwhelming wish to go home and tell his lover everything that had happened in the past weeks. Every little detail; every embarrassing secret. If he couldn't trust Aleksei to help him solve his problems, he might as well stay here and let the creature catch him.

The last line was a bit wobbly; his hands shook despite his effort to keep them calm. But the portal opened. The light illuminated the ground around him; an owl fled from the piercing glow with angry hoots.

"Yes!"

Gabriel took one last look back into the darkness—his head moved on its own accord, just as if the creature had taken it and turned it around.

He saw a shadow just outside the portal's light.

So damn close!

Come with me!

Gabriel screamed; his heart pumped adrenaline through his veins, and he jumped through the portal with one huge leap. He thought he could see movement from the corner of his eye.

An arm, claws, reaching out for him, touching him, trying to hold him back.

GABRIEL crashed onto the street, unable to stop his fall in time, and landed face-first on the pavement. For a few horrible moments he believed the creature had followed him through the portal and would rip him to pieces while he was still trying to catch his breath. Then the light vanished, the portal closed, and Gabriel realized he was alone. A lone streetlamp, an empty street, dark houses, and locked cars were all that was there.

He was back home. Whatever had been after him was gone.

He was too confused and too scared to think about it now. And he was cold.

He was also naked.

Dumbstruck, Gabriel stared at the clothes in his hands. They were dirty and wet, soaked with snow from another world. But they were clothes; better than nothing.

Still trembling, Gabriel forced his unwilling legs into the jeans, wondering in a very distant way why there were only two legs and not four. Closing the buttons of his shirt was equally hard; he didn't quite manage it, the last button not having found a hole. He must look terrible.

Staggering, Gabriel wandered through the deserted streets until he found the path leading to his home. His feet were numb with cold, which was good, because that way, he didn't feel the cuts.

At home, there was light in every window. The sight made him weak with relief.

He had run away. And only now, with proof that Aleksei was home, did he dare to admit his fear that his lover might have left him while he'd been playing hide-and-seek with a monster.

"I wanted to kill him." The memory was haunting. The voice had told him to do horrible things to his lover. So far he'd resisted, but for a moment, Gabriel seriously considered not going back inside. Everywhere else was safer than here. At least everywhere else, he couldn't hurt the man he loved.

Gabriel put one hand on the doorframe, not daring to go inside. He didn't even know how much time had passed since he'd left. Hours? Minutes?

He heard footsteps inside the house, pacing. Aleksei's footsteps. He would recognize them anywhere.

Okay, so Aleksei hadn't abandoned him. "I need to tell him what happened," Gabriel muttered, pushing the door open and forcing his unwilling feet inside. Running had taken him right into danger's way. No use trying it again. Better to sort this out. And Aleksei was the only one who could help him with that task.

Quietly, he crossed the hall, leaving wet, bloody tracks on the light planks. He didn't notice. He wasn't even aware that he wasn't wearing shoes.

When he entered the living room, the cat jumped up, startled. One look at Gabriel and he hopped off the couch, hissing, before vanishing toward the door and into the night.

Aleksei merely raised an eyebrow.

"Erm, sorry?" Gabriel tried, his arms wrapped around his body so Aleksei wouldn't see how badly he was shaking or how dirty he was. Probably, an apology would be a good start. "Didn't want to leave quite so abruptly. I was… confused. I think."

"Where have you been?" Aleksei asked.

"Don't know."

It was the wrong answer. Aleksei's eyes grew hard; obviously, he thought Gabriel didn't want to tell him where he'd gone.

"Listen, I really don't know! And I killed a deer," Gabriel blurted out. Saying it aloud didn't make it less embarrassing. "I sort of changed into a wolf. You know, the kind with fur and paws and fangs and, well, quite obviously a very empty stomach."

"Of course. I should have expected an unlikely explanation, but I must admit this one is even more creative than I thought it would be. If you don't mind, we'll talk about this later. The fae council requires my appearance."

"Ah. Lia calls and you come running. Good little doggie."

A fraction too late, Gabriel realized he'd said the words the voice had whispered into his mind aloud. True, he didn't like Lia, Aleksei's sister. But he would never call his lover a dog; he would never make such a nasty remark!

Only he just had.

"Sorry," he stammered. "I didn't mean that, I—"

"Whatever you meant, I have to go." Aleksei put his coat on and was at the door when he turned around once more. "You have changed tremendously in the past few weeks, Gabriel. And you do not trust me enough to tell me about your worries. I truly do not know how to go on. Or if I want to go on at all."

Suddenly, Gabriel noticed his naked feet and the tracks he'd left on the planks. "I—" he began, but he didn't know what else to say.

His legs gave way, too weak to carry his weight any longer, and he sat down right in the middle of the living room floor.

Wrapping his arms around his middle, he began to laugh until tears ran down his face. In any case, laughter was better than the overwhelming urge to cry. Yes, he had messed this up, but much worse than he'd initially thought, which became apparent the moment Aleksei shook his head and left the house, closing the door behind him quietly.

CHAPTER SIX

IT WAS the first rainy day after an eternity of blazing sunlight. The air smelled fresh and new, the light was dim and rather gray, and surprisingly enough, the dragon was in the mood to see the ocean.

He hadn't been in the mood for anything lately. Or to be precise, for anything else but glooming. Life was bad; light and sun and summer were bad. Breathing hurt, and thinking and remembering. No use getting up from his nest until it was absolutely necessary. No use going anywhere, seeing anything, spreading his wings, or, for that matter, finding some food.

But this morning he'd woken up craving fresh fish. And he wanted to change his form, something else he hadn't done in a very long time. Not since his mate had died.

He missed her so badly it tore him apart, still, although a substantial number of months had passed since her death. Maybe even years—for a dragon, time ticked differently. Dragons lived a very long time, centuries, millennia, even.

His mate, T'gani, had chosen to live in the mountains. And he'd been happy to oblige. The mountains were safe, especially if one hoped to raise young ones. One could see for miles.

Today, he missed the sound of waves lulling him to sleep, the cry of the seagulls, and, of course, the taste of fresh fish.

A seagull, then. Had he ever chosen this form before? He couldn't remember, and anyway, it didn't matter. He'd always enjoyed changing into other forms when he was younger. He certainly remembered how it was done. A bit of concentration, a bit of rune magic, and here he was, a small, swift seagull with sharp, beady eyes, a black beak, and, well, ink-black feathers. He could change into anything he wanted to, but he could not change his color. The dragon was black, so the seagull was black as well.

Spreading his wings, he felt the air brush across the feathers. When he tested his voice, he found his cry to be long and lonely, echoing over the mountaintops.

Quite appropriate for a seagull. Maybe he was a bit bigger than average, but that didn't matter. He would avoid other seagulls. Black wasn't really their color; they might attack him, and he wasn't in the mood for a fight.

For a moment, the dragon considered not going. It was a long flight. Fish was overrated. It was a rainy day; he would get wet and cold and—

Annoyed at himself, he ruffled his seagull feathers, feeling slightly disorientated because of the change in height and weight. *You decided to go*, he told himself, *so go.*

He was sick of being lonely. As a seagull, he could at least flee the mountains and pretend there were others out there who looked like him and accepted him as one of them, despite the fact he wouldn't even try to get near them.

The rain was cold, washing away the dust and the still-present heat. His feathers got wet, and flying was less fun than it would have been in his dragon form. The larger wingspan would have taken him to the ocean much faster.

You're a seagull now, he thought bitterly. *Enjoy it!*

Small as he was, he was also swift. He could smell the ocean already. Apparently, it wasn't as far away as he'd thought. Or maybe it was just that he'd underestimated how fast a seagull could fly.

The smell of rain and salt water mingled until he couldn't tell them apart anymore. But the sound of the waves crashing on the shore, whipped up by the wind, made his heart lighter. Last time he'd visited the ocean, T'gani had been by his side. They'd mated above the endless ocean, watched by no one but the waves.

Diving into the waves, he pushed his memories of her to some darker, hidden areas in favor of catching the fish he'd seen. Memories hurt. If only he could erase them from his mind for good, but of course that was impossible. He was, along with the few others left of his kind, the keeper of memories. Forgetting was not an option no matter how much any of them tried.

The fish wanted to wriggle out of his beak; however, he was too hungry now to let it go. Shaking off the water, he gobbled it down, dwelling on the delicious taste, and went to get himself a second one. This one he carried in his beak until he could find a place to sit so he could rip off the pieces and discard the bones and the head. He was a dragon, after all, not a seagull. They didn't mind the bones. He did.

Cruising above the surf felt so good he nearly forgot he was looking for a landing place. Only when the fish twitched in his beak did he take a closer look around and promptly spot a small rock in the middle of the ocean, breaking the surface of the water by only a few feet.

The dragon landed, spreading out his webbed seagull feet so he wouldn't be washed away by wind and waves. The ocean could be wild at times; when it rained, it rained heavily, and the rock was slippery despite its rough surface.

Unbelievable, but he had to catch his breath, glad to have found a place to rest his wings. He had neglected his health of late, depression having claimed his soul. The black mood dampened his senses, and it had a lot to do with his age.

One day at the beginning of summer, he had understood on a deep, painful level that he would spend not only the summer but also the autumn and winter alone, with his bones aching from the cold and his heart frozen from lack of company. Alone and cold, his nest empty with no chance of a new mate or offspring. There was no other he could share his remaining years with. He had known this before; he'd spent the previous winter alone, and autumn, too. Only this time, with the heat drying up the earth, he had felt it in his bones and his heart as well, and the knowledge had stabbed him.

Alone forever.

After that, he had stayed in his nest most of his days and nights. His wings had gone weak, and now his heart thundered in his chest, the tiny, thin seagull chest so vastly different from his real form.

The fish twitched again, nearly dead. He needed to eat it now or throw it back into the sea.

Maybe the fish had offspring. Most likely it would; there were myriad fish in the ocean, of all kinds and sizes. They didn't have only one child, they had many, millions and millions, in the short span of their lives.

It seemed unfair.

Maybe the fish children would miss their parent.

Ridiculous thought. Still, the dragon dropped the fish back into the sea and hoped it wouldn't get eaten by a shark.

Just when he was about to take off again, the wind caught him by surprise. He was half-airborne, and his wings came dangerously close to being crushed between water and rock. He tumbled and fell, hitting the rock's edge hard. He nearly slipped into the water, but at the last minute, he somehow got a grip. He realized he was not only scared and dazed but humbled, as well.

He shouldn't turn into a seagull if a bit of wind was a threat!

Crying out his dismay, the dragon caught his balance, clinging tightly to the small rock and even using his beak to keep himself steady. Clawing and cursing in his mind, he finally managed to pull himself fully back up onto the rock, knowing only too well a normal seagull would just have taken flight, fleeing the rock as well as the ocean. As he wasn't a normal seagull, he was glad the waves hadn't taken him, and wished the wind weren't quite so forceful.

The stone hummed underneath his feet, and he turned his head in surprise. He hadn't noticed the hum before. He must have been too occupied with the fish and then the wind to notice.

Another hum, deep and persistent. Now that he was aware of it, it was impossible to ignore it. He knew what the hum meant: forgotten memories, and the dragon was very responsive to that kind of hum. It must be an important memory, strong enough to survive in the stone, strong enough to pierce the barrier around his mind that shielded and protected him from the abundance of memories the worlds held. Without the barrier, he would go mad. As he heard the hum, he knew it was not the memory of a crab scuttling across the stone or a fish scratching its fin against the rock.

This was a memory that contained emotional turmoil, pain and hope and fear.

He used his beak to peck at the stone, hoping to find some blood or a piece of bone, because those would perfectly connect him to the one who'd been here. The constant patter of rain on his head distracted him, but eventually, he found a crack, small and deep and bent.

The memories called for him. Deep down in the crack, he thought he could smell blood, and although he couldn't quite reach it, he believed the hum turned into something stronger, more real. Memories invaded his mind, bright as sunlight and equally as burning. The dragon lost his balance; the sudden shock threw him right into the waves and would have killed him if not for the sudden, blinding jolt of hope the memories brought.

One of my kind!

With the waves clinging to his feathers, he struggled to get back to the surface. He could sense a shark shearing through the water, hoping to get early dinner. It was fast; if he didn't get his seagull body out of the waves quickly, he would end up in the shark's stomach with no chance to find out if what he'd sensed in the stone was true.

Impossible.

Seagulls weren't good at swimming, at least not when they were several feet under water, but as he wasn't a seagull and remembered how it was to have much bigger wings and stronger feet, he managed to get to the surface and crawl up onto the stone before the shark could reach him. Distantly, he felt the hunter's angry, hungry disappointment, but it was wiped out by the hum greeting him the moment his feathers touched the stone.

If only changing his form were less strenuous. If only the water were an element he liked. It was too cold and drained him of his strength, and so all he could do was cope with what he had. His dragon body was much more sensitive to memories. But he couldn't change right now. The wind was too strong and the rain too heavy, and he was too exhausted already. Besides, the rock would be way too small for him. Not even a single one of his dragon toes would fit on it, not to mention a whole foot.

The seagull's form would have to do.

Anxiously, he wedged his beak back into the crack and listened, fearing what he'd learned before would turn out to be untrue, a mistake, a misunderstanding. Because in actuality, it couldn't be true. One of his kind on this rock? One of his kind *bleeding* on this rock? His kind didn't bleed easily.

Closing out the sound of the wind and the rain wetting his feathers, the dragon listened to the hum. A memory rose up from the stone's cold depths, a memory containing pain, closely followed by more pain.

Human, the dragon realized in awe.

The second memory was more difficult, as it was much more complex. Fear, mostly, but also joy at having escaped a life-threatening danger.

The dragon frowned, as much as a seagull could frown, of course. What could be more life-threatening than being trapped on a tiny rock in the middle of the ocean with broken bones, bleeding while sharks circled around you?

Human. Male. Young, even for his species, and not able to think straight due to blood loss, fear, and the fact he'd crossed through a portal without proper guidance.

The dragon's heart leapt when the stone revealed the memories, one by one and painfully slowly. Humans, like all other species apart from his own, needed guidance to cross the portals lest they rip their souls and bodies apart. But this one had gone through not only one but two portals without grave consequences.

Completely, totally impossible. Humans were unable to use the portals like dragons did. *No one* was able to use the portals like dragons did!

One of my kind. Wasn't that what he'd thought the moment the memories had broken through his barrier?

Human. And dragon.

Both.

Neither.

A rush of longing soared through him. Unexpected, forbidden longing, because his mate hadn't been dead long enough for him to be longing after someone else!

But—a human dragon! One of his kind, in a way.

He hadn't known there were any humans left who could be called his kind. The few he'd known about had died centuries ago, and all of them had had twisted minds and twisted souls, not recognizing what they were and using their powers to do evil. Having offspring with humans had been a desperate experiment in the first place, and it had gone terribly wrong.

The dragon swayed, tormented by memories, each one more brilliant than the next. How dare there be a human dragon! How dare he end up in this world only to disappear again! He hadn't died on this rock. The human man had stayed for a while, fantasizing about water and food and rescue and creating a portal that would take him back home.

Unfair, unfair, unfair! the dragon's mind sang, for this one would have qualified as a mate, if only he hadn't escaped this world so quickly after he'd arrived.

He didn't die here. He's alive. He can be found!

Treacherous thoughts. He couldn't do that, could he? Kidnap a human? Force him to live in another world, force him to leave his life behind in order to adjust to a new one?

I wouldn't be lonely anymore, the dragon thought, and listened for the hum that would tell him more about the human. Desperately, he drilled his beak into the crack, searching for the blood. The blood he thought he'd smelled. The blood would tell him more. It would tell him where to find the human dragon.

There: another memory. A bleeding hand and a seagull, a real one, pecking at it, mistaking it for a fish.

If he found the human, he could bring him here, into this world, into his nest, and turn him into a real dragon.

Maybe it was because the rock was old. Maybe his beak was stronger than he'd thought. Maybe it was because the rain had ceased, and with it the constant patter on his head. But whatever the reason, he suddenly managed to touch the single drop of blood encased in the rock's stony heart.

A shiver ran through the dragon as the memory seeped into his flesh. Suddenly, he was the seagull, the one who'd spotted and pecked the prey displayed on the rock beneath him. His brain became tiny and focused on nothing but flying, wind, waves, and food. He saw flesh clinging to a bit of rock in the middle of the ocean. Soaring down, he circled the prey, waiting for it to move, and when it didn't, he landed and pecked at the flesh. The rock bit into his foot, barely perceptible. A drop of his seagull-blood welled up and disappeared in one of the cracks.

The prey's blood tasted strange, but good enough to hope there would be more. But the prey was not dead yet; it moved, and the seagull hopped away, hoping it would die so he could pick at the flesh and the eyes and take home a bite so his young ones could eat as well. It was too sweet, that blood, not like fish blood.

But the prey refused to die. It yelled at the seagull and it moved, so the bird decided to hover above it and wait for it to become still. Very annoying, flesh that moved. It would be a lot easier to peck out the eyes if there wasn't any resistance.

The dragon blinked once, disentangling the seagull's memories from his own. That the blood he'd found was not that of the human man he hadn't even suspected. Had it not held one interesting bit of information, he would have been very disappointed. But it did, just one, hidden underneath the urge to eat, to fly, and to hunt.

The human dragon had been here not too long ago. A few years at the most, which, to a dragon, wasn't much more than a heartbeat.

I could find him. If he hasn't died since he was here, I could find him.

The dragon cried a seagull's cry of impatience and swung himself up into the air and changed. Air was his element. Air gave him strength, air warmed him and protected him, and although he was tired, he was also determined, and so taking back his dragon form turned out to be much easier than he'd feared.

His wings grew. Feathers turned to black scales covering thick, leathery skin. The beak vanished and so did the plump black feet. Instead, he grew a tail, long and strong enough to turn a whole tree into sawdust with one swing. Claws sharper than a shark's teeth had left deep scratches in the rock, which was rapidly disappearing behind him.

Swiftly, the dragon flew back to his nest, unaware of the newly starting rain, unaware of the late hour or the hunger growling in his stomach. His thoughts were occupied, filled with hope and plans and a little more hope. Anything could happen now he'd found those memories.

Trying to find the human dragon would mean he'd have to change into a human himself. He would need to go into the humans' world. Going there would mean walking on soil he hadn't walked on in centuries, if not longer.

One last beat of his wings, and he landed on the brim of his nest. It sagged, but only a bit. True, he had neglected repairing it recently. He was old. Repairing nests wasn't what he liked to do.

The dragon didn't want to admit it, not even to himself, but the thought of changing into a human scared him. Humans were so fragile, and their minds were often ruled by their bodies. Besides, he would not fit into their world. He didn't know anymore what their world looked like or what new inventions they had come up with.

No use pondering it. Finding the one of his kind among other humans wouldn't be easy, if it could be done at all. Maybe there were hundreds of thousands of humans nowadays.

We shouldn't have stopped visiting them, the dragon thought, curling up in his nest and drying his wings with a simple thought of heat. *We shouldn't have stopped visiting any of the hidden worlds. Fleeing once our experiment failed was craven. Maybe they don't even remember us anymore.*

No. Surely that was impossible. The dragons were the most important race. They ruled the portals; they even had a seat at the fae council.

Well. Used to have.

How to find him, then? the dragon wondered. *How to find one man among thousands of others?*

He lifted his head, an idea sparkling up in his sleepy mind.

He could ask for help.

Now that was, apart from going for a flight this morning, the first decent idea of the day. Help was good. The fae council would point out someone to him who was good at finding people.

The dragon drifted gently off to sleep, for once not thinking about the missing warmth of his dead mate. Tonight, he would rest. Tomorrow, he would open a portal and remind the fae of his existence and their ancient promise of offering help in exchange for letting them have the knowledge of runes.

His tail twitched with amusement. Seeing him after the dragons had vanished centuries ago would certainly shock them to the core.

CHAPTER SEVEN

EVENTUALLY, Gabriel managed to drag himself into the bathroom and under the shower. He made the water as hot as he could stand it, dropped to his knees, and waited until the dirt and the blood washed away.

But he didn't get warm in the process.

Shaking violently, he wondered how his life could have taken a turn for the worse in such a short time. A couple of weeks ago, all had been fine. He loved his life, he loved Aleksei, he loved his job. What more could he want?

Eventually, the water turned cold, but Gabriel didn't get out of the shower. He'd sunk down and now just sat under the icy spray, listening to his chattering teeth and thinking about his lover, wondering where he'd gone and if he would come back. After all, he was fae; this world was not his. The house and most of his possessions were just the trappings of his assumed identity, and neither the car nor the furniture meant all that much to him, although he'd spent weeks to find the old Jag in just the dark green he wanted. Whenever he liked, Aleksei could go back home and live with his own people. His sister pestered him on a regular basis to do just that, using every opportunity to deride his choice to live among humans.

Even Gabriel didn't understand why his lover lived here and not in the fae world.

"Don't know if he's still my lover."

Of course, no one but the soap was there to listen, and even that was currently getting washed down the drain.

Maybe those were tears mingling with the water. He wasn't sure. He wasn't sure of anything anymore. He'd turned into an animal, for crying out loud! How sick was that? Okay, he was, in theory, a shapeshifter, but he'd never been able to change. That he liked his meat bloody was one of the few attributes of his wolf nature.

Or had been. Lately, it seemed he liked to eat his meat not only bloody but raw. Ideally with the fur still attached.

His stomach heaved at the memory of bones crushing between his teeth.

Leaves blocked the drain. The water in the shower had risen, not enough to flood the bathroom, but enough to freeze him to the bone.

I should get out, Gabriel thought distractedly, but he couldn't bother to move as much as a finger. *Out of the shower and out of the house and out of his life. Who wants to live with a shapeshifter who turns into a wolf whenever he smells something nice to hunt?*

It did occur to him that that wasn't the problem at all. The problem was he'd run from Aleksei. The problem was he'd lied to a man he claimed to love. Again. He'd withheld information, had betrayed him—he could go on with the list.

"Shit. Fucking, damn shit."

And he still couldn't remember exactly what had happened in the club. Not enough to know whether it had been rape.

The cold water made his muscles cramp, and as if in response, his stomach cramped too. Quicker than he thought he could move, Gabriel was out of the shower and at the toilet, where he was violently sick, clutching the porcelain with both hands, not caring if his hair got in the way. He threw up everything he'd eaten in the past twenty-four hours, which was a lot given a deer had been on the menu.

When he was done and lay curled up in a fetal position in front of the toilet, too weak to even care about the smell of vomit, he noticed a small bit of fur under one of his nails and threw up again until his stomach produced nothing but acid-tasting saliva.

On all fours, he crawled back to the shower, chucked out the leaves blocking the drain, and filled his mouth with water until the dreadful taste of vomit was gone. With soap and shampoo he cleaned himself, washing his hair not once but three times, the thought of finding more deer bits making him paranoid.

Bed, he thought vaguely. *Sleep.*

How long since Aleksei had left?

Faint light shone in through the window. The sun was rising.

Shit. He wasn't ready for a new day, not at all. First, he had to deal with the old one. First, he had to figure out what exactly had happened, where he'd been, and then, what that foul-smelling creature had wanted.

Rotten thing. Sneaking up on me like that. A little closer....

He didn't dare to continue that line of thought. A little closer, and he would have been dead.

His legs trembled, freezing under the cold water. His body ached. Really, it was time to—

The door of the shower opened, and his heart leapt with sudden panic. It took him many long seconds to realize it was Aleksei, exquisitely dressed as always and looking decidedly annoyed.

"Don't tell me you've been in the shower for the last two hours," he said.

Gabriel's teeth chattered.

"Your lips are blue, as are your fingers. Great. You look awful, Gabriel. The smell makes me assume you've been sick. Now will you share what really happened last night, or do you prefer to continue telling me lies?"

Under any other circumstance, Gabriel would have had some pointed opinions about who was usually lying to whom in their relationship, but he was too weak and too scared and too damn tired. He remained silent and tried to persuade his body and mind to get out of the shower.

He couldn't. "You said.... I thought... you wouldn't come back," he stammered. "I thought... when the door opened...."

Aleksei's look of annoyance changed to a look of concern. "You thought what? That a monster would walk in?"

Gabriel's throat worked but no words came out. On shaking legs he stood pressed to the back wall and thought of snow and hunting and that rotten smell, and he would have been sick again if Aleksei hadn't reached out and turned off the water.

"Get out," he said—or rather, ordered—and Gabriel obeyed.

Shaking, he stood in the middle of the bathroom and allowed Aleksei to wrap a towel around him. Without resistance, he let the fae steer him into the living room. Patiently, he sat on the couch and waited while Aleksei fetched him the thick, warm blanket from the bedroom.

Finally, Aleksei handed him a cup of hot chocolate. "Drink," he prompted when Gabriel stared at the cup as if he didn't know what to do with it.

The sweet, rich taste helped him shed some of the panic; the first sip warmed him up and calmed his still upset stomach. "Thanks," he croaked. "Can't guarantee it will stay down."

"So you have been sick." Aleksei shrugged out of his coat, throwing it carelessly over a chair, then slipped off his shoes and sat next to Gabriel on the couch. He kept his distance, usually something Gabriel would have respected, but right now, he didn't care. Hoping Aleksei wouldn't mind, he edged closer until he was near enough to put his head on his lover's shoulder.

He sighed deeply, feeling safe for the first time in hours. When Aleksei didn't push him away, he nearly cried with relief. "Remind me never to eat deer again," he said, glad it didn't come out with a sob.

"Deer? Whyever not?"

"It's the reason I was sick. Ate too much, and the fur tasted gross. Not a good thing, eating raw deer." He had to stop talking about it or he would need to rush back to the toilet.

By the way Aleksei's muscles tensed, Gabriel knew his lover didn't understand a thing he was saying. Deliberately trying to relax, he swallowed hard and pushed the most vivid memories out of his mind before saying, "I told you I killed a deer, didn't I?"

"Yes." The single word was laden with doubt.

Gabriel grinned humorlessly. "Chased it, killed it, ate it, threw it up. Truly made my day, it did."

He turned in his lover's arms. "I know you don't believe me. I know you are disappointed with me running away and that you think I don't trust you. But you are wrong. You are the only one I trust or I wouldn't be here. Wouldn't... have come back. Problem is, something is wrong with me, and I don't know what. Neither do I know how to explain it without sounding like a complete idiot. I don't even know where to start!"

Aleksei pulled him closer. "Start at the beginning," he suggested.

Great. When had it all begun?

Gabriel looked at the wall so he couldn't see the doubt in Aleksei's face. "A few weeks ago, maybe? At first, I thought I had gone through portals too often. I didn't think much about it.

"Then I felt like I was being watched, even when I was alone in a room, and then here at home, on the streets, in the office... everywhere. Plus, I can hear a voice in my head calling me. Drives me nuts, that voice. Can't think of much else. And now that I think about it—maybe it was the voice that made me run away earlier. I didn't really want to. I wanted to stay and talk about those damn bugs. Only the voice told me running would be a great idea, and because I was freaked out already, I did run away, and then I changed and killed the deer, and I think whatever called me was there too. I felt it coming, I smelled its rotten stink, and if I hadn't opened a portal at the last minute, it would have caught me."

"The moment you were out of the house you opened a portal? In which world did you end up?" Aleksei asked.

Gabriel sighed. "No idea," he said, and placed his still half-full cup on the table. "You wouldn't believe it. I don't even believe it myself. Yes, I opened a portal, but not to a world I have ever been to before. I have never used the Portal rune before and could swear I never saw it in one of your books."

"Ah," Aleksei replied. "Again."

Gabriel cast him a humorless smile. "Yeah, again. Like that one time when I ended up in the ocean and nearly got eaten by a seagull.

Sorry, Doc. I don't know what's wrong with me." He looked at Aleksei. "The voice—it is calling me now. It wants me to come back."

"What about your turning into a wolf?" Aleksei sounded calm and in control, as always, and not at all concerned about the voice. "You cannot change your form, Gabriel. I would have noticed in the past few years had you grown a tail at the full moon."

Gabriel's head began to throb, a low, steady pain. At least it dimmed the voice calling him back to the winter world. "As soon as I was gone, I turned into a wolf. A real one. One with paws and fangs. I killed a deer. Hence the blood. Hence me being sick."

Getting up on wobbly legs, Gabriel dragged the blanket tighter around himself. "Should clean up the bathroom," he mumbled, too tired to think straight. "Leaves on the floor, and I'm not sure that damn deer got flushed down the toilet properly."

He swayed, and then Aleksei was next to him, putting a steadying arm around his waist before he knew he'd moved. "You're in no condition to clean up. You are injured. Sit."

Injured. The word made no sense. But given how weak he was and how tired, Gabriel allowed Aleksei to lead him back to the couch, watching in fascination the bloodied outlines his feet left on the floor.

Why were his feet cut?

"Barefoot," Gabriel mumbled. "Ran through the woods barefoot. And the thing… creature… beast…." His voice trailed off.

He was barely aware of Aleksei pushing the blanket away, running his hands over Gabriel's body, touching old scars as well as new scratches the branches in the unknown world had caused. "As unlikely as your story sounds, I am not unwilling to believe you. Can you show me the Portal rune you used for getting wherever you have been?"

Gabriel blinked, managing to focus on the cup sitting on the small table next to the couch. He dipped his finger into the rest of his cocoa and drew a pattern onto the surface without feeding the lines with power.

Aleksei looked over his shoulder at the pattern. "Impossible," he stated calmly. "This Portal rune does not exist. It wouldn't have taken you anywhere."

Gabriel just shrugged his shoulders. Absently, he rubbed his hand along his leg, not surprised it hurt. Everything still hurt.

"This creature you mentioned, did it touch you?"

Aleksei's hands were on his hips. Gabriel didn't even recall him pulling the blanket away.

"Maybe," he managed, feeling a blush creep into his cheeks, which was ridiculous given how often Aleksei had seen him naked.

Hands on his skin—Aleksei's hands, searching for whatever clues he might find. Eventually, he dropped to his knees, his face inches away from Gabriel's thigh.

Gabriel shivered, his hands twitching. It was hard to keep them under control. Hard not to put them around his lover's throat and strangle him because, how lovely, the voice was really insistent now, whispering poison into his mind again.

"These are claw marks," Aleksei said just then, tracing his fingers from Gabriel's hipbone down to his knees. "Someone tried to catch you but didn't quite do so. Someone, or something." Swiftly, he drew a rune over the marks. "This should reveal what animal left those wounds," he said, leaving Gabriel to wonder why he bothered to explain himself. They'd had an argument, hadn't they? There had been something about bugs, and he'd run away, and damn it, he was too tired to think straight! His brain felt like wet cotton, which was just as well, because not even the voice could persuade him to do something stupid right now.

He frowned. There was something he had wanted to ask.

Ah. Yes.

"What was it, then? The thing chasing me?"

Aleksei took him by the shoulders and steered him to the bedroom. A good sign. If he was allowed to sleep in their bed, it could mean Aleksei wasn't afraid of him turning into a wolf and eating him up.

"Who am I kidding?" he mumbled as Aleksei pushed him down onto the mattress. "I wouldn't eat you if you paid me."

"Why would you want to eat me?" Aleksei asked, pulling the blanket up to Gabriel's shoulders.

Gabriel frowned. "We argued. You left. And the voice, the… thing… wants you dead. Don't want to kill you. Did I really know about the bugs? How could I forget something like that?"

Aleksei sighed. "You have a problem, beloved. A big one, if the rune didn't lie. Will you sleep now, please?"

Gabriel smiled at him. Aleksei smiled back. Did smiling mean all was well between them? "What was—" he began, but before he could finish the sentence, he was asleep.

HIS sleep, not surprisingly, was disturbed by nightmares he couldn't recall when he awoke. In fact, the moment he opened his bleary eyes to the light of the day, he felt as if he hadn't slept at all.

Stretching, Gabriel sat up, only to see Aleksei sitting next to the bed, a big volume on his knees.

"Hi," Gabriel said, vaguely wondering if they'd had an argument.

No. Stupid idea. They never argued. Not really.

Aleksei put the book down. "Good morning," he replied. "You didn't sleep well."

What a strange thing to say. "No, I didn't, but how did you know?" Pulling his knees up under the blanket, Gabriel was surprised at how badly his muscles ached. He must have been running for longer than usual. Much longer.

"I've been watching you toss and turn for the past few hours." Reaching out, Aleksei put a hand to Gabriel's forehead. "No fever, at least. How do the wounds on your hip feel? Do they hurt?"

"Wounds?"

"Yes. Wounds. From the creature that chased you last night. You went to a hidden world. You turned into a wolf, killed a deer, and were injured. Remember?"

Moments ticked by, during which Gabriel stared at his lover openmouthed, wracking his brain to find any meaning in what the fae had just said.

"Erm," he finally came up with, "I think I can remember bits and pieces, but not clearly. Did we… did we argue?"

Aleksei took the book, turned it so the pages were visible, and placed it on Gabriel's knees. "Briefly. I was angry when you ran away and surprised you returned relatively soon. If the fae council hadn't required my immediate appearance, I wouldn't have left, but then, I didn't have a choice. And I was still angry, of course."

"I thought you wouldn't come back."

"You said so last night. Ridiculous assumption, though. You are the one who turns your back to problems, not I. And you do have a problem." Aleksei raised an eyebrow, as if encouraging Gabriel to tell him everything there was to tell.

Gabriel glanced at the book. "The thing chasing me?"

"Yes."

"And—" Memories flared up in his mind, just like that. In a matter of seconds, Gabriel knew what had happened the night before and couldn't believe he'd forgotten it in the first place. He rarely forgot things!

"I remember being a wolf. Running. The deer." He swallowed. "What is this? Why isn't my brain working properly?"

"And there we have the next problem," Aleksei replied. "The main one is you were hurt by a creature that is believed to be extinct."

"What's it called?"

"It was a banshee—a death fairy. The rune was certain. According to my sources," Aleksei said, nodding to the book on Gabriel's lap, "their world is lost forever, their race killed by the dragons. One who heard a banshee's scream died in less than a day, and if they took an interest in you, it was better to kill yourself than to wait for the creature to get you. It is unclear whether they were male or female, but mostly, the banshee is referred to as 'she'."

Gabriel gulped at the sight of the picture in the book. The creature had no eyes, a hole instead of a mouth, long, sharp claws, and it looked vicious. "How lovely. Remind me not to have a row with a banshee again." With a quick thump, he shut the book and pushed it away.

Aleksei carefully took the volume. "This book is ancient, written by at least three different authors who claim different facts to be true, and I hesitate to believe everything that is said about the banshee. However, there are the claw marks on your skin, and my rune told me what hurt you *was* a banshee. You were violently sick, and I saw deer bits in the toilet. Something is profoundly wrong. Enough reasons to believe what you told me; enough reason to believe in the existence of at least one banshee."

"Whatever's wrong, it has nothing to do with you!"

"I am slowly beginning to believe that as well," Aleksei said with a crooked grin that made Gabriel's heart leap out of his chest.

"So, to sum it up, I've been to a world that doesn't exist and got chased by a creature that doesn't exist, either. I turned into a wolf, even though I am not capable of changing, and I escaped only because I am a lot better with runes than I have any right to be."

Aleksei nodded. "Precisely."

"Then can you tell me why you… we… had cameras installed in the house?" The question had been nagging at him ever since he'd woken up.

Aleksei's ice-blue eyes softened with amusement. "We had them installed for our protection, beloved. We are both dealing with strange people. Some of them are dangerous. Cameras seemed the logical choice. That you forgot about them worries me as much as the possibility of existing banshees, the voice in your head, and your capability of creating new runes."

From out of nowhere came the smell of blood, fresh and tantalizing in Gabriel's nostrils. It came with sound, too, the sound his paws had made on wet ground and the sight of softly falling snowflakes. "It scares the shit out of me, Aleksei," he breathed. "All of this. Last night, when we were at the *Poison Prince*, I totally lost it. I turned into a wolf, only one without fur and paws. I... I think I raped you. In some ways, I can't understand how you can manage being in the same room with me. *I* would run from me if I could. Why don't you?" He frowned. "Come to think of it, what did the fae council want?"

Aleksei leaned back in his chair. "They asked me to hear out a riddle that's been bothering them. For several weeks now, people crossing through the portals have been going missing. Not everyone, but enough to make them worry. Lia sounded urgent; otherwise, I wouldn't have left."

Pulling the bedcovers a bit tighter around his body, Gabriel cast a shy look at him. "Which leaves the question as to why you are still here," he said carefully. "Did I... rape you?"

Aleksei shook his head. "You did not," he said, and he said it in such a way that Gabriel just had to believe him. "And now, I think, I need to put a bit more time into my hobby should I hope to ever find out what's going on here."

"What hobby?" Gabriel asked, lowering the blanket just a bit.

Aleksei raised an eyebrow. "You're a bit slow today, beloved," he mocked. "Trying to find out what exactly you are. It might at least provide some answers. I think we should find a relative of yours so I can get blood for further examination."

Gabriel looked at him blankly. "A relative? My gran is dead, I guess, and my dad is too. No one else left."

Aleksei sighed deeply. "I've taken care of those scratches. And I think you should get up now. You need breakfast. Afterwards, you should call Monique and arrange for Billy to make some inquiries concerning your mother. Not that I am telling you how to do your job, of course."

Gabriel stared after him openmouthed long after Aleksei left the room.

BOTH Monique and Billy looked at him with concern written all over their faces.

"You don't look well. Are you sure you should be back in the office?" Monique asked, pushing her glasses firmly back up her beak-like nose.

Billy put it more bluntly. "You look like shit, man."

Gabriel couldn't help but notice the blotch of tomato sauce on Billy's not-overly clean shirt. Apparently, Father Barley had served spaghetti today. Billy loved food, any kind of food, but he could never manage to prepare it or eat it without damage to his clothing.

"Skip it," Gabriel snapped. "I know how I look. Didn't sleep well, that's all."

He'd gone to his office once he'd made it out of bed. Aleksei had tried to talk him out of it, arguing that a phone call would do just as well, but for once he'd insisted, although all he'd wanted to do was crawl back between the blankets and sleep until this nightmare was over.

Eating hadn't been an option, although Aleksei had made pancakes for him.

Now Gabriel sat behind his desk, hands pressed flat against his stomach and eyes fixed firmly on his secretary. His stomach, like his head, was still upset; his secretary, if not watched closely, might decide to get personal and prepare breakfast for him, which he couldn't deal with right now.

"First of all, I need to inform you I won't be in the office on a regular basis for a while. I—"

"For how long, Mr. Jordan?" Monique interrupted him. She had a pen and a notebook in her hand, ready to scribble down dates. "There are three new clients awaiting your advice. In order to reschedule their appointments, I need to know when you will be available." She pursed her lips, waiting for his answer. It was always a bad sign when she pursed her lips.

Better to put his hands flat on the table, where he could watch them should they start to develop claws. Or sprout fur. "I don't know for how long," he bit out, already losing his patience. A nice run would be good. A long run through snowy woods....

No. Definitely not.

"Are you ill?" Billy slumped into a chair, stretching out his legs and fishing for his tobacco pouch. He didn't smoke anymore, but he still rolled between ten and fifteen cigarettes each day, only to hand them out to whoever needed one. "You look ill. Tell us how we can help you."

A bit of fresh meat wouldn't be too bad.

Gabriel gulped. "I need you to find someone," he said over the voice telling him to get out of there and seek out the winter world and forget about his worries. "My mother, in fact. It's urgent. All other cases have to wait until I know where she is. Alive, I hope, although I wouldn't be surprised if she has overdosed by now. She's been a drug addict ever since I was born."

And now he began to shiver as if he himself were an addict going cold turkey.

"Coffee, Mr. Jordan?" Monique put a cup in front of him. Gratefully, Gabriel wrapped his hands around it, inhaling the scent and warming his fingers. He burned his lips at the first sip, but what the hell; for the time being, the voice was gone and so was his urge to get up and run.

If coffee did the trick, he'd drink gallons of it, although he usually preferred tea.

"How old's your mom now, and what's her name?" Billy was done with his first cigarette and was about to start a second one, then changed his mind and looked at Monique. "Can I have a coffee too, sweetie?" he said, flashing her a big smile, which revealed his rotting gums. He'd been a hooker and a user until some years ago, when one of his tricks had beaten him and left him to die. Ever since then, he'd worked at Father Barley's mission, taking care of everyone who needed help, cooking as well as nursing. He was one of Gabriel's few friends. Even Monique, who liked practically no one, had a soft spot where Billy was concerned. She even blushed at not having offered him coffee earlier and rushed away to get him a cup.

Gabriel massaged his temples, glad there was one less person he had to concentrate on. "My mother's name is Tessa Rose Jordan, née Parker. She had me when she was seventeen, so she's in her late forties by now. For a while, she worked on Park Street, but I assume that's not the case anymore. She's far too old to attract paying customers."

"Yeah, you're right there, man. No one older than twenty-five working on Park Street. You gonna tell me why you want her found all of a sudden?"

Damn thing with friends was they had a right to be curious.

"Let's just say I ran into trouble and need her to sort it out. And if anyone can find her, it's you. Call me as soon as you know where she is, be it day or night. You've got my cell number. Use it."

Billy grinned. "What's in it for the mission, man?" he asked. "We could do with a new kitchen."

The good thing about Billy was his needs were so very straightforward. He never asked for money for himself, always for the mission. Sometimes, Gabriel wondered what Father Barley would do without him.

"A new kitchen is a bit more than I can afford right now," he said. "How about a new fridge and oven for starters, and as soon as I've solved a few more cases, the rest will follow?"

"Deal." Billy grinned, reached across the desk, and brusquely smacked Gabriel's shoulder. "Take care of yourself, Gabe. This doesn't have anything to do with your man, does it?" Billy had met Aleksei only a few times but liked him a lot. He always feared they'd split up and Gabriel would land on the streets again—he'd said so more than once—and on his once handsome, now-broken face, Gabriel could see his worry.

"Nothing to do with Aleksei," he said, not sure whether he was lying. In a way, Aleksei was definitely part of the problem. "You just find my mother, okay?"

Billy nodded and got up just as Monique came in with his coffee. "If she's still out there, I'll find her," he said as he wrapped his arm around the secretary's wiry waist and led her out of Gabriel's office.

"Talk to you soon," he called over his shoulder before closing the door behind him.

The sudden silence came as a shock, and it hurt because now the voice calling him was so clearly audible it made him wince.

Come to me!

"Shut the fuck up," Gabriel said aloud. "Stay out of my head. I'm not coming, hear me? Whatever you are, I am not falling for the same trick twice!"

HIGH up in the mountains, the banshee was frantic with hate. Her child was not responding as expected! He refused to follow the call, and he refused to do as ordered!

By now, the child, her creature, should be sitting at her feet and worshipping her. Instead, he was still in that horribly loud and bright world, so warm and full of life it made her sick with disgust.

Her child was a lot more hardheaded than expected.

Although last night, the boy had followed her call. He had listened, he had obeyed, and he had opened the portal even though he had wanted to go to a different world, one with trees like this one but without snow. He had wanted to run, not hunt.

That he'd turned into a wolf had been unexpected. As a wolf, he was nearly immune to her calls, just like his grandmother. It was the only reason he'd escaped.

But as she knew his name, he obeyed her, on a certain level, at least. She could invade his mind. Call him. Persuade him.

The balance of the portals was already suffering. Some were damaged upon opening. People had gone missing.

Not her concern.

She'd come down from the mountains to meet him. She'd seen him devouring his catch, and she'd already reached out for him when his wolf instincts had sensed her.

And he'd run away.

The banshee screamed, rattling the icicles on her cave's ceiling and upsetting the egg slumbering in its nest. The boy, her child, had run away from her, although she had ordered him not only to stay but to embrace her!

Obey *her*. Do as *she* wished.

But the boy refused to obey in his human form as well. Even then, his wolf instincts worked as a protection, kicking in whenever the pressure became too great. Hadn't she wanted him to hurt his lover? But he hadn't. True, he had been forceful in his lovemaking, but not cruel. She had watched them; she knew.

She had to increase the calls. She needed to strengthen her power over him.

She looked at her claws. There was blood on them. His blood. Gabriel's blood.

He had tried to flee, and he had managed to get away from her. But she had scratched him right before he'd jumped through the portal. This was his blood on her claws, and she would use it to call him.

More portals would be damaged; the balance would be close to shattering for good.

This time, he would have to obey her. And once he was here, with her, he would willingly sacrifice his life so she could finally, after decades—centuries, even—get her revenge on the dragons.

CHAPTER EIGHT

THERE had been a lot of talk last night. That there was something wrong with the portals. That people felt insecure before drawing the required rune; that they were scared of them.

The wise one had crossed through hundreds if not thousands of them during his lifetime. And he had listened last night.

"The portals are killing people," they'd said, but he'd walked away instead of arguing. They were young, he'd told himself when walking home through the forest. They didn't have a clue about runes.

"They're dangerous. Did you know they could rip you apart? Did you hear of that one guy who got lost and couldn't find his way out, and when he did, he was an old man?"

Nonsense, of course. "Rubbish," the old fae murmured to himself. "Idiocy. The portals were given to us by the dragons. They are safe, always have been, always will be."

Last night, some of his people had claimed to have seen people vanish into the portal, screaming. Some, people whose friendship he treasured, whom he'd known for a long, long time, people he trusted, had said that sometimes, the color of the portals were wrong.

And the discord. They had talked about it last night. Endless discussions about whether it was true or not or if it was even possible for something like a discord to exist.

"Time to find out myself."

"What did you say, wise one?"

Ah. His pupil, of course. The one who was supposed to make sure he didn't do anything foolish. Head of the council he might be, but his son considered him too old to go investigating on his own and had saddled him with a young woman to look after him.

"Nothing," he replied briskly. "I'm going to open a portal now. Do not touch it. Just observe. Can you do that?"

The pupil looked affronted. "Yes, wise one. I can observe. I can even be quiet should you wish it."

Sarcasm. He smiled. The young woman already showed great potential for a career in fae politics.

The first portal was all right. So was the second one and the third and the tenth. They were all good, all golden, all as they should be.

"What are we looking for, wise one?" his pupil asked eventually, when the sun stood high in the sky. It was time for lunch. She looked like she was wondering how long this might take.

"I don't know."

Another portal, and another, and....

And this one was different. The discord was there. The color was wrong.

This one made his head ache.

This one upset the balance of the universe. No other way to describe it.

"Wise one?"

He looked at the young woman with watery eyes. Was he just old? Was he imagining things?

"Can you not hear it? Can you not see how wrong the portal is, how damaged?" Desperate for her answer, he even put his hand on her arm, shaking her, trying to make her see and hear and feel what he saw and heard and felt.

The only response he got was the confusion written all over her face.

"Children," he grumbled. Then he threw his walking stick away and moved a little bit closer to the portal. "Blind and deaf."

Damaged as it was, the portal still looked beautiful. It glowed, just as it should glow. The difference in the color was tiny. And the discord... now he wasn't sure he'd heard it at all.

"Strange," he said, and he took another step. "I could have sworn.... Maybe it is the sunlight. Or that third bowl of strawberries I had for breakfast."

Sure enough, his stomach was behaving as if it was not fond of food. He felt like throwing up.

"Maybe... I need to take a closer look. Damn eyes. Just another little step...."

"Wise—"

It was the last word he heard before he died.

CHAPTER NINE

PACING the living room from wall to wall didn't really help; nevertheless, Gabriel paced, hour after hour, no matter how tired his legs were becoming. Pacing, moving, seemed the one thing that kept his mind from snapping.

He would have preferred to go running, but he didn't dare leave the house. Outside, there were woods. Outside, there was soft grass and mellow sunlight and fresh, crisp air. Outside, he could stretch his muscles properly, not cramp them up like he had to in this small, useless room.

"Shit," he murmured. Even thinking about going outside was clearly not an option.

Raking his hands through his hair, Gabriel realized with horror that he was getting more and more restless, and it wasn't even lunchtime yet. He wanted to leave. He wanted to follow that call to the other world, the one with the snow and the deer. He wanted to obey.

What it would be like at sunset, he couldn't even imagine.

"Fine. Seems I'm going crazy. Any idea what I should do now, Doc?" Being aware he was talking to an empty room didn't stop him at all from doing it. Actually, talking felt good. All right, only crazy people talked to people who weren't there, but what the hell. He'd gone through worse times. When he'd started living on the streets for good and hadn't known where his next meal was coming from. When he'd sold his ass for the first—and only—time so he wouldn't starve. When Aleksei's brother had captured him, and when Aleksei had plunged a knife into his heart. Yep, that had been bad. Being nervous and restless was peaches compared to knives.

Only it wasn't.

The creature was calling him. Its voice sang in his blood, and he wanted to follow.

Luckily, Aleksei hadn't been home upon his arrival. Gabriel had fled the office once the more pressing questions had been taken care of. Billy would find his mother; Monique would rearrange his appointments. Nothing to worry about.

The house had been empty when he'd arrived home, which was good. He hated Aleksei, his presence, his smell, his taste….

"Bullshit!"

Gabriel ran into the opposite wall headfirst, not slowing down a bit. His head connected; his skin cracked and blood ran down his face.

"I do *not* hate him, do you hear me? Stop messing with my brain!"

The pain seemed to clear his mind a bit. Not much. Just enough to realize what he had been thinking only moments ago.

This wasn't him thinking and feeling those things. The creature was dropping poison into his thoughts, and since he'd been in its world, it had gotten worse.

Staggering backward with one hell of a headache building up behind his forehead, Gabriel fell onto the couch.

He'd been in the creature's world. It had touched him. The scratches along his hip and leg were proof it had really happened—the scratches that, right now, were throbbing with pain.

You hate him. He's bad for you. Leave him.

"Shut the fuck up," he said wearily. "You're a liar, whoever you are, and I don't believe a word you say."

There was no response.

"I can't stay inside for much longer." Staying inside was driving him crazy. Well, crazier than he already was.

He could take the bus out of town. There would be trees and fields and lots of animals to chase and to hunt. If he was quick, he could be back before Aleksei was home. He would never need to find out.

Or even better, he could go to that other world again. He didn't even have to turn into a wolf. The creature—the banshee—would surely accept him as he was.

He knew it wouldn't be long before he gave in to the calling. The voice was too strong. Gabriel almost believed Aleksei would be better off without him.

Fucking great.

"I need to do something," Gabriel murmured, still rubbing his head. "There must be a way to block out that voice. All I have to do is find it."

He went to the bedroom and stared at the smooth blanket and the perfectly set pillows.

Sex? No. Last time had been a disaster; he wouldn't touch Aleksei before he knew what to do about the wolf problem.

He needed to find inspiration. He thought best when there was chaos around him, but Aleksei had cleaned up before he'd left, so there was no help to be expected in that direction. No scraps of paper, no open books, not even a single sock lying around.

The kitchen was equally clean, and in the workroom only the microscope sat on the workbench, patiently waiting for its master to come home and do some more research. Right now, Aleksei was discussing whatever catastrophe with the fae council; he wouldn't be back for another hour at least.

"Could check some blood samples. Maybe find a solution."

Stupid idea. He never had gotten the hang of the thing, nor did he have the patience needed to stare for hours through the tiny lenses.

Television, then? Find an answer in one of the daily soap operas? Surely not.

Computer? Maybe.

His laptop was open and waiting for a command when Gabriel realized he had no idea what to do now. Search the Net for information about—what? Banshees running after him in the darkness? Voiceless calls? Werewolves?

He was just about to slam the lid shut when he remembered the recording Aleksei had brought back from the *Poison Prince*. So far, he hadn't watched it. The few glimpses in Tanith's tiny office didn't count, but now seemed as good a time as any to do it. Maybe he could learn something. In any case, it would help him remember what had happened that night. And as remembering was a major part of his problem, he might even get the much-needed inspiration.

Aleksei had put the CD on the bookshelf; it still sat there next to a large collection of strange music he liked to listen to, so Gabriel fetched it and put it into the drive.

"Nothing else to do today," he said as his finger hovered over the play arrow, refusing to hit it. "Go on. Watch it. Aleksei says he loved every bit of what I did to him. Couldn't have been that bad, then."

At first, it wasn't that bad. But as the recording continued, he watched with his mouth sagging open, and it stayed that way until it was over.

He had done *that*?

"Fucking shit!" he breathed.

He remembered now. All of it. He remembered the voice in his head ordering him to hurt Aleksei badly enough for his lover to end up seriously injured. He remembered how the hairs on his arms and neck had stood up, and he remembered growling.

A vague idea crossed through his burning mind, pestering him for attention.

The screen was frozen on the scene where they were both on the floor, right after he'd unchained Aleksei. On the floor next to them was the leather string he'd used to bind him.

Aleksei's skin patterns were glowing. And on his neck stood out a dark line of blood from where Gabriel had bitten him.

Blood magic. Now there was a spark of inspiration he really hadn't expected. Blood magic was illegal. It messed with people's lives, and because of it, Aleksei had once very nearly died.

Still….

Deep in thought, Gabriel pushed up the sleeves of his shirt. He'd gotten tan over the summer, having renovated the roof of their house, which had taken him half of July and all of August. His skin was smooth and nearly hairless; around his wrists, faded scars could be seen where Aleksei's mad brother had bound him with runed ropes.

"Maybe not Blood magic. But something like a Binding rune could do the trick. An anchor, keeping me in this world and knocking out the damn voice in my damn head."

He hadn't heard the front door opening. Usually, he would have sensed Aleksei coming home minutes before his car turned into the driveway. So he jumped in total surprise when his lover put a hand on his shoulder.

"What binding?" Aleksei asked while putting down the bag of groceries he'd been carrying. "And why are you watching porn in the middle of the day?"

"It's our porn. I thought watching it…. Anyway. It sparked an idea. Are you up for an experiment?"

Aleksei put the groceries in the kitchen, came back, and closed the laptop lid. "What sort of idea?" he asked. "What sort of experiment? I've been with Lia all morning and just went shopping. The only experiment I can think of enjoying is lunch."

Come to me!

Gabriel's head snapped up. The voice was like a slap in the face, and instantly, the need to obey returned. It made his feet ache, and his heart too, and it surely made thinking harder than it already was.

He clenched his teeth and fought hard to ignore the voice's demand. Seeing this through was important.

"The voice is calling me," he said aloud. In his head, the banshee screamed with anger at his betrayal. "Hard to resist. I think my wolf part is trying to run away. I think… I think the wolf and the banshee don't like each other. When I was a wolf, I didn't hear the call. And in the *Poison Prince*…. Before I lost it, before the wolf took over, the voice wanted me to hurt you."

"You didn't hurt me."

"I know. Now. Because I watched the film. But I can't be a wolf permanently unless I want to end up like my mad grandmother. I need another way to block out the voice."

Aleksei nodded. "Logical reasoning," he said. "So what about that experiment?"

Gabriel tapped his finger on the closed lid. "The leather string triggered an idea. I thought, what if you bind me too? You're my anchor anyway, Aleksei. Bind me to you and this world, make it clear I belong to you and that no one else, especially not a disembodied voice, has any power over me."

Aleksei paled. "You're talking of forbidden magic here." He shook his head vigorously. "Not only is it illegal to use, I couldn't do it anyway. Those kind of Binding runes require hate, beloved. I do not hate you. I do not wish you harm."

Gabriel grabbed his lover's collar. The voice became louder by the second. "That thing is out there, and it is calling me. I will follow its call if you don't hold me back somehow. And anyway, I am not talking about the forbidden runes. I'm talking about a new one."

"I can't—" Aleksei began, but Gabriel didn't let him finish his sentence.

"I'm losing my mind. Now. This very moment. The creature makes me believe I hate you. After I watched the video… I was so close to using all those toys on you. I was *that* close to hurting you really badly. If the wolf hadn't taken over, I would have. But in the long run, not even the wolf is strong enough. Hold me back, Aleksei. Please!"

"But I cannot!"

It was rare for Aleksei to shout. He was a man who won arguments through reasoning and logic and, sometimes, with a kiss. Shouting was just not part of his character.

"I cannot bind you, Gabriel," Aleksei repeated more quietly. "I am willing to do everything and sacrifice everything to save you, but a binding…. No. Never."

"If this is all about finding a way to do it, I think I can make something up." Before Aleksei could hold him back, Gabriel was in the workroom. He took a sheet of paper and a pen—both much more suitable for painting runes than cocoa spilled on a table—and scribbled lines without even bothering to sit down.

I shouldn't be able to do this, he thought, nibbling the pen's end. *But it is all so clear. All I have to do is… here, this line, and that one. No. Doesn't work that way.*

His knowledge of runes was fragile and pitted at best, and he would have been the first to admit it. He used them without knowing how they worked, he crossed the portals without even bothering to protect himself, and whenever Aleksei tried to get him to talk about it, he quickly changed the subject.

Inventing runes should be—according to his lover, the fae council, and everyone else—impossible.

He did it anyway.

It was so easy. Stupid, really, that no one had ever tried before. All it needed was—yes, if he began with the Protection rune but altered that line so the lower part of a Hiding rune could be added….

"No, still doesn't work yet," Gabriel mumbled, pushing stray strands of his hair behind his ear. "Got to erase that bit here. Now. That's more like it. Can't remember which rune that part is from, but what the hell. Should work anyway."

"I cannot believe you're doing it again." Leaning against the doorframe, Aleksei was watching him with a mixture of amusement, doubt, and faint jealousy on his face. "You have no idea how desperately people in all worlds try to do just that: invent new runes. It never works. It is impossible to feed them with power. They stay what they are, lines on paper. And then you come along and scribble not one but several new runes down just like that. Runes that work!"

"Hmm. Sorry." Gabriel flashed him an apologetic smile. "If you keep this to yourself, I won't tell anyone either. Ah. Now, that's better. I'm not done yet, but I want your opinion. Come here and take a look."

Aleksei stepped next to him, looked at the paper, and traced the lines with his fingertips. They were glowing faintly, not enough to do what they were designed for, but enough to make it absolutely clear they were more than ink on paper. "This one here was your first try, yes?"

Gabriel nodded. His fingers itched for the pen so he could continue his work, but right now, he understood it was more important to explain what he'd done. "It didn't feel quite right," he said. "That line is too long and that one there doesn't fit at all."

"I can see the difference with the second one. But I don't understand how you could know the first one wouldn't work. I cannot feel runes. I know by looking at them if I did them right and then I feed them with power."

Gabriel shrugged his shoulders. He couldn't explain it any better than that, just as he couldn't explain to a blind man what the color red looked like.

"The rune you invented to find the cameras—could you show me how it is drawn?" Aleksei raised a questioning eyebrow, and Gabriel couldn't help but smile.

"Sure. It's easy. Look," he said, and he drew a few lines underneath the runes already on the paper. "That one you need to draw in the air or it won't work, just like the… let's call it Binding rune… has to be drawn on naked skin. Try it. Think of something you want to be found and that's it. Easy."

"I have mislaid one of my—"

"Hang on! Even better… let's see if I can alter this a bit—yes. Perfect! Now, you know how you always talk about filing all your books so you can find references to certain subjects more easily? Or so I can find them more easily since you know all your books by heart, anyway, and I can't even remember the title I'm looking for?" Gabriel's cheeks were glowing with excitement. For lack of paper, he used the pen to write on his palm, rubbed out wrong lines with his thumb and a bit of spit before finally thrusting his hand in front of Aleksei's eyes. "There. Imagine you want to find books containing information about shapeshifters. Draw the rune."

Aleksei never hesitated when it came to runes. He'd grown up with them and had a natural knack for mastering their powers. No other fae, and probably not even the oldest elf, knew more about them than he did.

He hesitated now. Only when Gabriel waggled his fingers encouragingly did he take a close look at the lines and then paint the rune with a few smooth movements. From the doubtful look on his face, Gabriel knew he didn't really believe it would work, which made him grin—he hadn't believed in runes when he'd first met Aleksei. Since then, he'd learned better.

The rune began to glow and then exploded. On the bookshelf, volumes were marked with small bits of it, one after the other until ten or more glowed with the same light as the rune.

"Told you so," Gabriel said proudly. It was the first time he'd outsmarted his lover on his own turf, and it felt great.

Aleksei took down one of the books, leafing through it and making sure it truly contained the required information. He did so with every other marked book before nodding in satisfaction. "Had you told me about this a week ago, I wouldn't have believed you," he said. "This rune did not exist until you created it. Amazing."

"Well, now that you know it works, will you bind me to you?" He'd finished the rune while Aleksei had checked the marked books. It would work, he was sure of it. "No Blood magic. Nothing dangerous. Just a way to keep me sane." Not waiting for an answer, Gabriel undid the buttons of his shirt. "Unless, of course, you prefer to hunt me down once I turn into a wolf or follow me straight into the banshee's cave."

Aleksei's face went blank. "You should not joke about this, beloved."

"The alternative to joking about it is for you to do as I ask." Gabriel shrugged off his shirt. "Do it, Aleksei. Kick the banshee's voice out of my head. Bind me. Now."

The fae closed his eyes for a brief moment. "You don't know what you're asking of me. Just because one of your runes worked doesn't mean another one will as well. You don't know if there are any side effects. And even if it works as intended, have you thought about the consequences? What if you cannot take a step anymore without me knowing about it? What if you want to leave me, but I could stop you? I would not be an anchor but your prison. A binding, as I understand it, means you'd belong to me. Fully."

A chill ran down Gabriel's spine. "I think it won't happen," he said. "At least, I didn't create the rune that way. But even if so, it would be worth it. I belong to you anyway. And that damn voice makes me do things I don't want to do. I kissed Conchita, for example. And I nearly fucked a tree nymph a few weeks ago." He gulped; he really hadn't wanted to confess his sins that way. And now that it was out, it sounded as if he wanted to blame his guilt on this unknown creature.

Great. Surely Aleksei wouldn't buy *that*.

Briefly, Aleksei closed his eyes, pinching the bridge of his nose as if a headache was building up behind his forehead. "Anything else you would like to tell me?" he asked, surprisingly calm. "For now would be an ideal time. I knew you were hiding something from me. I didn't expect it would be quite that much."

"Nothing else," Gabriel whispered, studying the floorboards. "I think. I keep forgetting things, you know. If there is something else, I'm not hiding it on purpose."

It became harder by the second not to twitch and shuffle his feet, not to rake his hands through his hair and rip it out, to stand still as if this were a normal conversation and not something his sanity depended upon.

Come to me! You betrayed him. He doesn't want you. Come to me!

"No." Gabriel dropped onto Aleksei's chair in front of the microscope and dug his nails into the workbench's wood. Not looking up, he said, "I'm sorry, for everything. Only I can't talk about it any longer with the banshee in my head. You need to do the binding. And I think it's only fair. When you suffered from the Blood rune, I was there to keep you sane. Now I suffer. Now *I* am about to go insane. Help me, Aleksei!"

Slowly, Aleksei took the sheet with the runes from the workbench. He stared at them for a long time before finally putting his hand on Gabriel's chest.

Or rather, he moved to place his hand on Gabriel's chest, but Gabriel jumped up and out of his reach before he could be touched, toppling over the chair and smashing several glass vials in the process.

"If you don't want me to do this, you shouldn't try with all your might to make me," Aleksei said dryly, but with an underlying note of concern.

Gabriel could feel his heart hammering in his chest, and he heard the voice calling louder than ever before.

He wants to hurt you. He wants to kill you. Come to me, you'll be safe with me!

"I won't come, I will stay here, and this will be the last time you meddle with my brain!"

"Beloved," Aleksei said, but Gabriel had already moved, pinning his lover to the wall forcefully before he could continue.

"I want you to bind me," he bit out. "This thing wants me to believe you are about to kill me. Tell me you won't do me any harm, Aleksei, because if you don't tell me and if you don't make me believe you, I'm out of here."

His heart was going to break out of his chest at any moment now. It beat too fast and too hard and occasionally skipped a beat. Gabriel realized this must have been how his grandmother felt before she'd gone mad, trying to go about her daily tasks only to see herself fail.

She'd turned into a wolf for good. Hopefully, she was living happily in a nice, thick wood with lots of game. For him that wasn't an option, although the thought did have its appeal. One half of him believed the man before him hated him and wanted to hurt him. The other half wanted to run and hide. Only a thin slice of his mind told him not to believe the bullshit he was thinking. It wouldn't last much longer before the two halves ground it into dust.

"I love you," Aleksei said, and painted the first line onto his skin. It began to glow brightly, and it hurt like hell.

The screaming, hateful voice in his head shredded his mind into little bits of bleeding meat. Gabriel fell to his knees and tried to crawl away and out of the workroom.

With a leap, Aleksei landed on Gabriel's back, pushing him down flat onto his stomach. His left hand caught one of Gabriel's, and with a grunt, he flipped him over, pinning both his arms to the ground with his knees. "You're not going anywhere, Gabe," he said. "Not before I'm done." Swiftly, he painted another line, trying to finish the rune.

And a third. Aleksei glanced at the piece of paper lying only a few feet away from him on the floor. With its help, he managed to draw the rune Gabriel had created, slowly, but accurately.

When the rune was more than half done, the pain ceased. What was more important, the screaming voice in his head had diminished.

"Works," Gabriel breathed and relaxed under his lover's hard grip. "Another one. Put it onto every inch of my skin."

Aleksei covered Gabriel's chest and abdomen with the rune. Then he turned him over.

More runes, and with each one, Aleksei could draw them faster. With each one, the voice became quieter, until Gabriel couldn't hear it anymore. But it was looming in the back of his mind; he could feel it still.

Something was missing.

When there was no skin left unmarked, when Gabriel was glowing as if bathed in fire, Aleksei went to get up—and was held back.

"Finish the binding," Gabriel rasped. "You need to finish it. Make me yours." Fighting with his belt, he tried to wriggle out of his jeans but failed—Aleksei was still sitting on top of him.

"Finish. The. Fucking. Binding!" Gabriel shouted, reaching out and pushing Aleksei off. "Fuck me!" Finally, his belt gave way and he kicked off his jeans. The coldness of the floor bit into his flesh. He wondered vaguely if he'd already gone insane, demanding what he was demanding, but then he was naked and hungry for his lover's touch. Gabriel spread his legs and shifted his pelvis. "Fuck me, Aleksei," he repeated hoarsely.

More than likely they'd both gone mad, because Aleksei was above and inside him within a few moments. No more discussions, no more reasoning. He pulled up Gabriel's legs until they were around his hips, and he thrust slowly and deeply into him, a maddeningly lazy rhythm that made Gabriel forget his own name and each and every one of his worries on top of it.

"You're mine!" A thrust, a hold. "You belong to me." Thrust. Hold.

Gabriel tightened his grip, pulled his lover down and deeper inside him with his arms and legs.

"I bind you." Aleksei's voice whispering into his ear. Aleksei's cock filling him, claiming him.

The runes burned their power into his flesh, carved their way through his skin into his heart, his mind, and his soul.

Gabriel heard himself scream. Whether it was from pleasure, pain, or fear, he couldn't tell.

The banshee's voice in his head screamed too. Outraged, disbelieving, and hateful, the creature tripled its attempts to stop him.

In vain.

"You're mine," Aleksei whispered, holding him tight. "You have been mine from the moment we met, will always be mine, and I will never release you!"

They came together; they held each other, their hearts beating fast in perfect sync.

Silence at last.

Afterwards, arms spread wide in total surrender, Gabriel lay on the floor, a disbelieving grin on his exhausted face.

Aleksei kissed him tenderly. "I didn't know you had a thing for tree nymphs," he said earnestly.

Gabriel managed a shaky laugh. "Nor did I. I'm so damn sorry."

"I believe it was nothing you were craving. Although it is said tree nymphs are exceptional lovers. Very affectionate. Very... skillful."

"The voice is gone," Gabriel murmured. His skin was glowing. "But this isn't over yet, is it?"

Brushing red strands out of Gabriel's face, Aleksei looked down at him. "No, it isn't," he said. "I think it has only just begun."

THE next morning, they took a shower together, Gabriel dwelling in the silence that filled his head. No more voices speaking nonsense to him and no pressing need to go for a run. He was home with the man he loved. Together with Aleksei, who was washing his back, and not shying away from his touch.

The knock interrupted them just when they had finished drying each other, both contemplating the pros (many) and cons (none) of a lazy morning spent in bed.

"Are you expecting a visitor?" Aleksei asked, pulling on a dressing gown. His clothes were still scattered all over the workroom floor.

"No one but Billy telling me he's found my mother. But he'd rather phone than come all the way out here." Gabriel found a more or less clean pair of jeans in the corner of the bathroom and pulled them on. "I'll get the door. You close the door to the workroom."

Barefoot and without a shirt, Gabriel padded to the front door, thinking about a meal more than who was at the door. A salesman, probably. He hoped he'd be able to get rid of him quickly, because he was hungry and looking forward to breakfast.

He should have looked through the viewer, but he didn't. He just blindly opened the door.

"You," the tall, dark-haired woman said. There wasn't even a hint of a smile on her face. "I see you are still living here, then, shifter. An unpleasant surprise. I need to see my brother."

Gabriel stared at her for several seconds before his mind caught up. "Lia," he managed eventually. "Talk about unpleasant surprises. Would you believe me if I said Aleksei isn't home?"

The fae woman bared her teeth at him. "If I were allowed to, I would make you forget you were born."

"Good to see you too," Gabriel replied with a sigh. "Do come inside. It is always a pleasure to have my lover's family around."

Chin raised and fists balled, Lia stalked into the house, making sure not to get too close to Gabriel. "Go and do human things," she said dismissively. "What I have to talk about with my brother is none of your business. And put a shirt on. The sight of you is an insult to my eyes."

Gabriel frowned and looked down at himself, then raised his hands. Each finger was covered in runes, and in the dim hall, the shine of his skin lit up the walls.

"You mean you can't see them?" he asked.

Lia turned. "See what? You? Your chest? I can see both, and what I see disgusts me."

"Oh, wow," Gabriel murmured, closing the front door. "This is gonna be a lot more complicated than I thought."

CHAPTER TEN

L<small>IA</small> was a tall woman, taller than her brother and even taller than Gabriel. She had a knack for dominating any room she entered, and she expected obedience and respect from everyone who dared to even look at her.

Gabriel wished she hadn't come to visit. Usually, a visit meant trouble, and what he didn't need right now was more trouble than he already had on his plate.

On the other hand, the voice in his head was still inaudible, which was really good news. He could deal with Lia if he had to, so he followed the fae woman into the living room, where Aleksei sat on the couch, one of the books he'd marked with the Finding rune on his lap.

When his sister towered above him, he looked up with mild surprise on his face. "Lia. What brings you to our home? Last time you honored us with your presence you made it very clear you never wished to return." He wore his dressing gown; his hair was wet, and Gabriel knew from the disgusted look on her face what Lia was thinking: that they'd just had sex.

Well, she's wrong. We just had a shower, Gabriel thought with a grin. He took a chair and sat down, not bothering to put on a shirt as ordered. That Lia couldn't see the gleam of the runes on his skin irritated and fascinated him. She knew a lot about runes and had never failed to show off her superiority on the subject.

"Aleksei," she said with the smallest inclination of her head. She wore her hair short. It covered her head like a helmet, the dark strands streaked with a lot more gray than Aleksei's. She was twelve years older than her brother, and she carried a lot of responsibility on her shoulders, being one of the most influential members of the fae council.

"It is true I did not wish to visit this place again. The human world is too dirty for my taste, and too loud. You living here is something I do not understand. But I did not have a choice."

Aleksei put the book aside. "Take a seat, sister. Tell me what worries you."

Watching the two together was like watching a fight where not a single fist was raised. On the outside, brother and sister looked very much alike: both had fair features, their skin bearing a silver shimmer. Both were slender built, and both their skin patterns were beautiful and rich.

But where Aleksei's eyes were blue, Lia's were green. Where he was gentle and caring, she was demanding and cold. He would give his life to protect the ones he loved; she would send an army to get what she desired.

They couldn't be more different.

"Send your human toy out of the room," Lia demanded, still standing. "What I have to say is private. And in my presence you will take off the necklace you're using to obscure your true looks. Living in this awful world is bad enough; not showing what you are is even worse."

Gabriel hadn't even noticed the necklace. To him, it was just a piece of jewelry. To Lia, it was an insult. She couldn't see through the rune's disguise, something Gabriel hadn't known until Aleksei had told him.

Aleksei casually took off the necklace; Lia's shoulders lowered a fraction, something like satisfaction showing on her face.

"Gabe," Aleksei said, "would you be so kind as to fetch my sister a glass of water? She will wait with what she has to say until you are back."

"I told you I want him out of the room."

Aleksei raised an eyebrow. "I just made it clear I want him to be a witness to your words. Do you really think you can tell me what to do in my own house?"

Lia bit her lip, clearly trying not to spit out the sharp reply hovering on her tongue. When Gabriel gave her the glass—a wine glass, as he hadn't been able to find another one—he saw her knuckles turn white and knew it was from the effort not to break the stem. Or throw the glass back at him.

"Were you to live in our world, where you belong, brother, you'd know how to behave in the presence of a member of the fae council." She turned away from Aleksei, her long, plain dress brushing over the light wooden planks. With a single gulp, she emptied the glass. "But you chose to flee, little brother. You chose to leave your responsibilities behind like a sulking child. You should have been a member of the council yourself. You should have wielded the power that comes with that post instead of living in this petty little house with your petty little toy."

Aleksei sank back into the cushions. "You call my partner a toy once more and I will personally throw you out into the street no matter what you have to say, Lia." His voice was friendly; his eyes were hard.

She whipped around. "You wouldn't dare. You never—" But there she stopped. "Maybe you would," she mused. "After all, you erased our brother's mind, reducing him to a babbling infant. And only because he threatened *him*."

"His name is Gabriel," Aleksei said. "I think I've told you as much."

Having taken his place on the chair again—backward, this time—Gabriel simply watched them and wondered how he deserved to be so fiercely loved by a man who obviously could have chosen any one of the richest and best-looking fae.

Instead, Aleksei had chosen him, a man with no family and no past, someone who'd lived on the streets like a wild dog for years.

With a contented sigh, Gabriel put his arms on the back of the chair, placing his chin on top of his hands. Watching those two was always a very special experience. Maybe if Lia could control her anger for a moment or two, she would tell them why she had actually come.

Lia put her glass down swiftly on the small side table next to the couch. She did it carelessly, and Aleksei reached out to steady it before it fell. "What is it I can help you with, sister?" he asked. "I trust you came here with a purpose? Or perhaps you wanted to join us for breakfast?"

The look of disgust that flared up in Lia's green eyes was gone as quickly as it had come, and Gabriel had to grin. She'd only eaten with them once, and she hadn't enjoyed a single bite.

Not surprising, since Gabriel had done the cooking. The only thing he was good at was spaghetti, and that hadn't been on the menu that day.

"Another one is missing," Lia bit out. "This time, the incident was witnessed. Apparently, he wanted to investigate the rumors concerning the failing portals. Before he died, he opened many portals, one after another, until one of them… sucked him up. He screamed; then he was gone. He has not turned up on the other side, nor anywhere else."

Aleksei steepled his fingers, looking first at his sister, then at Gabriel. "I told you about the missing people, did I not?"

Gabriel frowned. Had he? He wasn't sure, so he shook his head.

"I thought I did. Anyway. It appears that for a few weeks, the portals have been unreliable. People are vanishing. Some of them turn up dead. Some never turn up at all."

"I cannot believe you are involving him," Lia said. "He knows nothing of portals or runes. Why are you telling him things he won't be able to understand?"

Her arrogance was getting on Gabriel's nerves. "I can hear you, Lia. And I'm not totally dumb. I know what portals are, I can open them, and I can use them. Who's gone missing? And how many?"

Lia just shrugged her shoulders.

"We know of twelve people who have gone missing, but I suspect there have been more," Aleksei said.

"And I say they didn't know how to protect themselves from the portal's powers," Lia interjected. "Most of the missing were uneducated fools. They didn't know the proper Protection runes, and the portals ripped them apart." She stood before the bookshelf, tracing her fingertips along the books' spines. It was close to a caress; she was clearly as fond of books as her brother.

"Bullshit."

Gabriel said it before he'd thought about the effect it would have; Lia as well as Aleksei turned and stared at him, waiting for an explanation.

Having two impatient fae facing him wasn't something Gabriel was fond of. "I mean, it's unlikely," he stammered.

"Why?" Aleksei asked.

"Because... well, for one, there are people out there who can handle portals better than others. Me, for example. I don't ever bother with protection. I just step through. I can't be the only uneducated fool handling the portals."

Lia snorted; Aleksei continued looking at him. "Go on," he said.

"And why so many in such a short time? If what Lia said is true, people would go missing all the time. But from what I understand, they don't. So twelve in a few weeks is suspicious. There must be another reason."

Aleksei cast him a smile. "Precisely my opinion."

"Plus," Gabriel added, "if Lia really believes what she said, she wouldn't be here right now. She'd be thinking that new guy who's gone was just another victim of his own stupidity. She would've dismissed him and stayed home. But instead, she's here. Question is: who's the guy, and why'd he die even though he knew everything about portals and protection?"

Both Aleksei and Gabriel looked at Lia.

It was funny to watch her fighting for words. She clearly wanted to tell her brother what had happened; she did *not* want to tell Gabriel.

Eventually, and because Aleksei had made it so very clear he wanted Gabriel to hear it as well, she bit out a name: "Rohan."

Aleksei's eyebrows shot up. "Impossible!"

"But true. One of his pupils was with him when he vanished. A very bright pupil, I have to say. I have no reason to doubt her report. We want you to investigate, Aleksei. No one knows more about runes and portals than you. No one else has your connections. No one else can be trusted in this matter. If the portals have become dangerous, if the runes are failing to work...." Her voice trailed off, deep concern written on her sharp-angled face.

If the portals couldn't be used anymore, there was no way to predict what would happen to the hidden worlds. Social, financial, and emotional ties were tight among many of them. Some wouldn't be able to survive without the help of others, their natural resources being too limited to provide for their inhabitants.

"Rohan was head of the fae council," Aleksei said, visibly shocked. "A good man and a fair trader. He wouldn't make a mistake when it came to portals."

"Will you come home with me?" Lia asked. "Will you help solve this mess?"

Aleksei was quiet for a long moment. He looked at Gabriel, who could practically hear him thinking.

He doesn't want to go because of me. His first priority right now is to find out who's calling me, not investigate portal riddles.

Aloud, he said, "Go ahead, Doc. I'm okay, at least for now."

Silently, he wondered if he would remain okay or if the Binding rune would lose its power the moment Aleksei was out of sight.

"Leave, Lia," Aleksei said. "I need to talk to Gabriel. I will be with you shortly."

"Do not dawdle," Lia answered, and moments later, they heard the front door close.

"At least she was polite enough not to open a portal right in our living room," Gabriel said. "Maybe I'll understand one day why she hates me so much."

Aleksei frowned. "It's obvious. You are, as far as she is concerned, of low social status. You are partly human, you are not fae, and most importantly, you are male."

Gabriel watched him go to the bedroom, shed his dressing gown, and search for something to wear. He could tell how distracted and absentminded his lover was by the way he stared at the shirts for several moments before eventually choosing one that didn't match his socks.

"So Lia's homophobic. And… humanphobic and peasantphobic. Lovely. I suppose she'll begin to like me when hell freezes over."

Aleksei laughed. "She's not homophobic as such. That is, she doesn't mind me living with you in general. The point is that we cannot have offspring. As much as she knows how much I love you, she also knows I won't ever leave you for, say, a nice fae woman with wide childbearing hips. Our line has come to an end, neither she, nor Petresh, nor I having children. That is why she hates you. Don't take it personally." Sitting on the bed, he put his shoes on.

Gabriel came in and sat next to him. He waggled his fingers, admiring the glowing runes on each digit. "Did you notice how she couldn't see these?" he asked. "It made me wonder if they are real. And if the binding is truly working."

Aleksei quickly put a hand over his. "*I* can see them," he said. "They are real. I bound you; I sealed the rune you created by making love to you. Do not doubt its power, beloved."

Gabriel gulped. "Wish I could believe it," he murmured. "Wish you could stay. But this is important, isn't it? This guy—what was his name?"

"Rohan."

"Yes. Right. My memory's getting worse every day. Something else we have to sort out. This Rohan mystery needs to be solved. So go. But be back soon, okay?"

The sheer thought of the house being empty in a few minutes made him uneasy.

Aleksei pulled him into a hug. "There is nothing I wish more than to stay with you," he said quietly. "But yes, Rohan is important. What's more, he was the one protecting my somewhat unique status among the fae these past decades. Not many of my kind leave our world, Gabriel. The few who do are considered outcasts and not allowed to come back.

I am the only exception, and I wish to continue to be able to go home every now and then. If I find out what happened to Rohan, Lia will put in a good word for me."

Gabriel returned the hug for a few heartbeats before breaking it. "Could it be you've kept a few secrets yourself, Doc?" he mocked. "A few lies you've haven't told me about yet?"

"Like why I left my people or why I am the exception to the rule?"

"Like that, yes."

"Or why Rohan took a special liking to me?"

"Or that."

They were both grinning now, remembering the lies Aleksei had told Gabriel at the beginning of their relationship. Some of them had been fairly ridiculous, like the one claiming Aleksei was the owner of an umbrella factory.

"Rohan was my teacher," Aleksei said. "He taught me everything I know. Simple, really." Aleksei leaned over and kissed him. "Promise me you will stay away from portals," he urged. "Promise me you will be here when I get back. I have the feeling you and that portal problem are connected, which is another reason why I am willing to sacrifice my time for my sister's wishes. The fact that you were being called, turned into a wolf, and have created completely new runes around the same time the portals became dangerous cannot be a coincidence."

Admittedly, Gabriel hadn't even thought about that. "I might go to the office," he said, "and grab something to eat afterwards. I'll be here when you come back, promise. And I swear I will not go anywhere near a portal."

Then a thought struck him. "Aleksei, how do I know *you* will come back? What if the portal eats you up or something?"

Aleksei, who was already painting the first line of the Portal rune, froze. Then he carefully wiped out the line. "You are right. I was stupid and arrogant not to consider that possibility. If it's true the failing of a portal has nothing to do with one's skill, then the portals are dangerous for everyone."

Sagging to the floor, he raked his hands through his short hair, looking decidedly lost. "And I truly thought I knew everything that could be known about runes."

Quickly, Gabriel knelt next to him and drew random lines onto the planks. "The Portal rune must be the basis," he murmured. "And I need a bit of a Protection rune, and half of the Binding rune from earlier on. Yep. Good. Hey, this gets easier each time I do it!"

Aleksei sat next to him and just shook his head.

The rune he was creating was a Portal rune, and it wasn't one. Once finished, the portal exploded in light rather than emerging in a pleasant, gentle gleam like a common portal. It also looked more solid. "The altered rune will stabilize the portal, and it will change its color should it be unsafe to go through." Rubbing his head, Gabriel only now realized how strenuous creating the rune had been.

"I'll use this rune upon coming back," Aleksei said. "Hopefully, talking to the council won't take too long. Last time... well, last time we couldn't find a solution. We might today." He got up, stepped through the portal, and was gone.

The portal closed right after him. The light vanished, and somehow, the air seemed to be much colder now that Gabriel was left behind, alone.

"Shirt would be good," he murmured to himself. "Shoes. Office. Breakfast, maybe. If I stay home, I might do something really stupid. Like... wash the windows. Do some cleaning up. Yeah, much better to go to the office and have a chat with Billy. Maybe he's found my mother by now. Maybe Monique has a nice and easy case for me."

Maybe he should stop his wishful thinking.

"YOU look—"

"Awful. I know," Gabriel said as he tried to get past Monique before she could make a more thorough observation. He was unsuccessful, as his secretary grabbed his wrist the moment he entered her office. Her grip was iron hard. She'd worked for a vampire for more than a decade; she knew how to handle tricky and unresponsive bosses.

"Not as bad as last time, I was going to say. Still, you could do with a decent night of sleep, proper food, and less worrying. What's wrong, Gabriel?"

Oh, damn. She only called him by his first name if she was truly angry or—more likely, given the look of concern on her face—unhappy with him.

He considered his options only to realize there weren't any. What she wanted to know she eventually figured out, and so far, he hadn't found a way to successfully lie to her.

"And don't you even *think* about wriggling your way out of it again," she snapped as if she could see he was trying to think of a believable story. "I can imagine lots of things are bothering you. What I want to know is which one has taken away the spring in your step."

Gabriel blinked. He hadn't known it was that obvious. "What would you say if I told you I had turned into a wolf a few nights back?" he asked.

It was impossible to lie to her.

Monique impatiently tapped her fingers on her desk. "Continue," she simply said.

"And that there's a strange creature calling me, driving me crazy, and trying to separate me from Aleksei?"

Monique sighed.

Gabriel dropped into the chair in front of her desk. Sometimes he wondered why he came in at all. He was there to do the footwork—find the missing person, drag them back if possible, and deliver the file. Monique was the brains. She ran the office, placed the ads, answered the phone, talked to potential clients, set his appointments, and cashed the checks. If she had been able to use runes, she wouldn't need him at all.

"Look, it's too complicated, and I don't even know where to start. Once I know, I promise you'll be the first to get the details. But the wolf problem and the voice problem are the reason for... everything."

Monique snorted, got up, and poured him a glass of whiskey. When he raised his hands to indicate it was way too early for alcohol, he noticed they were trembling.

So did Monique. "I have never seen you like this," she stated. "Drink the whiskey, Gabriel. Have you had breakfast? No? I thought so. However, it's past noon and it will calm your nerves. I'm sure whatever your problem is, it can be solved."

The liquid in the glass sloshed gently against the side. "I don't drink," he wanted to say, and "I don't like whiskey," but he didn't. He just sighed and downed the glass's contents, bracing himself against the burning alcohol.

When his eyes stopped watering and he got the cough under control, he realized he felt better. Not much, just enough to lean back in his chair a bit more comfortably. "Lia came round earlier," he told Monique, who sat patiently behind her desk waiting for an explanation. "She's Aleksei's sister. Now he's gone with her, and I have to deal with my problem alone."

"You told Dr. Tennant it was okay to go?" Monique asked.

"I was lying."

The secretary's cool, pale eyes softened. "I am sure he will be back soon."

"Don't count on it." Gabriel sighed. "Once Lia has him in her claws, she's bound to keep him as long as she can. Might take days before he's back, especially if the fae council wants to have a word as well."

Only when Monique's silence stretched out did he rethink what he'd just said.

Then it hit him. "Oh," he murmured, unable to keep an embarrassed look off his face. But it was definitely fascinating to see Monique speak through pursed lips.

"Can I assume Dr. Tennant isn't entirely human?"

His blush deepened. He'd told Monique about his shapeshifter genes—apart from Aleksei, she was the only one who knew—but hadn't revealed anything about his lover. To her, Aleksei was an ordinary human man with a few too many kilos on the ribs, thinning hair, and a charming smile. She probably even believed the umbrella factory story.

"He's pureblood fae," he muttered, suddenly inclined to tell her the truth. "He doesn't look like you think he looks. He's taller and much slimmer and... well, he looks different."

Monique again tapped her fingers on the table. "Will he mind that you told me?" she asked. "Because I do expect an invitation to your Christmas party, as always. And if you do choose to invite me, I need to know whether or not I can let on that I know about his race." Lips still pursed, she awaited his answer, and once more, he felt like a schoolboy who was expected to solve a particularly complicated math problem in front of the entire class.

"He likes you." Gabriel shrugged his shoulders. "I'm sure he won't mind, and of course you don't have to lie about it. Should have told you long ago, Monique. Sorry."

She granted him one of her rare smiles. It made her look younger than her fifty-three years; it also made her look slightly mischievous. "I am quite curious to see if I can persuade him to show me his true looks," she said. "For now, I need you to take a look at this new case. A couple wanting to know about their missing daughter. I set an appointment for tomorrow morning at ten. They e-mailed the basic information, so you might be able to give them an estimate as to how long it might take you to find the girl. Oh, and Mr. Taylor called. He wishes you to be present when he meets his mother. He said, and I quote here, 'Tell him I'll throw in a club membership if he agrees.' Any idea what that's supposed to mean?"

Gabriel grinned tiredly. The day was turning out to be better than it started, with Lia on his doorstep before breakfast. "A club membership." He had no idea how to feel about that. "Well, let him know I'll be there if he manages to match the appointment with my schedule."

Gabriel had just gotten up to go to his office when the door burst open. Billy strolled in, a waffle in his hand and chocolate sauce dripping all over his chin and sweater.

"Got a minute?" he asked between bites. "Have some news about your mom. Or even better, you invite me for lunch and I'll tell you what I found out completely for free." Winking at Monique, he stuffed the last bite of the waffle into his mouth and wiped his hands clean on his trousers. Or sort of clean, given how badly his trousers needed a wash.

"Lunch. Good idea." Gabriel's stomach began to rumble with a vengeance. "Monique, I'll take the file about the missing girl. I'll be there for the appointment tomorrow. See you, and thanks for listening."

"Always, Mr. Jordan," she replied briskly.

BILLY was already downstairs when Gabriel caught up with him. At the corner of the street, a small bald woman pushed herself off the wall and flung herself into his arms. "Hi, Gabe," she chirped, smacking a kiss onto his cheek. "You're stubbly. But you smell nice, all warm and safe. I missed you!"

"Missed you too, Marita," he said, realizing he'd forgotten to shave this morning. He lifted her up and swung her around; she was like a child most days, happy to be alive and not caring about tomorrow. That she was a skilled silversmith was only one of the many intriguing facts he'd discovered about her over the years. Marita had helped him make the bracelet Aleksei wore. He had no idea how she earned her daily living other than staying at Father Barley's mission and helping in the kitchen whenever she was in the right mood. She didn't whore, and she didn't steal. Occasionally, she did a bit of begging, but not nearly enough to keep her fed.

Seeing her hugging Billy more tenderly than she'd hugged him, he suspected the crooked-nosed man had something to do with her well-being.

"Come for lunch with us?" he asked.

Marita slipped her hand into Billy's. "Can I have a burger? Are you rich enough to buy burgers for all of us?"

"And fries," Billy added. "And Coke, and a milkshake for the sparrow here."

Marita's eyes widened. "He can't be *that* rich!" she objected, but Billy only grinned.

"He could afford *two* burgers for each of us," he whispered into her ear, sharing a glance with Gabriel. "And cake for dessert!"

Marita beamed from ear to ear, grabbed Gabriel's hand as well, and pulled them along. Like anyone else eating at the mission on a regular basis, she was eager to eat elsewhere, and burgers and a milkshake proved to be just what she wanted today.

Another bit of tension left Gabriel's body. The banshee's voice was pleasantly absent, and he felt normal, neither like a wolf in a human body nor like a puppet on strings. "Guess the binding works even when Aleksei is not around," he murmured under his breath and smiled when Marita glanced at him curiously.

The small café was half-empty when they entered, and the waitress was eager to give them one of the better tables. She didn't bother to hand them a menu; she simply recommended the daily specials, which consisted of pancakes, burgers with fries, and cheesecake. "Homemade," she said, beaming. Her hips swayed as she walked away.

Watching his friends eat, Gabriel had a burger and took a fry every now and then, listening to their chatter and news about Father Barley and the newest boys who had been accepted into the mission. Despite his empty stomach, he'd decided to take it easy with food given what had happened the last time he'd been too greedy.

Gabriel supported Father Barley with regular checks, having relied on the mission for food and shelter himself only a few years ago. Now that he earned more money than ever before in his life, he made sure the mission's roof was intact and waterproof and that there was enough food for everyone who was hungry.

"Father Barley asked about you," Marita was saying. "He says he hasn't seen you in a while and wanted to know if you would like to pay him a visit. I thought you had coffee with him a week ago?" She wiped her mouth clean and slurped down the rest of her milkshake.

Gabriel grinned. "Been there, done that. It's just that the good father's brain resembles swiss cheese more than anything else. He never remembers me."

It used to bother him, the rune on his neck that made it so very hard for him to make friends or be recognized by his foster parents or even the occasional one-night stand. Since Aleksei, who never had any problems recognizing him, had become part of his life and he'd been working as a private investigator, he cherished being more or less invisible.

"Now, will you tell me the news about my mother, Billy, or do I have to buy you another Coke?"

Billy flashed him one of his gaping smiles, most of his teeth having rotted away after years of drug use. He was clean now, and he used his grin to make it crystal clear what awaited a good-looking boy who chose cocaine over vegetables. "Didn't find Tessa, if that's what you'd hoped," he said. "She's still alive, though. Not whoring anymore, as far as I know. Too old for that. She's living on the streets, and man, she's fast when it comes to running. Twice I nearly had her. So she knows someone's after her, and maybe she even knows it's you. Dropped a few hints here and there. And that there's a bit of cash involved. She might get the word. Sorry, buddy, but that's all I have for you."

Gabriel nodded a brisk thanks and got up to get him another Coke and one more milkshake for Marita. He needed to get his emotions under control, and it was easier without the two of them staring at him expectantly.

His mother. Tessa Rose, who'd given birth to him at the tender age of seventeen. The woman who'd dumped him in the garbage the moment she'd set eyes on him. Maybe she'd dumped him because she saw he was different. Maybe because she hadn't wanted him in the first place.

His palms were sweaty when he returned to the table, and his heart beat too fast: he had mixed feelings about Tessa Rose, and he couldn't believe the simple mentioning of his mother's name could turn his emotional state upside down. As a boy, he'd been thrilled to see her the few times she'd visited his grandmother. She always seemed so tall and lovely, and she looked so beautiful in her tight skirts and big earrings. At least, he'd thought so. Once he got older, he'd found out she worked as a hooker and was always on whatever drug she could find in order to forget her life and her defective son.

Because in her eyes, that's what he was: defective. Tainted blood.

He sat down heavily, staring at his half-eaten burger and only partially listening to whatever Marita was talking about, and Gabriel realized it still hurt after all these years.

He tried to recall her face but failed. A faint memory of her smell was all he got: a mixture of alcohol, sweat, dirt, and, strangely enough, honey. He realized he wouldn't even recognize her were she to stand in front of him right now.

She could be anywhere. And the chances she'd agree to say hello to him, not to mention donating some of her blood, were pretty slim. She'd probably try to kill him first and then kick him heartily in the kidneys once he was down.

"Don't look so sad, Gabe," Marita said, putting her hand on his. "I don't know where my mama is, either. You've got us to comfort you, and Doc Tennant."

"Where is he, anyway?" Billy asked. "He must be mighty busy with him spending so much time away from you."

One day I'll tell him the truth, Gabriel thought. Aloud, he said, "Actually, he's waiting for me," and got up. "I need to go. Billy, let me know if you manage to catch my mother. Marita, take care of yourself. And pop by my office tomorrow. One of my clients will be needing a present for a newly found relative. I'm sure your skills would be welcome."

Marita clapped her hands. "Wonderful! I'm in the mood for some work. I'll be there, promise!"

Gabriel left them sitting in the little café, glad to be out in the fresh air. He decided to walk home even though it would take an hour, if not more.

The sun was still high in the sky as he wandered through the streets, keeping away from the main roads and sticking to smaller streets with less traffic. When he crossed through one of the main parks, he took his shoes off, enjoying the cool, damp grass beneath the soles of his feet.

He smiled. There was no urge to run and no voice calling him. When he lifted his hands in front of his eyes, he could see the Binding runes glowing gently, even against the sunlight.

Neither Monique nor Billy nor Marita had seen them, but they were there. He could feel their weight, not on his skin, but on his soul, and he knew he was safe.

For now.

He arrived home slightly out of breath, hoping, unlikely as it was, to find Aleksei in the living room. Fumbling for the keys, which were, as always, hidden in the depths of his knapsack, took all of his attention. The house was in an industrial area, with office buildings surrounding it, and was heavily locked and barred. Even during daylight, this was one of the quietest areas in town, and so far, neither he nor Aleksei had ever been bothered by burglars.

So when a hand grabbed his wrist, it came as a shock, and instinctively, he slammed his would-be attacker into the front door.

He expected his opponent to recover immediately; he expected a fight, and his fists were balled in defense. He wasn't what one would call a good fighter—he didn't follow any sort of technique or rules—but he was strong and fast, and if he was forced to fight, he tried to win by getting it over with as quickly as possible.

But this person, who had slumped to the ground after hitting the door, wasn't getting up again. This one sat with his back against the door, wiping a sleeve over a bleeding nose. The sun was shining brightly in his face, making his features indistinguishable, but Gabriel could smell the blood, just as he could smell the alcohol, the sweat….

And honey.

His fists dropped limply to his sides. The blood rushed out of his face, and his knees became weak.

"Mom?" he heard himself say, already kneeling next to her. The thought that the woman sitting before him was his mother seemed ridiculous.

"Piece of shit," the woman rasped. Then she lifted her head and spat right in his face.

CHAPTER ELEVEN

GABRIEL dropped his keys; when he reached out to pick them up, her foot landed in his stomach.

Skittering backward and out of her way, Gabriel got to his feet, his arm clutched around his middle.

"Dumb and just as ugly as you were when I pushed you out. Looking for me! Risking people finding out I'm connected to you! My fucking life is hard enough without something like *you* making it worse!" Slowly, she got up, rubbing her face from where she'd hit the door.

Tessa Rose Jordan was smaller than Gabriel expected her to be, with ridiculously bushy gray-brown hair and eyes hard enough to cut through glass. Her face was heavily lined after decades of drug abuse. She wasn't even fifty years old, but she looked older, mostly due to the bitterness and hate that tarnished her features.

"Should have killed you the moment you began mewling," she said.

"You tried," Gabriel said, keeping his distance. "Remember, you dumped me in the garbage when I was barely a few minutes old. Gran told me. You couldn't have done much worse, other than putting your hands around my throat."

Tessa hissed at him like an angry cat. Her teeth were small and sharp, just like her fingernails, as Gabriel found out when she lashed out and raked them across his cheek. Not enough distance, apparently. "Should have smashed your head in. But no, I was stupid. I thought dumping you would be enough. Stupid, stupid, *stupid*! Your worthless father found you and brought you back. Even beat me for trying to get rid of you."

The hate in her voice sent a chill down Gabriel's spine.

"My father found me?" he asked, his brain still slowly wrapping itself around the concept of being in his mother's presence.

"He changed. Into an animal. Right in front of me." The bewilderment in her voice was nearly comical. "Tobias came home shortly after I'd given birth. I was covered in blood and slime. I hurt all over, and he had nothing better to do than ask for you. I told him you'd been stillborn and I'd dumped you, and he went frantic. Sniffed me, can you believe it? Like a dog sniffing a bitch, and then he changed and ran out. He came back with you between his fangs. I was half dead, but there wasn't even a scratch on your skin."

Dirty hair, dirty clothes. Her shoes had holes in them, and she wasn't wearing a jacket. A thin blanket was wrapped around her bony shoulders. Rail thin as she was, it was obvious she didn't eat on a regular basis.

She's like me a few years back, Gabriel thought. *Living on the streets, stealing food, not caring what others think as long as they leave her alone.*

"I knew my father was a shapeshifter." He had to say something or the unspoken words would choke him. "I didn't know he could turn into a wolf. Nor did I know he saved my life."

Tessa growled, a low, dangerous sound. "Useless bastard. Worthless piece of shit, just like you."

"And you came here just to tell me this? How nice." Gabriel was close to strangling the woman. His gran had hated her. He was pretty sure he hated her as well.

Tessa crossed her thin, rash-covered arms over her barely existent bosom. "You're looking for me," she snapped. "That guy of yours, that Billy, he's after me. Can't let that happen. Customers get scared of people like Billy. Ex-street guy. Ex-hooker, himself. Now he's working for that Father Barley, telling my kids to go to the mission whenever they're hungry. Lost more than one because of fucking Billy. Why're you looking for me?"

Gabriel was about to reply when a thought crossed his mind. "Do you want to come in?" he asked. "Have a drink and maybe something to eat?"

Briefly, Tessa narrowed her eyes in suspicion. She glanced at the house, at him, and at the key in his hand. "So you live here?" she asked. "This your house?"

He nodded. "Mine and Aleksei's."

Instantly, she took a step back.

"He's not home," Gabriel assured her. "Just you and me. And I won't hurt you. I just want some answers."

"Aleksei," Tessa said thoughtfully. "Your lover?"

"Yes."

She grinned a nasty smile. "He took you in, I bet. Found you on the streets and offered you a meal and a bed in exchange for a fuck."

Damn her, Gabriel thought. *She doesn't even know how close she is to the truth.*

"Whore," she hissed. "Just what I expected from a monster like you."

"Big words from you, Mom," Gabriel repeated coldly. "You whored until you got too old, didn't you? Billy said you're not in the business anymore. From what you just said, I guess you're a pimp now? And not a good one, given the state of your clothes. Fine, let's stay out here."

"Monster. Animal. Tainted blood," Tessa singsonged, the words drilling holes into his soul, something he hadn't expected given she didn't mean anything to him. Her clawlike fingers were clutched around her upper arms as if she wanted to prevent herself from attacking him.

Touching him. Touching her defective child.

"I saw it," she continued. "The moment you were born, I saw you were not pure. Not *human*."

"What did you expect, with my father being a shapeshifter?" Gabriel was close to losing his patience. If he didn't manage to shut her up soon, he would slam the door in her face, whether or not he got some of her blood. "I mean, you knew what he was, didn't you?"

She was fast; she hit him again before he realized she was moving. This time, her fist cracked his lip. "I knew he was different, but I didn't know your fucking father was an animal until he changed, idiot! I would have killed him had I known!"

"You touch me one more time and I'll beat you unconscious," he bit out, wiping the blood from his lips.

"Your lousy father *raped* me," Tessa hissed. "When I got pregnant, he cried and begged for forgiveness, and because of the pressure I got from my mother, and because I hoped to get a bit of freedom, I married him. Hoped I'd get some money out of him. Stupid idea. He thought we could build a happy little family. Forbade me to drink. Forbade me to do drugs. Forbade me to smoke. Forbade me to go out. I left him before you were born. Hoped you'd be normal. But no, you were like him. Just my luck I give birth to—"

"An animal. Yes, you've already mentioned that." Gabriel had never wished he could turn into a wolf on command, but right now, the idea of changing and ripping her apart was quite tantalizing. "Look, I had Billy trying to find you because I've run into a problem. I need a blood sample, that's all. Sorry if Billy threatened your little business. I'll tell him to back off. But I promise, if I do not get a blood sample from you, you'll spend the rest of your days behind bars."

He could smell her fear and hear her increased heart rate. She didn't like to be threatened; he wouldn't be surprised if she turned and fled.

Instead, she raised her chin. "Came here to tell you to leave me alone. You're no child of mine, monster. And whatever your problem is, it's none of mine. Can't have my blood. Got no diseases. Just leave me alone."

Without warning, Gabriel grabbed her hair and pushed her against the wall, using his height and additional weight to immobilize her. "I need a blood sample," he breathed into her ear. "Because, you know, I think there's more to you than you say. Not many people know what I am. Apart from Aleksei, no one has ever even guessed that I have mixed blood. And you say you saw it the moment I was born. You knew my father was different. Strange, don't you think?"

She struggled in vain. As frail as she was for her age, as well as underfed and weak from years of mistreatment, it was a surprise she'd made it all the way out to their house in the first place.

"Let me go," she croaked. "Don't touch me, monster! Look at you, all shiny in your nice clean clothes and new shoes, with your hair all washed and combed! Deep inside, you're just a filthy beast. You're even marked like an animal with those symbols on your skin. Did the one who fucks you put them there? Are they like an invisible leash so you can't run away?"

Her accusations were so very wrong and so close to the truth at the same time that Gabriel had to laugh. "No, Mom, they're not like a leash. They're runes, and they keep me—" He stopped dead. "Hang on. You can see the runes?"

Tessa aimed for his balls with her knee but missed as he shifted his hips at the last moment. "You bet I can see them," she bit out, fighting against his grip. "All over you, on your face, your hands. Looks awful. Heathen. God wouldn't approve of this. Should have killed you."

"As if you believed in any kind of god," Gabriel said, shaking with suppressed rage. "I wonder why you visited me at Gran's place from time to time. Drunk and out of your head on drugs. You hate me? Surprise, Mom. I hate you too."

Tessa struggled, spitting and clawing at him.

Gabriel tightened his grip. He needed to see this through or the scene would follow him into his nightmares. "The thing is," he said, staring at her, "no one except me and Aleksei can see these runes, and I think Aleksei can only see them because he drew them. So the question is, why can you see them?"

Her heart was racing in her chest. The smell of fear became overwhelming. "Don't know," she wheezed. "Let go of me!"

He didn't want to kill her, and he didn't want to scare her any more than necessary. He knew he should let go of her, but he didn't.

A Sleeping rune. Yeah. Good idea. She'd doze off and he'd be able to take a blood sample and then take her back into town.

Maybe a Forgetting rune as well? She wouldn't remember a thing the next morning, not that she'd come to see him, not that they'd argued, and not that she'd seen the runes on his skin.

Another thought made him hesitate. "How did you find me, anyway?" he asked. "It's not as if I advertise where I live."

"You were in the paper," she bit out, wriggling in his grip, "your name and picture. You kept the name your father gave you. Gabriel, like his granddad, he said. It was easy to find you. That business you own? I told one of my kids to watch out for you. She called this morning and said you were a few streets away grabbing something to eat. Now take your filthy fingers off me!"

He made a mental note to ask Monique for camera surveillance outside his office, and then blushed when he remembered the fuss he'd made about the cameras in his house. Billy would have an entire day's work soon, putting them back up.

He couldn't make her forget him, he just couldn't. A Forgetting rune was a tricky thing to handle, as Aleksei had warned him more than once. If done sloppily, it could erase not only the memories of the past hour, but of days, months, or even years. Worst-case scenario, he might wipe out Tessa's entire brain, leaving her in a condition like Aleksei's brother, Petresh, who'd forgotten how to talk and feed himself after Aleksei was done with him.

Tessa might forget him completely. And that was something Gabriel didn't want to happen.

"My hands aren't filthy," he clarified. "*I* am not filthy, unlike you. And I am not an animal. I will get that blood sample, Mom. And before I drive you back to town, I want to know why my dad killed himself."

He saw her swallow and her eyes narrow, as though she were calculating the odds of getting more out of him than just a ride. "Give me some cash and you can have what you want," she said finally. "I'm your mother. I need support in my old age. And you're rich. You can afford—what?—a hundred a week?"

This time, he lifted her off her feet. She didn't weigh more than a child. But she struggled and kicked until he put his arm across her throat. "Don't ever try to blackmail me again or you'll find out what it means to mess with me," he said quietly. "You'll go to sleep now, Mom. Count yourself lucky if you wake up again tomorrow. But first tell me about my dad!"

She gurgled, but he knew she was only putting on a show. His grip wasn't hard enough to stop her from breathing. "Said he heard voices," Tessa finally croaked. "Said they were driving him crazy. Hung himself in his mother's house. Best thing he could have done."

It wasn't easy to draw the Sleeping rune, as Tessa began kicking and screaming the moment he moved his fingers. His shins would undoubtedly be blue in another hour.

The rune's first lines glowed golden when he fed them with power, and his heart clenched with pain at the simple fact that his own mother had nothing but hate for him.

Nothing he could do about it. At least his grandmother had loved him. And, apparently, his father.

Who'd heard a voice.

Think about it later, Gabriel reminded himself, and he finished the rune.

There. Done. The rune hovered above Tessa's head, but she didn't fall asleep as she should have. Nothing happened beyond her eyes getting a bit glazy and the stream of obscenities slowing down a bit.

Gabriel frowned.

"Filthy beast with filthy magic," Tessa hissed, trying to scratch him. "Doesn't work on me, your magic. I'm immune to it. You better let me go now, or I'll bite you and give you all the diseases I have."

"Aleksei couldn't make me sleep," Gabriel murmured, holding the struggling woman in his arms and wondering when exactly the police would be showing up. "And you said you don't have any diseases."

This was a quiet area, but it was broad daylight, and there were offices in the neighborhood. Right now, someone might be watching them; right now, someone could be calling the cops.

"Help! Rape! Murder!" Tessa screamed—she must have seen his glances toward the buildings across the street and come to the same conclusion. Her voice wasn't particularly loud, but her thin, fragile voice was so full of hatred it made him snap nevertheless. Gabriel brought his elbow up and knocked her out, hoping he wouldn't break her skull.

Limply, she hung in his arms. The stench of her unwashed body and half-rotten clothes bit into his nose, and he briefly considered just dropping her on the doorstep and going inside for a bucket of water he could dump over her.

Instead, he carried her into the garage, wrapped her own blanket tightly around her, and put her on the backseat of Aleksei's Jag. He rarely drove the car, but there was a spare set of keys hidden in one of the tool drawers, which he retrieved before slipping behind the steering wheel.

As an afterthought, he turned and drew the Sleeping rune over the unconscious woman. Now that she was out, she couldn't fight it any longer. Once it was done, she began to snore.

Somewhat dumbstruck at how peacefully she slept, Gabriel needed a moment to remember why he had wanted to find her in the first place. Then he rushed upstairs to the workroom, searching through the drawers until he found a syringe. Aleksei kept them by the dozen. Over the years, he'd taken blood samples of nearly everyone he'd met, Gabriel included.

A shirt lay half-hidden under the workbench, and briefly, Gabriel smiled, tracing one of the runes on the back of his hand. He was bound. Safe. There was no voice in his head telling him lies and shouting, "Come to me."

Good.

He took the syringe and went back to the car, taking a blood sample from the vein at his mother's elbow and storing it securely on one of the shelves. He could get it later; for now, he needed a place to drop Tessa.

Gabriel was about to leave the garage when he realized he had no idea where to go.

"Can't put her on the street," he said to himself, leaning into the soft leather and inhaling the faint scent that proved his lover was the one who used the car on a regular basis. "She'd be dead by morning. If the cold doesn't finish her off, someone will rob and kill her." He turned in his seat, looking at her. "Not that there's much to steal."

He didn't even know if she had a place to stay. Somehow, he guessed she wouldn't be sleeping outside in winter, but he had no way of finding her hiding place.

That left a hotel.

Great. They would ask questions he couldn't answer, and most likely, they wouldn't let her in anyway given her looks. Not even the really cheap hotels.

"Just when I think I've solved all my problems, I run headfirst into another one."

He could take her into the woods, wrap her up warm, and hope she'd find her way back into town. Or he could take her into one of the hidden worlds, a warm one, clean her up....

No. He'd promised Aleksei to stay away from the portals, and anyway, Tessa would go apeshit were he to kidnap her. She was freaked out enough about him; no way to predict her reactions if she met up with a harpy or a centaur.

"Could take her upstairs and put her into bed."

Only he didn't want to. He really, really didn't want this woman anywhere near him or anything that belonged to him. The sheer thought of her in the living room, the kitchen, or the bedroom was unbearable.

His eyes fell on the cell phone lying on the passenger's seat. Aleksei must have forgotten it. He tended to leave technical devices where he'd last used them, which was the reason it was nearly impossible to reach him by phone. The thing was simply never where he was.

And apparently, neither was Gabriel's. He was sure he'd taken his cell phone this morning, but when he patted himself down, it wasn't there.

"Maybe," Gabriel murmured, picking up Aleksei's phone. "It's a silly idea, but then again, I can't think of anything else."

Quickly, he dialed the number, hoping he remembered it correctly. He'd only spoken to the man a few times, and he wasn't even sure he didn't change his number on a regular basis. Many businessmen did, and this one was well known to fiercely guard his privacy.

The phone rang twice before it was picked up.

"Yes?"

The voice on the other end was sleepy, cautious, but not hostile— luckily, or Gabriel would probably have hung up immediately.

"Mr. Taylor," he said carefully. "This is Gabriel Jordan speaking. I have a problem. You might be able to help me solve it."

Silence answered him. Then a brisk "Go ahead" allowed him to continue.

"You don't own just the *Poison Prince*, do you?" Gabriel asked. "You also bought a hotel chain a few years back, as my secretary found out when doing the background check on you. Do you still own it?"

"Yes." Taylor sounded as if he was about to lose his patience.

"I need a room for twenty-four hours and no questions asked by anyone. One guest. Asleep. Dirty. Female."

Gabriel could practically hear Taylor tighten his grip on the phone. "Who is she?" he asked.

"My mother. I'll pay for the room. And I'd owe you a favor."

He could hear Taylor breathing, thinking it over.

"The address is 5 King Street, Hotel Babylon, room forty-two," Taylor finally said. "You've got half an hour to get there. I'll meet you at the back entrance." With that, he disconnected.

"Yeah, fine," Gabriel said. Then he threw the phone back onto the passenger seat and backed out of the garage.

BRIAN TAYLOR was already waiting when Gabriel drove into the parking lot.

Carefully, Gabriel lifted the sleeping Tessa out of the back. With the blanket wrapped around her, the smell was bearable, but he still turned his head away so she wouldn't breathe directly into his face. It had turned to late afternoon without him even noticing.

Taylor opened the back door and let him in. They went upstairs to the fourth floor and found the room Taylor had reserved.

Gabriel was about to lower Tessa onto the bed when he realized he couldn't bring himself to do it. She stank. She probably had lice. Her clothes would ruin the sheets for good. One of her shoes dropped off and lay on the floor accusingly.

"Could you run her a bath?" he asked, not even embarrassed. This woman might have given birth to him, but she meant nothing to him. He was only taking care of her because no one else would, and he would be damned if he repaid Taylor by putting a filthy wreck in one of his beds.

Wordlessly, Taylor went into the bathroom and turned on the hot water. When Gabriel carried Tessa in and dropped the blanket to the floor, Taylor stepped out of the way so no part of her could touch him. He watched as Gabriel undressed her and put her into the tub; he watched as Gabriel washed her hair and her body, drained the dirty water, and refilled the tub a second time.

He watched but didn't comment when Gabriel drew a second, stronger Sleeping rune. Only when he placed her clean body, wrapped in a towel, on the bed and covered her with blankets, did he say, "Your mother, yes?"

"Yep."

"I do hope mine will be less quiet when I visit her." For a man of his reputation, it was a strangely mild remark.

Stretching his back—although Tessa was small and light, carrying her and bathing her hadn't been an easy task—Gabriel finally looked at Brian Taylor. "I appreciate this," he said. "There was no one else I could ask, and I needed a solution fast."

"You could have let her sleep in your bed, I assume." Taylor's dark eyes, in combination with his clothes and pale complexion, made it easy to believe there was vampire blood running through his veins. It was abundantly clear he had better things to do than waste his time by watching a sleeping drug addict taking a bath.

On the bed, Tessa didn't stir. If it weren't for the gentle rising of her chest, one might have thought her to be dead.

"She refused to come inside when I asked her. I saw no reason to force my hospitality on her once she'd passed out."

Paying Taylor for the room first, Gabriel left some money on the bedside table as well and was at the door when Taylor said, "A word about that favor you owe me, Mr. Jordan."

Slowly, Gabriel turned back to him. "You want that one quickly," he said. All he wanted to do was to go home and take a shower. Hopefully, Aleksei would be back by now. More than a shower, he needed a hug.

"Skip the favor," Taylor replied. "I want answers. Now. One of my employees told me she fell asleep in front of the screens. It is her job to watch the rooms and make sure no one gets injured. Or at least, no more injured than he or she begs for. Tanith has been in my employ for nearly three years. Never failed me. Never been sick a single day. She enjoys watching the members of my club, Mr. Jordan. Especially the males; even more so if no females are involved."

"So?" Gabriel knew what would be coming now but decided not to say any more than he had to.

"So imagine my surprise when she mentioned she couldn't remember watching you and your partner. What was his name again?"

Gabriel was about to answer when he remembered Aleksei had given a false name. And that he couldn't recall which one it had been.

Damn.

"You don't know your partner's name?" Mild amusement laced the words, barely covering the cold anger.

There was nothing he could say, so Gabriel kept quiet.

"And Tanith can't remember you leaving the club, either. Or show me the files from room number eight. It appears they are gone, even the backups."

Casually, Taylor turned to the sleeping woman in the bed. Every movement spoke of the gentle, wordless threat he was using to make Gabriel talk.

Gabriel briefly closed his eyes. He guessed that if he wanted to, and with his connections to Senator Dubaku, he could cause Taylor a shitload of trouble.

But what for? The man just wanted some answers. He had helped him take care of Tessa without asking more than the basics.

Fine, he would get answers.

"We took the files. All of them. Or rather, we took the CDs and had Tanith erase the files. Aleksei used a Forgetting rune on her. It's not her fault she doesn't remember a thing. She did watch. She did her job and did it well. She even fought against the rune, but of course, she didn't stand a chance."

"Why did you do it?"

"Because it was a strange night for both me and my partner. Because I sort of lost it, and because we didn't want anyone to know what happened."

Taylor just looked at him. "Did anyone get hurt?" he asked. "You or your partner?"

Surprised Taylor would comment on that part of it over all others, Gabriel shook his head. "No. For my partner, it was an exceptionally erotic experience. For me, it was weird and scary for reasons I cannot explain to you. Neither he nor I got hurt."

A flicker of relief showed in Taylor's dark eyes. "I wasn't sure," he murmured.

"Sure of what?" Gabriel asked.

"Rule number one in my club," Taylor mused. "No one gets hurt. That's why there are cameras in every room. That's why my employees watch and listen to what happens. Each member knows the rules. Allowing you to use one of my rooms although you are not a member was an exception. Because I trust you. Still do, by the way. Thank you for telling me the truth, Mr. Jordan. Understandably, your partner didn't want to get caught on camera, not with his skin patterns so clearly visible at the height of his lust."

That one took a moment to settle in.

"How the fuck do you know about Aleksei's skin patterns?" Gabriel felt the small hairs on the back of his neck rise, just as a wolf's fur would bristle when the animal was under attack.

Taylor placed the room keys on the table next to the money. "I was curious," he said. "I thought I'd watch you for a while myself. Of course I saw his patterns once he'd taken off the necklace. And I saw you. I must admit I don't really know what I saw. In any case, it is why I offered a permanent membership. Anyone who can keep control during such a wild, rough act, I don't need to worry about."

THE drive seemed longer than usual, but maybe Gabriel only thought so because he had far too much to think about. Luckily, the car knew where to go, or he would have ended up on the other side of town. As it was, he drove on autopilot, thoughts and words and accusations and insults hopping up and down in his mind like crazy bunnies.

He barely managed to drag himself upstairs once he'd parked the car. He was tired, and the headache was back.

His father had saved his life, and he had heard the banshee's voice.

His mother was a filthy pimp who still hated him after all these years. And she could see the runes on his skin.

The binding worked. The voice, which had bothered him for so long, was gone. No calling, no idiotic demands, no threats.

His father had killed himself because of the voice.

Great. Wonderful prospects for him should the binding cease to work.

Aleksei was still not home. The darkness of an early autumn night and silence were all that greeted him, and right now, he couldn't stand darkness and silence.

Gabriel went to the workroom with the syringe of his mother's blood clutched in his fist. "Should take a look," he murmured, trying to remember where Aleksei had put those little glass things whose proper name he could never remember. "Just one drop, switch on the microscope, and I'll see what makes her so special she can see my runes."

But he was too tired. It was dark outside. Where had the day gone?

He needed to sit down, just for a moment. Aleksei's chair was just the place, just for a sec, just for resting his—

He was asleep before he knew it, his head sinking down next to the microscope, his feet wrapped around the chair's thin legs.

CHAPTER TWELVE

THE mirror of ice reflected the banshee's empty eye sockets. She'd been looking into it for a long time now, determined to call her child to her world once more.

She had failed. Although she knew his name, although she had his blood, he couldn't hear her anymore.

It was the fae's fault. He had bound her child. He had taken him, marked him, and made him his entirely. She had watched; she had witnessed their mating. She'd seen her child fall into the fae's arms, willingly offering himself and helplessly crying out his lust and his lover's name.

His skin soiled with runes. His mind blocked against her voice.

There had been no way to prevent it. Her child, of mixed heritage as he was, was developing unexpected skills. Inventing runes—no. She hadn't planned on that happening.

Hear her, yes. Obey her, of course. But not oppose her. Not disobey her.

Never to choose the fae over her.

At first, the two falling in love had been a convenient coincidence. She couldn't have forced love; it had happened just like that.

At the beginning, their relationship had confused her. Then she realized that without the fae, Gabriel wouldn't have learned about the runes, would never have stepped through a portal, and would have stayed lost to her forever.

But then their love got in the way, and she had tried to break them apart. Like his father before him, she'd ordered Gabriel to do what he didn't want to do. Kiss someone else. Touch someone else. Surely if he was unfaithful to his lover, it would end their relationship.

It hadn't. Though she constantly whispered into his mind all sorts of lies and temptations, she had been unsuccessful.

Under different circumstances, she would have admired his strength. As it was, it only annoyed her and made her angry.

And now this binding. It was a problem. Her child was out of her reach. He belonged to his lover now, fully, body and soul. She no longer had any chance to come between them.

Briefly, the banshee touched the mirror. Gabriel was asleep, felled after a long day. The fae was nowhere to be seen.

She saw him twitch in his dreams. That he was probably dreaming of her nearly made her smile.

If only his grandmother hadn't managed to disobey her for so long. Maybe, if she had known the boy's name sooner, she would have been able to lure him into her world without needing the fae's help.

No use regretting what had already happened. His grandmother was dead, and so was his father. His mother was useless to her. She was twisted and broken and deaf to her calls. She'd just come in handy for creating a child that would serve her purpose.

Of course, Gabriel's father had needed to be forced into taking the girl. *Rape*, he'd called it. A necessity, in her eyes.

Carefully, the banshee touched her sleeping egg. It was her first; she was not sure yet whether it was a good idea to have it.

Vaguely, she remembered the day she'd touched Gabriel's grandmother for the first time. Back then, the woman had been young and stupid, tumbling into her world by accident. Altering her genes so they partly resembled hers had been so very easy. And the woman had screamed so nicely.

Cold clouds formed before the banshee's mouth. They froze in the cold air and covered her egg with icy dust.

A young one. She wouldn't be alone anymore.

She liked being alone. And a young one would need caring.

The banshee stared into the mirror, watching Gabriel sleep. She touched the ice again.

He's bound.

Her ageless, icy voice echoed through the mountain.

He's not mine.

In many ways, he was more important to her than her egg.

Her nails made a sharp, screeching sound on the ice. If she couldn't get to him directly, maybe she could try to get to the one who dared to keep him away from her?

After all, a binding worked in both directions. She had a link to her child. And through him, to the fae.

Gabriel will follow his lover.

It was worth a try.

CHAPTER THIRTEEN

CHANGE into a human. Do I really want to do this?

Sitting on his nest, the dragon had been pondering this question for days now. Changing into an animal was easy. Changing his form allowed him to go to places where, as a dragon, he wouldn't fit, and to do things he wouldn't, as a dragon, even consider. As a wolf, he ran for hours and played with the other wolves. As a bird, he forgot who he really was and enjoyed the now without worrying about yesterday or tomorrow.

Animals were easy. Their minds, though simple in the common sense of the word, were more focused and less apt to contemplate complex things, like life.

Or death.

Humans weren't easy.

The dragon put his huge black head onto his huge black paws and stared holes into the air, trying to make up his mind.

He needed to find the one of his kind. His sheer existence was a miracle; not finding him, not trying to lure him into the dragon world, would be a crime against his race.

Strange creatures, those humans. Fragile and loud, rude and... different.

And the boy was human, or mostly, at least. There were traces of other races in his blood, faint and not strong enough to be determined without direct physical contact. He was a gem in a world of worthless pebbles. He must be found.

Human. Walking on two legs. No wings. Unable to fly, and due to his mixed heritage, probably unable to use runes properly.

The dragon sighed. It would be risky to change into a human. Changing always meant taking on not only the body but also the character of his chosen form. As a seagull, for example, he was fond of fish, and his concentration lasted only from one fish to the next if he wasn't careful. It was harder to think, as flying was much more important to a seagull than using its brain.

As a wolf, he was fast and wanted to run, to hunt and kill. The taste of blood in his mouth dominated his mind, and he was always part of the pack.

Humans were so… strange. They talked a lot. Most of the time, they couldn't hear their own thoughts because of their ever-babbling mouths. They lived fast and died young. They didn't walk their ways for centuries, only mere decades, if they were lucky.

Another sigh, deeper this time and a tad scared. The dragon couldn't really remember what a human shape did to his mind. It might diminish him, make him think in ways he didn't want to think, force him to make rash decisions. The human form was a strong one; they possessed a more complicated brain than animals. They could think, if they wanted to.

The dragon stretched, spread his wings wide, and yawned. He had been pondering this for a long time now. Thinking could solve neither the fact he had to change nor his fear about it. Which left only one option: change despite his worries and hope everything would go well.

He concentrated, blocking out the wind and the sun blazing down from the sky, the chirping birds and his lingering fear. The act of changing itself was easy, but it was important not to let one's mind wander when between forms. Once, as a young dragon, he'd allowed his mind to get distracted by a mouse while planning to change into a weasel. The result had been embarrassing, to put it mildly.

His heartbeat began to race. Humans were always so restless, even when standing completely still. His dragon heart beat twice a minute; a human heart was more than thirty times as fast.

His body shrank and stretched. His wings became shoulder blades, his paws arms and legs. No scales, just skin, soft and vulnerable. Feet not made to walk due to feeble soles inadequately protected by a thick layer of calluses. At least the changing didn't hurt, although it was uncomfortable.

The wind made him shiver, and, confused, he looked at his hands and feet. Nakedness. He had forgotten about that part. Animals didn't need clothes, nor did dragons. But humans tended to react strangely upon seeing one of their kind unclad.

The sun was gone; changing had taken time. Still, the remaining light pierced his eyes and his brain. Human eyes were more sensitive to light; on the other hand, they had barely any sense of smell.

The dragon inspected his new body. It appeared to be tall for a human, although it was hard to judge when being suddenly only a fraction of one's usual height. Also, he was slim and bony, which he should have expected, as in his true form, he had been neglecting food recently.

Fingers, toes, and short, stubbly hair. Not too bad. At least he seemed to be complete.

He knelt, bending over a patch of water. The surface reflected his face.

A thin-lipped mouth, a slightly crooked nose, and almond-shaped eyes. High cheekbones and an angular chin.

Not too bad at all. This body would do for what he planned.

He stretched again, only this time he had to keep his balance or he would have fallen out of his nest. The missing wings were something he would have to get used to quickly. And his nakedness. He hadn't known how cold the air could be.

With chattering teeth, he opened a portal simply by thinking the rune, pleased it worked just as well as it did when he was in his dragon form. He'd feared he would lose his power over the runes. Luckily, he'd been wrong.

Maybe the human shape wasn't quite as tricky as expected.

Clothes, he thought. *And information.*

Not the human world. He needed to go there eventually, but not right now.

Thoughtfully, he waved his fingers over the portal, changing its destination by doing so. Which world would be best to visit first?

The centaurs' world? They were clever and respected the dragons.

No. They were hunters and might kill him before he could ask his questions. And it was even colder there than here.

The fae world, then. Yes. There had once been a council that tended to the problems of all races. If anyone knew how to find a single human in a world full of humans, it would be them.

The portal changed its destination once more. Just before he stepped through, the dragon added one more rune to his body. The color of his skin faded to a light brown. His eyes, always hardest to disguise, took a bit more effort. Eventually, they were plain black.

Turning his hand in the faint light of the first stars, he was satisfied. He looked human. No one would be suspicious.

TO HIS utter surprise, the fae world hadn't changed much since his last visit. There were still many trees, and the sky was as dark as he remembered it. There couldn't be cities anywhere nearby, or the lights would have spoiled the night's velvet softness.

The grass was soft and wet under his naked feet, and he shivered in the gentle breeze. He sighed. It had been centuries since he'd last taken human form. Back then, there had been people who knew what he was. They had helped him and guided him. Tonight, no one was there holding up a robe to cover him or serve him food his body could digest.

Were humans able to hunt and devour raw flesh? Did they like fish, bony and cold?

The dragon shook his head and took a step. When he lost his balance again, he involuntarily spread his wings so he wouldn't fall, only to realize he didn't have wings anymore. Only arms, thin and feeble.

Ungracefully, he landed in the dirt, facedown, with aching knees and hands.

Embarrassing. He didn't even remember how to operate this body!

Slowly, he made it back to his feet, brushed some earth off his skin, and took another step.

Better. The body learned fast. Or maybe it just didn't want to keep getting hurt.

Step by step, the dragon made his way to the nearby forest, where he could smell smoke and hear voices. It seemed fae still liked to meet under the stars rather than in houses, which was convenient; it would be easier to overhear their conversation.

A moment before he would have entered the circle of light in the middle of the forest, he remembered he still wasn't wearing any clothes. Surely the fae would frown at him were he to step among them naked. Surely they would be reluctant to answer his questions were he to offend them.

He turned away from the fae circle, observing with pleasure how quickly his mind was adjusting to the body. Walking was easier; it was fun, even. He had long, strong legs, and he thought he could walk for hours without tiring.

He was wrong, of course. Soon, his stomach began to rumble and his legs to tremble from the unaccustomed exercise. The wood's ground was uneven, covered with leaves, hiding rabbit holes and branches. More than once, he fell. A break was due, and food.

He'd followed a track; now he saw there were houses high up in the trees. Out of one, angry voices could be heard. A fragile-looking rope ladder hung down to the ground, swaying gently in the wind.

Hesitantly, the dragon put one hand to the first step of the ladder. Closing his eyes, he listened, inhaling deeply the scent of the two fae up in the house, the sound of their words, the crackling emotions heating up the space between them.

He might look human, but he was dragon. He could still do things no one else was capable of. He could see without using his eyes, and he could taste the tension between the brother and sister arguing over whatever nonsense fae might argue about.

Closing his eyes, the dragon saw them as clearly as if he were with them in the treetop. One wore a rune disguising his true looks, but of course it meant nothing to him. He could see through all disguises, all runes, and this one was no different.

This one had been created to cover the man's skin patterns, to make him ordinary rather than extraordinary. He was tall underneath the rune. His hair was black and curly at the ends. Ice-blue eyes matched his pale features.

His sister—they looked very much alike—was tall as well, and no runes were hidden in her wide garment. Her eyes were hard, her voice demanding.

"I said take it off," she hissed, and the dragon was reminded of how unpleasant a voice could sound. "You didn't wear it before the fae council; you never wear it outside the human world. Only in my presence, and only to insult me!"

His name is Aleksei, the dragon knew. *He feels familiar.*

Aleksei crossed his arms over his chest. "I'm about to go home. True, I could put it on once I arrived, but I am not willing to risk my cover just to please you, Lia."

And he's stubborn. That felt familiar too. The dragon smiled. His mate had been stubborn. Instinctively, he took a liking to the male fae, no matter that he didn't know him at all.

Lia pursed her lips. "You shouldn't live in that world. Or with that human."

Bemused, the dragon opened his eyes. Ah, this was about love. He couldn't have chosen a better place to get in contact with the world. Love was always the most fascinating subject.

He felt his heart speed up a bit, and his smile deepened. Maybe it hadn't been a bad idea at all to become human.

"I live where I like and with whom I like, Lia. And you know that too. I will not discuss either subject with you."

"And you know I cannot have children, Aleksei! It is your duty to do so instead. It is your duty to take your place amongst your people. You must sit next to me at the fae council, you must stop Rhys and his lot from banning the use of portals now Rohan is gone, and you must end this foolish relationship with the human!"

"This is precisely the reason why I left in the first place!"

The dragon could hear the pain in his voice; the fae didn't like to talk about this, not at all.

"You trying to command me. You trying to live my life for me. I refuse to live in this world simply to satisfy your demands, Lia. Fulfilling all of your wishes is impossible. I came to understand and accept that years ago. Leaving the human world is not an option. I like my job; I like my house and my car. Leaving Gabriel is not an option. You will have to live with the fact that neither you nor I will have offspring."

Oh, yes, there was a lot of love involved here.

"And thanks to you and your pet, Petresh won't have children, either." Bitterness laced Lia's words. "If he had killed your little lovetoy—"

The sharp sound of a slap made the dragon frown. This Gabriel was clearly a very tender subject for Aleksei if insulting him made him hit his sister.

No more arguing followed the slap, and with a sudden shock, the dragon realized that the two up there were done with each other, at least for now. One or both would come down at any moment, and he was still as naked as he'd been upon his arrival. He rubbed his hands across his bare arms, but it did nothing to warm him. He needed clothes, and soon. There were other treehouses around, all of them dark. He guessed the owners were at the clearing where he'd heard the voices earlier on. Quickly, he climbed up a different ladder, found a soft, wide robe, and pulled it over his head. Immediately, he felt better. Not only warmer, but decent as well.

Time to find the fae council. Time to show himself.

After jumping back to the ground, he noticed both the fae and his sister were gone; he wondered vaguely whether he would see either of them ever again. He was, he admitted to himself, curious without having a particular reason. But somehow, he thought he should keep track of them, or the male, at least.

Still barefoot, the dragon wandered silently through the dark wood in search of the light and the voices, but it took him longer than he'd expected. He could see neither the sky nor the stars. Only the moon shone through the leaves every now and then, helping him find his way and avoid stumbling over the most obvious roots.

Finally, he smelled smoke and heard the voices again. Through the undergrowth, he fought his way to the clearing, pulling his robe free every now and then. Truly, flying was a lot easier than walking.

The fire had burned low. Not that many people stood around it, warming their hands, and the ones present looked tired. He must have lost more time in the woods than he'd thought.

The fae woman, Lia, was there. She and five others sat on the tree stumps closest to the fire. A visible gap separated them from the rest.

One tree stump was kept empty, and the dragon's heart leapt with joy at the sight. They kept a seat for him; after all these centuries, they still kept a seat for a dragon!

Silent and unnoticed, the dragon mingled with the small crowd. He wanted to listen; he wanted to learn what had changed during his absence.

"We cannot close the portals," Lia said. "They are our sole connection to the other worlds. We would lose too much should we declare them unsafe."

The dragon frowned. She'd mentioned the portals before, but he'd been too cold to listen properly. Now he wondered why anyone would want to close the portals. They were the dragons' gift to the worlds. Closing them made no sense.

The fae next to her rubbed his hands across his eyes. He looked as if he hadn't slept in days. "I have said this before. I say it again. Rohan was head of the council, and now he is gone. Devoured by a portal he opened with his own hands. They are not safe anymore. We need to give word that using them is prohibited, effective immediately. And Aleksei agrees with me. We've talked this through a dozen times, and even he, knowing most about runes and the portals, sees no other choice."

His words met with disapproving murmurs as well as agreeing nods.

Lia got up. "Without the portals, we cannot trade. Without trade, our wealth will wither. Our children need food, clothing, education. They need the contact with other races. *We* need it. Shutting off trade, closing the portals, means the death of our people."

Her words were greeted with cheers.

"Your brother is of a different opinion."

"My brother is a fool, Rhys," Lia snapped. "He listens to a human, one who grew up in the gutters of his world, one who thinks runes are toys to serve his needs. I do not care about Aleksei's opinion, no matter how much he knows about runes. He does not live in our world. He has no seat on the council. I demand his voice not be heard."

"*You* brought him here," Rhys replied heatedly. "You went and ordered him to stand before the council. He did. He gave his opinion. Had he declared the portals safe, you would have listened, Lia. Just because his vote goes against your wishes, we cannot ignore it."

Few fae nodded. Most looked as if they'd heard this discussion a few times too often.

Wracking his brain, the dragon tried to remember if the portals had ever turned against people before, but could not think of a single occasion.

Using his elbows, he made his way to the front of the crowd, ignoring the angry looks he got and admiring the beauty of the flames as well as their warmth. The robe covered his nakedness; it did not really keep the cold from seeping into his body through his bare feet.

"We need to come to an agreement." Lia crossed her arms over her chest. "Now. We've talked about this long enough."

"I would like to ask Aleksei a few more questions," another woman said, which caused the crowd to groan and Lia to shake her head.

"He decided to go back home," she said, and the dragon wondered whether she was lying. "But even if he were here now, I say do not listen to my brother. Use your brains. The portals have been safe from the beginning of time. They are safe now. I don't know what killed Rohan, but I am certain it wasn't the portal."

"Others before him have vanished," someone pointed out, but Lia just waved the comment aside.

"Youngsters. Uneducated fools. Thieves. They didn't know how to protect themselves. It is a well-known fact that not just anyone can step into another world. It takes training and skill and knowledge. Let us vote now. Let us vote for keeping the portals open."

The dragon took another step. Some people looked at him oddly when he went to the front. Maybe they didn't like a stranger among them?

But he was a dragon. The portals were his responsibility. If there was something wrong with them, he needed to know.

Wait, he said, not with his voice, but with his mind, because that was how dragons communicated.

Some people gasped. Some didn't react at all. Lia and the other council members continued conversing without even noticing him.

Hmmmm.

Then he remembered about the voice problem. It was a stupid way to communicate. But obviously, if he wanted to be understood, he would have to use it.

"Wait," he said aloud, or rather, croaked. Briefly, he closed his eyes in embarrassment, then cleared his throat and again said, "Wait."

Lia turned to him. "Who are you? You are not fae. How dare you be here tonight?" She turned to a guard carrying a spear. "Why has no one informed me of a human being amongst us?"

Men and women moved away from him, leaving him standing alone before Lia's wrath. After centuries, a dragon stood before the fae council again—and they didn't recognize him!

It was an odd feeling.

"It is not your right to decide about the portals," the dragon declared, refusing to feel intimidated by the dozens of eyes on him. "It is mine alone. Tell me what is wrong; tell me about Rohan and the others."

Ah, his voice adjusted quickly to talking. Maybe he could have said those words a bit louder, but then, these were the first words he'd spoken in centuries. He was allowed a small amount of time to relearn this special skill.

Rhys got up from his trunk. "Who are you?" he asked. "You must be crazy to believe what you've said. The fae council makes all the decisions about everything connected with runes. It is our right to do so, ever since the dragons left the worlds. We know most about runes. Leave now, stranger. Do not bother us, and do not talk about things you clearly do not understand."

The dragon blinked.

"We have left the worlds; we are not dead," he said indignantly. "We live; we fly. True, we've neglected our duties as guardians, but I am here now, and I want answers."

An elderly woman got up, went around the fire, and took his hand. The dragon was so puzzled he didn't resist.

"Let me take you to a quiet place," she said soothingly. "You seem to be hungry. We have food and wine. When you've slept, we will take you to any place you desire to be."

She talked to him as though he were a demented child!

He hadn't spoken in a long time. It had been even longer since he'd been truly angry. Back then, his mate had quarreled with him, and they had fought to settle their argument.

Snatching his hand back from the woman's, he spread his arms wide. The robe slipped open, revealing his nakedness. Some giggled; some blushed.

Furious at his own stupidity of believing nothing had changed since the last time dragons had walked among people, furious at those stupid, feeble creatures, furious at his own inability to obtain the respect he deserved, the dragon roared out his frustration and his anger.

Then he changed. He hadn't planned to do so; all he'd wanted to do was to find someone who would help him locate the one human who was of his kind. His wings spread, his fingers became claws, and he dropped the disguising rune so everyone could see what he really looked like.

He pushed over trees and made the fae run for cover. His claws digging deeply into the ground, he focused on Lia and Rhys.

Someone screamed.

I am dragon! he roared into their minds, and this time, they all heard his words. *The portals are mine. The runes are mine. Tell me what I desire to know!*

First Rhys dropped to his knees, then Lia, with obvious reluctance. There was shock written all over her face, but doubt as well, as if he might not be a dragon, as if he were only forging his looks and pretending.

He stared her down easily, the fire of his eyes making her go pale.

Two-legged, stupid animals. A nuisance they were, at best. Pity he needed their help!

With a last shake of his wings—did it feel great to have wings again!—he changed back into his human form. He'd proved his point. They knew now what he was, and frankly, the clearing was too small for him, broken trees poking at his scales. In a matter of moments, he had his feeble, fragile body back and bent to pick up the robe. Slipping it over his shoulders and holding it tightly closed with his left hand, he pointed a finger at Lia. "Open a portal," he demanded. "Let me see if there is truly something wrong with it."

Lia, barely daring to look at him, didn't move a single muscle.

He must have looked furious, because Rhys staggered toward him. "Lord Dragon," he whispered. "We did not mean to insult you. We thought… we were sure…."

"A portal," the dragon just said. He was tired. And still hungry. Maybe he should have taken the old woman's offer of food and a bed before becoming angry.

Rhys dropped to his knees. Shakily, he drew the Portal rune to the elves' world into the grass. He didn't get up when it was done, just waited for further orders.

Not completely stupid, that one, the dragon thought, and circled the portal.

He saw it immediately. The change was tiny, barely recognizable. Anyone who stepped through the portal would have been safe. But the discord was there. And sooner or later, it would topple over the balance of another portal and kill the one who wanted to cross through it.

Disgusted, the dragon vanished the portal. Someone was messing with the powers. Now he not only had to find the human dragon, he also had to find a criminal.

He sighed.

"Do not use the portals until I say otherwise. The word of the fae council is the law. The other races will listen to you. Send messages through the portals—no people, only parchment—and tell them... tell them I'm back. Tell them of my will."

People murmured all around him, and Lia fought hard to find a way to answer him without becoming aggressive. He could see it: her face was white with suppressed fear as well as anger at his intervention.

"All but the humans will listen." Her voice was harsh. "They rarely use portals, and when they do, it's only to raid and kill. They do not accept our authority. They will not stop using the portals whatever we say."

Thoughtfully, the dragon lowered his head. "I will take care of the humans." It was time to leave, anyway.

They backed away when he walked toward the tree line. Some averted their eyes; some stared at him hungrily, reaching out to touch his robe when he walked past. It was shockingly obvious how badly they wanted him to stay, to take his seat among them, to guide them.

His kind truly had been gone from the worlds for too long. Maybe he could even bring himself to come back here once he was done with his task.

Just when he was about to vanish in the darkness, he turned around one last time, a thought crossing his mind. He'd come here for a reason, hadn't he?

"Lia," he called, and he saw the woman pale once more. "Your brother, Aleksei. Where do I find him?"

CHAPTER FOURTEEN

SOMETIME during the night, Gabriel wondered where his arms had gone. They didn't seem to be attached to his body anymore. At least, he couldn't feel them, nor his hands or fingers.

Sleepily, he pondered the possibility of his arms having turned into paws and walked away from him. Stupid things, paws.

Thinking about his missing arms woke him up. Waking up made him aware of his body, still sitting on the chair. He ached all over.

"Wss't?" he mumbled, not sure what he wanted to say.

Then he felt himself slip, and someone caught him. He wasn't alone. Someone was with him in the darkness.

Luckily, his nose caught up with reality before his brain could, giving the all-clear a heartbeat before he would have panicked.

Aleksei. Smelling of grass and smoke, smelling of the fae world, smelling awake and bemused.

Why bemused?

"Would you like to tell me why you fell asleep on my workbench?" Aleksei asked, steadying him lest they crash to the floor together.

Ah. That's why.

"Tired," Gabriel managed, trying to get up. Luckily, Aleksei kept him steady—he'd just found out he'd lost his legs as well.

"Obviously. Would you like me to take you to bed?"

Though more asleep than awake, Gabriel could hear—or sense?—the precaution humming in his lover's body.

No surprise there. Not too long ago, he'd told Aleksei how he'd betrayed him. Not too long ago, he'd admitted how he believed the fae wanted to kill him. If precaution was all there was, he would consider himself lucky.

"Bed would be good," he murmured, relaxing into his lover's embrace. "And a cuddle?"

He could feel Aleksei's smile more than he could see it.

"Bed and cuddle. As you wish, beloved. Can I take this as proof no voices are whispering lies in your ear? That no tree nymph is lurking somewhere in the house? Can I assume the binding has worked as intended?"

"Hmmm." Gabriel stifled a yawn. "No voices. No tree nymphs. Binding worked out fine."

Hands on his body, undoing buttons, taking off his shirt and his trousers and finally his underwear. Hands on his shoulders, pressing him down onto the mattress. His head upon the pillow and the bed dipping when Aleksei got in.

Arms cradling him. Aleksei pressed against his back, holding him tight.

There was just no better feeling in the whole world.

Just when Gabriel was about to drift back to sleep, a thought struck him. "Where've you been?" he managed through the web his oncoming dreams were weaving.

Confusion, sharp and clear. It jostled him awake a bit more, but not enough for him to open his eyes.

"Lia came and demanded my presence at the fae council," Aleksei said quietly. "Don't you remember?"

Lia. Who was Lia? Ah. Of course. "She doesn't like me." His tongue was too heavy to speak. "Sure. How did it go?"

"We argued. Again. I spent hours trying to convince the council the portals needed to be closed, but they did not follow my advice. Again. Eventually, I left the council and had an argument with Lia. After which I took a walk in the woods to calm down. I came home a few minutes ago."

Aleksei pulled him a bit closer, which was good, as he was cold and weary and longed for the contact with his lover.

No voices apart from theirs. No urge to go anywhere.

No desire to change into a wolf.

Gabriel drifted off to sleep, unaware Aleksei stayed awake for a long time afterward.

FIRST, the dragon needed to find Lia's brother Aleksei. He felt a strong connection to the man, though he hadn't even seen him properly and knew nothing about him other than his name and that he wore a rune to disguise his true looks. The idea of finding him first and requesting his help was appealing. True, he could grab the nearest fae and force him into answering his questions. But he didn't want to. His instinct told him to seek out Aleksei, and he'd long ago learned to listen to his instinct.

Aleksei was the one he needed; Aleksei was the one he would find.

The dragon walked through the night in the fae forest for a while before he admitted to himself he was a bit scared of crossing into the human world. Leaning against a huge old oak, he looked into the sky and felt the ache in his heart telling him that although the dragons were not yet extinct, they soon would be. Another few centuries, and the last of them would be dead. They grew old, but they were not immortal. And for some reason even the dragons hadn't been able to figure out, no living young one had been born in ages. They hatched from their eggs—and died. Or, as in his mate's case, the mother died even before the egg was laid.

Mating with other races hadn't worked so far.

"But this new one, this human dragon, is out there, and he is good. I need to find him. Nothing else is as important." He had to believe it or go back to the black depths of depression.

Staring at the moon, the dragon suddenly felt insecure and lonely. *I wish T'gani could be here*, he thought. *She would know what to do next. She would not be afraid.*

But his mate was dead. The young one had died with her, within her, leaving him behind, grieving and dwindling.

He drew the rune with a set jaw. He would not fail her. There were so few of his kind left; he couldn't afford *not* to find this one.

Determined, he finished the rune and was startled when he sensed the strangeness in the portal more clearly than before. Not that he hadn't expected the false tone to grow clearer, but not this quickly. Not in portals to two different worlds.

Well, it didn't matter. Stepping through the portal might be a bit unpleasant, but he would endure it. He was, after all, the master of the portals.

The dragon had imagined trees upon drawing the Portal rune, the easiest and safest way when not knowing where exactly one was going. In every world, there were trees, even in the merpeople's. And should there truly be a world without a single tree, the portal simply wouldn't open.

This one had opened without a problem. The human world lay beneath it, and when the dragon took the required step, he felt the stinging sensation of someone—or something—interfering with the portal's magic. As he passed through, he couldn't really make out what it was, but faintly, he thought he heard a voice.

Later, he needed to take care of that voice, but not now. Now, he was out to hunt.

There were trees, quite a lot of them. Not precisely a forest, but close enough. There was also noise. The stars in the night sky couldn't be seen, as there was false light all around him. Not immediately near, but close enough to lighten the darkness.

A city. Hundreds of thousands of houses. It was what Lia had told him when he had asked for her brother; she'd been torn between fear and disgust and curiosity as to why he wanted to talk to Aleksei.

A city with millions of inhabitants was an abomination of nature. Humans surely couldn't be that stupid, crowding their world until there was no air left to breathe?

Seeing the light in the distance, the dragon feared Lia had been right.

His instincts wanted him to go where the night was darkest. Just a few steps, and he could be lost in the woods.

But he stopped. He was seeking a specific human in an ocean of other humans. There was no use dwelling in the darkness, no matter how much he longed for a good night's sleep. He had a task to fulfill, and another one after that. There was no time for sleep.

So he turned right, toward where the light was brightest, and reached a path that brought him out of the trees soon enough. Apparently, he hadn't been in the woods at all, as there seemed to be houses all around it.

A... park?

The idea sparkled in his mind, and he realized with sudden frustration that his body knew more than his mind did, adjusting to this world quickly, just as it had adjusted to walking. The body was aware of the concept of cities and parks and those stinking, ugly, noisy things now rushing past him.

Cars.

Ah.

The dragon left the park and walked down a street, looking in awe at everything he passed. He stared and was stared at.

So many houses. So many people, even though it was nighttime.

Though, come to think of it, dawn was close. The sun would be up soon, so most likely, some of those people weren't still up, but up already.

Interesting.

The dragon walked on for a few hours until he believed the whole world was up around him. People pushed him aside, cursing him for being in their way. People stared at him, sneering at him in obvious disgust upon seeing his plain robe. He didn't wear what they wore, and no one apart from him was barefoot. People everywhere, and even more cars on the street, so many that they couldn't move anymore.

What is the use of those things? the dragon wondered, disregarding his body's insistence that they were made for taking people from one place to another.

Maybe they were small houses for people of lesser wealth?

Eventually, he had to sit down, as his feet ached and his stomach demanded food with painful clarity.

Over there. The small house with the open door.

The smell of bread wafted toward him, making his mouth water. He went inside, finding tables and—what a surprise—more people sitting at the tables with tall mugs in front of them and paper napkins laden with small rolls, bread, sweet pastries and colorful… other things.

Muffins.

Fine. Muffins.

He had forgotten how the chosen body picked up information from others of the same kind. As a wolf, he knew what a wolf knew simply by being among them. As a human, he knew what they knew the same way. As they knew a lot, it was like standing in a tide of new words and ideas, trying not to drown in them.

Then he became aware of the silence spreading through the little café, and that it was because of him.

He looked down at himself, knowing his face underneath the disguising rune he used looked harmless and friendly. A streak of mud had managed to soil his garment, and his feet were not only naked, but dirty as well.

Someone sniggered.

He nearly fled. These people weren't fae; they didn't know about dragons and would only scream in terror should he change into his true form right then and there. Given how aggressive some of them looked, they might even try to harm him. There would be no respect and no understanding.

Quickly, he snatched one of the muffin things and devoured it in two bites. The woman who owned it was too dumbstruck to do anything about it, so he took the second one as well, and her coffee too.

Then he turned and fled.

THERE was a moment of utter confusion and a panicked *Who is this guy?* upon waking up and seeing the sleeping man next to him, but it was gone so quickly Gabriel refused to believe it had been there at all. It was impossible that his memory was getting worse now the Binding runes were doing their job! This was Aleksei; he was in their bed, their house, and honestly, he'd forget his own name first before admitting he'd forgotten his lover's.

"Hey, you," he said, leaning over and trailing kisses over the sleeping fae's neck. Pulling the bedcovers away, he quickly glanced at the clock. Not yet seven in the morning. Enough time for a bit of cuddling.

Aleksei stretched and yawned, and only then did it occur to Gabriel how odd it was that he was still in bed. His lover was an early bird, always up long before sunrise.

From somewhere under the bed came a soft purr; the cat liked hiding there, and Gabriel smiled, relieved the little fur ball was content in his presence again. Maybe that meant the wolf problem was solved for good; maybe it meant that touching Aleksei was allowed again even without the necessity of Binding runes.

"You get in late last night?" Gabriel asked, putting his hand on his lover's hip and rolling him over.

Aleksei didn't resist. He flopped onto his back and gave Gabriel a sleepy smile. "Early rather than late, beloved. I found you in my workroom, dragged you to bed, and watched you sleep for a while. I cannot remember what time it was when I fell asleep myself."

"Then should I get up and make some coffee so you can go back to dreamland?" Gabriel offered with a mocking grin. He knew only too well how much Aleksei loved to be woken up with kisses and the obvious intention of more.

"Try," Aleksei replied. "You won't get far."

They made love slowly and tenderly, sleep-warm and dream-hazed and not thinking about anything else but one another. It was more about being close and aware of the other's wishes than the actual climax, more about reassuring and strengthening their love than finding release, and when they were both sated, they lay on the rumpled bed, not talking, just enjoying each other's company.

Only when the phone rang did they separate, and then reluctantly so.

"Who calls this early?" Gabriel grumbled into the phone only to hear Monique's brisk voice reminding him of the appointment she'd set for him at ten o'clock.

"Which appointment?" Gabriel asked, just barely aware of a slight nagging feeling he'd forgotten something important he needed to tell Aleksei.

"Mr. and Mrs. Brisbane," Monique told him. "The couple looking for their daughter. You agreed to have a look at the file and see them today. If you don't feel up to it, I will reschedule, but…." She let the sentence hang between them. Monique always had a way of making what she expected of him crystal clear.

"I'll be there," Gabriel agreed with a sigh. A look at the clock told him he had about forty-five minutes to get ready and into town. Manageable. Just. But only if he didn't go back to bed. Which was a serious temptation given that Aleksei still hadn't got up.

The fae had pulled the bedcovers up to his chest and watched with one arm propped under his head as Gabriel got dressed after his far too short shower. "I hoped we could have breakfast together," he said. "Do you feel well enough to go to the office?"

For a moment, Gabriel didn't have a clue what he was talking about.

"Feel great," he finally said, remembering with dread how lousy he'd felt only recently. "The binding worked much better than I dared to hope."

"We still need to talk about this. A binding is not to be taken lightly. I did it because there seemed to be no other choice; I do not feel comfortable at the thought of having used a rune I did not and still do not know."

Gabriel wanted to agree but got distracted by the way Aleksei's leg and hip showed under the blanket when he moved. "Sure," he managed. "Tonight?"

"Tonight. And so you know, Billy will be coming round today to install new cameras. Monique informed me you asked her to arrange this." Aleksei ever so slightly raised an eyebrow as if to suggest now would be the right moment for Gabriel to flip out over this.

Had he asked Monique to arrange this? Probably, only he couldn't remember it. In any case, the cameras were for their own safety. He had no problem with Billy installing a fresh set as long as it wasn't in the bedroom.

Bending down for one last kiss, Gabriel nodded, grabbed his keys, and was out the door before he could reconsider his agreement about going to the office. He was halfway to town before he remembered he hadn't mentioned a word about his mother to Aleksei, or that her blood awaited examination.

Fishing for his cell, he realized it was Aleksei's, still in his pocket from when he'd taken it out of the Jag the previous day. And when he called home, no one picked up. Most likely, Aleksei was in the shower and couldn't hear the phone ring.

He could have left a message, but he didn't. Talking about his mother was something he preferred to do in person, and anyway, Aleksei had better things to do than stare through the microscope all day. He'd probably rather be thinking of…. Gabriel stopped, trying to remember what Aleksei was in the middle of. Something to do with the portals.

Well, they'd talk tonight, and Aleksei could bring him up to date then.

THE problem with the clothes became more pressing as the weather grew worse. On a sunny, warm day, the dragon would have stuck with the robe, since the soft fabric pleased his skin. But instead of sun, there were clouds, and instead of a gentle breeze, there was a nasty, biting wind. His toes had turned to icicles hours ago, and they were aching and filthy. Humans tended to leave their rubbish lying in the streets where unprotected feet could get cut up easily.

At least his hunger was satisfied for the moment. Apart from the two muffin things and the coffee—it had tasted awful but had warmed him nevertheless—he'd managed to steal a sandwich and something called a burger from unsuspecting people. His stomach was filled. Now he needed new and warmer garments before he could concentrate on finding Aleksei.

He paused, causing a gentleman to bump into him. Although by the way the man swore, the dragon doubted he was a gentleman at all.

"Best I should get out of the way," he muttered to himself and stepped closer to the house behind him.

This Aleksei—he had to admit he wasn't sure why he had asked Lia about him. True, he had been amused by the man's fierce defense of a lifestyle he'd chosen against the wishes of his family. Still, he didn't know the man, and he had no idea if he could help him to find one man amidst thousands. But he did know that he felt drawn to the fae.

It would have to do. At least he had a name, and he knew he was in the right city. It was better than nothing. And although it would have been nice to open a portal right into the fae's living room, Lia had flat-out refused to do so, and even the dragon understood how very impolite that would have been. Besides, this little journey through the city gave him an opportunity to adjust to this world. It didn't matter whether he found Aleksei now or in a few days.

The dragon sighed, rubbing one cold foot against the calf of his other leg. "Clothes first," he reminded himself, and then noticed a shop on the other side of the street with dolls in the windows wearing things the dragon wouldn't consider proper garments for any kind of creature.

Well, hopefully they had warmer, more appropriate things inside.

Crossing the street proved to be easy. The cars stopped for him with screeching brakes, as though the mindless metal recognized and respected his true form.

Shivering—no, shaking—he stepped into the shop, grateful for the warmth that greeted him. As he'd expected, the humans inside looked at him oddly, but he was used to it by now and it no longer bothered him. There were more clothes in here indeed, warmer and better-looking than the rags on the dolls in the window. Those long trousers should do, and the sweater over there, and thick woolen socks to keep his toes from freezing and falling off.

A woman approached him as he was feeling the warm fabric between his cold, numb fingers. She was actually the first who talked to him at all.

"You need to leave," she hissed, tugging at his sleeve. "If my boss catches you in here, if he sees you *touching* things, I'm fired. No beggars allowed in the shop!"

The dragon let the robe slip off his shoulders. After all, how would the woman be able to provide him with clothes that fit properly without measuring his human body?

The woman turned white. Another woman in the back of the shop gave a small shriek, grabbed the man with her, and fled the shop.

I need..., the dragon began, then mentally slapped his forehead. Stupid humans needed their stupid ears to hear him talk!

"I need clothing," he began again, profoundly satisfied his voice sounded less hoarse each time he used it.

"Yes, I can see that," the woman said faintly. The dragon wondered why she avoided looking at him until he remembered he stood naked before her.

"Do you... do you plan to hurt me?" she whispered.

The dragon frowned. "Why should I? Do you wish me to hurt you? Is this a human thing?" He was, once again, confused. If things continued like this, it would take him a lot longer than planned to get anything done.

"Don't hurt me," the woman pleaded. A tag on her blouse told him her name was Alice. "You want clothes? Come along, then, away from the windows. And the really expensive stuff. Everyone can see you!"

He turned. True enough, a few people had gathered, staring at him and pointing and laughing. One pulled out his... his—

Cell phone, his mind prompted.

—and talked angrily to someone the dragon could not see.

"The police will be here shortly," Alice said, no longer scared since the dragon had used a small, harmless rune to calm her nerves. "Come on now. There's a lot of traffic today. It'll take them a while to get to the town center. What do you want? Jeans? Or something more formal?"

From his blank look, she drew her own conclusion. "Jeans, then. And underwear. Yes, underwear first and the rest will be peaches." She pushed him into a small cubicle with lots of light and mirrors, rushed off, and left him behind.

The dragon peeked after her and saw she was locking the front door. Clearly, she did not wish anyone to disturb them.

Or maybe the rune had prompted her actions. In either case, they were alone in the shop.

She was back quickly, bringing an armful of clothes with her. A pair of underpants dangled from her outstretched hand.

"These first," she huffed. "And then the jeans. You need to hurry a bit. And all I found for shoes are these boots. Not the latest fashion, but somehow, I don't think you really care about fashion."

Warm.

He sighed with relief as one garment after another found its place on his body and kept the cold at bay. "This is fun," he said, surprised at himself. "I did not expect fun."

Alice's eyes became glassy and her pupils got more dilated the more he looked like a normal human man in normal human clothes. She stared at him longingly, and one of her hands touched his shoulder. He sensed her wish to come even closer.

Dragon charm. It only worked on some people. He was lucky it worked so well on her.

Grateful for her help, the dragon allowed her to lace his boots, wondering if it would have bothered her under other circumstances to kneel before him. In the past, all races had knelt before dragons. Now, even most of the fae had remained standing when he walked past them.

Something had gone seriously wrong in the past centuries. It was high time the dragons returned to the worlds.

Alice still knelt, a small, happy smile on her face, when the dragon opened the door, ready to face the world once more. At the last moment, though, he turned and said, "Do you happen to know where I can find food without having to steal it?" For some reason, he was already hungry again.

BARELY making the bus by running the last half block, Gabriel paid for his ticket, though the driver didn't even notice him, and fell onto a seat. He would be just in time for the appointment; carefully, he put his knapsack between his feet and sighed contentedly. This day had begun very pleasantly.

Putting his feet on the opposite seat, he wondered why it had slipped his mind to tell Aleksei about his mother. It was important news, no matter how badly he tried to convince himself it could wait until evening. Aleksei would be thrilled to have her blood for examination. And he… well, he wondered if there were other things he'd forgotten, more important than his mother, perhaps even crucial for his survival.

The thought made him uneasy, and he hunched his shoulders, trying to get more comfortable on the hard plastic seat. "I don't forget things," he said to himself, glad there weren't many people on the bus. "Never have. I can recall every rune I have ever seen. I never mix them up, I always—"

But he'd forgotten about Pandora, the gorgon with four legs and a nasty temper. When Aleksei had mentioned her, he'd had no recollection of her whatsoever.

And the cameras were even worse! He'd gone totally postal because of them, and without any reason at all. Aleksei had told him. Like he'd told him this morning Billy was going to come around and install a new set. Now he remembered. *Now!*

And then… this morning, just a few hours ago, he hadn't been able to remember Aleksei's name. Just for a moment, he hadn't even known his own name.

He'd been wrong. The binding had worked, but this was getting worse nevertheless. He was just not ready to admit it.

"I'm losing my mind." And now he was talking to himself again. Great.

On the other hand, Aleksei would know what this was all about. Aleksei knew everything. And tonight they would talk.

Tonight. The thought calmed his mind and his emotions. *Tonight!*

With a sigh, Gabriel took the file out of his bag, the one Monique had ordered him to read. Something about a missing girl. Brisbane, the girl's parents were called, if he remembered correctly. But then, his memory was clearly nothing he could count on at the moment.

When he opened the folder, a girl stared at him with big, angry eyes. She was young, not yet fifteen years old, according to the birth date written on the back of the photo, but her eyes were hard and forbidding, as if she'd been in many fights and lost most, but not all of them.

One of those kids. Eager to leave home when not yet fit for the world. Eager to make choices they couldn't yet make, have experiences they shouldn't yet have. Eager to say yes when they should say no, and vice versa. Luckily, he didn't get many of these cases.

If she was alive, he would find her.

A glance out the window told him he had another stop to go when movement caught his attention. A couple of people stood before a shop window, laughing and pointing and nudging each other with their elbows, although it was clear all of them should be somewhere else: businessmen on their way to work, housewives laden with shopping, even a few school kids much too late for lessons.

"Wonder what they're up to," the man two rows in front of him said, and from his lack of effort to keep his voice down, Gabriel knew the man didn't realize he wasn't alone on the bus.

Damn rune, Gabriel thought with a sigh, but with less bitterness than he used to feel.

The bus stopped at a traffic light, and Gabriel looked back at the shop, wondering what was causing the crowd to linger. It wasn't easy to catch anyone's attention in this town.

"Probably some poor fucker wrestling with the cops 'cause he tried to steal a cigarette," the man in front of him murmured.

Gabriel silently agreed with him and went back to reading his file.

MISSION was written in bright, large letters above the door, which stood invitingly wide open. It was a large building, not new, but in perfect condition as far as the dragon could see. Some of the structures he'd passed today had been rotten, the roofs half falling down, the walls infested with mold. This one here—this place had someone who took care of it. Even better, the smell of food emanated out into the street in thick, fragrant waves, engulfing the dragon and making his mouth water.

A man passed him, entering the building without hesitation. He just went through the doors and vanished inside, as if he lived there. Could he do the same?

Alice had explained it. "The mission serves everyone in need, and the food is decent. Clean place, don't ask me where they get the funds from. Father Barley runs it, and he never minds another mouth to feed. He's a good man; he won't mind you, even though you're older than the usual lot of teenage hookers that show up there."

The dragon hadn't asked what a hooker was. Instead, he'd headed down the road, using the shop's emergency exit to avoid the few remaining people awaiting his reappearance from the changing room. And the police, the siren distantly roaring its threat just as he slipped away from the shop.

"You gonna stand there much longer, or you gonna come in?"

The dragon hadn't expected to be addressed, so he flinched at the words only to find the man who had said them smiling in a friendly, inviting way. He was tall, with blond, spiky hair and bad teeth, but he was obviously an authority concerning this place.

"I would like food," the dragon said, thinking it best to pronounce his needs as bluntly as possible.

The man laughed. "This'd be the right place, then, buddy. Good food here. Curry today, if my nose is right. I've been busy, so Oscar did the cooking. Come on in. Father Barley is bound to be messing around in the kitchen, but you can meet him after you've eaten. You look like you're starving." He stepped aside and bowed slightly, a gesture much to the dragon's liking until he realized it was a mock.

So what? He wouldn't be staying in this world forever, and anyway, he didn't come here to find worshippers.

Inside, he saw a single large room with lots of freshly scrubbed tables, most of them occupied. Some of the guests were eating, but most just talked or enjoyed the peace the place offered. Even the dragon felt it—this place was safe. Nothing bad could happen here.

Runes. He could practically smell them. Someone was protecting this "mission."

"Come on, buddy, sit down," the blond man said, leading him to an empty table. "My name's Billy, by the way. I do everything that's needed in this place. I cook most days, I clean, make the beds, and take care of the washing and the shopping. Only the finances are solely in Marita's hands. She's better with figures than Father Barley and makes sure there is enough in the bank should something bad happen."

"Nothing bad can come upon this place," the dragon said, glad his dragon charm worked so well on the young man. Otherwise, he wouldn't have given so much information.

Why did he have the feeling he'd been here before?

Billy laughed, a sound full of warmth. "You should have seen this place a few years ago. It was falling apart. But we found a donor. Provides us with money and everything else we need. Got us a contract with the hospital down the road, as well. They treat our people for free because of a favor our donor did for their boss. But I know what you mean. This is a good place. Ever since we repaired the roof, it doesn't even smell moldy anymore."

The dragon listened with only half an ear. *There*, he thought, looking at the outer left corner. *There is a rune protecting the wall.*

It wasn't the only one.

A small smile spread on his face. He'd not expected runes in this place. But there they were, and they made him feel at home. Could it be he was closer to finding Aleksei than he'd thought? Could it be he was drawn to this place because there was an underlying connection?

Billy had taken advantage of his absentmindedness to fetch a bowl and some bread. When he put both in front of him, he said, "It's hot," and he laughed again when the dragon blew at the indefinable mass. It was mostly yellow, with meat and rice added to a thick, strong-smelling sauce.

"Hot as in spicy, buddy. You're not from around here, are you?"

"Not quite," the dragon replied. He was ravenous. Talking would need to wait until his belly was full.

The first spoonful was an experience he would never forget in his entire life, and for a dragon to say so, that meant a lot. The food exploded in his mouth, flooding his taste buds with flavor and heat, and even more flavor; then it went down his throat and exploded again in his stomach, wonderful as fire, unique as a sunrise. True, he had never eaten a curry before, but he wouldn't have thought mere food could make him speechless.

"Like it?" Billy asked, and the dragon realized he wasn't mocking him this time.

"Very much!" he wheezed and emptied the bowl without wasting another word. "More," he demanded when he was done.

He got more, and more bread as well, and he begged for water, which totally failed to quench the fire on his tongue.

Finally, he was sated, really sated, not like a few hours back when he'd eaten the muffins. This here had been truly good food, and he didn't think he would need to eat for another few hours at least.

With the last bite of bread, he wiped the bowl clean, then sank back and folded his hands over his belly. "Billy," he said, "I am grateful for your service. How may I thank you?"

Unexpectedly, the man narrowed his eyes in suspicion. "Telling me who you are would be a good start," he said. "You're not a hooker.

I doubt you're a pimp or a cop. Got an eye for those. So what d'you want here?"

The dragon knew none of the words Billy had used, but he guessed they were insults. "I am searching for someone," he said slowly. "I do not mean any of you harm."

Before Billy could reply, the kitchen door burst open and a girl swept in, carrying a huge tray with small cakes. Everyone cheered, and when the plate was empty except for three cakes, she flopped next to Billy onto the bench, took one cake, and devoured it. "Other's for you," she mumbled between bites. "Who's he?"

Now the dragon was the center of two humans' attention, and he disliked it. The woman, though visibly harmless, had elf blood running through her veins. She might recognize him; elves tended to see through disguises, but then, she was young and the elf blood not very strong.

Still, when she focused on him, the dragon felt uneasy. "Who are you?" she repeated. "What is your name?"

A direct question by an elf's heir. He couldn't ignore her, but maybe he could avoid answering by asking questions of his own. "I'm not here to cause trouble," he said hesitantly. "Someone pointed me to this place. It feels familiar. It feels as if I have been here before. Runes are protecting it. Would you tell me... does either of you know of one Aleksei Tennant?"

Immediately, the woman grinned. "Doc Tennant. Sure, we know him. If you're a friend of his, you're a friend of ours."

"Marita!" Billy hissed. "We don't know the guy. What if he's not a friend? Gabe will kill us if something happens to the doc!"

Marita dismissed his concerns by getting up and hugging the dragon tightly. Obviously, her elf blood wasn't that thin, for she clearly knew from the bottom of her heart she could trust him. "Can't you see it?" she asked Billy. "He's not what he seems to be. Can't describe it, only that he's different. Just like Gabe is different. But he's okay. Promise!"

For a moment, doubt dominated Billy's beaten-up features. Then he relaxed. "If you say so, sweetie, I believe you."

The dragon followed their conversation with an eager heart, all the while trying to deal with the woman being so close to him. He wasn't used to being hugged.

Still, this one felt good.

"This Aleksei," he said. "Would you be willing to show me the way to his house?"

Billy glanced at Marita. When she nodded encouragingly, he said, "More than that. I'm on the way to his place. I can give you a ride if you promise to behave yourself. Father Barley is very particular about his car."

CHAPTER FIFTEEN

FIGHTING a strong and somewhat irrational urge to pop by the mission, Gabriel forced himself in the direction of his office, knowing he was already late for his appointment. The bus had taken longer than expected, and there had been a few traffic jams and too many red lights. If he didn't hurry, the couple would probably give up on him, which would result in Monique scolding him for aggravating the clients.

If at all possible, he tried not to aggravate his secretary.

Taking two steps at a time, he rushed upstairs and burst into the office, wiping sweat off his brow.

Monique looked him up and down with pursed lips. "You're late," she declared. "Well. We don't want the Brisbanes to think you're too ill to work. I recommend you catch your breath and braid your hair lest they think you are incapable of basic grooming. At least you've shaved."

Still out of breath, Gabriel grinned at her, bent, and pecked a kiss onto her cool, paper-dry cheek, which made Monique blush and Gabriel grin even more. He went to braid his hair as ordered and wash his hands and face, with half his mind contemplating the runes still decorating his skin. He'd already gotten used to them. They reminded him of Aleksei's skin patterns, of the binding, and the fact there was still nothing but blissful silence in his head. Now all he had to do was remember the important bits.

"What is their name again?" he asked Monique just before he opened the door to his office.

"Brisbane," she whispered brusquely.

A couple in their forties stood when he entered. They were plain and looked remarkably alike, being the same height and wearing the same hopeful expression in their brown eyes. Her hair was slightly longer than his, but her shoes seemed to be the same size, and her handbag could as easily have been carried by a man.

They blinked at the sight of him, taking in his flaming-red, waist-length hair, his strange, unsettling eyes, and his frugal clothes. "We are waiting for a Mr. Jordan," the man said hesitantly, reaching out his hand, clearly unsure whether to trust Gabriel's identity.

Gabriel took his hand and shook it. "That would be me," he said. "Sorry for being late. And don't judge me by the way I look. You won't find anyone in town who knows more about the hidden worlds and people gone missing in them. Your daughter has been using portals, according to the file you gave my secretary?" Shaking the woman's hand as well, he gestured for them to have a seat.

Mrs. Brisbane took a tissue from her handbag and dabbed at her eyes. "She's a good girl, our Sally," she said hoarsely.

"A bit wild, maybe, on occasion," Mr. Brisbane added.

Even their voices were alike.

"She's been seeing this… creature, this… horse-person," Mr. Brisbane continued, and Gabriel would have chuckled had the situation not been so serious. Centaurs. Girls just couldn't resist their world once they found a way into it.

"Ever since she was three, she's opposed us, trying to do everything her way even when it was clear she'd only get hurt. Always voicing her opinion no matter how it might offend others." Mr. Brisbane kneaded his hands as if they were dough. "She's a good girl, our Sally. Something serious has happened. Something bad. She'd be back by now otherwise!"

As tactfully as possible—which was still, in his opinion, rather blunt—Gabriel asked, "Have you ever seen who she's meeting? Or do you know how she met the centaur in question?"

The parents shared a look, then shook their heads in unison. "Just the light when the—what do you call it—a door? A gate?" Mrs. Brisbane looked lost.

"A portal," Gabriel said.

"When the portal opened. It shone underneath the door to her room. She'd forbidden us to come in when her friend was there. She said if we ever dared to come in she'd leave home and never come back. I… once I peeped through the keyhole." Mrs. Brisbane blushed. "I saw fur and the tail and a mane." She gulped.

"She said she couldn't open the portal herself," Mr. Brisbane continued. "That her friend was doing it. She was so excited about it, no matter how much we warned her that friendships with other… races could never replace the friendship with one of her own kind."

Gabriel feared the man would break his fingers if he didn't stop kneading them so vigorously. At least he had a basic picture of what had happened. A kid from the hidden worlds had found out he could open portals, gone on a few excursions, and bumped into Sally with her hungry, angry eyes and her need for something more than her parents' simple, plain world. And now Sally was gone and he needed to get her back. It sounded easy, but only in theory. Teenagers fought like warriors when someone tried to drag them away from their friends.

"She's been gone for over twenty-four hours now," Mrs. Brisbane whispered and wiped away some more tears. "We called your firm the moment we heard her scream. We burst into her room, no matter she'd forbidden us to. She was gone. We hoped she'd be back, and your secretary couldn't give us an earlier appointment, but that portal thing is still gleaming, and she is still screaming, and I cannot stand another night like this!"

The hairs stood up on the back of Gabriel's neck. "What do you mean, the portal is still gleaming?" he asked. "They close immediately after someone crosses into the chosen world."

He didn't ask about the screaming. That part was clear enough.

Rohan, his mind whispered, and just like that, he realized he'd forgotten all about him until now. *He's gone,* Lia had said. *Devoured by a portal.*

Did he scream as well? Did the portal kill him?

Another glance shared by terrified parents. "That portal is still in her room," Mr. Brisbane said. Now he was crying too. "It did not close. It looks as if there is a rip in the fabric of the world and it has eaten up our daughter. That's why we called and asked for an appointment. We thought—Sally is screaming, so it could mean she's hurt. We want you to find her and bring her back to us!"

Mrs. Brisbane, pale and shaking, took her husband's hand. "Please," she added, as if she thought Gabriel needed to be persuaded. "We didn't dare to go after her ourselves. What if the centaurs are torturing her? We took a second mortgage on our house this morning. We can pay whatever your rate might be. Just bring back our girl!"

Somewhat stunned that they'd stayed in a house where they could hear their daughter screaming for hours without doing anything, Gabriel nodded. "I'll try," he said. "You've got a car? I need to see the portal."

He opened the door and found Monique cleaning the coffee machine. "I'll be at the Brisbanes' house," he said. "Call Senator Dubaku. Tell him he needs to go live and declare the use of portals as potentially deadly. He has a daughter in one of the hidden worlds. If he says it is too dangerous to visit her and his grandkids, people will listen to him."

"Mr. Jordan—" Monique began, but he interrupted her.

"And call Aleksei. I still have his cell phone, so it will be hard to reach him. Tell him I cannot keep my promise, but I will take care not to be harmed. And—shit. There are other things I wanted to tell him myself. Damn! Tell him the vial filled with blood on his workbench is from my mother."

Alarmed, Monique dropped the cloth she'd been holding. "When will you be back?"

Shrugging his shoulders, Gabriel ushered the Brisbanes out of the door. "Don't know. This is an emergency. As soon as possible?" And with that, he was gone, the stunned parents following close behind.

His mind racing, he ran downstairs, cursing under his breath. A portal unwilling to close. A screaming child. Screaming for hours, apparently, and not because the centaurs were torturing her. They didn't torture children.

Rohan missing, and others gone missing too. The portals damaged. And him having forgotten to tell Aleksei about his mother this morning. Damn his faulty memory!

"Should try to call him again," Gabriel murmured, fingering Aleksei's cell phone as Mr. Brisbane drove through the streets as fast as the traffic would allow. "But he'd only try to talk me out of this. No, better Monique tells him what happened. Let him yell at her."

It turned out the Brisbanes lived closer to his office than he thought, so even if he'd wanted to call Aleksei, there wouldn't have been any time to do it. Mrs. Brisbane had already opened the front door to their small, plain house but was so obviously unwilling to go inside that Gabriel saw no other choice but to take the first step himself.

The air smelled stale, which was strange, as there was a window open in the kitchen and Gabriel could see a breeze moving the curtain. He could smell toast and coffee and saw two filled cups and two untouched slices of bread.

No surprise with that underlying smell polluting the air. It was not just stale. It was threatening, like the smell of acid or smoke.

A sound was making the walls hum. He wasn't sure if he really heard it or if it was just his imagination, but in any case, the sound was making him sick. Something was profoundly wrong in this house.

"Sally's room is upstairs," Mrs. Brisbane said from the open front door. She hadn't set a foot into her own house yet, and by the way she clung to the door handle, she wasn't planning to in the near future.

Gabriel turned to face the couple. "I want you to go back to the car and wait for me," he said as calmly as he could, though his skin was itchy with uneasiness. The prospect of getting close to *that* portal didn't help at all. "I'll try to find your daughter by using the portal she went through. In any case, don't come inside until I'm back. And be warned, it might take me a while. You... you just wait."

Taking two steps at a time, he went upstairs, opening the doors to each room. The first was the bathroom, plain and small with a tiny window. The second was the parents' bedroom, equally plain, just a bit bigger, with the main color being a boring light brown. And the next was a guestroom. A quilt lay on the single bed, plain brown and beige.

I can't blame the girl for wanting to break out of here, Gabriel thought, and opened the last door.

All colors of the rainbow greeted him, overshadowed only by the golden light the portal cast. Bright, sunny walls, deep red carpet, a purple bed with emerald bedding, a black desk, and a ceiling that was painted a light blue, just like the sky. The clothes lying discarded on the desk chair spoke of rebellion, just like the girl's eyes had. A tight skirt flashed a colorful wink at him, as inappropriate for a good girl as this room and very much unlike anything her mother would have chosen for her.

No surprise this one had befriended someone from a hidden world. She probably would have befriended a vampire or a hooker or a prisoner just to shock her parents.

Gabriel's attention snapped back to the portal. He'd never truly examined one. The first time he stepped into another world, it had been in Aleksei's company. Ever since, he never even thought about taking a really good look. Portals were opened and crossed. Passing through them took less than a heartbeat. They were tools; he would as soon examine a kitchen spoon.

This portal, though, was damaged. Badly damaged. He would have known that instantly even without the harsh screaming emerging from beyond the portal

It wasn't the light, which was as it should be, golden and clear. And it wasn't the appearance, though it was smaller than usual. It was the resonance it caused deep inside him. The portal made his teeth ache and his head hum. It made him wish he'd stayed in bed this morning, safely cuddled up in Aleksei's embrace. It made him wish he'd never set eyes on a portal, and it made him wish he could turn and run as far away as possible. Anything but move closer; anything but even think about stepping through it.

"Fuck," he breathed, unable to imagine spending another minute close to that thing, not to mention an entire night.

The scream unceasingly pierced his head. There weren't any words, just a basic, urgent call for help from a terrified fifteen-year-old. It caused shivers to run down his spine.

"Sorry about this," Gabriel said to the empty room, with his lover in mind. Taking a deep breath, he stepped into the portal.

USUALLY, the step into another world took no more than the blink of an eye. It was over before one could think about it, and there it was, a different universe under a different sky, where the trees didn't quite look as they should and where people had hooves, or horns, or a tail instead of legs. This was how it always was, and until now, Gabriel would have sworn it was the only way portal travel happened.

In his experience, the portal had always been two-dimensional, flat like a mirror with no space in between. So it came as a shock to Gabriel to find himself stuck somewhere in the middle, caught between his world and the centaurs'.

Color did not seem to matter in this strange twilight zone. It was there, but at the same time not. What really caught Gabriel's attention was the smell—flat and stale, just like the smell that dominated the Brisbanes' house—and the discord, which made his blood boil. The combination invaded his nose and eyes and went straight to his brain, shutting down his other senses and making it hard, if not impossible, to think.

If he could have, he would have given up and gotten out of the portal. Except there was that scream, more urgent now, more pleading, and it was impossible to turn his back on it.

Anyway, he didn't know where the exit was. Distance and movement didn't matter inside the portal. It was hard to feel his body, and when he touched his face, he couldn't tell whether it was warm or cold. The sheer thought of walking toward the scream seemed ridiculous. His feet were gone, and so was his sense of direction. So how to get to the girl, how to find her, and, should he find her, how was he going to get her out of here?

Odd, Gabriel thought when suddenly the screams seemed to be coming louder from what seemed to be his left. *There's no left or right in here.* He floated like a feather between the two worlds, but now he was floating with a purpose—toward the screams, the girl, and hopefully the exit.

The longer he was inside the portal, the harder it became to plan his next action. At times he couldn't even remember why he was in here or where "in here" actually was, and then he would be yanked out of his stupor by the girl's screams once more. "The girl. Sally," he mumbled. "Got to find her."

If only the screams didn't seem to be coming from all directions. Only a moment ago, he thought he had drifted closer; now he believed there weren't any screams at all.

Enough.

Had he thought that?

What the hell. He was sick of this place! If it even was a place; it was more like one of his nightmares. Maybe he was just asleep and not caught inside a damaged portal.

Damaged. There it was, the word he'd been looking for. This was not a normal portal, and whoever was caught in here would be too disoriented to expect normal portal behavior.

A scream to his left. Not knowing how he did it, he reached out and caught it, holding it in the hollow of his hands like a scared little sparrow.

Another scream. It was easier to detect its origin, and easier to catch it.

Soon he had a handful of screams to care for. They were heavy and restless, and they glittered in all colors of the rainbow.

Had he thought color was unimportant in here? He'd been wrong. The screams sparkled, yet none of the colors were the gold of a portal.

There, just one last bit. Emerald green. Gabriel caught it and thought he'd fall to his knees with the sudden weight. It pulled him down, made him stumble. Clutching at the screams, he took a step, and his foot fell upon harsh, cold snow.

Face-first, he fell, and only then did he realize he held a body in his arms, warm and breathing, the living sum of the screams he'd been gathering for the past—

How much time had passed since he'd stepped into the portal?

He nearly crushed the girl as he quickly rolled off her and tried to wrap his mind around the fact that there was snow all over him and that he was not caught in the portal anymore. And that he wasn't alone.

He hated the cold; he hated snow. Apart from the physical discomfort the damn stuff caused him, it also brought back memories of Aleksei lying bleeding on the ground. He could do without snow.

But right now he didn't have a choice. The portal was gone, he hadn't landed in the Brisbanes' house, and he truly did not have the guts to open another portal and take the girl back home.

Getting up on his knees, Gabriel noticed the snow had soaked his jeans and the wind was shaking more snow out of the surrounding trees.

He'd landed in a forest. Surrounded by lots of snow and with an unconscious girl at his side.

Great. Anyone finding him like this would probably come to some pointed conclusions and shoot him the moment he dared to breathe.

Then he saw a boy lying facedown in the snow only a few feet away from him.

Oh, fucking shit, he thought. *I should have stayed in bed today!*

First things first. Methodically, he checked Sally's pulse and breathing and found she was, at least, alive, with a strong heartbeat and a flushed face.

Her hair's green, his mind tried to tell him. *Emerald green, like the last scream I found.* But he didn't listen to this thought because a girl's hair color was truly of no importance to him. But gathering screams—he was sure that had been nothing but a hallucination.

When he was sure Sally wouldn't die on him—at least not right now—he crawled over to the boy. He hadn't moved yet, didn't even seem to be breathing, but then he was half-covered with snow the wind had blown over him. He had hooves and a tail, distinctive of a centaur. Yes, no use denying it. Definitely one of Kyril's lot.

This day was getting better and better. In fact, if someone attacked him right now, he would sigh with relief at the distraction. A teenage centaur boy and a teenage human girl, both unconscious, both nowhere near home—anything would be better than this. Centaurs were deadly creatures in the first place. When it came to their families, and especially their children, they became nothing less than cold-blooded killers. As he was the only adult here and the only one conscious, the centaurs would consider him guilty of having committed horrible crimes upon the kids.

The girl stirred. One moment she was out like a light, the next she was on her knees, shaking her head to clear it. "Who're you?" she mumbled.

When she saw the centaur boy, her eyes narrowed. When she flung herself at him with fists flying, all he could do was protect his face.

"What have you done to her? Why's she lying there? Is she dead? Have you hurt her? If you've hurt her, I'll kill you!" Her fists, small and hard, hit his shoulders and chest. If she weighed a bit more and had a clue about aiming before punching, she might even have broken his nose.

Gabriel finally got hold of her wrists and held tight.

She didn't stop yelling at him, though. "Bastard!" she spat and kicked at his shins. "Swine. Idiot. Piece of shit. Let go of me or I'll tell the police you've molested me!"

"Do you see any police nearby?" Gabriel snapped, and he pushed her back hard enough to make her land in the snow. "Or streets? What about cars or houses? You're not at home, Sally. There's no one here to save you except for me. Quit behaving like a fool!"

He'd never been good with children. He felt quite lucky he didn't have any of his own. And if she even had a clue he considered her a child, she would begin hitting him again.

"I know where I am," she spat. Then she crawled on all fours toward the centaur.

"Erm," Gabriel managed as he knelt down next to her, checking the centaur teenager's pulse again. "That's a girl, you say?"

"'Course it's a girl! Did you think I'm stupid enough to talk to one of their boys? They think humans are useless, and they think I'm too young to handle a bow, and they snigger behind my back. This is Ylis. She's my friend. What have you done to her?"

Gabriel carefully touched the centaur girl's neck, searching for a pulse. It was there, but faint, and when he tried to move her so he could have a better look into her face, she winced, apparently close to waking up. "I think her arm is broken," he said when he was finished with his examination. "Might have happened when she crashed to the ground. There's a branch underneath her, see? I think she came out of the portal too quickly, stumbled, and fell. And I had nothing to do with it, just for the record."

The wind bit into his skin and played havoc with his hair. Only now did he realize he was not too far from the place where Aleksei had been wounded some years back. The woods looked familiar, as much as trees and snow were able to look familiar to him. These trees were taller and older than any he'd ever seen and loomed too much for his liking. They blocked out the pale sunlight, but not the wind.

Just great.

Gently, Sally brushed the hair out of Ylis's face. "Can you hear me?" she whispered. "You need to wake up. It's too cold. We need to get you back home, hon!" Her hands fluttered over the centaur girl's chest and the rough fur of her flanks, smoothing out the tangles of her mane.

Her deep concern for her friend's condition allowed Gabriel to sit back and catch his breath. He was exhausted, though he'd done nothing but step through a portal. Sure, he'd hunted down Sally while passing through, but he shouldn't feel quite so old and ache as much as he did.

At least it wasn't snowing. Grateful for small mercies, he took off his jacket and draped it over Sally's shoulders. She wore only a sweater, bright and colorful and maybe even warm enough if she were running or hunting, but not warm enough for sitting in ankle-deep snow.

He wasn't exactly dressed warmly enough either. Again.

"I hate this world," he murmured, hugging himself and wondering how on earth he was going to explain any of this to Aleksei. Unlike him, the fae would have been able to deal with this easily. Last time, he'd had an arrow sticking out of his shoulder and still he'd managed to ease the situation with a few well-placed words.

"I won't leave her," Sally said categorically. "I know you're thinking about getting out of here. It's written all over your face. You're a coward. The centaurs are friendly. They don't mind my friendship with Ylis; they even gave me a fur coat so I wouldn't freeze in this weather, and anyway, she's injured. If we leave her, she'll die!"

"Centaurs are hard to kill," Gabriel replied absently. He was scanning the tree line, watching out for torches, listening for the sound of hooves. Centaurs had a knack for turning up at the worst moments, usually in full gallop and heavily armed. They were fast and strong, and their females were hard to tell apart from the males. Both were of the same height, both wore their hair long, and not all the men had beards. A female centaur with large breasts was unheard of. No wonder he'd mistaken Ylis for a boy.

Nothing but silence. They were alone except for a few squirrels playing in the treetops.

Ylis stirred. At first, only her eyelids fluttered; then her legs moved as she tried to get up. A centaur never lay down, not if it could be helped, not even for sleeping. That way, they could attack whenever danger lurked, and Ylis was no different. As soon as her brain told her she was horizontal, she struggled and was up on shaking legs only a few seconds later. Her flanks shivered; her tail twisted nervously. When she touched her arm, she gave a low moan of pain.

"Sally?" she said. "Sally, are you okay?"

"I'm here," Sally said, and Gabriel was glad neither of the girls started to cry. "What happened? One moment I was next to you with my hand on your back, the next moment you were gone and everything went strange. I didn't know going through a portal could hurt that much!"

"I heard you scream," Ylis replied, clearly confused. "I lost you. I think I was lost myself for a while, but then I saw the snow and ran, and then I stumbled. Next thing I know I woke up on the ground. Who's that?"

"Gabriel." It was probably best not to expect the two of them to trust him, but at least they should get his name. "Your parents asked me to find you, Sally. You stepped through the portal yesterday, and you've been missing for over twenty-four hours. The portal didn't close after you, and your parents heard you scream. So I went after you, found you, and here we are. Don't ask me how it happened. The main question is how to get both of you to a warm and safe place."

Sally and Ylis simultaneously narrowed their eyes at him. They stood next to each other, close enough for their shoulders to touch.

"Bullshit," Sally said.

"You are lying," Ylis added.

Gabriel looked from one girl to the other and didn't know what to do. "I'm not lying," he finally said. "Why do you think I am here, freezing my ass off?"

"My parents don't care what I do, and anyway, I told them they'd better not go in my room." Sally edged a bit closer to Ylis. The cold was getting to her even though she had wrapped Gabriel's jacket tighter around her body.

Gabriel sighed. "Parents tend not to listen to their kids if they think the kid is in trouble," he said as calmly as he could manage.

"And besides," Sally continued, unimpressed, "I stepped through the portal only a few minutes ago. They wouldn't worry, not that quickly, and I'm always back for dinner." Apparently, Sally had no desire to listen to anything he was saying.

Gabriel shrugged his shoulders. "Fine. It's sheer coincidence I'm here. Go on, do whatever you usually do when you meet. Hunt or play or giggle or whatever little girls do. I'll go home."

From the hateful looks on their faces he gathered he shouldn't have called them little girls. Or accused them of giggling.

Despite her broken arm, Ylis brought out a long, vicious-looking knife. It trembled a bit because she was clearly in pain, but it didn't stop her from threatening him.

"I am able to open and use portals," she hissed. "My mother taught me everything I need to know to protect myself and the ones with me. Sally is safe in my company! Losing time in a portal, especially as much as a day, never happens to me!"

"Then why did she scream?" Gabriel snapped back. Not that he'd ever had full control over this conversation, but he was losing more ground by the second.

Ylis frowned. "I do not know," she admitted. "And I agree we need to get somewhere warm. My arm hurts. We're wet and tired. Sally, would you take the horn from my bag and blow it? My mother will come and get us, and she will make sure this stranger here does not escape. He did something to us. Maybe Kyril will take care of him personally." She said the last words with a malicious sneer.

"Kyril. Just the man I want to see," Gabriel murmured, but the girls didn't hear him over the loud, low sound Sally produced with the horn. It wasn't a large horn, just the right size to be carried in a bag, but surely it would be heard for miles.

With sudden force, Sally sank to the ground, her legs giving way beneath her. She'd gone pale; the horn slipped from her fingers and vanished in the snow. "I'm not feeling well," she said weakly.

"You haven't eaten in a day," Gabriel pointed out. "You were lost in the portal, Sally. I know you don't believe me, but that's what happened. And you," he said as he turned to Ylis, "you better not think of hitting me or stabbing me with your knife, okay? I'm in a lousy mood. I shouldn't be here. I promised my partner I wouldn't go to the hidden worlds. All I want is to get home, understand? So no tricks. I might not look like much of a threat to you, but I am good with runes, and you'd both be sleeping before either of you knew what was happening."

Ylis snorted. "You're human. Humans are dumb when it comes to runes. Everyone knows that."

"I'm more than just human. I can, and you better shut up."

Finally, the sound of hooves could be heard thundering through the woods—Ylis's mother, Gabriel assumed, had heard her daughter's call for help and was rushing to her side.

No. A single centaur wouldn't cause that much noise. More than one, then. And if things went really bad....

Yes. Gabriel recognized the first centaur, the tall one with the braided hair, the dark, wild beard, and the charcoal black eyes. He wasn't taller than any of the three others next to him, but he radiated power and thus seemed taller and much more dangerous, though he didn't even carry a crossbow.

He stopped only a few feet before Gabriel. One centaur rushed to Ylis's side—her mother, Gabriel realized after a moment. Concern was written all over her face. She didn't ask her any questions. It seemed Kyril would do the talking, just like last time.

"You again," Kyril said. "I cannot remember having given you permission to visit this world again."

"I don't need your permission," Gabriel said.

Kyril focused on Ylis. "You are hurt. What happened?"

Her mother put an arm around the girl's shoulder. "Tell him," she ordered. "Everything."

Ylis was clearly intimidated by Kyril, but she stood her ground now that her mother was next to her. "I opened a portal," she admitted. "I know you said I am too young, but Sally is my friend, and we cannot meet otherwise. Occasionally, I pick her up and take her into the woods, where we hunt and run for a few hours. Nothing bad has ever happened."

"But this time, something went wrong." It wasn't a question. Kyril's face didn't show any emotion, but Gabriel could feel the centaur's tension as if it were his own.

Sally, still sitting in the snow, began to shake badly.

"I lost her," Ylis whispered. "She screamed. And she didn't come out of the portal after me. I fell and broke my arm. I must have been unconscious for a while, because when I woke up, there she was, and that man there as well." She pointed to Gabriel with her uninjured hand. "I think it was him who did whatever made the portal stop working properly."

A thin smile appeared on Kyril's lips. "The fae council has declared the portals unsafe. They have to remain closed until further notice. If you had not been so stupid and left the group without permission to do so, this would not have happened. Gabriel had nothing to do with this."

"Thank you," Gabriel said. "I guess I can be glad you didn't shoot me. Aleksei sends his regards, by the way. His shoulder has healed nicely."

The regards were a lie.

Kyril nodded to one of the other centaurs, who picked up Sally in one swift move. In his arms, she looked like the child she was, small and scared and injured. Not as obviously injured as Ylis, but still definitely not well.

"Carry her to the camp," Kyril said. "Amara, take your daughter home. I will think of a punishment once she's better."

"But—" Ylis began, only to get shushed by her mother.

Hooves stirred up snow. A few moments later, only Gabriel and Kyril were left, and Gabriel's jacket, which had slipped off Sally's shoulders when the centaur had picked her up.

He put it on despite the fact it was wet and cold. Better than the wind, anyway.

"Now what?" he asked through chattering teeth. "You gonna kill me for saving this girl's life? And what did you mean about the fae council having prohibited the use of portals? Aleksei was there last night. He would have told me."

What if you forgot about it? Or... didn't he say he went wandering through the woods instead of staying at the hearing?

Kyril was watching him. "You are still with Aleksei? He promised to pay me a visit. I would greatly appreciate his insight into this portal problem. I assume you don't know anything about it?" Amusement faintly but clearly laced his words. Gabriel heard as well as saw it in the centaur's face.

"Nothing," he replied lightly. "I know how to use them, that's it. Dumb human, remember?"

Kyril's eyes narrowed. "Shapeshifter," he countered. "And Aleksei was willing to risk his life for you. There is more to you than meets the eye. I would like to know what. You will come with me, Gabriel Jordan. I have questions, and I want answers."

"So do I," Gabriel murmured as he followed Kyril through the snow, hoping the camp was somewhere nearby.

How did I manage to save the girl? he wondered. *Why didn't the portal kill both of us?*

CHAPTER SIXTEEN

RIDING in a car was much worse than the dragon had anticipated, and that was saying a lot for a creature who could live among wolves and whales should he decide to do so. The human world hadn't been short on strange, frightening experiences so far. So many people, so much noise, not enough nature—but the car topped it all. And the way Billy handled it was way too fast for the dragon. It felt like flying without wings, and the thought alone made his stomach heave. Too close around the corners—there were people and houses and other cars and those big things—

Buses.

—buses, which looked nearly as bad as the trucks.

When Billy finally stopped the car, the dragon stumbled out. He had to lean against the house for support or he would have sunk to his knees.

I prefer being a dragon. Or any kind of animal, he thought as he suppressed his urge to throw up.

"Here we are, buddy," Billy said, jingling his keys. "Aleksei's house. And Gabe's, but he'll be at the office. You okay there?"

The dragon managed to nod.

"Cool." Billy took two stairs at a time and knocked loudly on the front door.

He had a bag over his shoulder and another one in his hand. In the car he'd talked about bugs, but the dragon hadn't been able to concentrate on anything he'd said. Or anything else besides the curry sloshing around in his stomach.

Slowly, the world stopped spinning and the dragon was able to take in his surroundings. There was less noise here, and hardly any people on the street. He could even see a few trees wearing their autumn colors. The sun glanced through the clouds, and the street, compared to other places he'd seen today, was practically beautiful.

"They live in an odd place, don't they?" Billy said, having followed his gaze. "Too far away from the center, but they like it. Don't worry, I'll take you back to town later on, and we can have something to eat together, if you like."

Food was a subject the dragon definitely did not want to think about right now.

The door opened, and a man stood there, plain and ordinary, with mousy brown hair and a beer belly. Billy grinned at him and shook his hand, and then the dragon's eyes widened when his senses caught up with reality.

Black hair, not brown. Ice-blue eyes and a pale complexion. No beer belly, but long, slender limbs and narrow hips. Silver patterns all over his skin, and yes, there it was, the pendant dangling from the fae's neck, the rune that hid his true looks, the rune his sister, Lia, had been so angry about.

He's skilled. And the rune he wears is really strong.

Without thinking about it, the dragon strengthened his own rune, the one hiding the color of his skin and eyes. He wanted to observe the fae without being observed by him. He wanted to walk through his house without having to answer questions.

"Hi, Billy," Aleksei said, not even looking in the dragon's direction. "Come inside. You know what to do, right?"

"Yep." Billy took his bags and went into the house, then turned and gestured toward the dragon. "This is Aleksei," he said. "Doc Tennant to you, I s'pose. You want to talk to him, this would be the time."

Hesitantly, the dragon came forward, but he needn't have worried. His runes worked perfectly. To the fae, he came across as someone unimportant, someone to forget right after being introduced.

Aleksei reached out a hand. "Welcome. Are you a friend of Billy's?" The raised eyebrow showed slight curiosity, but no suspicion. Perfect.

The dragon nodded. It was not the truth, but neither was it a total lie.

"Then you're welcome in my house. Billy won't be long."

He'd never been in a human house before. The houses he had visited—fae treehouses, vampire cave houses, riverghost houses floating on the waters of their world—were very different from this kind of house. For one, this was much larger. A family of ten could live here without getting under each other's feet, but as Billy had explained, this place was inhabited by only two people. Then there was the shape of it: square, and made of stones. Riverghosts and the merpeople lived under or near the water, and most of the other races used wood for their buildings. Only vampires preferred to be surrounded by stone, but only if the stones came in the form of caves.

I need to find out what is so special about him, the dragon thought.

While Billy got to work, the dragon inspected the house. At first, he just sat on the couch in the living room, enjoying half an hour of quiet time. His stomach, still upset from the car ride, calmed, and when Aleksei surprised him by placing a cup of tea in front of him, he was as good as new after the first sip.

Aleksei took the chair opposite. "I usually avoid getting into the same car as Billy. But he's a nice guy and perfect for installing bugs."

"Bugs?" the dragon asked. Billy had mentioned them. He was no wiser now why anyone wanted bugs in his house than he had been before, but the subject was as good as any if it gave him the opportunity to talk to Aleksei.

"Cameras and microphones. For security reasons. My partner and I live a secluded life, and this area is not particularly safe."

Aleksei frowned. "Did you tell me your name?" he asked. "I cannot remember, but you must have. I would have noticed had you not done so."

The dragon quickly leaned forward, and their knees nearly touched as he looked deeply into the fae's eyes. "I told you my name," he said calmly. "You just can't recall it because it is complicated. And asking me again would be rude."

Gradually, Aleksei's breathing deepened. "Yes, you are right." He sounded sleepy. "Would you like another cup of tea?"

The dragon smiled. The fae was hard to convince, but of course he did not stand a chance against runes woven by a dragon. "No more tea. But I would like to have a look around while you take a nap if you don't mind."

"Go ahead." Aleksei leaned back in his chair and closed his eyes.

"Thank you."

He went into the kitchen first, touching the knives and the oven, opening the fridge and taking out a tomato. Now that the nausea was gone, he was hungry again. And the tomato tasted very fresh and juicy.

The kitchen seemed to be a place where the fae and his partner liked to be. It was tidy, but the atmosphere spoke of many happy hours. It was also completely uninteresting. Nothing about it told him about either inhabitant's profession, about their secrets and sins. Occasionally, a memory stirred up upon touching a utensil, but only faintly—these things were handled on a daily basis. It was impossible to pick out a specific memory.

The dragon didn't even know what he was looking for. All he knew was that he'd come here for a reason. He'd followed Aleksei from the fae world to this one. He'd found the one place where people knew his name and address. There was a connection between them he couldn't explain, and the dragon didn't like not knowing who or what was pulling his strings.

"He's just an ordinary fae," he murmured. "I should stop placing so much importance on this meeting."

Instead of leaving, he went into the bedroom.

Ah. This room spoke of love and passion. It was bright and airy, with several candles on the windowsill and bookshelves, and the bed was big enough for two.

There was a fragrance too. Were he in his dragon form, he would have been able to smell it properly, but a human's nose was insufficient to catch the elusive scent, and so all he could do was stand there in the middle of the room with his eyes closed, sniffing like a dog.

The hair on his arms stood up.

The fragrance was familiar. Which was impossible, because he had never been in this house before or met the people who lived here.

I am not here by accident.

Obviously not.

Quickly, he went over to the bed and pulled back the covers. The place where people slept and loved was the place where fragrance as well as memory was most prominent. Surely—but no. There was no fragrance on the sheets. The bedclothes were freshly washed. As he was about to open the wardrobe, he was interrupted by Billy's footsteps, and he left the room just before the young man reached the living room.

"Gotta go, buddy. Done with the bugs. You coming with me, or you staying for a chat with the doc?" His eyes were glassy, his speech just a tad slurred, results of the rune the dragon had used to make him leave willingly and without asking too many questions.

"I will stay," the dragon said, glancing toward the bedroom.

"Well, the doc seems to be asleep. Tell him it was a pleasure working for him," Billy said, and the dragon saw him to the door. Then he went back into the house, eager to get back to the bedroom while the fae was still sleeping. But something caught his attention as he passed the dining room.

Runes on the bookshelf. Filled with ancient volumes, the bookshelf was a wonderful sight, dominating the room.

Several books were marked with runes. And not just ordinary runes everyone could use. Special runes, new runes, runes he had never seen before.

Impossible. Nobody could invent runes.

But these were new. Simple as that.

The dragon carefully pulled out one of the marked books and opened it. Nothing special inside. It was a book about shapeshifters, basic information accompanied by some nicely drawn pictures.

He pulled out and opened one marked book after another. All the marked books were about shapeshifters. None of the other books he chose had the same subject.

Heart pounding, the dragon recreated the rune. It sparkled, then marked the same volumes he'd already laid upon the table.

Dumbstruck, the dragon stood there, arms hanging limply at his sides.

No one but dragons could invent new runes.

How great was the chance he'd bumped into the one man who could lead him to the human dragon the moment he set out to find him?

"I need to be sure," the dragon murmured, and went back to the bedroom, where he opened the closet. Clothes, freshly washed, were inside. He buried his face in them. He smelled which ones belonged to the fae and which ones didn't.

The other one's fragrance was very familiar, yet so strange at the same time it took him off balance. With the hugeness of the possibility stretching out before him, the dragon dropped the faded T-shirt he was holding, suddenly overwhelmed, and made his way back to the living room. He knelt next to the sleeping fae and put his hand on his knee. *Wake!* he ordered. *Answer me!*

Aleksei opened his eyes. He blinked, staring first at the hand on his leg, then into the dragon's face. "Who are you?" he croaked. "Why did you make me fall asleep?"

I am dragon, the dragon told him, and wasn't surprised the fae understood him without a problem. *Tell me about your partner.*

Now his questions would be answered. The fae would surrender to his will and would tell him what he needed to know. No sniffling out memories that didn't belong to him. No spying on someone he didn't even know. Just simple questions and equally simple answers. He would find the one he was looking for and take him back home, to his nest, the only place a dragon belonged and the best place to court his mate-to-be.

The dragon truly believed it would happen that way. So he was most surprised when the fae kicked him hard between his legs, added a second blow to his chest, and held a knife to his throat before he knew what had happened.

"I won't tell you anything before I have your name," he hissed. "And if you are the creature who's already injured my partner, then chances are slim you will survive until lunchtime."

THE sun was high in the sky, the snow gleaming in its beams, but Gabriel didn't see much of it, as he was being held in a hut, his clothes still wet and his arms tied behind his back.

"This is silly," he said aloud for the fifth time. "Kyril, do you hear me? This is silly!"

"Be quiet, human," Ylis hissed. "You'll wake up Sally."

Up until now, it had never bothered Gabriel to be called human. On the contrary, it was reassuring that other people did not realize he had a predator locked inside him. Here, though, with centaurs all around him and no way to get home anytime soon, it disturbed him. Ylis, Kyril—everyone here loathed humans. Moreover, they considered them stupid as well as dangerous, a nasty combination and the reason Gabriel felt more and more uneasy.

"I shouldn't have allowed them to tie me up," he muttered, glancing toward the bed of fresh hay upon which Sally lay.

"As if you could have stopped Kyril from doing anything he wanted to. He could have killed you just like that, and you could have done nothing to prevent it." Ylis sounded proud as she rebuked him.

"I know what he is capable of, thank you very much. He nearly killed my partner the last time we were here. And you will get punished too, just for the record." Twisting his wrists in the bindings, Gabriel was pleased to notice it was easier to do so than half an hour ago. A few more minutes and he would be free. Not that he'd know what to do then. He was held prisoner, stuck with two girls and surrounded by centaurs. He couldn't leave Sally behind, which was the reason he hadn't objected too much when Kyril had bound him. Free hands wouldn't make much of a difference.

Okay. It would be more comfortable.

He sighed and was about to ask Ylis for something to eat when a rush of heat washed over him, surging through his body and leaving him breathless.

Something's wrong.

He struggled to get to his feet and swore because he couldn't use his bound wrists to push himself off the ground. If only he knew a rune to vanish the rope… but he didn't and couldn't think clearly enough to make one up.

He broke out in a sweat, though moments ago he'd been cold.

Something was really, *really* wrong. Something bad. Something back home.

Aleksei.

"Fuck."

"What are you doing?" Ylis asked, alarmed at his sudden attempt to get free. "You need to stay here. Kyril said so."

Ignoring her, Gabriel shouldered the door open. As it was made of branches and grass, it wasn't much of a problem. The centaur standing guard outside took aim with his spear when Gabriel appeared.

"You are not allowed to—" he began.

But by then, Gabriel could only think about Aleksei and a way to get home. This very moment. The centaur stood in his way, so he shouldered him aside too. As a result, three others aimed their spears at his back a heartbeat later… after they'd grabbed him and thrown him to the ground.

"I need to go home," he tried to shout through a mouthful of snow.

"The use of portals is forbidden," Kyril said, not sounding in the least bit surprised at Gabriel's attempt to escape.

Had he wanted to escape? He hadn't really thought about it, just left the hut so he could get back to Aleksei.

The runes on his skin flared up. "Someone is with him, someone strong, someone dangerous!" Of this, he had no doubt. It was happening, and it didn't matter how he knew about it.

Gabriel craned his neck. "Let me go," he pleaded, but Kyril only laughed.

It drove him crazy being helpless like this. He didn't have time to mess with centaurs or kids or the spears holding him down! "I need—" he wheezed, only to realize that speaking with a hoof and several pounds of centaur on his back wasn't easy.

"—need to leave," he managed to finish.

And because it wasn't good enough, and because now the other centaurs had begun to laugh as well and no one was taking him at all seriously, he made a stronger effort.

Let go of me!

He hadn't said it aloud. It hadn't been a thought. But the centaurs backed off, shock written on their faces. Kyril had stopped laughing.

Cut me loose!

Someone did; Gabriel could feel the knife in the centaur's hands shaking and hoped he would only cut the ropes, not his skin. As he got back to his feet and brushed snow off his jeans, they stared. Silence surrounded him.

"What?" he bit out, annoyed and nervous, a finger pointing at Kyril. "If you hadn't tried holding me back, I wouldn't have needed to do that."

"What exactly *did* you do?" Kyril asked. "I could hear you in my heart and in my soul, but I could not hear you with my ears. What did you do?"

"S'CHN TG'AI."

"I beg your pardon?"

"You asked for my name. That is it. A dragon does not give his name easily. Treasure it."

This was not going as planned. The fae should have surrendered to his request without a fight. He especially shouldn't have been able to push him away. So either Aleksei had extraordinary powers, or he had dealt with dragons before.

The implication of the latter made him shiver with excitement.

"I did not harm your partner."

The fae stood calmly, waiting for further explanation.

"Your using a Sleeping rune on me tells me I have no reason to believe you." Aleksei said. "Your ordering me to give you information about my partner. Your coming into my house in disguise, come to think of it. Because this is not how you really look, is it?"

The dragon's eyebrows shot up. "You can see the rune which alters my appearance?" he asked.

"No. It was an educated guess, and you just confirmed it."

"My true appearance would scare you. I do not want to scare anyone. All I want is to find the one who belongs to me."

Aleksei grew still. "Belongs to you?" Coldness was creeping into his voice. "Then you just confirmed my suspicions. My partner was close to going crazy because of your calling. Get out of my house, and expect the fae council to deal with your attack on him as well as me."

Aleksei moved his fingers. A rune flared up and attached itself to the dragon's hand. A small golden patch, hard to see, impossible to remove.

Amused, the dragon touched the rune. "You've tagged me? You really think with this rune you can find me again wherever I go?" Then he smiled. He had been right. "I have not called your partner. I do not know him; I have not yet met him. And without his name, his image, or his blood, a calling is next to impossible, even for me."

"Even for you—what's that supposed to mean?" Aleksei raised an eyebrow, a gesture the dragon found strangely irritating. "Why are you here? What do you want?"

The dragon shook his wrist as if something wet were upon it. The rune sparkled, lost its color, and then was gone.

Aleksei's eyes widened. "No one should be able to do that," he said flatly. "It is impossible to get rid of a tag!"

"I am dragon," S'chn Tg'ai replied, not hiding the pride in his voice. "My kind are the masters of the runes, just as we are the masters of the portals. Nothing you come up with could bind me to this place or keep track of my steps. Should I wish to leave, I could. But I do not wish to leave. I wish to meet the other person living here with you. Billy called him Gabe."

Aleksei hadn't changed his posture, but the cold hostility radiating from him didn't surprise the dragon. Hadn't he already learned upon overhearing Aleksei and Lia's argument that this was about love?

Two people lived in this house. Two slept in the bed he'd seen.

It did not matter. If this Gabe was really the human dragon, he belonged in the dragon world, not with the fae. He belonged to him.

Crossing his arms over his chest, Aleksei nodded slowly. "Dragon. Do you have a blood sample for me? I would very much like to verify your story before as much as thinking about continuing this conversation." Given he spoke the words through his teeth, he still seemed surprisingly calm.

S'chn Tg'ai ignored the request. "He creates runes. No one but dragons have such powers. I saw the ones that mark your books. I was drawn to you because of your link to him. Has he created other runes? What else is there you can tell me about him?"

Aleksei just looked at him. "I think I just made clear I won't tell you anything before I verified the dragon part of your story. A blood sample would help me do just that. I could find out what you are not, and I could compare it with my partner's blood. There are traces in his genetic code I have not been able to classify yet. Helping me—"

"I've tried to find him ever since I learned of his existence," S'chn Tg'ai interrupted him, trying hard to suppress his urge to strangle the fae for his unwillingness to cooperate. "I went to the fae world; I asked your sister about your whereabouts. At that time, I did not know why I wanted to talk to you and no one else. Now, it is clear." He shook his head; he wasn't used to explaining himself. "I'm drawn to you; I'm drawn to him, to Gabe, because I caught a glimpse of his memories. The rune on the books is new. He created it, although he is not even fully dragon. Please," he said, nearly choking on the word. Dragons didn't beg. "Please tell me where he is. Please let me meet him."

Maybe it was the way he'd said it; maybe Aleksei was susceptible to his pleading. Maybe it was his dragon charm. Or maybe Aleksei had simply decided that working with him rather than against him was the easier course of action. However, the fae got up abruptly and vanished into a small room next to the kitchen. The dragon heard him rifle through some papers and was about to follow him when the fae returned. In his hand he had a single sheet. Without a word, he held it out, waiting for the dragon to take it.

S'chn Tg'ai caught a glimpse of the runes. He swallowed hard. No! This couldn't be true!

"Take a closer look." Aleksei's voice was cold and insistent at the same time.

The dragon's hand didn't shake when he took the paper. He did not pale when he set eyes on what was scribbled there. But his voice was rough with emotion when he said, "Binding runes. Strong ones. Are you telling me you've used them on Gabe?"

"You're either an exceptionally good liar, or you really didn't know."

"Know what?"

"Someone was calling him. He cannot hear the voice anymore, and it is because of those runes. He came up with them when the threat posed by the calling became unbearable. He begged me to use them, and I agreed, as I saw no other way to help calm him. He is bound to me, but it is a temporary solution, of course. He belongs only to himself."

The dragon opened his mouth, but no words came out.

Aleksei cast him a thin smile. "I can see you are shocked about the binding."

Slowly, the dragon nodded. "A human dragon is beyond rare. It is unheard of. He would be—" He broke off in midsentence, unwilling to tell Aleksei how important this really was for him.

Aleksei sighed. "The blood sample, please. If what you say is true, there should be a similarity between your blood and Gabe's blood.

It won't prove you're not the one behind the calling, but at least it would be a start."

Slow, steady breaths seemed most helpful to keep calm. "I did not call him," S'chn Tg'ai said, feeling trapped and helpless. "I did not even know anyone had that power over him. Calling a dragon is dangerous. Most times, we would not even hear it, but then, Gabe is not fully dragon. That you do not seem to know who's behind the calling is disturbing."

His heart was beating too fast, and his skin felt hot as well as sweaty.

You're shocked, his mind told him, and he could do nothing but agree. He *was* shocked. The one sane child of his kind was bound. Forever unavailable. Out of his reach, whatever the fae might say. Gabe belonged to Aleksei. The binding—this kind of binding—could not be undone.

"Are you all right?" Aleksei asked, and to the dragon it sounded as if he were talking through a thick wall of cotton. "You look unwell."

The dragon blinked away a tear. "Not really," he said. "I did not expect this outcome to my quest. I only learned of the human dragon's existence a short while ago. If he is the one I am searching for, of course." Taking a deep breath, he forced his muscles to relax. "I think I would like to be on my own for a while, now."

Aleksei just snorted. "After everything I've just learned? Hardly."

"Will you at least allow me to meet him?"

For a moment, the fae pondered the question. "Legend says that dragons were able to extract memories from any given object. I have two blood samples for you. One belongs to my partner. The other one he collected last night. His secretary claims it is his mother's blood." He raised an eyebrow. "Gabe is not home. You still haven't told me why he is so important to you. I still want that blood sample from you. Helping me would give weight to your story."

"His mother?" Sudden, unexpected excitement, sweet and poisonous, thundered through the dragon's veins. *There might be another of my kind. There might still be hope!*

And of course he could not tell Aleksei his reasons for wanting to meet Gabe.

He followed Aleksei into the same room where the fae had gone to get the paper with the Binding rune. Aleksei stepped over to the workbench and picked up a small vial. "This is what my partner brought home yesterday. Tell me what you make of it."

As a dragon, S'chn Tg'ai would have simply devoured the whole vial, knowing the glass couldn't harm him. But as a human, with human flesh and human flaws, he was not able to do so. He had to uncork the vial and tilt a drop onto his finger. He had to taste it and be watched by the fae, even though there was so much hope in his heart, he could barely swallow.

The sweetness of the blood hit his tongue, and he swayed.

Female.

Adult.

Ill.

The dragon spat, hope being replaced with disgust. Gratefully, he accepted the glass of water Aleksei offered him, but it was hard to get the foul taste out of his mouth.

"Dragon," he finally managed, fighting an urge to scrub his tongue clean by raking it against a wall. As a dragon, he would have done so, using a tree or rocks or anything else that was rough enough. "She's bad. Her body, her mind, her soul—everything is wrong in her. Were she to see me, she would go mad. Were she to touch me, she would die. Impossible to have offspring with her, of course. Just like the others who were born with both human and dragon ancestors."

Aleksei took a glance through the microscope on the table. "Her blood is very similar to Gabriel's," he said. "Not identical. The stripe through her cells is thinner, it is broken in places, and the color is wrong. Close enough, though, to say she's very likely his mother."

Aleksei took a second vial and held it out wordlessly, waiting until the dragon took it. "Gabe's blood," he explained. "I took a sample the day we met. I knew he was different from the moment I laid eyes on him. He could see through my disguise. As much as I tried, I could never figure out what he is besides shapeshifter. *You* tell me."

Again, the dragon smiled. "You are responsive to his dragon charms. Not many are, but you are certainly an exception. I can see through your disguise as well. Any dragon could. You are tall, with black hair and blue eyes. Much more appealing than the plain brown you currently wear, and the belly."

"Another riddle solved." Aleksei sighed, still holding out the vial.

Gabe must be the one, the dragon thought. *But what is the use in knowing? I cannot take him with me. He is bound. He will never be mine.*

But of course he was the one. Otherwise, he would not have felt drawn to his bound partner, would not have followed Aleksei, and would not have ended up in this house amidst millions of other houses.

It did not matter. Finding one of his kind in the human world, a sane heir of the dragons, after centuries of being alone, would be a relief beyond words. It would be proof there was a chance, a small chance, the dragons did not have to go extinct.

If there was one, there might be others. If one could be found....

Carefully, S'chn Tg'ai took the vial. But before he could taste the blood, a portal opened in the middle of the living room, making him forget all about it.

GABRIEL stood surrounded by centaurs, waiting for them to attack. They were keen on attacking, and they were good at it. If they put their heart into it, his survival was not an option.

But for some reason, their spears and bows remained at rest. For some reason, he was still alive.

"I need to leave," he pleaded.

Kyril came forward. He seemed tense yet somewhat more respectful than before. "The use of the portals is prohibited. Fae council order, and we are bound by vow to obey their orders. You cannot leave."

"I have to," Gabriel replied, and pushed past him. A moment later, he began to run, away from the camp and away from the centaurs and Sally, expecting an arrow or a knife to stop him at any moment.

His fingers moved of their own accord. *Home*, he thought with all of his might, and there it was, the golden glow of the portal, awaiting him, urging him on.

He jumped, fearing the centaurs would catch up with him before he made it through, but apparently, they had the sense not to follow him. He would have fought and most likely would have killed one of them before being brought down.

What if the portal is damaged?

Trust his stupid brain to throw questions at him at the most inconvenient moment!

Too late. He was caught by the light, the forward momentum making it impossible to stop.

Come to me!

He heard the voice and nearly soiled himself upon realizing he'd drawn the wrong rune again.

"Shit, shit, shit!" he screamed, but the portal had already swallowed him up, spitting him out a second later onto the snowy ground of the banshee's world.

Gabriel stood, taking in his surroundings, his head splitting with sudden, blinding pain. He couldn't draw another rune; right now, he couldn't even remember what the rune that would take him home looked like.

He was higher up in the mountains than last time. There were no trees around, and it was daylight. A cold, bright day with a pale sun hanging in a dark-blue sky. Since his clothes were still wet from the snow in Kyril's world, his bones ached from the chill and his teeth chattered.

Well, he definitely wasn't home, and Aleksei wasn't here. Nothing else mattered to him. Aleksei was in danger; he'd sensed it clearly.

He should turn on his heel and try to draw the proper rune no matter how badly his hands shook and his head ached. On the other hand, he knew that the banshee was here, somewhere, waiting for him. What if she followed him back into his world, back to Aleksei?

Better not take the risk. Better sort this out here and now.

There was no wind, not this time. It was quiet, and because there were no rustling leaves and no water rushing over stones, Gabriel could hear his own heartbeat, his harsh, ragged breathing, and his thoughts, which were telling him he should run.

The wolf inside him stirred, alarmed. Alert and aggressive, it came forward and wanted to take over.

You're here.

The voice was everywhere and nowhere, echoing off the rocks, bouncing back and forth in his brain. He whipped around, but there was no one. He was alone with nothing but sky, a few clouds, and tons of rocky mountains surrounding him.

It was hard to keep the wolf in check, but Gabriel managed to do so. This was not the time to run, nor was it the time to attack. "Listen first," he muttered to himself and the wolf. "Maybe you can find out what this thing wants."

You are here. Finally, you are here.

"Where are you?" Okay, he croaked the words rather than spoke them calmly, but what the hell. He wasn't calm. He was scared shitless. "Show yourself!" he challenged. "Talking's a lot easier that way."

Hadn't you come to me of your own accord, I would have called the fae. He would have followed my call, and you would have followed him. But now you are here. I do not need him. Come to me. Serve me.

"Fuck off. I'm not serving anyone, certainly not a creature that isn't even brave enough to show itself."

A small path led downhill just a short distance away. Barely visible, it was probably used by rabbits and foxes. It would do. The path would lead him out of the mountains. Once back in the woods—and far away from the banshee—he could open another portal and get back home.

He took one step, then another.

Serve me!

With the words came a pulling sensation, and Gabriel struggled—if the creature had thrown a lasso around him, it couldn't have been more effective. Toward the mountain wall he was pulled, away from safety, and now came a smell, strong and awful, rotten and dead.

He knew that smell. He'd smelled it before, when he'd been a wolf, when he'd run from Aleksei and ended up in this world. Back then, he'd barely escaped the creature, the scars along his thigh proof of how close it had been.

The wolf, as scared as himself, struggled against his grip. *Run*, it demanded. *Now!*

Dropping to his knees, Gabriel dug his hands into the gravel, simultaneously glancing toward the path, wishing with all his might he were home. He could hear its slithering steps. He could smell it....

Much faster and smoother than last time, his hands changed, then his feet, and finally his whole body.

The wolf twitched his ears. Far too close by, he could hear the creature howl with rage.

Run.

His body did the thinking, just like last time. Leaving his clothes, his shoes, and even his knife behind, he fled, tail between his legs, ears pressed tightly against his skull.

Run!

And he did run. The creature was not fast enough to catch a wolf. It reached out; its claws caught nothing but emptiness.

Trees. Soft leaves, warmer ground.

Home.

A portal. He didn't know where it came from—he certainly hadn't stopped to scratch a rune into the ground—but it was there nevertheless. It glowed invitingly, and it would take him back to Aleksei, and it didn't matter that he'd arrive on all fours and unable to speak. Aleksei knew he was a shapeshifter. A bit of fur wouldn't bother him.

He hoped.

Gabriel jumped, still able to hear the creature's howls and faintly feeling the pull of its thoughts. But they weren't strong enough.

Somehow, when he was in his wolf form, the creature had less power over him, its voice less strength.

He landed hard, paws slipping on smooth planks. Crashing into a bookshelf, he felt his ribs crack, and his tail got caught underneath him at an awkward angle, forcing a whine out of his snout.

The portal closed, cutting the voice out of his life and his mind as if it had never existed.

Hands held him, safe and familiar. He knew that fragrance. It was always with him no matter where he went. Sleeping next to the man who owned the scent had become his pleasure as well as his anchor in a world that was unpredictable at best and dangerous more often than not.

What was his name again?

Aleksei.

Of course. How could he have forgotten?

"Hi," he wanted to say, but he couldn't. A wolf's snout was not suited for words. Nor could he touch his lover, not with paws, not with claws.

"Gabriel?"

There was something he needed to do, but he couldn't remember what it was.

So he simply passed out.

CHAPTER SEVENTEEN

THE banshee shivered with excitement, anger, and hate.

Her child had been here! She'd seen him, could have touched him if she hadn't been too slow. His image was still bright and sharp in her mind, and so was his taste. His fragrance was everywhere; the cold air was laden with the smell of his hair, his skin, his blood.

Especially his blood. It had rushed through his veins, and oh, how she longed to shed it!

His arrival had been unexpected. It had shocked her to see the portal open; it had shocked her to sense his presence when she was not ready for him, when her body was slow and weak. She hadn't eaten in days, her mind being otherwise occupied. She hadn't slept out of fear that nightmares would torment her with hopes of a peaceful future.

She'd even neglected her egg, but then, that was all it was: an egg. She could have another one should this one die.

So when Gabriel arrived, she could do nothing but hide lest he overpower her and render all her century-old plans to ashes.

At the memory of his refusing to serve her, she growled. He was so strong! She hadn't expected that. Her other children—the ones without dragon blood, the ones with nothing but her genetic code imprinted upon them—had been weak, unable to resist her orders, unable to flee from her. Even Gabriel's grandmother, who'd for so long managed to evade her call by turning into a wolf, had been helpless in her presence.

Not so Gabriel. He'd fought, and for the second time now, he'd run from her.

The cold soothed the pain in her joints, but it still took many minutes to reach the place where he'd knelt, digging his fingers into the ground shortly before turning into an animal. She stood there, gasping for air and fearing she'd die right there and then. She needed to eat soon, today. But first, she needed to see if he'd left anything behind. The blood on her claws was no longer fresh. It hadn't lost its power, not yet, but it would eventually.

Footprints in the snow, partly melted from his body heat. Paw prints, blurry and barely recognizable because of the change of form and his efforts to flee. No fur; no fresh blood.

But a single, long lock of red hair, half-hidden under snow and caught against a rock, drew her attention.

Not as good as blood, but in combination, it would work perfectly. With blood and hair, she could call the fae.

Carefully, she wound the strands—no more than four or five hairs—around her claw, where they touched the blood. A bolt of excitement rushed through her, dimming her hunger to a mere inconvenience. Her child was out of her reach; his lover wasn't because of the link they shared. And although she hated having to do it this way, she was well aware that she didn't have another choice anymore. For a long time, she'd believed she could call her child without using tricks; now she accepted that it was not possible.

With the hand that held the hair, she drew a circle in the snow. It melted, leaving a gleaming mirror of water under the pale sun. She didn't like the sun—it dried out her brain and made it hard to think—but seeing through the mirror was easier that way.

A breeze stirred the water, blurring the picture. Still, she continued staring into the small puddle and spied on her child and the fae because it was her right to do so. They both belonged to her now.

Come to me, she whispered, and saw the fae's head whip around. He'd heard her. Of course he'd heard her. Her child lay unconscious at his feet, once more out of her reach now that he didn't breathe the same air as her. The fae's hand rested on Gabriel's chest, and he was worried about him. Not much was stronger than worry. Love, maybe. But she didn't understand love, so she focused on the worry and called him.

The fae, at least, would obey her. No dragon blood ran through his veins, so he stood no chance against her wishes. He would be here soon, and Gabriel would follow.

And this time, when she had his lover in her claws, her child would not dare to run from her.

CHAPTER EIGHTEEN

"He is in bad condition."

"I know. Until a moment ago, he was covered with fur."

"That is not what I meant. He's crossed through an unstable portal. More than one, actually. A dragon does not pass out easily."

"When he crossed through portals for the first time on his own, he lost days in the process and was half-dead once he made it back home."

"Understandable. He is not fully dragon. You should not have allowed him the use of portals without showing him how to handle the runes."

Voices. There were voices all around him. He could hear them, but what they said made little sense to Gabriel. Dragon? Portals? Runes? He didn't know the meaning of any of them.

He did know he hurt, though. And that he was cold. And that what was underneath him was hard and uncomfortable.

His thinking was a bit fuzzy around the edges. He opened an eye slowly, ready to shut it again if he didn't like what he saw.

Blue eyes. They might be familiar, but he wasn't sure. And the face.... Did he know the man who was looking down at him?

I should know him, Gabriel thought. *But I can't remember from where.*

He tried to speak but couldn't. *Thirsty,* he thought distractedly, and was glad when someone held a glass to his mouth and helped him drink.

Warmth spread through him, and a second later, when fire exploded through his throat and down into his stomach, he began to cough and pressed his hands to his ribcage. Tears ran down his face, and the taste of whisky dominated his senses. Wheezing, he sat up, supported by arms belonging to the man whose name he couldn't recall.

His eyes fell on his legs, and curious, he waggled his toes. It felt strange. Should he have toes? Come to think of it, should he have legs, and should they be naked?

Gradually, Gabriel realized he was sitting on the living room floor with only a blanket around his shoulders. "Why am I naked?" he croaked.

The question broke the barrier in his brain. His eyes widened, and he coughed some more to cover the burning red that was crawling into his cheeks. "Aleksei!"

"Here, beloved."

There was no way to avoid it. "I'm losing it," Gabriel said, pulling the blanket a bit tighter.

Aleksei raised one of his delicate eyebrows. Had he not felt so downhearted, Gabriel would have hugged him just for that. Instead, he let his head hang.

"Until a moment ago, I couldn't remember your name," he said quietly. "I'm forgetting things. Little stuff, like Pandora, and big stuff, like telling you about my mom. And now your name. I was wondering who you were, and then it goes *pop* and it's all back again. I'm losing it. Simple as that."

"You don't need to worry about losing your memory," a new voice said, darker than Aleksei's and somewhat strange and foreign.

Gabriel didn't want to see who else was here. He'd just fled a world he didn't know after fleeing a bunch of angry centaurs, and all that after he'd somehow saved a girl from one of those damn portals. Anyone else but Aleksei was currently too much to bear, even if this anyone sounded so strangely familiar.

But—a stranger in their house?

Against his instincts and definitely against his will, Gabriel turned his head, expecting to see someone he didn't know, a stranger to scowl at so he could make clear he didn't want company or advice right now.

But when he saw the dragon, his heart skipped a beat and his breath caught in his throat. Eyes threatening to pop out of their sockets, he was on his feet and backed up against the bookshelves before he even realized he'd moved. The blanket fell to the ground; he didn't care about nakedness, merely wondered whether he would survive the next few minutes. Or seconds.

"What's that?" he croaked, pointing a shaking finger at the stranger and unaware of Aleksei's surprised expression.

"The usual question would be 'who's that?', Gabriel," Aleksei admonished, picking up the blanket and placing it once more around his shoulders. "And the answer would be 'he's a guest.' His name is—"

"I don't give a fuck who he is or what he calls himself." Gabriel moved away another few steps. "That is not a 'who'. I don't know what he is, but he's not human, or fae, or anything else I've met so far."

At first sight, the creature seemed ordinary enough, wearing jeans and a sweater and boots, his arms crossed over his chest, his face open and friendly. His eyes were strange. And his hair was… blond, maybe. Or black? He seemed to be totally human.

Only he wasn't. His image wavered like a badly tuned television; it was hard to focus on him, and insisting on doing so gave Gabriel a headache. He'd had far too many headaches recently.

Underneath, the stranger looked very, very different.

Gabriel's eyes began to water, and his stomach made some unpleasant somersaults. "Do you remember, Aleksei," he bit out, still staring at the thing, "when we met, I thought your hair was brown although it was black."

"Because of the necklace I wear."

"Yeah. But I could see through your disguise. I can see through his as well, only his is much stronger. And he… and he…." His voice faltered because he really didn't know how to describe the creature underneath the rune.

"What do you see, Gabe?" Aleksei had an arm around his shoulders, steadying him, and it was of great necessity, or he would have run from the room by now.

Running seemed to have become his favorite pastime recently.

"He's black," Gabriel stated, turning his head for a brief moment so his stomach could calm down a bit and his eyes could rest. "I think he's black, that is. Hard to say with the disguise. Makes me sick looking at him. And his eyes... his eyes...."

The dragon had heard enough. "He is right," he said. "Of course I do not look human. I also told you I did not wish to scare you, so I use a glamour to hide my true appearance. If you wish, I will drop it."

"Anything's better than the way you look now," Gabriel croaked. His knees were weak, and he was grateful for Aleksei's support.

The dragon stood still, taking a deep breath. "Do not scream," he pleaded.

Like he were slowly dropping a mask held to his face, he revealed his entire body. A small shiver ran through him when his disguise was gone.

His human form was black, like the inside of a cave is black, or the night when one wakes up after a nightmare. His skin tone held not the smallest trace of brown, and his face and hands were scaled. His hair—black. The palms of his hands—black. The whites of his eyes—black.

His irises were red. At least.

"Fascinating," Aleksei just said. The one word, dryly spoken, broke the tension, and Gabriel laughed out loud, ignoring his still-present headache as well as his still-heaving stomach.

"What *are* you?" he asked again, ridiculously amused by the uncomfortable look on the stranger's face. "And why are you here? Oh, and what do you know about me losing my memory?" Staggering to the couch with Aleksei's help, he dropped onto the cushions and pulled his legs up, managing to pull the blanket completely around him so only his head was visible.

The stranger made him uneasy. He also made him wish he could get up and touch him in order to investigate his black, alien body. Made him wish Aleksei weren't here, wish he had the freedom to get to know the stranger better. Much better.

The stranger inclined his head. "I am S'chn Tg'ai. I am dragon," he said. "You are of my kind. Dragon blood runs through your veins and makes your heart beat. Now that I see you, it is obvious to me that you are the one I was looking for."

Gabriel shifted closer to Aleksei, hoping his disturbing attraction to the stranger would vanish. "This is a joke, isn't it?"

S'chn Tg'ai sighed deeply. "It was a mistake to retreat from the worlds," he said quietly. "People believe we've gone extinct. The members of the fae council were shocked when they saw me last night. You are shocked. I can see on your faces that you think this is a trick or a nightmare. But I am not a nightmare. I came to find you because I stumbled over your memories in my world."

"I have never been to your world!"

"You have. You fled from a murderer, and your mind instinctively opened the portal to your true home. You landed in an ocean and bumped into a rock. A seagull attacked you; your memories and your fear seeped into the rock. I learned enough from the remaining traces to find you." Briefly, S'chn Tg'ai closed his eyes. Even more quietly, he added, "Now that I have, I cannot say how much I regret coming here."

Aleksei asked, "You met the fae council? Last night?"

The dragon nodded, his red eyes gleaming. "I met your sister, Lia, and I forbade the use of the portals. Right now, they are too dangerous to use. The balance is upset. It is the discord that disrupts your memory, Gabe. Others have been killed by it. The memory loss will not be permanent, but you ought not to use the portals until I discover the source of the discord."

The way the dragon said "Gabe" instead of using his given name made Gabriel tremble with sudden longing.

"I did, just this morning," he said, rather than jumping up and tearing the clothes off the dragon's scaly skin. "Went into Kyril's world, found a missing girl, and on the way back lost my way again. I ended up in that creature's world, the one who injured me last time I was there. This time it talked to me too. Seems whenever I'm tired or scared my brain gets fucked up and I draw a Portal rune to a world I never even knew existed."

The dragon cast a smile laden with sadness. "The first time, your mind led you home. I do not know about the other times."

Gabriel snorted. "My home is *here*."

"You are dragon. Your home is where dragons live."

"I am also a shapeshifter. And human. Don't you tell me where my home is and where it isn't!" Gabriel took Aleksei's hand. "My home is here. You aren't the first who has tried to tell me otherwise. Lia would love to see me gone so she could lure Aleksei back into the fae world. That creature calling me, ordering me to serve it. And now you. Fuck off, dragon. I am not of your kind. Got no scales, see? My skin is not black, my hair, neither; my eyes are gray. I bet you are making this up!"

But he wasn't, and Gabriel knew it. There was a connection between him and the stranger he couldn't deny. And S'chn Tg'ai confirmed it by saying, "You're attracted to me, although you're bound. It is only natural. You're drawn to me because we are of one kind."

Briefly, Aleksei squeezed his hand. "It makes sense, beloved. More than anything else. I checked your blood against all other races. No match. You don't look like him, but you can travel through portals without protecting yourself. You create runes, although it is impossible. You saw through my disguise. No one else, not even my sister, is able to do that. I've always known there's something special about you. I just didn't expect it to be quite so special. So although I did not yet have time to check your blood against his, I do believe you are dragon. Just like him."

A hint of sadness laced his last words, gone before Gabriel could be sure he'd heard it at all. "Bullshit," he said weakly.

"I can prove it." Invitingly, the dragon held out his hands. "So your doubts will vanish. So you can see for yourself I speak the truth."

"Yeah?" Gabriel asked, his eyes drawn to the dragon's hands. His nails were black, like the rest of him, but long and curved, like claws made of obsidian glass. "How?"

S'chn Tg'ai obviously considered the question to be permission to proceed, which hadn't been Gabriel's intention. Swiftly, the dragon crossed the distance between them and took his face between his hands.

I should have told him to leave and never come back was Gabriel's last thought, but of course, once it was too late, it was simply too late. He was frozen to the spot, unable to as much as lift his little finger in defense.

"I will not hurt you," S'chn Tg'ai said, and with a glance at Aleksei, he added, "forgive me," before he leaned forward and pressed his lips to Gabriel's.

Gabriel grabbed the stranger's shoulders and dug his fingers into the strangely fragile frame, not knowing whether he wanted to break bones, leave bruises, push him back, or pull him closer. The dragon tasted so different from any other person he'd ever kissed. Sweeter, in ways, but also wilder, with subtle notes of air and ocean and something he could not identify.

Dragon, he thought, only dimly aware of Aleksei next to him, watching him.

Had he thought about it—no. That was a lie. He *had* thought about it, only moments ago. How those lips would feel. Cold, maybe, or rough, given the scales? Disgusting, like a dead fish?

S'chn Tg'ai's lips were warm, but not as soft as human lips. Gabriel could even feel the scales. They were tiny, each one touching him with feathery delicacy.

It wasn't a skilled kiss. Gabriel had never kissed a dragon, and the dragon had never kissed anyone at all.

Dragons didn't kiss.

She's dead. His mate is dead and he's lonely.

The thought was just there, and Gabriel knew it was true.

More memories flooded him. S'chn Tg'ai held him close, his fingers strong against his neck.

Memories, centuries of memories, a whole lifetime poured into Gabriel's mind, a life so different from his own he thought his head would explode. He saw dragons, whole clouds of them covering the sky and blocking out the sun. He saw young ones hatch and old ones die. He experienced thunderstorms so vicious even a dragon could only barely withstand them, and he witnessed firsthand how it felt to mate in the open air.

An eternity of joy, shared with his mate. Grief after her death. He saw her die, and he was helpless, useless. He saw her vanish in the floods, sinking to the ocean floor like every dragon who'd died so no one and nothing but the ocean floor would ever touch their bones. He knew why the dragons did not walk among the other races anymore. A disease had fallen upon the dragons, killing the young ones within their eggs. The dragons, for the first time ever, had failed to find a cure. They could not stand how easily fae, elves, humans, merpeople, and centaurs conceived, how full their worlds were with young ones while the dragon race dwindled no matter what desperate steps they took. Even mating with humans, the only race, for some reason, that was at least partly compatible with them, turned into a failure.

A tear ran down Gabriel's cheek when S'chn Tg'ai let go of him. He opened his eyes, momentarily blinded by the light and the fact he was in his house, with no open sky above him and no wings attached to his shoulders, his lips still burning from the dragon's kiss and his head pounding with too many memories.

"You're so lonely," Gabriel said, his voice cracking with grief.

"You're so much in love." S'chn Tg'ai sat down right in front of him, pulled up his legs, and wrapped his arms around his knees. His chin rested on his folded hands. "I have forgotten how wonderful love feels. All I remember is pain when thinking of my mate, even though it's been a long time since she died."

Gabriel crouched down next to him. "I grieve with you," he whispered. "And I know why you came here, now I know. To find me, and to take me with you."

"You could turn into a dragon," S'chn Tg'ai said. "The knowledge is in your blood, in your genes. Buried; sleeping. You have turned into a wolf in the presence of danger; you could change into a dragon just like I changed into a human. You could fly."

Longing and temptation made Gabriel's throat dry and his hands sweaty. And maybe he would have done something stupid had his nose not picked up a smell that very moment: Aleksei's fragrance. Not that wild, compared with the dragon's fragrance, but wild enough for him. Not that sweet, but familiar, and more than that—loved.

"I cannot," Gabriel said.

"I know." The dragon wiped the tear off Gabriel's face. "You are in love. You are bound. I know it because I saw it in your memories, and I know it because I see the runes on your skin."

So far, Aleksei hadn't uttered a single word of his own on the matter. Gabriel got up, sought once more for his hand, and found it, holding it tight until he felt grounded and safe once more.

"I created the runes because of the creature calling me," he said. "The one I met before returning home. The one that scratched me. I don't know what it looks like or what it wants, other than my blood. Any idea why I end up drawing the rune to this creature's world?"

With a fluid movement, the dragon got up as well. "I will know it soon," he said. "I hold your memories now, all of them, but of course there are too many to recall all of them at once, or even a small part of them. Let me find the one memory where you talk to this creature, the one where you drew the rune to its world." He turned his back to Gabriel and Aleksei and strolled to one of the windows, putting his long black hands on the sill.

The dragon's silence gave Gabriel the time to face his lover. "I don't even know where to start," he said helplessly.

Aleksei raised an eyebrow. "Start what?"

"Explaining this. All of it."

At least Aleksei didn't pull his hand away. He should have, though, in Gabriel's honest opinion. After all, he'd just kissed another man right in front of him.

Well, dragon.

"There is no need to explain anything. Or, more precisely, to explain anything that has to do with S'chn Tg'ai. I heard what he said. I saw what happened. I have no reason not to believe anything he, or you, just said."

"I kissed him!"

"He kissed you. For me, there is a big difference."

Gabriel blushed, remembering the kiss he'd shared with the tree nymph as well as the one with Conchita.

"I broke my promise," he said, glancing at the pondering dragon. "I went into Kyril's world. Missing girl, desperate parents. I heard her scream. The portal for some reason hadn't closed after her. I had to find her. Kyril is probably pretty mad at me. Fled from his camp, threatening him on the way out. Left the girl behind and—oh, shit. Her parents are still waiting for me to report back!"

Aleksei held him back as he tried to leave the room. "Get dressed first," he said firmly. "I will call Monique, get the number of your clients, and call them. Is the girl safe?"

"I think so. She's alive, if that's what you mean. At first, she was conscious and able to talk. But then she passed out. Exhaustion, I think. She was sort of lost inside the portal, if that makes any sense to you. Is it true the use of the portals has been prohibited by the fae council? Because that's what Kyril said and why he wouldn't let me get back home."

A brief flash of bitterness shone in the fae's eyes. "How would I know?" he said. "After my argument with Lia, I left, preferring the peace of the woods to more arguments with the council. I do not know what happened, and certainly Lia did not inform me about any decisions that were made. S'chn Tg'ai told me he forbade the use of the portals. Too many have gone missing; too many have died in the process of crossing from one world to the other."

"So not only did I break my promise to you, I also ignored the fae council's decree."

Aleksei cast him a smile. "You didn't know. And a child's life is more important than any promise you gave. As for the fae council's decree—since you appear to be partly dragon, I believe their wishes are not relevant to you."

Gabriel tightened his grip on Aleksei's hand. "I still believe I'm losing it. This memory loss worries me no matter what he says. I didn't even know how bad it was until I woke up here, saw your face, and couldn't remember your name." His throat was tight. Admitting it was harder than he'd thought.

And now, upon glimpsing part of his naked feet, he remembered something else. "I turned into a wolf again!"

Another smile. "I know. You came through the portal as a wolf. Impressive sight, I must admit, though slightly unexpected. You changed back while unconscious."

"I lost my knife!" Frantically, Gabriel patted down his body, hoping against hope the knife's shape would show underneath the blanket.

"It is just a knife," Aleksei said calmingly, taking his hands and holding them still. "It can be replaced. You can't."

Fighting back an urge to scream, Gabriel just shook his head. "More than that," he managed. "It was a present, it—" Suddenly, a thought struck him. "Are you jealous?" he asked. "Of... this? Him kissing me? Because you don't need to be. You are the only one I love."

A tiny flare lit in the fae's eyes, and had Gabriel not been looking for it, he would have missed it.

"You *are* jealous."

Aleksei sighed. "Of course I am. What did you expect? A lot has happened in a very short amount of time. We did not have the luxury to talk about any of it. Not about what happened in the *Poison Prince*. Not about the calling. Not why you didn't tell me sooner. Not about the memory loss you suffer from or, for that matter, your admission of having cheated on me."

There it was, the edge in his voice, the pain, the disappointment, and the fear. Fear of losing him showed in his lover's eyes. Aleksei's face was rarely that open and unguarded. Now it was, and it spoke volumes.

"I never," Gabriel stammered. "I mean... I didn't mean to hurt you with any of this! Keeping things to myself is the way I am, Aleksei. Not sharing my fears or uncertainties is how I was brought up. You know this. You know *me*!"

Gabriel saw Aleksei frown, then turn his head as if he heard something, a small noise, or maybe a nagging thought chirping up at the back of his mind. "I thought I did," the fae said somewhat coldly. "I was wrong. You are dragon, Gabe, partly, in any case. I am not your future. He is. S'chn Tg'ai offered you wings. How can you deny the truth? Staying here, staying with me, is not what you want. Following him is." Aleksei let go of his hand and stepped back, putting some distance between them.

"You don't mean that!" Gabriel started to reach out, pull Aleksei into an embrace and make him take back the stupid words he'd said, only to see his lover back away from him.

"I should have seen this from the beginning," Aleksei mused, crossing his arms over his chest as if to keep his body in check. "Freedom was always what you treasured most, was it not?" The frown on the fae's face deepened, and he rolled his shoulders, turned his head ever so slightly. Listening to an inaudible voice?

"You've always run from the ones who cared for you, be it your foster parents or lovers or your few friends. You ran from me more than once. You even turned into a wolf to get away from me faster. Denial does not suit you, Gabriel. You might have loved me at some point in the past. I am certain you stopped loving me a while ago, or none of this would ever have happened."

With a nod toward the silent figure at the window, Aleksei indicated that "none of this" mainly meant the dragon.

"You don't mean that," Gabriel replied weakly, not knowing what else to say and not understanding why Aleksei was so different from his usual self all of a sudden.

A faraway look had claimed Aleksei's eyes, and lines appeared on his face that had not been there before. Around his mouth Gabriel saw a hard twist he did not recognize.

A glance at the dragon told him S'chn Tg'ai was not yet ready to join the conversation. He would have liked to ask the dragon if he saw something strange in Aleksei. But the dragon stood with his back to them, head low, eyes closed, lost in thought. Or memories.

What had the banshee said?

I would have called your fae. Through the binding, I can reach him.

Remembering the creature's threat made his blood freeze.

"Are you being called?" Gabriel asked, barely daring to ask the words, and Aleksei reacted as if he'd been slapped: he slumped onto the couch and dug his hands into his hair. A low moan escaped him.

"Fuck," Gabriel said, dropping beside him. "This is my fault. The banshee has gotten to you. Seems I'm safe, but you are not. I'm so damn sorry!"

On Aleksei's face, suspicion and hope and fierce anger fought with each other. "I can hear a voice," he said, desperation in his voice. "Right now, it's faint. I cannot make out any words. But it feels as if I should get away from you, as if…." His voice faltered.

"I cannot let that happen," Gabriel murmured. "I won't allow this beast to meddle with you."

The dragon glanced over his shoulder, frowning as if he wondered what they were talking about.

Gabriel's fingers were already moving, but he got them under control just in time. By now, he knew the pattern of the rune he needed. He'd drawn it twice subconsciously; he could draw it again with his mind focused on the task.

"I'm getting dressed," he said, and went into the bedroom, where he found a pair of jeans and a shirt. He should have put on shoes as well, for where he was going the ground was frozen, but then, his shoes were in the hall, and putting them on was not an option, not if he wanted to avoid questions. And the thought of walking around in drenched socks… no. Barefoot it would be, no matter how cold it was.

I'm going to die.

Great. Just the thought he'd been waiting for. So very reassuring. And, probably, so very true.

He would die, and soon. He'd known it for days, weeks now. The creature waiting for him would see to it.

The portal opened just as Aleksei looked up. "Don't!" he called out, jumping up, but Gabriel closed the bedroom door in his face. He had to do this or it would never end. Or worse, it would end with Aleksei's death.

"Love you," he said to the empty room. Just as he felt snow underneath his feet and felt the portal close, he heard a door burst open, the door to his bedroom.

Too late.

CHAPTER NINETEEN

SO MANY memories.

The dragon hadn't expected this. After all, Gabriel's life only spanned a few decades. How many memories could a man gather in such a short time?

But he was wrong. When his lips touched Gabriel's, memories flooded into him, drowned him, each one brighter than the next. Many were sad; some were cruel. But many were also happy, and the happy ones, nearly all of them, were connected with the fae. In a matter of moments, S'chn Tg'ai learned everything there was to know about Gabriel—his childhood, his years on the streets, his relationship with Aleksei, his job, as well as his travels to the hidden worlds and the background concerning Petresh and Lia.

Lots of memories, so much brighter, so much more intense than the memories of ordinary humans. And all of them tumbling down upon him in one single, painful avalanche.

The kiss lasted longer than planned. Usually, a quick peck was all that was needed. Humans just weren't—

But of course, Gabriel was not human. He was dragon, and that alone made his life so much richer.

So many emotions. Overwhelming, frightening emotions.

I cannot deal with this, the dragon thought upon breaking the kiss. *I need a moment to… think!*

Stepping, or rather fleeing, to the window, he put distance between himself and them. His fingers trembled when he put them on the sill, treasuring the cold sensation of the marble against his skin.

He thought about T'gani, his beautiful mate. What would she do with the information at hand? Would she test the ties that bound Gabriel to his lover? Would she try to convince him no matter that he was neither free nor willing to go?

No. Stupid idea. She would have turned her back on him by now, knowing she'd lost.

But he didn't.

"You're so lonely," Gabriel had said, and it was true. S'chn Tg'ai was dying of loneliness. It ate him up from inside, devouring his heart and his soul, and the only reason he was still alive was because he'd found one of his own kind. Not a pureblood dragon, but still a member of his own kind.

We should have looked for children like Gabriel before, the dragon thought. *We might have found others like him, others as sane and stable as he is.*

But they hadn't looked, not after the first few attempts at having mixed human-dragon offspring had gone so terribly wrong. Not after it became clear that children of dragons and humans were damaged, like Gabriel's mother.

The windowsill under his palms warmed from the heat of his hands. In the background, he could hear Aleksei and Gabriel talking. Vaguely, he was aware of the sudden tension, the change in their conversation, but he was still too much occupied with the new memories to take proper notice.

Where was the one memory where Gabriel talked to the creature he'd mentioned? It was buried under other memories, like how he'd changed into a wolf and that he'd saved a girl with green hair. There was something interesting in that memory. It tasted different than the others; he felt the discord and knew it had to do with the portal.

Later.

No, not the memory of sex that had taken place in this house only recently. Especially not that memory.

Ah. There it was. A soundless, disembodied voice threatening Gabriel under a pale, weak sun.

The dragon's hands turned cold.

Impossible.

He knew that voice, and he knew the world.

Not her!

Gabriel muttered something behind his back, and the dragon turned, shooting him a glance. He nearly asked what had happened, but right then, another memory came bobbing up—the moment when the voice had grown claws, leaving three long scratches on Gabriel's hip and thigh.

Not many creatures had only three claws. Most had four or five, some none at all; some had fins or wings instead of them. But three?

"You should have told me the creature calling Gabe is a banshee," S'chn Tg'ai said with a deep sigh, turning from the window. "Had I known.... But anyway. She is dangerous. And she is the one damaging the portals."

GABRIEL had chosen the woods for his arrival, remembering the place where he'd killed the deer. The smell of blood was still fresh in his mind, the feeling of snow underneath his naked feet—it was easy to imagine the spot and even easier to open a portal half a step away.

Nothing was left of the deer's corpse. It was just a patch in the middle of woods, and for a heartbeat, Gabriel wished he could turn into a wolf right now, hunt down another deer, and ignore the task ahead. Which, in his honest opinion, consisted of him getting killed.

"Damn," he murmured, and set off toward the mountains instead. The banshee was waiting for him.

Come to me!

"Oh, just shut the fuck up, will you?" Gabriel shouted. He wasn't surprised that now he was back here, he could hear her voice again. "Who asked you to turn up anyway, huh? That damn dragon offered me wings a little while ago. Aleksei thinks he's better off without me because of your fucking meddling with his mind. The dragon's nothing but a big, sad lizard stuffed into a human body, you're a fucking nuisance, and actually, you can both go to hell and leave me alone, thank you very much."

He was pretty sure neither banshee nor lizard could hear him.

The mountain seemed even higher and steeper now that he was heading uphill. The air grew thin, and the cold bit into his naked feet. Despite the sun and the exercise, he began to shiver. The wind picked up, playing with his hair and cooling the sweat on his skin whenever he stopped to catch his breath.

"Couldn't this thing live on the plains?" he growled, wishing he were up there already so he could sit down on a nice rock and relax his trembling legs. Too much running lately, and none of it done in proper running shoes.

Things shouldn't have happened so quickly. A few weeks back, everything had been fine. He loved his job; he loved living with Aleksei; he loved working with runes and traveling to the hidden worlds. He was good at what he was doing! He found missing people, he reunited families, and every now and then he got an extra treat like the look on Taylor's face when he'd told him about his completely harmless mother. And now all the good parts were over because some strange creature had decided to interfere with his life.

Probably, he shouldn't have been such a hothead, running off instead of talking with Aleksei and the dragon and coming up with some sort of a plan. But then, who knew how quickly the banshee could call his lover into her world and what she would do with him once she had Aleksei in her claws? Better not to risk it. Better to act before she had a chance to do any more damage. And plans were overrated, anyway.

"Hope Aleksei remembers to call Monique. I bet the girl's parents are still standing in front of their house, awaiting my return."

It was good to talk aloud in the silence around him, with only the wind whispering and a few birds' lonely cries above him.

At least he remembered his lover's name. But the name of the girl he'd saved from the portal was gone from his mind, as were the names of her parents. Which day of the week it was, he hadn't a clue, nor to which hotel he'd taken his mother.

"Got a brain like swiss cheese nowadays." He needed to draw breath twice to finish the sentence, and even then, it came out as a faint wheeze.

Maybe wings wouldn't be so bad after all. He could fly up the mountains, sail above the peaks, and search for the creature with the foul smell.

Sinking onto a rock, Gabriel laughed, only then remembering that his ribcage should be sore. He had cracked his ribs, hadn't he?

Carefully, he lifted his shirt, sucking the air in sharply when the cold hit his heated, sweaty skin. His hair, having long slipped out of the braid he'd forced it into ages ago, clung to his temples and got between his lips. Salty and bitter. Like tears.

He guessed he would have cried had he had the time.

Faintly, he saw the Binding runes covering his skin. There were bruises beneath them, all down his left side where he'd hit the bookshelf. Tracing them hurt, but they were already mostly healed thanks to the rune on his neck. "Wish I knew who put it there," he mused, tucking his shirt back in.

There was a lot he would've liked to ask his mother. Over a cup of tea, ideally, and without her spitting and swearing.

Idle wishes. He wouldn't see her again, nor Aleksei, nor anyone else. Not with the appointment he had looming with the banshee.

"Aleksei," he sighed. He knew his lover. He knew Aleksei would follow him. "Shit. Can't sit around any longer. Got to find the banshee before they come after me."

Gabriel got up, looked downhill one more time, and then ran, only this time, not from the creature, but toward it.

ALEKSEI broke down the bedroom door in a matter of seconds, but he was too late. Gabriel was gone, having taken the glow of the portal and the shape of the rune with him.

"You fool," he breathed. "You think you can do this on your own. Once more, you have made the wrong decision."

Well, he knew Gabriel acted on instinct more often than not, and his actions were nearly always unpredictable. But he would always fight for the ones he loved and put himself in the line of danger rather than standing aside and letting someone who was better suited for the job act on his behalf. He was strong and stubborn, fiercely loyal, and so far, Aleksei had never had a reason to doubt his love.

"And I thought he would leave me for the dragon," he muttered under his breath, staring at the spot where but a moment ago Gabriel had been.

"He would not do that," S'chn Tg'ai said quietly behind his left shoulder. "Nothing could ever part him from you. Nothing but death. Which is what he is facing right now. It was stupid of him to follow the banshee's call, but then, I cannot blame him. She is mad with hate. Her calls must be very tempting. She is the last of her kind, even older than the oldest living dragon. Weak, but vicious. And angry enough to upset the balance of the portals by calling a dragon."

"Gabriel could hear her call for a while. Then I bound him to me and her voice was gone." Aleksei touched the floor where the portal had been in hope of seeing, *sensing* a glimpse of the rune Gabriel had used. If he could, he would be able to follow him. Together, they might yet defy the banshee.

"I believed her," he said, shaking his head in disbelief even as the words dropped from his mouth. "Hearing her voice struck me as odd, but I believed her words. In a way, I still do. On a subconscious level, I believe Gabriel never truly loved me, that he treasured his freedom more than what is between us, that he would want wings rather than my arms holding him back."

S'chn Tg'ai placed a hand on his shoulder, soothingly brushing his hair back. "Wings are naught compared to love. I would cut off my wings for one last hour with my mate."

Aleksei looked up at him. "I want to follow him."

The dragon shrugged his shoulders. "It is not possible."

"It has to be!"

"He will die, fae. Soon. The banshee has been calling him for weeks, but he has refused to obey. I do not know about her plans, but I know they will be fatal. Gabriel has been in her world twice, and he has fled her wrath twice. I don't know how this is possible. For some reason, he is stronger than her call. But now he is with her of his own free will. She will kill him. It's what a banshee does, always, with everyone who gets too close to her."

"You wanted him to be with you! You came to this world to find him and take him with you. And now that he is in danger, you give up on him?"

The dragon's eyes burned a deep red. The scales marking his jaw line stood up, and nostrils flared, his breath coming in fast, harsh gulps. He did not say a word.

"There is something else, isn't there? Gabriel is human and dragon. He is shapeshifter. Didn't you say a dragon wouldn't hear a banshee's call? Then how can he hear her?" Aleksei stared at the dragon. "I want to follow him. I want him back."

"You can't." Quietly, the dragon turned his back to him.

GRADUALLY, the rotten smell became more prominent. Gabriel was so high up in the mountains by now that even the low, sorry-looking bushes had given up trying to grow. His feet were so cold he couldn't feel them anymore, and his breath formed clouds in front of his mouth.

"Should have taken a jacket. And shoes. Or maybe thought this through instead of leaving in a rush. Stupid beast truly should have chosen a warmer place for messing with my life."

Come to me.

"Yes, yes, on my way. Can you think of anything else to say? Gets a bit boring, always hearing the same sentence over and over."

He was annoyed rather than scared. It felt like hours had passed since he began to climb. He was beyond tired, given he hadn't slept much the previous night—or any night in the past few weeks—and he was hungry and bored.

"Yeah. About to face a deathly enemy, and I don't even consider it to be all that interesting."

This habit of talking to himself was annoying too, come to think of it.

But this *was* boring. Nothing but rocks and snow. No attacks. No sign of the creature he was looking for.

"Maybe I'm imagining it. Maybe I went mad weeks ago, and this is nothing but a nice, pleasant little nightmare."

Just a bit higher, little one. There is a cave at the end of this path, surrounded by sky. Come to me, come—

"Oh, shut the fuck up," Gabriel snapped, and broke into a slow trot. "And don't call me little one. You're not my mother. Although you can't be much worse."

I'm more than your mother. I'm the one who created you. Without me, you would not exist.

"Blah, blah, blah." The sun reflected off the snow with blazing light. It blinded him. His eyes were watering, burning; tears ran down his cheeks. "You can tell me all sorts of rubbish, beast. Doesn't mean I believe a single word you say."

Silence answered him, dumbstruck silence. Gabriel grinned, his lips cracking in the cold air. Apparently, this creature was not used to being argued with.

I killed your grandmother.

"So you say, sweetie, so you say." Another bend and he would reach the end of the path. He was at the top of the mountain now. No more peaks blocked his sight. He could see for miles, although what he saw was pretty dull. Rocks, mainly, and the plains, far away. The trees were tiny, no larger than grass from his position. In the distance, there might even be water, but he couldn't be sure. Might just be the horizon.

The last barrier vanished as he dragged himself around the last turn. The narrow path opened to a wide plateau surrounded by low rocks and nothing else but a hole in the ground at the far end. Only the path Gabriel had chosen led to this place; only the path would take him away again.

The plateau was empty.

She was small toward the end, the voice whispered into his mind. *An old woman way beyond her years. Mad and lonely. She'd nearly forgotten about you, Gabriel. For your safety, she left you. For your safety, she had you marked with a rune. In the end, she still followed my call. In the end, she gave me what I needed—your name. Do you know how important names are for my kind? No? I thought not. No one knows. Names are the key; names are everything.*

Gabriel was out of breath, but even if he hadn't been, he wouldn't have known how to answer.

Do you believe me now, little one?

"No."

Puzzled surprise made his fingertips tingle. The creature obviously didn't understand the concept of denial, either.

How else could I have called you?

"Who cares? Maybe you liked my hair color. Maybe you were bored. Doesn't matter, really. You called. I came, eventually. Now tell me what it is you want so I can go back home."

But the creature still struggled with his "no." Gabriel could feel it. The thing, wherever it was, wanted him to understand its reasons.

Fine for him. The longer it talked, the longer he lived.

On the other hand, the longer it talked, the more time it gave Aleksei to follow him.

Shit.

"Look… thing. Beast. Whatever you are. Why don't you just spill the beans, tell me what's going on, and be done with it?" It took a bit of an effort not to shout, but he managed it. Barely. Shouting was probably not the best thing to do when facing a potentially deadly enemy.

Not thing. Not beast. Banshee.

"Banshee, yes? Lovely. Must have forgotten, but then, I tend to forget a lot, recently."

I am a banshee, and I am part of you. It is why you heard my call, although you are also dragon; it is why you will obey me.

Gabriel staggered and realized he couldn't feel his feet, or his knees, for that matter. His jeans were wet up to his thighs. The fabric was frozen and covered with snow.

"I just learned I'm dragon," he bit out through gritted teeth so they wouldn't chatter from the cold. "Always knew I was shapeshifter. And now you come along and tell me I am—what was it? Banshee? Take a ticket, sweetie. I have to learn how to fly first before I can even consider adopting that rotten smell of yours."

There it was again, the confused silence. Only this time, it had a center—the hole at the end of the plateau.

The creature was in there, hiding.

Gabriel took another step, not an easy task given that his legs were trembling as well as seeming to be disconnected from the rest of his body. "You honestly expect me to obey, don't you?" he asked. "You really thought once you had my name I would come running."

You did not.

"'Course not. You've got nothing I want. You've got no power over me!" Another step. He wasn't that far away from the hole now. The rotten smell overwhelmed him, and on the ground he could see bones, feathers, and blood.

Amusement mixed with annoyance washed over him. *No power? Then who poured hatred into you at the sight of your lover? Who made you believe you loathed him?*

A pause, short but meaningful.

Who made you wish you could take him with force, make him bleed, make him scream with terror as you came inside him?

Gabriel lost his footing and fell. His palms scraped on the frozen ice and bled onto the white snow.

In his mouth, fresh as when he'd just bitten him, he tasted Aleksei's blood.

"You made me do that to Aleksei?"

Hesitation. An urge to agree but fear that the lie would be detected.

Gabriel made it back onto his feet, but just barely. "Tell me!" he shouted. "Did you make me hurt him?"

You did not. Reluctance, and something like shameful admission. *I wanted you to hurt him so he would be torn from your side. Had you killed him, it would have suited me too. But you evaded my control. The wolf took over. I watched. I witnessed. There was no pain. No reason to leave you. No death.*

As though from a distance, Gabriel watched the blood from his cut hands soil the snow. He heard a ringing in his ears, overlapping the creature's voice.

He took a handful of snow, fresh and cold, to wipe his face clean. To slake his thirst, he ate some as well. He couldn't get any colder anyway.

No pain. No reason to leave you.

No wonder the creature was disappointed.

"How do you know?" Gabriel finally asked. "That I didn't hurt him. That I—"

I told you: I watched. I have been watching you for years, Gabriel. I could not call you, not without a name. But I knew of your existence from the moment you crossed through a portal. I witnessed many moments of your life. Once I had your name, I influenced you as well. And once I had your blood....

The creature didn't finish the sentence. It didn't have to. The scars along Gabriel's thigh began to hurt as if the claws had only just slashed them.

"You really killed my grandmother?" Not that he wanted to know, but somehow, talking seemed to distract the creature. If he got close enough before it noticed, he might be able to kill it instead of the other way round.

Slowly, he stood back up on shaky legs.

I did. It took her a long time to come to me. As a wolf, she was nearly deaf to my call. Eventually, she had to listen. My blood ran in her veins. My blood ran in your father's veins. It runs in yours too.

"So I'm a dragon-banshee-human-shifter. Great. Explain that to anyone who believes in the purity of the races. And I know of a few people who always wanted to know which creatures had shaped me."

I shaped you. I brought together your mother and your father. She was dragon, immune to my calls. He was partly banshee. They did not want to mate. I forced him. You were the result. You are unique. No one else unites my blood with dragon blood. Because of my blood, you hear and obey me. Because of the dragon inside you, you will serve your purpose.

"And what purpose would that be? To scratch your back? To get you some more pigeons? Seems you like them, seeing there's all these feathers covering the ground."

Another few feet, and he'd be at the hole. Another few feet, and he could reach inside, drag out whatever was in there, and break its neck. He had never killed anything with his bare hands before, and he didn't look forward to doing it now, but kill this thing he would. It had threatened him, it had threatened Aleksei, and anyway, if he didn't find someplace warm pretty soon, he wouldn't have to worry about serving or obeying any longer, because he'd be an icicle.

Sudden movement made him stop an arm's length from the hole. A shadow fell onto the snow, and where nothing but thin air had existed a moment ago, a shape now emerged from the hole. The rotten smell flooded his senses and brought him to his knees once more. Coughing, Gabriel pressed his arm to his mouth and nose. He tried not to breathe, which didn't work, tried to get used to the stink, which didn't work, either, and finally tried to crawl away, back to the path that had brought him here.

Claws grabbed him by the hair and pulled him back like a fish on a hook. What was worse, he didn't fight it. He was helpless, his traitorous blood responding and obeying its master.

Against the blue sky and the sun, the banshee's face was nothing but a black, shadowy patch. Deeper shadows indicated holes where eyes should have been, and another indicated something of a mouth. Sharp teeth blinked; only some were rotten, and only a few had fallen out.

Your purpose is to die, little one, the banshee hummed. *You will open a portal for me. I found your grandmother when she was young, long before her only child was born. I changed her. Through her, I made you. Dragon blood is needed to fulfill my last and only wish. You are what I need. Useful to me even against your will. You will open the portal, and the knife you lost last time you ran from me will end your life. Your blood, dragon blood, shed upon the portal's opening, will destroy them for good.*

Funny, but what the banshee said made sense, in a strange, crooked sort of way.

Yes, destroy the portals. After all, it was his destiny. After all, it was the sole reason for his existence. Besides, they were damaged already. Better to shut them down for good.

The banshee let go of his hair, allowing him to kneel before her. Her claws held his knife.

Someone had given it to him once, a lifetime ago, but he'd forgotten his name.

Didn't matter. Soon he would be dead, and he wouldn't have to worry about names ever again.

A lazy smile crossed his cracked, bleeding lips.

Perfect.

CHAPTER TWENTY

"OPEN the portal to the banshee's world." Aleksei was pacing the living room, tense with fear and nervousness. His muscles hummed with the need to move, to follow Gabriel, but the dragon hadn't lifted a finger yet. "Or are you telling me you don't know the required rune?"

The dragon didn't seem to be listening to him. "She is strong," he said, a frown on his face, as if he were trying to figure out why he was talking about banshees at all. "Deadly. We forbade her kind the use of the portals. We denied them the knowledge of the runes, for we knew they would have invaded the worlds and destroyed them. We locked them in their world and waited, knowing they could not leave. I thought they had died long ago. She, the one who is calling, must be the last one, or the hate that hums throughout the portals would be much stronger."

Digging into the pocket of his trousers, Aleksei came up with a crumpled piece of paper. "Gabriel created this rune. He said it stabilizes the portals enough for a safe journey. I used it upon coming back after meeting my sister. It requires a lot of power; using it on a permanent basis would be impossible for me. So if this is about safety—use it. Take me there!"

S'chn Tg'ai didn't even bother to look at the rune. "It is not about safety. I can take you anywhere without risking your life or your health. The problem is we forbade visiting this world. Even I cannot go there."

"Gabriel went there," Aleksei argued.

"He did not know." S'chn Tg'ai lowered his head, shaking it sadly. "We did not teach him the rules. We abandoned him. But—"

Aleksei flicked a rune into the air, opening a portal without taking his eyes off the dragon. "Lia?" he called, not getting too close to the portal. Around the edges, it shimmered black, and it wavered in the air like a mirage. Not stable, not safe enough to pass through, but still a connection to the fae world.

From the other side, a voice could be heard. "Aleksei? Do not come through, brother! This portal—"

"I know. I need you to do me a favor. Talk to the council and get permission to search through the old books for a Portal rune leading to a lost world where the banshees live. If someone can find this, it is you. I need your help, Lia. I would be immensely grateful."

Lia's voice spoke clearly of surprise as well as triumph. "And if I find the information you require? Will you do then what is expected of you?"

"You never waste an opportunity to blackmail me, do you?" Aleksei muttered under his breath, but before he could agree—and he would have agreed—S'chn Tg'ai shattered the portal to pieces simply by blowing at the glowing outlines.

"You will not do this. She does not approve of your relationship; she would demand that you leave him. And anyway, finding what you are looking for would take her too long to save Gabriel's life."

"I know."

"You are stubborn and stupid!" The dragon came to stand only inches from Aleksei, towering above him but still not managing to intimidate him. "Do you not understand that following Gabriel is not an option? The fae council will learn about the breach of the law now that you have asked your sister about the lost world. She will learn that the punishment for ignoring the law is death. And she won't have a choice but to tell the fae council. First you will see Gabriel die, should you follow him. Then you will die yourself."

Aleksei was at his throat in a matter of seconds. His hands locked around the dragon's neck. Underneath his fingers he felt the scales, the heat the alien skin radiated, and the slow, strong pulse. "I don't care about the consequences. If there is the smallest chance to find him... save him...." He gulped. "Take me there, or I swear there will be one less dragon amongst the worlds."

They stood close, like lovers. S'chn Tg'ai could have kissed him had he wanted to, or head-butted him into unconsciousness, for that matter. Instead, he embraced the fae, wrapped his long arms around him and pulled him even closer. Aleksei thought his spine would break under the pressure as the dragon tightened his grip, breathing hotly on his neck.

"As you wish," S'chn Tg'ai whispered. "I will take you to your lover's side so you can watch him die. But not without witnesses. Others need to be present to see for themselves what the banshee is capable of and why we forbade portals to be opened into her world. There will be witnesses so no rumors will spread afterwards about what happened and what did not."

THE sky above the banshee's cave was a blurring whirlwind of pale yellow, white, and gray. A storm was brewing, mere minutes distant, and it had already washed away the various shades of blue usually seen in a winter sky. Pale beams of sunlight beat down to the ground, not strong enough to melt the snow or chase away the cold.

Sweet, tempting chill, laden with triumph, the banshee thought, embracing her child, her weapon. *I won. He is mine.*

Gabriel knelt before her, his head bent, his long hair brushing the frozen ground. He did not shiver, as if he no longer minded the cold.

The banshee knew better. He still felt cold, but his body had forgotten how to express its discomfort, just as it had forgotten how to run. Not even the wolf inside him could interfere with her wishes anymore.

Forgotten; all gone. He knew nothing but his need to serve her. Touching him had convinced him, and now he believed it. Maybe the dragon part in him still fought her, but as he was of her blood as well, it stood no chance.

Now, the banshee thought, and then screamed it out loud, the first word that had left her mouth in centuries.

"Now!"

Distantly, she felt Gabriel's curiosity at her announcement and brushed a claw across his head. "I have waited for so long," she croaked, somewhat amused at her urge to speak, to use her voice rather than her mind for talking. "Now my waiting is at an end. You have come to me, as ordered. You—"

A portal opened, interrupting her speech and shocking her to the core. No one was allowed up here, so close to her home, no one but her child. He alone could walk through the barriers she'd set.

The portal's golden gleam conquered the sun's beams, only to be overshadowed by black and terror.

A dragon. Here. Now, of all times!

"No," the banshee whispered.

More portals opened, three in all, right behind her barrier. Through each, someone stepped—or rather fell—into the banshee's world.

A centaur. A fae. A tree nymph.

And the dragon, that cursed dragon, tall and black and disguised as a human, with human arms and legs, a human head, and without wings or claws. Only his skin was proof of what he was, together with the scales and the red of his eyes.

He could see right into her soul with those eyes. He would know of her plan; he would know she had called others, although forbidden, and that they had followed. He would kill her for ignoring the dragons' law.

Fear threatened to paralyze her. Fear rushed through her veins, numbing her mind.

But then she felt the knife, Gabriel's knife, heavy in her hand. She had no need to fear. The barrier between her and the dragon would hold until she was done.

Smoothly, the banshee touched Gabriel's throat with the sharp knife, coming dangerously close to the main artery. One flick, and he would bleed; in mere minutes, he would be dead.

But it was too early. He had to open a portal first, and not just any portal. He had to open the portal to the dragon world.

Carefully, the dragon stretched out his arm, touched the barrier, and nodded in recognition and acceptance of the banshee's powers. "Let go of him," he ordered, and only then did the banshee see yet another fae with him, struggling against the grip the dragon had on him.

The banshee winced. She remembered only too well how unbreakable a dragon's grip could be. She'd been chased and caught by a dragon for no reason other than her very existence. They'd trapped her and her kind in this world.

Hate flared up inside her, and she spat on the ground, hissing through her teeth. "Mine," she bit out, and spat again. "You cannot save him."

The fae woman, tall and dark-haired, spoke up. "Why are we here?" she demanded to know. To the banshee's irritation, she addressed the dragon rather than her. "You forbade the use of the portals, and yet one opened right in front of me, pulling me through to this place. An explanation would be welcome." Belatedly, a slight bow of her head took the edge off her words; a moment later, she lowered her eyes, avoiding looking at the dragon directly.

Nervously, the centaur flicked his tail. "I can only agree with you, Lia of the fae council. Who is this?" he asked, glancing at dragon as well as the banshee, "and why are we here?"

The tree nymph didn't say a word.

Bitterly, the banshee watched as the dragon turned to them, as if he were in charge, as if it weren't she who pulled the strings. Her grip around the knife's handle tightened.

"You, Lia, are here as a representative of the fae council," the dragon said. "Watch, and report back to your people what happens here today."

Pursing her lips, Lia nodded. "Why's Kyril here?" she asked. "And who's the tree nymph?"

"They are here as witnesses too. I do not know them, but in one way or another, they are important to Gabe. I learned of them when I tasted his memories. I decided there should be people who care for him to witness his death."

The fae in the dragon's grip redoubled his efforts to break free. Gabriel's lover. The banshee'd only ever seen him through her mirror of ice, but it was undoubtedly him.

She nearly chuckled. She had an audience. They hoped to save her child! They truly thought there was a way for him to survive.

How ridiculous.

The dragon raised his arms, roared, and even the banshee cowered. Black, garment-covered arms turned into wings, nails into claws. The human face melted away and was replaced by a huge reptilian head with fierce fangs longer than the height of a man.

The banshee raised the knife, ready to cut out Gabriel's heart should the dragon try to break through her barrier.

Upon changing, the dragon let go of the fae, who'd fallen to his knees and was about to throw himself against the barrier. He couldn't see it, only feel it; it would still break his skull should he try too hard.

"No!" the fae screamed. "No! He cannot die. You mustn't let him die, *I* will not let him die!"

The dragon's claw closed around him just as he was about to break into a run. The fae fought. To no avail.

"I will not just stand here and watch!" Aleksei's voice broke.

To the banshee, it was a wonderful sound, worth another little bit of delay. She hadn't had so much fun, and attention, in all her life.

"He is gone already." The dragon's voice was soft. "So close to the banshee, he has forgotten who he once was. His name; his origin. What brought him here and who he was before he arrived. You. The love he had for you. If I could, I would save him. But I cannot. Let him die."

No emotion showed in his words. The banshee flinched in disgust at his lack of interest. Clearly, her child meant nothing to the dragon, no matter he was a child of the dragons as well.

But the fae still fought, watched in silence by the three witnesses until the fae woman spoke up. "Compose yourself, Aleksei," she hissed. "You're bringing shame on our family by insisting on trying to save your lover even though the great dragon says it is useless."

Aleksei turned to her, madness in his eyes. He might have shouted at her, insulted her, but the dragon beat his wings, once more demanding silence. "Gabriel is dragon. Blood of my blood, kin of my kin. Caring for him is nothing to be ashamed of, nor is loving him or trying to save him."

Another beat of his wings. Lia paled and fell to her knees.

Without effort, the dragon kept his balance although he had only one leg to stand on; the other kept Aleksei under control, preventing him from running right into the banshee's barrier. His great wings overshadowed the plateau, stirring up the snow so it whirled up like dust, mingling with the clouds above. A flash crisscrossed the sky, closely followed by deafening thunder.

And the banshee laughed for the first time in her long, lonely life. Maybe the dragon did care, after all. In that case, it might not be so bad that he was here to witness Gabriel's end.

"Your blood, dragon, yes. And mine," she said aloud, so everyone could hear it. "Shared in one fragile human. Long planned and finally accomplished." Talking was easier than she'd thought it would be. She had everyone's attention, and they all listened.

"What for?" the dragon asked.

The banshee let the knife touch soft skin, drawing a single drop of blood. "For this," she hissed. "To kill him. Had his useless grandmother not hidden him from my eyes as a child, this would have happened years ago." The banshee exposed Gabriel's neck by yanking him off his knees by his hair. "This rune"—she pecked her claw to the tiny spot on the back of Gabriel's neck, piercing the skin as she did so. He hung in her arms like a rag doll—"hid him from my eyes. Made it impossible to see him, to follow him, to direct his steps. I thought I had lost him. Then he stepped through a portal, and I found him. I watched him. And finally, I learned his name so I could call him."

A glance at the sky showed a whirlwind of clouds; it would rain soon. The banshee focused on her child. His eyes were half-closed, his mouth hung open, and he was so pale one might think him drained of blood. He was not unconscious, but quite close to it, unable to talk or to fight and definitely unable to think.

She lowered her head, breathed in his scent, and wished she'd eaten enough to throw up. He stank! He stank of humanity and maleness. He stank of life, and he stank of dragon even stronger than he stank of wolf.

She hated him.

Up until this moment, she would have sworn he meant at least a little bit to her. Hadn't he been her sole reason for living, even more so than the egg sleeping back in her cave? He was her child, her creation. She had watched him for more than three years now, and before that had witnessed his birth and his first few years in his grandmother's care. She had believed he meant more to her than her own life.

She had been wrong. Hate was what drove her. Hate for him and what he represented. She wanted revenge on the dragons.

I wish I could kill him right now, the banshee thought, tightening her grip to the point where she could have broken his neck, just like that. Only she had waited so long for this moment. She had planned so carefully and been so patient. She wouldn't throw it all away because of a bit of hate.

"And why?" she mused, kicking Gabriel to the ground, where he lay motionless, staring at the snow in front of his eyes. "It is so obvious. Can you see why, dragon?"

She bent to whisper into her child's ear. For a long moment, he just continued to stare at the snow; then he moved, came slowly to his feet, and stood before her like a living shield.

"I cannot wield runes. You took this away from my kind because you detest us. But he can, and he will." Her claw curved around Gabriel's neck, keeping him upright.

The dragon beat his wings. "He will open a portal." It was not a question, and the dragon's voice held no surprise. "Your kind was worse than the plague, spreading like mold, cruel and deadly to everything and everyone you touched. You don't deserve to know about runes; all you deserve is to die here, old and alone."

"But I am not alone," the banshee hissed back. "You are here, dragon. Your witnesses are here; my child is here. *Our* child." She cackled, an awful sound above the rolling thunder. "And you will stay here and die here, with me, because once my child has opened the portal to your world, I will slay him and push him into the light. His death, the death of a dragon, will close the portals forever. All of them, to all worlds. You'll be trapped, dragon, just like me, and because this is a cold world, you will freeze to death."

"No." Nothing but a whisper from the dragon, but an outraged cry from Lia.

"Yes." The banshee stood up a bit straighter, although standing for so long hurt her more than she cared to admit. "For all the years I was doomed to just *watch*. For my family, dying one by one, leaving me behind. For the hate I have for you, dragon. I watched your kind visit the human world. It is all I can do, watch through a puddle of molten ice what others do. I saw the disease spread, and my heart sang with joy. I watched dragons couple with humans, and I watched their offspring go crazy or cruel or both. It was not enough. Now all you can do is watch—and witness. And cry."

The last word she said tenderly, madness flaring up on her face. Her grip, strong on Gabriel's neck, loosened just a bit, not enough for him to get away from her. "Open a portal," she whispered into his ear, and he looked up at her, wide-eyed like a child.

"A portal," he repeated dreamily.

"Yes. It is important. Open a portal to the dragon world. Your world. The rune is in your heart. It is warm there, and safe."

"Safe." He just repeated her last word, clearly without understanding a thing the banshee was saying.

"Gabriel!" The shout was louder than the approaching thunder, louder even than the dragon's outraged roar. "Gabe! Beloved! Do not listen to her!" Once more, the fae tried to free himself from the dragon's grip—in vain.

"Her," Gabriel repeated, and the banshee patted his head.

"Draw the rune," she hissed, blocking out the noise around her as well as the wind that carried with it the sweet smell of destruction.

It would rain soon. The storm loomed above, hot and demanding, too hasty for ice and snow. It would rain; her ice would melt and her cave would flood.

Her egg was in there. The rain would drown it.

If she released Gabriel, she could save it.

No. The egg was of no importance. Her revenge was the only thing that mattered.

Open the portal! the banshee said right into Gabriel's mind, pressing the knife to his throat, demanding his obedience once more. What if he refused to do as he was told? What if he was stronger than she thought, if the dragon blood was superior, what if—

But there—he moved his fingers. Golden lines appeared in front of them, forming a rune.

A Portal rune.

"Gabe!"

Her child looked up, right into his lover's eyes.

Nothing. No recognition, no regret. The grip she had on his mind was perfect.

Briefly, he looked at the others, lingering for a moment on the tree nymph. Then he shrugged his shoulders and drew the last line.

The rune was complete. Silently, the portal opened, bathed in golden light, promising a new life, adventures, a whole world of possibilities. The female fae as well as the centaur tried to break through the barrier but failed.

The dragon just watched while the male fae sank to his knees, crying.

"Now," the banshee whispered, and dragged her child toward the portal.

Flashes lit up the darkened sky; thunder made it impossible to hear anything now, no matter how loud it was screamed.

Unspectacularly, the first drops of rain hit the frozen ground.

CHAPTER TWENTY-ONE

GLEAMING silver caught his eyes. Powerful silver, bright like the moon. Sharp, by the looks of it, and less strange than, say, his own hands and feet.

Who am I? The question formed in his mind but made no sense. *Do I have a name? A purpose?*

The grip on his neck was unpleasant. He wished the pain were gone. Without pain, everything would be well.

Sunlight, pale and mysterious, was sucking up the color of the day. The people standing in the distance, watching him, appeared like mere shadows. One was a female, tall and angry, her short dark hair a halo around her angled face, a spiky crown for a dangerous queen.

He smiled. Then he thought, *Queen? What's a queen?*

One man, caught in the claw of a dragon. Also tall, also dark-haired, and very upset about something. He was the one doing most of the shouting. But the dragon didn't let go of him no matter how hard he fought.

The man meant nothing to him. He was just a man and hopefully would stop shouting soon. It hurt his ears.

The creature held him tight. She had called him. Obeying her was his sole purpose, his only yearning. Whatever she had in mind for him would be his ultimate pleasure to fulfill. When she spoke, he felt his body hum with her words. Occasionally, she became angry, and then her grip tightened. It did not matter. He was hers. If she wanted to hurt him, it was her right to do so.

Again, his gaze fell on the man in the dragon's grip. Had the man seemed familiar, if only for a brief second? But looking at him was painful, so he stopped doing it.

There was something the creature wanted him to do. If only she would tell him what it was so he could do it and be done with her. She didn't smell good. But she was powerful. Powerful was good. She would protect him should the dragon dare to attack.

Dragon.

The word caused a flame of pain to shoot up in his head. Tears ran down his face; he didn't notice them. But he moved closer to the creature, safe in her embrace. She would not allow the beast to get to him.

Only, only, only… something worried him.

Important.

Just a word, echoing in his empty mind and gone before he could think about it.

Suddenly, he felt the cold creep upward through his naked feet.

He looked at the man, the silent one. Something… the silent man… and the silver knife….

He frowned. Maybe the creature felt his confusion, but if she did, it didn't bother her.

The silent man stood a few steps away from the others, staring at him intently. He was younger than the others, and he wore different clothes. If one could call leaves and twigs and a bit of cloth around the loins "clothes."

Loins. Hmmm. Why did this feel uncomfortable?

There was something behind that cloth that bothered him.

Open the portal.

It took him a moment to remember what a portal was. His fingers obeyed the order and were already moving while his mind was still pondering.

And his feet were ice blocks.

A portal. Right. Golden light glowed, and he thought, *Sure, why not?* This place was too cold anyway. His toes were numb; his teeth were chattering.

Death was his destiny, wasn't it?

But... the silent man. He held a secret he needed to unravel before he died.

A tree nymph.

He didn't know the man's name, he was sure of it. Not that he had forgotten it; he had never known it.

Forgot to ask him, he thought. *I kissed him and nearly fucked him and couldn't bother to ask for his name.*

What sort of man didn't ask the name of his bed partner?

A bastard, that sort of man.

Golden light distracted him from his thoughts. It was awfully easy, it seemed, to distract him.

Damn, but the creature stank!

I kissed him, he thought.

The sudden noise of thunder and lightning made him jump. The last line necessary to complete the rune turned out a bit wobbly; the golden light became a little less golden, just a tad, not enough to be noticed.

The creature held him tight, her claw on his neck, in her other the silver knife.

My knife, he thought. *Not hers. Mine. It's silver. Like the moon.*

Deep inside him, the wolf growled his response.

She wants to kill me.

The small hairs on his back rose. Gone was the feeling of safety. Gone was the reassuring knowledge that nothing would happen to him as long as he stayed close to the creature behind him.

My knife! She wants to kill me with my own fucking knife!

The portal opened, and it was damaged. He could taste the flaw in its pattern, feel the discord down to his bones. Surely the banshee could too?

The tree nymph smiled at him over the distance. The man in the dragon's grip sank to his knees, crying.

I need to end this.

Slowly, he turned to the creature and remembered what she was. A banshee, a death fairy. He'd dreamed of her for weeks and months; he'd known he'd be dying in her grip for a long time now. Looking at her face, it was hard not to flinch at the sight of her empty eye sockets.

She lifted the claw that held his knife, standing on the portal's threshold. He could feel its pull, and he could feel its wrongness. If he stepped into it, the portal would rip him apart. That last line he'd drawn was too crooked.

And the banshee didn't know.

Carefully, like a drunken man trying to accomplish a familiar task, he reached out and placed his icy palms on her stone-like cheeks. The surprise showing on her face was comical, as if no one had ever touched her, as if she'd been alone all her life.

"Have you ever stepped through a portal?" he whispered.

Puzzlement at the question was his only answer.

"Then you should now."

He took a step back and pulled her along with him, stumbling awkwardly into the waiting gleam with the banshee's face in his grip just as she brought down the knife, aiming at his throat.

The portal embraced him, the discord sharply cutting into what was left of his mind. A scream followed by sudden silence. A gush of blood splattering over him.

The wrong kind of light pierced his eyes. And the absence of pain in his head and neck was too good to be true.

The portal would rip him apart soon. The light tore at his soul, hacking him to pieces.

Where was the banshee?

She'd never gone through a portal before—he'd asked her just a moment ago. No one could go through a portal unprotected.

Only him. Because he was dragon. Just without scales and wings.

He laughed.

Headache. Again. It increased with every breath he took.

I'm dragon, Gabriel thought. *Didn't someone tell me we are the masters of the portals and that they cannot harm us?*

Like a feather, he floated through the light, and like small, nagging birds, the portal's power tugged at what was left of his consciousness. Each time, he felt a jolt of energy rush through him, searing off a bit of himself. He wouldn't be able to stand this much longer. Either he needed to get out of here soon or....

There was no "or." He didn't know the way out, so he would die.

Someone was waiting for him, only he didn't know who. Someone was grieving. A little longer, and he would surely remember his name. It was on the tip of his tongue.

Gradually, Gabriel lost the will to escape, only hoping it wouldn't hurt when the light consumed him completely. He kept his eyes firmly shut. It was all he could do. Maybe if he waited long enough, the light would cease?

Stop fighting! It's no use, and anyway, the dragon can find you again, just like you found the girl.

Good advice. Relieved, he finally gave up fighting. He opened his eyes wide and allowed the light to shine into his head and burn his mind to ashes.

He didn't know it, but the moment the light hit his brain, his body went limp, and the man who had once been Gabriel Jordan was gone.

BLOOD poured out of the portal, hit the ground, and created a steaming, ugly puddle. Raindrops hit it; eventually, it would either be washed away or freeze, depending on how long the thunderstorm lasted.

Dumbstruck, Aleksei just stared at it. He didn't move. Tears streamed down his face.

Gently, the dragon opened his claws, giving the fae a bit more leeway but preventing him from falling face-first onto the ground.

He needn't have worried. Kneeling, Aleksei was barely able to continue breathing, let alone do anything else.

Dragons couldn't cry. But Gabriel's death added to the grief S'chn Tg'ai already felt. His wings became heavy; his mood, black and bitter for a long time now, darkened even more. "He was dragon." Every word boomed across the plateau. "Blood of my blood. Kin to me and every other dragon still living. His death—his death is...."

He couldn't continue. He wished he could cry his heart out, just like the fae at his feet.

Lia, Kyril, and the still-unnamed tree nymph stood motionless, disbelieving, shocked.

"This means it is over? We are trapped here, forever, with no way to get home ever again?" Of course it was Lia who asked.

S'chn Tg'ai didn't bother to answer her. He stared at the steaming puddle of blood, at the portal's golden glow, and wished with all his heart he could have killed the banshee before she had killed Gabe. But her barrier had been too strong even for him.

"Let me go over there," Aleksei said hoarsely, and only then did S'chn Tg'ai notice the barrier was gone. Nothing but wind and rain whirled around them. A faint rotten smell from where the banshee had stood only moments ago wafted toward them.

The smell hadn't been there until now, the barrier having blocked it just like everything else except for sound and light.

S'chn Tg'ai didn't hold him back when Aleksei walked toward the portal. When he reached it, when he reached the pool of blood, he just stood, his arms wrapped around his body, shaking and crying.

One small, short beat of his wings brought S'chn Tg'ai next to the fae.

"Why's the portal still open?" Aleksei asked, his voice flat and lifeless.

Now that was a good question, and one the dragon hadn't yet considered. Actually, he hadn't even noticed. The blood had commanded all his attention, that and the immense feeling of loss and grief that flooded him. Now, he looked at the portal. Now, his attention shifted.

With his tongue, he touched the gleam, tasted it, and shuddered in disgust: the portal was damaged.

Aleksei took a step. "And why is the portal still open if the shedding of dragon blood is supposed to destroy them for good?"

S'chn Tg'ai frowned.

The portal was damaged. It was so very obvious to him that he couldn't understand how the fae could stand so close to it without cringing. Not only did it taste awful, but the light was too harsh as well, and….

S'chn Tg'ai embraced the portal as only dragons can do, wrapped his wings around the gleam, closed his eyes, and *listened.*

A heartbeat, feeble and small. Irregular. Desperate and lost.

Still—a heartbeat.

He wasn't aware of Aleksei touching his side, and he didn't hear the questions the others were asking, demanding answers, demanding rescue or at least some hope, demanding everything he couldn't give right now. He was aware only of the portal and the one caught inside, the one he had come to find, the one he had wanted to take with him.

"Gabe," he said, or he thought he just said it, although in reality he roared out the name. It echoed off the mountains. It made the thunder sound small and unimportant.

Portals had their own minds, and their powers, nearly as old as the dragons, were tricky and unpredictable. S'chn Tg'ai knew that Gabriel's body was unharmed; he also knew his mind was gone. Although it wasn't his blood on the ground, his soul had bled out of him.

He knew all of this. Grief gripped him, destroyed the last glimpse of hope in his heart, and made him forget that he could try to carefully gather the bits and pieces of Gabriel's soul.

With a roar, S'chn Tg'ai destroyed the portal. The light exploded, and Aleksei jumped back as a body dropped to the ground, limp and white as snow. Bloody bits of the dead banshee landed next to Gabriel in the pool of blood, a few bones, a bit of skin, this and that and things one wouldn't like to look at too closely.

Distantly, the dragon heard retching.

Like an afterthought, the silver knife dropped to the ground out of nowhere, as if the portal couldn't cope with its presence and spat it out rather than trying to devour it, just like it had spat out the man. The metal clinked when it landed half on the stony ground and half in the puddle of blood.

Raindrops hit Gabriel's body, soaking his clothes and his hair and washing the banshee's blood off his face. When he opened his eyes, they were empty, bereft of emotion, knowledge, understanding. Bereft of the soul that had once lived inside the body.

"Gabe?"

Hesitantly, Aleksei reached out to touch the face of the man on the ground, but Gabriel turned his head away, then propped himself up on his elbows and tried to crawl away.

"Beloved, you—"

"He is dead." The dragon said it harshly, and he wasn't surprised when the fae paid no attention at all.

"All is well. You're alive, you—"

"He is *dead*, Aleksei. The man you knew is gone. His mind is empty, only his body remains."

"He does not look dead to me." Lia, always curious and always trying to get the upper hand in any given situation, joined them. Swiftly, as if she'd never been afraid, never feared the banshee, she stepped next to her brother and put her hand on his shoulder. "Actually, he looks pretty well given all the blood on the ground. I take it the banshee didn't manage to stab him?" With the tip of her toe, she touched the knife, carefully avoiding soiling her shoes.

Aleksei snatched it up and cradled it against his chest, because it was clear he couldn't cradle the man on the ground. The man on the ground just stared at him without recognition, stared at the dragon, lifted his face into the rain, and screamed.

S'chn Tg'ai lifted him up before Aleksei could get to him. The fae's touch would have brought only terror, whereas his wings granted protection as well as safety. Gabriel's mind was shattered; his blood, though, still reacted to his. They were both dragon. And now, with Gabriel's mind wiped clean as a slate by the portal's powers, S'chn Tg'ai would be able to write a new story upon his soul, create the mate he had been looking for. He needn't be lonely ever again.

You're cruel.

The thought bore no surprise. Of course he was cruel. He was taking away another man's love, and that this love did not exist any longer didn't really matter.

When Aleksei stabbed the knife into his leg, the dragon didn't even flinch. It was a good knife, no use denying it, but it couldn't really do much harm to his dragon skin.

"He's bound to me," the fae said flatly.

"No. The runes on his skin are gone, erased when his soul was lost in the portal. Like you said, he does not belong to anyone. Not anymore." S'chn Tg'ai turned, ready to leave.

Aleksei held him back. "He is not yours, either."

"But I will take him with me nevertheless. I need a mate. I cannot stand being lonely any longer. I would not have stolen him from you had he survived this, but he has not. Not the part that made him Gabe. That part is dead."

Lia dragged her brother back a few steps. "This is all very interesting, but I would still like to know what will happen now," she said. "What about the portals? Are we trapped here or not?"

The dragon was usually a patient creature, but right now, he wished he could crush the woman with a well-placed step of his foot. He might even have done it had he not felt some mercy for the fae. The loss of his sister along with his lover would surely be too much for him.

"You are free to go, all of you," the dragon said, cherishing the weight in his arms. Gabe didn't struggle against his grip. That was good.

You could have saved him. You could have gone after him and gotten him out whole.

The dragon discarded the thought as unimportant. Maybe he could have, but he hadn't. Bad luck for everyone but him.

He opened a portal. It was perfect. Lia gave a cry of relief at the sight.

Another stab from Gabriel's knife, deeper this time. If Aleksei continued like this, he would have to do something about it.

A low growl emerged from Aleksei's throat, but before he could attack again—and he might have done enough harm this time to actually injure the dragon on a more permanent and painful basis—Lia reacted. She shared a gaze with the centaur, and they caught Aleksei and held him.

"You better go now," Lia shouted as more thunder rumbled over the plateau.

Kyril knocked Aleksei out and let him slip to the ground. Rain poured down, melting the ice just as the banshee had predicted. Behind them, the banshee's cave collapsed. Ice and snow blocked the entrance.

The dragon turned, his burden in his arm, eager to get home.

"One more question," Lia called after him. As she knelt next to her brother, the fae woman's face grew hard and calculating. "Aleksei will want to know what's happened to Gabriel once he wakes up. So tell me, or better promise me, if he'll be gone for good."

In her words rang something like a plea. It changed the dragon's mind profoundly.

I'm not a cruel creature. I do not steal love. I could have saved him had I not been so slow in thinking and so greedy in my needs.

On Aleksei's wrist, he saw the bracelet he'd noticed much earlier, when they had been in the fae's home, the bracelet Gabriel had given him.

Even if the fae had been conscious, he couldn't have stopped the dragon from snatching the bracelet from his wrist. S'chn Tg'ai's claw sliced open his flesh as the bracelet's catch opened under the pressure; smeared with Aleksei's blood, it then vanished in the dragon's grip. It was a tiny thing, but it was important.

"Take him home," the dragon said. "When he wakes, tell him I will bring back his love."

"Shit," Lia said forcefully.

CHAPTER TWENTY-TWO

THE air smelled of snow; winter would be early this year. Last year, the dragon hadn't bothered to warm the air, and he'd shivered with cold and nearly frozen to death. It was not easy to kill a dragon, but age, nature, or accidents sometimes did it.

This winter, hopefully, he wouldn't feel the urge to die. This winter, if everything went right, he would have a reason to live.

His wings beat the air. In the distance, he could see his nest, which was good, as Gabe, clinging to one of his claws, became restless and tried to escape. Of course it would mean falling hundreds of feet and shattering to pieces once he hit the ground, but as he had less brain than the average daisy right now, he didn't know that.

"Easy," the dragon said to himself as well as to his burden. "Not much longer, I promise."

Soothing words, meant to calm Gabe. They soothed him as well.

Until Lia had spoken, his plan had been easy. Take Gabe back home. Fill his empty mind with new experiences. Teach him how to turn into a dragon. Surely Gabe would have adapted to his new life quickly; surely he wouldn't have mourned the loss of his former life simply because he wouldn't have known he'd had a former life. Right now, he was like an empty vessel. Right now, it was possible to form him into whatever S'chn Tg'ai wanted.

Damn Lia and her carelessly spoken words. Damn her and her dislike of her brother's lover. She wanted Aleksei back in the fae world so badly she was willing to sacrifice his happiness.

Impossible. There was nothing more precious than love. Gabe did not belong to him, and that was why he would return his memories to him rather than create new ones, fill him with himself rather than a lonely dragon's hopes and longings.

It would work. It had to.

Crows had occupied his nest in his absence. When they saw his huge shadow blocking out the sun, the flock flew upward, fleeing in every direction and leaving behind feathers, bird droppings, and the fleeting memory of food and sleep.

Growling, S'chn Tg'ai reclaimed his home and used runes to clean it and warm it. Growling, he checked for other intruders and found none. Only he and Gabriel were here, the latter cowering in a corner and looking at him with wide, confused eyes.

"Don't be scared," the dragon said, and changed. It was an almost natural thing to do, with no pondering beforehand, no doubts, and a substantial lack of fear. He knew what he wanted and how to do it, and thinking about it wouldn't have changed his mind at all.

The first difference in his new human body was that he was less bony. This one had several distinct curves: at its hips, around the chest area, and where his new bottom was.

Definitely not bony.

Strange.

His legs were longer, and so was his hair. It reached down his back, tickled his annoyingly thin, tender skin, and made him sneeze when a lock brushed his nose.

A smaller, less crooked nose than the one he'd had as a male.

Curiously, the dragon touched his face, examined high, fragile cheekbones, almond-shaped eyes, and full lips.

Gabe, still sitting in a corner, was staring, mouth open.

S'chn Tg'ai had never turned into a female before. It was an interesting experience. Females seemed to move differently. Their center of gravity was where he hadn't expected it to be, and S'chn Tg'ai managed to fall flat onto his nose when he took the first step. The uneven ground of his nest was probably a reason as well, but the result was the same.

Rolling onto his back, S'chn Tg'ai looked at the deep blue sky, glad it wasn't raining here. Rain would have made seeing his plan through more complicated and less enjoyable.

A face swam into focus. Long red hair brushed the dragon's face, and a hand touched his cheek. Gabe's panic had subsided, and curiosity was getting the better of him. He'd crawled out of his corner and now seated himself next to the dragon.

His stare was intent.

S'chn Tg'ai felt a blush creep into his cheeks. Dragons had a completely different concept of mating in general. Dragons didn't touch, not like humans touched each other. They did not caress, and they didn't kiss. Dragons mated in flight, not in their nests, and when mating, there was no need for delicacy, tenderness, or chitchat. Mating meant wildness, fierceness, and dominance. Mating meant fighting and losing. Mating meant....

It meant he couldn't do anything he was used to here. It meant he had to suppress his instinct so he wouldn't change back and take flight. It meant he had to grit his teeth and see this through, although he didn't really want to and was pretty sure it would feel gross.

Just to make sure at least Gabe would enjoy it, he wove a few runes into the air above them and watched them circle the man's hair and body and sink into his mind.

A slow grin appeared on Gabriel's face, and he edged a bit closer.

Humans.

How could they become aroused without air beneath them and wind playing in their wings? How was it possible they enjoyed this close physical contact without using their teeth and claws? How could they become aroused at all with so many clothes on?

Gabriel seemed to think of that as well, for he suddenly got up and undid the buttons of his shirt with clumsy fingers.

The dragon watched. Soon, he stared, transfixed, wondering how humans managed to have intercourse at all without bursting into laughter, given how silly they looked naked.

He couldn't help himself. He had to touch Gabe's soft, pale skin, let his fingers run through the rough strands of his hair, and experience firsthand what touch could do to a man.

Gabe's hands found S'chn Tg'ai's hips, grabbing him and pulling him closer. He'd closed his eyes, inhaling deeply, as if trying to figure out what to do by using his nose rather than his sense of vision, which was fine for the dragon, because he was sure a hint of resistance was written all over his new, soft body.

Female, he thought. *How mad am I, really?*

S'chn Tg'ai shed his worries as well as the haunting memories and took Gabriel's face between his hands, looking at him intently. He would give back what he'd forgotten to save. He would not steal.

S'chn Tg'ai had never even thought of being with anyone else but his mate. She had been all he needed and all he wanted. He definitely had never thought of being with another male. Some dragons took this path, but he hadn't been one of them.

Gabe's human body was male just as his own was female. The problem was that his mind wasn't female. He did not know what to do or how to act, what to say if words were the custom, how to lead on to the next step. Should he try to kiss Gabe again, as he had done back at his house? But that kiss had been for a purpose, for sharing memories.

A gleam caught his eye; the bracelet he'd taken from Aleksei. Quickly, S'chn Tg'ai pushed it underneath some twigs. Then he nearly panicked upon realizing things were happening faster than he'd anticipated, but by then, it was already too late to stop and reconsider: Gabe pressed him onto a soft patch of feathers mixed with grass, forced his legs apart with an eager knee, and was inside him with a hard, determined push of his hips.

The dragon gasped and forced himself not to fight. This was painful and burning. It was, as expected, gross.

Gabriel's face was covered with sweat, his eyes closed. The dragon's rune made him want this, and he thrust fast, not caring about anything but his own need, and he held the dragon down with a surprisingly strong grip.

"Gently," S'chn Tg'ai bit out, his first words in this new body. "Look at me."

Their bodies joined but not yet their minds, man and dragon looked at each other, one confused and out of breath, one solemn and knowing.

Desperately, S'chn Tg'ai tried to find a more comfortable position. "Easy," he croaked. But Gabriel had no mind for gently or easy; he thrust a few more times, his hands digging into S'chn Tg'ai's upper arms. Then he shuddered, spilling his seed and collapsing on top of the dragon. His face was gray and haggard; his muscles trembled as if he'd just run a marathon.

The dragon, deeply relieved at least this part was over, embraced the man lying atop him. He had waited for this and was ready. The barrier that shielded every living being's mind vanished at the height of passion for a brief moment. Not even the dragons knew why this happened, but it was gone, and someone who was capable and willing to do so could access such an open, unguarded mind. S'chn Tg'ai could have shown Gabriel what it was like to fly, how easy and wonderful the life of a dragon could be, how desperately he was looking for a mate. He could have turned him into his puppet at that very moment.

But he didn't. "You're human," he whispered, using the physical link to find his way into Gabe's mind. And when Gabe struggled, he gripped him harder and forced his head up so he could kiss him again. It was how he had taken the memories; it was how he would give them back.

Gabe's breath caught in his throat when the first picture dropped into his empty mind like a pebble in a quiet lake. It stirred the surface, caused waves of connected memories to follow, and then there was a different kind of storm, one inside Gabe's head, silent and unspectacular but by no means any less violent than the most ferocious thunderstorm one could imagine. Myriad memories tumbled down onto him, crushing him with their weight.

It felt like an eternity, but the exchange lasted no longer than a few seconds. Much sooner than the dragon expected, Gabriel's barriers came up again. He slammed his hands against the dragon's chest and pushed, breaking the kiss as well as the contact. Fighting with teeth and fists, he managed to get away from the dragon, crawling away and collapsing in the same corner he'd chosen when they'd first arrived.

Seed trickled down the dragon's legs. Curiously, he touched it, rubbed the sticky substance between his fingertips, smelled it—and decided it wasn't worth further examination. As long as his body did not reject the seed, it could taste and smell as it liked.

"Gabe." The dragon faced the human sitting in the corner of his nest. "Gabe, look at me."

No reaction.

There were only Gabriel's clothes available. S'chn Tg'ai pulled on the jeans and shirt, noticing they didn't fit as smoothly as they would a male body. "I promised Aleksei I would bring you back," he said.

The name caused a reaction. Gabriel jumped up only to fall to his knees again, his legs refusing to carry his body's weight. Clutching his head, he howled like a beaten dog.

"You're in pain," S'chn Tg'ai said calmly. He had expected this, but not quite so soon. "A normal reaction. You brain has to adjust to the quantity of memories I gave back to you. It will take weeks to get used to the feeling. And it will be unpleasant."

"Banshee," Gabriel croaked. "Hurts. Death."

"She tried to kill you. That would be one of my memories, given to you to fill in the gap between the time I took your memories and the point where I gave them back. She was not successful."

"I'm naked."

"Yes."

"You... we...."

"Yes."

"Why?"

Before the dragon could answer, Gabriel howled again, louder this time, and longer. Blood spurted from his nose, and he fell against the dragon, who caught him and held him as he would have held a child. "Shhhhh," he murmured, well aware this voice was softer and much better suited for soothing than his rougher male voice had been. "I promise you an explanation. For now, I need you to relax." He took Gabriel's wrist. "Your head thinks it is too small for all the memories. Your head is wrong."

Fishing for the bracelet he'd taken from the fae, he mended the catch with a rune and closed it around Gabriel's wrist, making sure his nails cut a small wound beforehand. Gabriel didn't even notice. He'd dug his free hand into his hair and was pulling it as if trying to rip his head off. As the bracelet closed around Gabriel's wrist, the fae's blood, which had dried on the silver, came into contact with Gabriel's fresh blood.

The low howl turned into a scream. Runes began to blossom all over Gabriel's body, covering him from head to toe. Always the same rune, sometimes small, here and there big enough to cover the space between shoulder blades or ribcage and hipbone.

Binding runes.

"You're yourself again, Gabriel," the dragon said quietly.

Only Gabriel didn't hear him. The pain becoming too much, he collapsed and hung unconsciously in the dragon's embrace.

"You can be glad Aleksei's sister is a right bitch," the dragon said thoughtfully, cradling Gabriel in his arms and opening yet another portal. "Without her, you'd have wings by now, not remembering your name, your past, or your lover. But you still wouldn't belong to me."

He stepped through the portal into the fae world, a thin smile on his lips. He was truly looking forward to seeing Lia's face when she realized he was actually keeping his promise.

CHIRPING birds woke him up. They were loud and cheerful, and they clearly believed chirping was a good way to pass the time until the next worm turned up. It wasn't even close to sunrise yet. Why did the damn birds chirp in the middle of the night when everyone else was trying to get some sleep? And why did it smell like hay in his bed?

Thinking was becoming more difficult with each passing moment, so Gabriel turned over and drifted off again, not knowing where he was or when he was or, for that matter, why he was able to hear the birds at all. At home, there were no trees nearby for birds to chirp in.

It was still dark when he woke again. Or dark once more? Time seemed to be fleeting, for whatever reason. He couldn't even tell if it was early morning or late at night.

Voices he didn't understand, arguing over this and that. One deep and angry; one lighter, reasoning with cold calculation.

"He's been like this for weeks now. Time to accept he most likely won't come around."

"The dragon said he needs time to heal. This place is the safest place I know, fae healers are the best in all worlds, and he will get all the time he needs."

"He—"

"What would you like me to do? Put him out of his misery like a sickly horse?"

"You could go on with your life! Stop sitting by his bedside. Stop wasting day and night worrying and waiting for him to wake up. Mariam would so like to go for a walk with you. She came round again yesterday. Why not take the opportunity to meet someone else?"

"Shut up, Lia. Just shut up, will you?" The deeper voice sounded beaten and tired. Gabriel's heart went out to the speaker, but before he could even move a finger to indicate he was awake and willing to help, sleep took him into its arms again and carried him away.

Dreams haunted him, dreams of a black woman with fiery eyes and a booming voice. Dreams of a stone-cold creature stabbing at him with a silver knife. Dreams of drowning in blood. Dreams of kisses, and those dreams were the worst, because the kisses tasted all wrong. In his sleep, he fought the one who tried to kiss him; in his dreams, he refused to do as ordered.

The third time he awoke, he was covered in sweat, entangled in a woolen blanket, with his hair plastered to his skull. He smelled as if he hadn't washed in ages, he felt as if someone had beaten him to pulp, and the light shone blindingly bright.

Ow.

Headache. Had there ever been a time his skull didn't feel as if someone were trying to split it in half with an ax? If so, he certainly couldn't remember it.

He tried to sit up only to realize his body was inclined to remain horizontal.

Fine. Be stubborn, then, he thought. *Resting is good. Sleeping is good. But I'm thirsty, and I'm sick of sleeping!*

"—'lo?" he managed to say, not really surprised his voice sounded rusty and weak. "Anyone there?"

There was no answer, but he felt a presence with him in the room. A disdaining presence; someone who was not happy to see him awake.

"Lia?"

"And I really thought you'd have the decency to stay in a coma for the rest of your sorry, little life."

"Good to see you too," Gabriel croaked.

She stood in the shadows next to the door. With her lips pursed and her arms crossed over her chest, she was the picture of arrogant superiority. Some things never changed, no matter what happened.

What *had* happened?

"Where's...."

And he couldn't remember the name. Damn!

Lia noticed his confusion. Stepping out of the shadows, she was barely able to keep the triumphant gleam out of her eyes. "Already forgot him, yes? No surprise, given you arrived here naked. At least to me, it was obvious you'd betrayed my brother the moment the dragon had you to himself. You are like him, after all. It is only natural you crave to be with S'chn Tg'ai rather than a shabby, graying fae."

"He said he'd give me wings." The words escaped from his mouth before he could stop them.

"He looked more like a she, I can tell you that," Lia said primly. "And the dragon wore your clothes. My brother was shocked at the sight."

Gabriel wracked his brain for her brother's name, but couldn't find it in the mess up there for the life of him. He'd remembered Lia's name. Why the hell not her brother's?

"Can't remember much at all," he murmured.

His words forced a laugh out of the fae woman. "I bet you can remember everything," she said coldly. "You mutter in your sleep. You dreamt of a long-legged woman taking you, a woman with black skin and red eyes. A very precise description of the dragon's current human form."

Putting a single finger on his blanket-covered chest, Lia bent over a bit so he could hear everything she had to say. "You broke my brother's heart," she hissed. "Seeing you in the dragon's embrace, hearing you whine for his kisses, was too much for him. It took him a while, but well, eventually he realized I was right. He is not here, human, and if I have a say in it, he won't come back, either. At the moment, he's talking to the fae council. I persuaded them to give him a seat, but of course they will do that only if he swears to come back home. He will live in his own world again. Where he belongs, with people around him who love him, with a devoted wife by his side who will bear his children. Your influence—your nasty, destructive influence—is broken. Better call the dragon. Better tell him to carry you away. Live in the dragon world. Share your bed with S'chn Tg'ai, and keep your hands off my brother."

Gabriel opened his mouth, but no words came out. What would he have said, anyway? That she was lying?

But she wasn't.

Gradually, a few bright, sharp pictures bubbled up in his mind. The encounter he'd had with a nameless tree nymph. His lies. His constant attempts to run away. The loathing he'd felt for his lover and his eagerness to stay away from him. The man he loved wasn't living with his people; he wasn't married; he had no children. Whose influence could be worse?

Lia smiled as if she were reading his mind, saw what he saw, felt what he felt. "I can see you agree with me," she said. Her finger drilled a hole into his chest. "I can see there is some mercy left in you. Call the dragon. Leave, before my brother returns."

"I don't know how!" Tears were running down his face, born out of shame, embarrassment, and the general belief he had destroyed someone else's life. "I can't even move my fingers, never mind open a portal. Lia, I swear, if I could, I'd leave right now, but—"

"Damn." As if she hadn't heard his words, Lia stepped away from the bed. "Not a word," she hissed. "Pretend you're still in a coma."

Gabriel might even have done so, but the moment the tall, dark-haired fae stepped into the room, every coherent thought fled his mind. His heartbeat sped up to a racing gallop, his headache increased from a mere hum to a blazing inferno, and when he saw those ice-blue eyes....

"Aleksei!"

More memories tumbled over him, buried him, crushed his bones and his mind, but it didn't matter, because his lover was next to him, gathering him into his arms and shedding tears of his own into Gabriel's hair.

"Damn, fucking shit," Lia murmured. "I thought you were meeting with Rhys to discuss your future role in the council."

"I did." Aleksei did not turn toward her. Instead, he brushed the hair out of Gabriel's face, took a wet cloth, and trickled some water between his lips.

Bliss.

"And?"

"And we came to the conclusion that my role is unimportant compared to Gabriel's. I might take a seat at the council if it doesn't require living here. Gabriel, once he has fully recovered, definitely will."

Lia looked as if she didn't know whom to strangle first. "He has no role," she finally said through gritted teeth. "He's not fae. He's no one. I thought we agreed on that."

"*You* agreed on that. I didn't. And he's *not* no one, Lia. He's dragon. S'chn Tg'ai wants Gabriel to represent him in his absence, which might very well cover a decade or more."

Lia wasn't a young woman, but she moved fast as lightning now, throwing Aleksei against the wall, which was, as Gabriel noticed only now, made of twigs. "You're lying!" Grabbing the collar of his shirt, she shook him. "The dragon said nothing like that! He dropped him here, having no use for him anymore. He wanted to get rid of him, brother! Why would he want a human to take his place in the council? Why would he want to talk to you and not to me?"

Resolutely, Aleksei freed his collar from his sister's hands and pushed her back at arm's length. "Gabriel means everything to S'chn Tg'ai," he said in a low voice. "Bringing him back cost him a lot. And we did talk, Lia. For hours. Why he didn't tell you of his plans, I don't know. Ask him yourself should you ever see him again. Now, I think you should leave. This is *my* house, sister. You are not welcome any longer."

She paled. "I helped you build it!"

"I did not ask you to." Frowning, he added, "You should know I heard the lies you've been telling my partner. Leave now, or I will throw you off this tree with my own hands."

Lia was out of the treehouse before he could reach her.

With an audible sigh coming straight from the bottom of his heart, Aleksei looked at Gabriel. "I hate quarreling with my sister," he said. "But this time, she went too far. Just forget what she's told you. None of it was true."

Gabriel's throat felt too dry to talk, but he tried anyway. "Not everything," he managed. "Bits were true."

Aleksei raised an eyebrow. "Which parts?"

"The dragon." Disgust crept into his voice. "Carried me. Cradled me. Took... me."

"I know."

"Then I did break your heart! Then you do hate me, and I can't blame you for wanting to stay here and live your life without me and find yourself a wife and kids and... all," Gabriel finished lamely. Emotional outbursts sure were tiring. All of a sudden, he could barely keep his eyes open, and behind his eyes, a thunderstorm was shredding his brain to pieces.

Aleksei put his hand to his face, wiping the tears away. Gabriel couldn't stop him—not that he wanted to—because even moving his head took too much effort.

"You killed the banshee, Gabe. She died the moment you dragged her into the portal. I know," he said, shaking his head when Gabriel tried to say something, "you cannot remember right now. S'chn Tg'ai said this was to be expected. Don't force yourself. Your memory will come back with time. Also, the headache will cease if you don't allow yourself to worry and ponder too much." Taking the wet cloth once more, he trickled more water between Gabriel's lips.

"I remember... a woman."

Aleksci nodded. "The dragon took a female form to heal you, and to conceive. The portal had sucked up your mind. S'chn Tg'ai decided to give back your memories rather than making you fully dragon. Admittedly, I would have preferred a less physical way, but then, as it means I've got you back alive and well, I am not complaining."

The few drops of water had soothed his rough throat, but talking still wasn't easy for Gabriel. "I remember...." He frowned, trying to hunt down the pictures hopping around in his mind. "Touch," he finally came up with. "Heat. Scaly skin. Blood. Fear. And mostly, I remember not wanting to be touched." Once more, he tried to move and failed.

"If it is any help, S'chn Tg'ai told me he used a rune to arouse you."

"Lovely." It came out dryer than he'd intended. As a reward, Aleksei gave him one of his rare smiles.

"I'm glad to see your humor is back," he said. "It's about time. Nearly three weeks have passed since the dragon brought you back."

"Was I really naked?"

Aleksei's grin deepened. "Yes. And he was wearing your clothes. My sister was shocked speechless."

"Don't believe it. When it comes to a filthy mouth, she's as bad as my mom." Ah. Another memory was popping up. "I…. Did I tell you about my mom?"

"No. But I had the pleasure to meet her. A few days ago, when I was checking on the house and the cat, she was sitting on the doorstep with a bat in her hand. Persuading her not to smash in my head took considerable effort."

If only he weren't so tired, surely Aleksei's news would have had a different effect. As it was, Gabriel just managed a "really" while fighting to keep his eyes open.

Aleksei noticed his struggle. "You go to sleep now," he said. "I promise to be here when you wake up."

Something was wrong, something important. If only he could concentrate for another few minutes….

Sleepily, Gabriel noticed Aleksei wasn't wearing his usual clothes but fae fashion consisting of a bright-red tunic, tight, dark, linen trousers, and a belt woven from horsehair. "You look different," he mumbled.

Aleksei's hand was warm on his face. Something was wrong with his hand. Something important.

"It's not only Lia who takes offense when I wear human clothes." Aleksei sounded as if he were miles away. "For the time being, I look like fae. Until we're back home."

"But you won't come home with me." Gabriel was certain of it. "Your bracelet. You're not wearing it. You said… you said…." What had it been Aleksei had said?

"I said I would never take it off willingly."

"Right."

"And I didn't. The dragon took it. It is around your wrist, beloved, supporting your healing process and reminding your body and soul that you are mine. Do you hear me? You are mine, Gabe. No dragon, no sister, no mother can ever take you away from me. Don't you forget it. And now sleep."

A silly grin spread over Gabriel's face. Sleep was so close now he could feel its breath on his neck and, mostly, on his eyelids.

Just one more thing was bothering him. "Why… why female?" he mumbled.

Aleksei kissed him lightly on the lips. Then he said something Gabriel didn't understand because sleep was faster and once more snatched his mind away.

EPILOGUE

IT WAS autumn again, the first sunny day in weeks, and Gabriel had taken the opportunity to go jogging.

A year had passed since the banshee's death, a year filled with new cases, new worries, and many new quarrels with mothers and sisters and councils and the worlds in general. Sally, for example, had flat-out refused to go back home, so her parents had decided that a few months in another world could only broaden their horizons. By now, they'd learned how to make a fire, how to stop the rain from draining onto the floor of their hut, and how to disembowel the prey the centaurs gave them.

Not a single word from S'chn Tg'ai had reached them. The dragon had vanished from the worlds as if he'd never existed, and people might have gone on believing he was only a product of their imaginations had Rhys of the fae council not announced Gabriel was taking the vacant chair due to his heritage. Lia had looked as if she were about to puke right on the spot, and had refused to talk to him or her brother ever since.

Grinning at the memory of the shock written on Lia's face, Gabriel sped up, feeling the soft path under his feet, the wind in his face, and the sweat running down his back. It had taken him a long, hard winter to get back on his feet, an even longer and harder spring to walk more than half a mile without collapsing. Now that his body was back in shape, he enjoyed being outside again, away from cell phones and computers and demanding clients. Even away from home. Running gave him the opportunity to think, to let his mind wander; running was, to him, a very special and personal form of freedom.

Only today he felt he wasn't running fast enough. And his shoes were too tight, no matter these were the running shoes he always wore and which had fit perfectly until a few minutes ago.

He stumbled and would have fallen had he not caught his fall with both hands. On all fours, he gasped for air and wished he could run properly, swift and closer to the ground.

Run like a wolf.

"I wish," he murmured, spitting at the leaves and knowing only too well he couldn't change his form deliberately. He'd tried; it hadn't worked.

His legs trembled when he got up, and his muscles ached when he picked up a slower pace than before. "I wish I could run."

The shoes were definitely too small, so he pulled them off. And it was a warm day, too warm for the shirt and, well, much too warm for the trousers.

Naked, he took one step after the other, slowly at first, but he gained speed quickly. And why use a path when there was a perfectly good forest at hand?

It was only a park, but a huge one; it was late afternoon, and he couldn't see the harm in a simple run, not even when he was stark naked. No one would see him. No one would ever know he'd....

Paws instead of feet. A smaller, slimmer body, perfectly adjusted for uneven ground and densely growing trees. A tail to keep balance and lungs big enough to make him believe he could run forever.

The wolf howled, a deep, rich sound, full of joy. Had he thought he could not change? He'd been wrong. It seemed all he needed was the right motivation. A flock of crows took flight when he thundered past. He didn't move as quietly as a real wolf, but what the hell, he ran!

Eventually, the wolf slowed down to a trot, following his own trail back to where he'd shed his clothes. There was a spring between the rocks. Not much, but enough to quench his thirst. And the leaves on the ground were just perfect for a roll. A moment later, he had all four paws in the air, rubbing his back and seriously trying to get as dirty as possible, when he heard the soft chuckle.

"You're nothing but a big fluffy dog, beloved," Aleksei said, leaning against a tree and watching him. "Taller than the average dog, I give you that. But keen on playing, and keen on toys. I see the mark of your teeth on that branch over there, so don't you deny it."

Gabriel shook, trying to get the leaves out of his fur, but he failed. So he changed back instead without even knowing how he did it. As a human, he tried to scratch a spot behind his ear with his leg, lost balance, and landed in the brook.

"Shit, that's cold!" he exclaimed, and he hurried to get back onto dryer ground. "How long have you been here? And how did you find me?"

Aleksei grinned. "You might not believe it, but a wolf in this part of the park does not go unnoticed. I knew you'd gone running, and I know your usual route. Easy, really." In his hands he held Gabriel's clothes and shoes. "I've got news."

"What news?" About to take his clothes, Gabriel realized he was covered in mud. The occasional leaf stuck to his skin, and twigs were entangled in his hair. "I think I need a bath first."

Aleksei took a step and pulled him into a close embrace. "You definitely need a bath. But I need a kiss first."

"I'm sweaty and dirty!" Gabriel couldn't suppress the goofy grin that spread over his face when Aleksei totally ignored him and kissed him instead. Kissing Aleksei was wonderful. Gabriel's sense of smell was heightened so shortly after the change, but more important was that the kiss was solid proof everything was fine again between them.

There hadn't been much lovemaking lately. At first, Gabriel had been too weak. Once home, he needed to sleep more hours than he was awake, and activities in bed had mostly consisted of cuddling and talking. Their first time after S'chn Tg'ai had given back his memories had happened only a few months back and had been awkward, to put it mildly. Only a good sense of humor had enabled them to survive the experience. The dragon had been present at every moment in both their minds, and after that, they had skipped lovemaking for another few weeks.

Gabriel broke the kiss and grinned. "Let's get home," he suggested. "Dinner and a bath, and then a night in?"

Aleksei grinned back at him. "Home, before you freeze. I cook. You—" Then he stopped in midsentence. "No," he corrected himself. "I suspect that a quiet evening at home is not on the agenda for tonight. I've got a message for you, beloved. It's the reason I came looking for you in the first place."

"Important news?" His shirt had gotten damp, but, well, it couldn't be helped. "Can it wait until after dinner? I'm starving."

"How important the news is, I cannot tell. Here. This arrived shortly after you left home." From a pocket of his coat, he fished out a small stone. A single rune was engraved on it.

Surprised, Gabriel took the stone and placed it onto the palm of his hand. It was about double the size of his thumbnail. It was black. "Do you know this rune?" he asked, but Aleksei shook his head.

"There aren't many runes you can't place." Thoughtfully, Gabriel turned the stone between his fingers, trying to see what he was missing. The meaning of it stared him right in the face, but he still he couldn't solve the riddle. "I think… I think S'chn Tg'ai made this one."

Not really knowing what he was doing—as happened often when he dealt with runes—he traced the lines on the stone.

Together, they watched as it began to glow. Silently, a portal opened, consuming the stone as it spread wide enough to let a man pass through.

"Guess you'll be home late," Aleksei said, and only because Gabriel had been looking for it could he hear the slight tension behind the words.

"Guess so," he replied. "And so will you. I'm not going anywhere near him without you next to me." He held out his hand. "Coming?"

THE air was warm in the dragons' world, which was lucky, as neither Aleksei nor Gabriel was wearing entirely dry clothes.

A huge nest loomed right above the point where they arrived. The sight made Gabriel cringe. He remembered the nest, the sky above him;

he even remembered how the twigs had felt on his bare ass. About a year ago, he'd been up there with a dragon as his only company. "I think I would rather be back home," he whispered, but the moment the words had left his mouth, they heard the sound of spreading wings, and the dragon looked down at them.

About time you arrived.

"About time you learned to use your mouth rather than your nutshell of a brain if you want to talk to us," Gabriel snapped. "Anyway, what d'you want?"

Aleksei's hand on his shoulder tightened, reminding him to keep his temper in check.

"Okay, okay, I'll behave." Gabriel sighed. "It's just I don't like being here."

"I assume he has a reason for calling you. Let him speak, will you?"

Thank you.

Swiftly, the dragon brought down one of his wings, and before either Gabriel or Aleksei could react, he swept them up as if they were sand on a shovel. Safe, though a bit shaken, they landed in the nest.

"I do have a reason." Before their eyes, the dragon changed. It was different from Gabriel's changing, much more practiced, and faster. There were no in-between forms, no half dragon, half man images—one moment, there was the dragon, the next, a naked man standing before them, the same man who'd knocked on Aleksei's door, the same man who'd wandered through their world a year ago searching for Gabriel.

Aleksei raised an eyebrow, shrugged his coat off his shoulders, and handed it over wordlessly.

"Thank you," the dragon said again. "I do need a way to store clothes, it seems." He cleared his throat. "My apologies. It has been a while since I have used my voice. Talking mind to mind comes more naturally to me, and I know you can understand what I say."

"Glad you took on human form." Gabriel felt uneasy. "And really glad you didn't choose the female version."

The dragon's mouth twitched. "It is not necessary to be female anymore. I prefer to be male, and I chose the human form because a dragon's facial expressions are limited. Also, there is the significant difference in height. I wanted to talk to you, not scare or embarrass you."

"How very thoughtful." Gabriel crossed his arms over his chest, signaling his unwillingness to be in the nest at all. Somewhere deep inside, he feared he was rather beginning to like the dragon. There was a link between them he couldn't deny, so he denied it anyway and behaved rudely. "Now then. Is there something you wanted, or did you just fancy a chat?"

"I do not mind the chat, but in fact, I wanted you to be here for the big day. It was a good decision for you to come too, Aleksei. If I am right, you have as much to do with this as he or I."

"I think I have a vague idea what this is all about," Aleksei said, his hand once more on Gabriel's shoulder. "Your efforts were crowned with success?"

It was a disturbing sight to see the dragon grin. His teeth were too sharp despite his human body, his eyes lit up like a bushfire, and all in all, he looked much more dragon now than a few seconds ago. "They were," he said. "Today, she will hatch."

"Eh?" Somehow, Gabriel had lost the meaning of this conversation. "Which efforts? Who'll hatch?"

Aleksei leaned closer. "I did tell you why S'chn Tg'ai chose a female form to give back your memories," he said quietly. "To become pregnant. Don't tell me you forgot!"

"I thought you were kidding me!"

"I wasn't. Apparently, you will soon be the father of a daughter."

After a look into his lover's face, Gabriel realized Aleksei was fighting hard to suppress his amusement.

"But…," Gabriel said, only to see the dragon take a step and reveal a smaller nest inside the nest, not larger than the span of his arms and padded with feathers and fabric.

"Are these… these are my jeans!"

"And your shirt. For her to get used to your fragrance. Young dragons can be fierce upon meeting someone whose smell they don't recognize. I wanted to make sure she wouldn't eat you up."

"She." Suddenly, Gabriel had an urge to sit down. "You mean, that egg there…."

"Is the current home of your daughter, yes." Tenderly, S'chn Tg'ai brushed a black, long-nailed hand over the egg's shell.

"An egg."

The dragon's lip twitched. Next to him, Aleksei had pressed a hand to his mouth. Gabriel had the strong suspicion he would have burst out laughing otherwise.

"I cannot father an egg," Gabriel stated. "I'm human. Partly. And a bit shapeshifter. Okay, and another little bit dragon. Banshee, very deep down. But I do not father *eggs*!"

Intently, S'chn Tg'ai looked at the egg, bent, and pressed an ear to the dark, spotted shell. "I was born male," he said quietly, as if not to scare the young dragon inside. "But because of what I am, I can change my form and my gender. When I brought you here, I chose a female form so I could conceive. When my body did not reject your seed, I turned into dragon form but remained female until I had laid the egg. Easy, really. When you turn into a wolf, it is a similar principle."

Gabriel just shuddered. Changing into a wolf was one thing. Changing into a woman… no, definitely not.

"And what are you laughing at?" he hissed in Aleksei's direction. "This is not funny! Can you imagine a dragon coming to visit us? She'd eat up all your books!"

Aleksei couldn't stop grinning. "I just tried to imagine Lia's face upon hearing the news," he managed. "Not only are you sitting next to her at the fae council. Not only do you know a pureblood dragon who protects you and considers an insult to you an insult to himself. Now you are also a father to a dragon. She'll have a stroke!"

Well, he hadn't thought of that. "And… it's a girl?" he asked, taking a step forward and putting a hand on the egg's shell.

It cracked.

"Damn!" Gabriel exclaimed, snatching his hand back. "Sorry! I didn't mean to break it!"

"You didn't break it; she did. She's hatching," S'chn Tg'ai said. "Come here, both of you. I want her to see you so she knows you're safe and part of her life. And by the way, she won't eat your books. Not if you teach her not to."

Before Gabriel could ask what he meant by "teach her," there was a knock from inside the shell. Dozens of tiny cracks formed, and then there was a frantic fight, making the whole egg rattle. Gabriel could have pulled it onto his lap easily; the egg was no bigger than a very large cat. But he just sat and stared, feeling the sun drying his clothes and his heart speeding up with every new crack that appeared on the shell.

There—the tip of a wing showed, gleaming pale in the sunlight, pushing its way from darkness into the warm autumn day. And a claw, thin and small and sharp, slicing open the shell as if it were made of paper.

Then the shell cracked for good, the pieces raining to the nest's bottom as the little dragon stretched her body. A few bits stuck to her wings, some more to her back, and to Gabriel's surprise, he felt a strong urge to cradle the little monster and soothe it and assure it there would be food soon.

"Fuck," he breathed.

Hello, little one, S'chn Tg'ai said silently.

The little dragon turned to Aleksei. Pale red eyes met ice-blue ones. She hissed, took a wobbly step—and collapsed into his arms.

"Ah." S'chn Tg'ai smiled, not at all concerned when the fae began stroking her. Much to Gabriel's surprise, the little dragon responded with a soft and very catlike purr.

"I thought so," S'chn Tg'ai said, briefly touching Aleksei's shoulder. "Good. Had she not accepted you as family, she would have bitten your hand off. I am very glad she decided otherwise."

Impossible not to touch the tiny dragon. Impossible not to admire the softness of her scales and the pale white of her wings. She was already trying to flap them—at that rate, she'd be flying by the end of the day.

"She's beautiful," Gabriel said in wonder. "Totally, utterly beautiful."

The sound of his voice made the dragon child focus on him. She flapped her wings, and Aleksei supported her by lifting her up and placing her gently on Gabriel's lap. The soft purr increased. Simultaneously, she stretched her neck and touched Gabriel's face with a thin, lizard-like tongue.

Emotions flooded him. The first and largest was hunger, followed by a general joy—at the warmth, his hands on her back, the smell and presence of her dragon father, safety, and fatigue.

She yawned. Glancing at S'chn Tg'ai, the little dragon seemed to grin, then curled up and yawned again. One wing hung over Gabriel's leg; the other one was caught between her body and his—clearly, she didn't know yet how to handle them.

A moment later, she was asleep.

"She needs a name," S'chn Tg'ai said softly. "She is special, Gabriel. Like you, she is not entirely dragon. She—"

"These are fae patterns on her wings." Careful not to wake up the little dragon, Gabriel traced a fingertip over the fragile structure.

On the outer edges of the wing covering Gabriel's thigh, there were faint, barely visible lines. Blue, if one looked closely enough, resembling tiny dancing butterflies.

S'chn Tg'ai didn't have skin patterns. "Anything you would like to tell me?" Gabriel said to Aleksei. "Any secret meetings with this dragon while your lovely sister tried to poison me with her homemade soup? Nips into the dragon world so you two could hook up?"

He didn't mean it, of course—he was only teasing his lover—but by the look on his face, he figured he'd better stop now, for Aleksei was becoming paler by the second.

"How?" the fae asked the dragon. "Tell me how this is possible."

S'chn Tg'ai looked distinctly embarrassed. "I might have lied to you," he finally said. "I told you Gabriel was not bound to you any longer because the runes on his skin had vanished. But the kind of binding he created cannot be undone. Flattened, yes. Forgotten, for a little while, maybe. But not undone. So you were always bound. When I took his seed, you were bound. When I conceived, you were bound. You are part of him, Aleksei. So my daughter—our daughter—is yours as well, and it shows in the patterns on her wings. Once she learns how to take human form, they will show on her face and her body. If you teach her how to look human, that is. If you are willing to play a part in her life."

Gabriel didn't even get a chance to think about it. "Yes," Aleksei said before he could so much as open his mouth. "Of course we want to, and we will."

"Do we?" Gabriel turned to his lover, never taking his hands off his daughter. "Look at her. She's a reptile—no offense, S'chn Tg'ai—and even in human form, she'll never fit in. In my world, she'll be an outcast until she manages the glamour rune. And even then…."

"In mine, she'll be honored. In every world apart from yours. But even if not—does it matter? She's a part of you. Part of us. I am not willing to miss the chance to see her grow up."

"You're not willing to miss the chance to introduce her to Lia," Gabriel grumbled, and there was Aleksei's smile again, the one that increased the lines around his mouth and deepened the blue of his eyes. "She won't believe you, anyway."

"She will once she sees her." A pleading undertone laced the fae's words. One of the biggest points for quarrels between Aleksei and his sister was the fact that neither of them could or would have children.

Only now Aleksei's child was curled up on his lap, sleeping soundly. She'd grow quickly; she'd learn how to change her form.

Actually, seeing Lia's face when she met the little girl was something he wouldn't miss for the world.

Gabriel didn't need another reason to be convinced. "She's so beautiful," he murmured, touching one of her claws. "And naming her is easy. Pearl. Okay with everyone?"

S'chn Tg'ai sat next to him. Carefully, he stroked his daughter's wing. "Pearl. Yes, a very good name. The others will agree to it."

Aleksei raised an eyebrow. "The others? Do they know of her?"

A grin spread over S'chn Tg'ai's black face. "Of course they know. Several have visited my nest during the past year, making sure the rumors are true and a new dragon will fly our skies. There have been more discussions amongst us in the past few months than during the past five centuries."

"Good. Apparently, mating with humans wasn't a mistake after all."

"We are aware of that now. Right now, Aliss is in the human world, searching for others like you, Gabe. She is one of the younger dragons, if you can call anyone young at the age of 3,000 years. Aliss is thorough, and desperate for a mate. We believe that there must be others; we believe Aliss is just the right dragon to find them. And once we have, Pearl won't remain the only young one." Proudly, he looked at his daughter. "Although she will always be the one who gave us back our future."

Then he looked at Aleksei and Gabriel. "You can stay for the night, if you like," he offered. "Stay with her. She will want to be close to you once she wakes up again."

Aleksei and Gabriel looked at each other, then at the sleeping dragon, and finally at S'chn Tg'ai. "Sure we want to stay," Gabriel said, and knew it had been the right decision. An evening at home would have been great; an evening spent with his—their!—newborn daughter, was much, much better in a very special way.

IN ANOTHER world, rain poured down onto already soaked earth. The rivers flooded the meadows, trees fell over as their roots lost their grip in the muddy ground, and yet more rain hid in the clouds, rain and lightning and thunder.

Even the mountain caves had filled with water. All that had wings and legs had fled long ago; everything else had died.

The banshee's cave no longer existed. It had turned into a pool, the ice melted, the supporting rocks long tumbled down.

Howling, the wind chased away some clouds only for others to replace them. Never before had a thunderstorm this vicious and lasting tormented this world. But then, never before had a creature misused nature's powers to disturb the balance of the portals. In this world, balance was no longer known. In this world, the discord had remained, and it centered in the banshee's broken cave. Had it been possible to get in there before it collapsed, one would have seen nothing but bare walls covered in ice. Nothing personal; nothing colorful. A few bones on the ground, and more ice where the banshee used to sleep.

But one place was different. In the corner farthest away from the entrance, farthest away from light and sound, a low hole was carved into the ground. For an eternity, it had contained nothing. Now, with the cave destroyed, it again contained nothing.

The banshee's egg floated in the water, midway between ceiling and floor. It was gray, but from inside, a faint cracking sound could have been heard, had anyone been there to hear it. Although smaller than a dragon egg, it was less fragile, and perfectly able to survive a flood as well as lack of care. Sooner or later, the shell would crack and what was inside would hatch.

Another flash of lightning. Another rock broke loose and tumbled down, its fall slowed by the water. It hit the egg, tossed it aside, and made it drift to the outer corner of the cave, where it hit a sharp corner.

The shell cracked. The young one inside struggled when water pushed in. It might have survived even without someone to feed it had it been allowed to stay inside the egg for another few days. As it was, it stood no chance against the rising flood. The water broke the shell for good and washed out what had been inside. The banshee's child drifted through the flooded cave, pitifully small, pitifully dead.

And the discord finally echoed away into nothingness.

Also from SAM C. LEONHARD

SAM C. LEONHARD

TAINTED BLOOD

http://www.dreamspinnerpress.com

SAM C. LEONHARD is a journalist by profession who lives in Southern Germany. Writing has been part of her life since age twenty, but somehow it was never enough to report the latest news about small-town politics. She wrote short stories for friends and family until a few years back she discovered the world of fandom. The Petulant Poetess is where she feels at home; slash became an addiction as soon as she stumbled over the first story.

If not writing—which isn't half as often as she'd like—Sam takes care of her son, her dog, a few cats, the madness at work, and life in general. She likes to believe she's got some humor left after years of dealing with people who usually don't understand what she's talking about when she says she's writing fantasy and gay porn on top of it.

You can contact Sam at sc.leonhard@googlemail.com.

Fantasy Romance from DREAMSPINNER PRESS

http://www.dreamspinnerpress.com